"I'm sorry, Mr. Donahue, this really is a bad time for me,"

Daphne said crisply. "Could we get together some other time?" *Like in my next lifetime?*

Their eyes locked. A charge of electricity coursed through the air between them and sizzled across their skin.

Quinn's eyes narrowed. "No," he said softly. "I'm sorry if this is a bad time, but I wanted to see you again."

Daphne moved to go, but he was too quick for her, grabbing her arm before she could escape.

She jerked free and glared at him angrily. "How dare you! Get out of my house!"

He held up his hands. "I'm not a threat to you, Daphne. I give you my word."

She lifted her chin. "Your word? How do I know your word is worth anything?"

"You don't," he told her softly. "You're just going to have to trust me."

Dear Reader,

When two people fall in love, the world is suddenly new and exciting, and it's that same excitement we bring to you in Silhouette Intimate Moments. These are stories with scope and grandeur. The characters lead lives we all dream of, and everything they do reflects the wonder of being in love.

Longer and more sensuous than most romances, Silhouette Intimate Moments novels take you away from everyday life and let you share the magic of love. Adventure, glamour, drama, even suspense— these are the passwords that let you into a world where love has a power beyond the ordinary, where the best authors in the field today create stories of love and commitment that will stay with you always.

In coming months, look for novels by your favorite authors: Kathleen Eagle, Marilyn Pappano, Emilie Richards, Judith Duncan and Justine Davis, to name only a few. And whenever—and wherever—you buy books, look for all the Silhouette Intimate Moments, love stories with that extra something, books written especially for you by today's top authors.

Leslie J. Wainger
Senior Editor and Editorial Coordinator

LEE MAGNER

Song of the Mourning Dove

SILHOUETTE·INTIMATE·MOMENTS®

Published by Silhouette Books New York

America's Publisher of Contemporary Romance

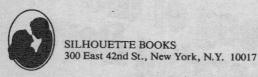

SILHOUETTE BOOKS
300 East 42nd St., New York, N.Y. 10017

SONG OF THE MOURNING DOVE

Copyright © 1992 by Ellen Lee Magner Tatara

All rights reserved. Except for use in any review,
the reproduction or utilization of this work in
whole or in part in any form by any electronic,
mechanical or other means, now known or
hereafter invented, including xerography,
photocopying and recording, or in any information
storage or retrieval system, is forbidden without
the permission of the publisher, Silhouette Books,
300 E. 42nd St., New York, N.Y. 10017

ISBN: 0-373-07420-4

First Silhouette Books printing February 1992

All the characters in this book have no existence
outside the imagination of the author and have
no relation whatsoever to anyone bearing the same
name or names. They are not even distantly
inspired by any individual known or unknown
to the author, and all incidents are pure invention.

®: Trademark used under license and
registered in the United States Patent and
Trademark Office and in other countries.

Printed in the U.S.A.

Books by Lee Magner

Silhouette Intimate Moments

Mustang Man #246
Master of the Hunt #274
Mistress of Foxgrove #312
Sutter's Wife #326
The Dragon's Lair #356
Stolen Dreams #382
Song of the Mourning Dove #420

LEE MAGNER

is a versatile woman whose talents include speaking several foreign languages, raising a family—and writing. After stints as a social worker, an English teacher and a regional planner in the human services area, she found herself at home with a small child and decided to start working on a romance. She has always been an avid reader of all kinds of novels, but especially love stories. Since beginning her career, she has become an award-winning author and has published numerous contemporary romances.

For K.T.
Thanks for helping me with
the baseball cards, sweetie.
Love, Mom.

Chapter 1

Quinn Danaker checked the luminous dial on his wristwatch and frowned. It was nearly 11:00 p.m. The courier was now an hour and a half late for the drop. Something must have gone wrong.

"Damn," he muttered softly.

He had a bad feeling about tonight, a sourness in the pit of his stomach. He'd gotten out of the clandestine side of the arms business just so he wouldn't have to go through this kind of garbage, and yet, here he was again. Waiting in the dark for a rendezvous with the unknown.

Danaker had been sitting on the wooden park bench, watching the lights flicker along the waterfront, while they rolled up the streets of Alexandria's quaintly upscale Old Town. He knew that it had become obvious to anyone who might have been watching that he must be waiting for someone. It was too late to be feeding the pigeons, much too dark to read, and since he was sitting alone, it was clear that he wasn't out courting tonight.

He put his arm along the back of the wooden bench and casually glanced toward the street corner where he and the courier should have rendezvoused at nine-thirty. All he saw was one lone couple, arm in arm, murmuring as they strolled away from the Indian restaurant there. Judging from the way they were swaying across the empty sidewalk, he concluded that they'd had more than enough wine for the night. He couldn't help smiling faintly at that. He and his late wife had probably looked like that in Rome on their honeymoon, he thought.

That seemed like a hundred years ago now.

Danaker heard the engine of a police car, and he smiled casually in its direction. The policeman stared at him suspiciously as he slowly drove past. He'd cruised by three times since Danaker had been sitting there, and each time he'd sent a sharper, longer look in Quinn's direction.

Danaker stretched and stood up. Casting a final cursory glance over his surroundings, like a visitor soaking up the last of the local color, he walked back up the cobblestone street in the direction of his car. The street had been permanently closed to traffic and was now intended for pedestrian tourists wanting to see the two-hundred-year-old houses, to browse in the quaint shops and to dine at the pricey restaurants in the Old Town neighborhood.

He could see a patchwork pattern of lights flickering behind drawn living room curtains on either side of the narrow lane. In the distance, an intermittent whoosh of traffic broke what was otherwise a very quiet night.

The relative silence in such a densely populated urban area was eerie, but Danaker noted it without much alarm. He'd faced far more deadly situations in his forty-five years. This should be a walk in the park, figuratively and literally, he thought, amused by the irony.

He walked with the firm stride of a man capable of handling whatever was thrown his way. Out of habit, he kept a close watch on every darkened alley and recess.

He had gone little more than a block away from the bench when he heard the sound of someone running. Broad, flat, leather shoes coming fast in long strides across cement sidewalk. A man, he guessed, from the sound of it, as he turned to see. The runner was silhouetted at the corner where the tipsy couple had been. From the way he was anxiously looking about, it was clear that he was being followed and feared being discovered by his pursuers. The man was wearing a beige jacket and a plaid tam-o'-shanter. Those had been the courier's designated insignia.

In the meager light, and heavily shrouded by the many fully grown trees, Quinn knew that he would be very difficult to see. He had worn dark trousers and a striped shirt in subdued colors. He whistled sharply in an effort to attract the courier's attention, to let him know where to run. They could both hide in the shadows while the courier made his delivery.

The man whirled, stared, then seemed to relax a little. He took one step in Danaker's direction, only to freeze at the sound of a car suddenly accelerating down the street. With a squeal of tires, it veered toward him. There was a bitter expletive, then the man broke into a run, trying desperately to reach Danaker and the cobblestone side street with its chain barring the way for any car.

Quinn sprinted across the rounded cobblestones, cursing as he struggled to keep his balance on the slippery footing. He leaped to the sidewalk, picking up speed on its flatter surface, trying to meet the man halfway. Maybe if they knew there was a witness, the men in the car would abandon the chase. There was a chance, he thought. It was the only chance at this point. He had no choice but to try it.

He squinted through the dappled darkness, trying to see who was inside the car that was bearing down on the man now sliding awkwardly over the polished stone street. There appeared to be two men in the front seat, but it was hard to be sure.

Two whining pings ricocheted through the night. Shots fired through a silencer. Quinn dropped and rolled instinctively, then lifted his head to see which direction the car was going before deciding which way to jump next.

But there was no next. The car shrieked down the street and careened around the next corner, disappearing into the darkness. From the sound, it was probably heading toward the nearest entrance to the beltway, Danaker thought. Then the eerie silence descended again.

Danaker got up and ran the rest of the way down the hill to the fallen courier. The man had been shot. Kneeling beside him, Danaker turned him over and felt his neck for a pulse. It was very faint. The man was barely alive.

His eyes were open. He looked surprised. His mouth was working, as he vainly tried to speak. Quinn had seen wounds like this before. Help was going to arrive too late. He heard the siren and saw the police car skidding to a stop.

"Call an ambulance," Danaker shouted at the officer. "He's taken two shots in the chest." He leaned down to try to hear what the poor son of a bitch was trying to say.

"Chri-ti-na..." he whispered. His lids began to slide closed.

Danaker felt the man go slack. The cop had arrived at his side.

"Ambulance'll be here any second," the officer said. "Who is he? Who are you? What happened?"

Quinn began CPR as the dying man began to fade. In the distance, he heard the wail of an ambulance. It grew louder, pulling to a halt next to him. Paramedics were suddenly on either side of him, taking over.

Danaker stood up and got out of their way. He wondered if the message or item the courier had been bringing was on him. And how the hell was he going to get it now? Had it been the cause of the ambush? Or had the courier been shot down for some other reason? The poor guy, Danaker thought grimly, watching as the paramedics worked hard to keep the unconscious man alive.

Damn. It was going to be complicated this time. And he thought he'd put complications behind him for good. Danaker clenched his fist. If his old arms-dealing colleagues were responsible for this, he'd personally see them in hell.

Lights were flashing on all over the neighborhood, and a soft hum of noise filled the air as people stirred to see what was going on. Blue lights flashed on top of the marked cars flooding the area from three directions. The place lit up like Christmas, and people stepped out into the street in their robes, asking what had happened.

As the paramedics loaded the mortally wounded man into the ambulance, the cop flipped open his notepad, pulled out a pencil and asked Danaker, "May I have your name and an ID, sir?"

"Quinn Danaker." He showed his license, shoving it back into his pocket when the officer had finished examining it.

"Could you tell me what you saw?"

Danaker told him in rapid-fire fashion.

The cop blinked. "You sound like a professional."

Danaker shrugged. "Just being clear and concise." Not quite true, but the uniformed cop didn't need to know everything. Someone in the police department would need to know eventually, but that could wait. "Look, if you wouldn't mind, Officer, I'd like to see how the guy makes out. Could I answer your questions at the hospital?"

"I guess." The cop looked at his notes, then frowned. "What were you doing here, by the way?"

The detectives pulled up and rolled out of their car, zeroing in on Danaker and the uniformed officer with the speedy precision of two hunting dogs.

"Whatcha got, Gallagher?" the bigger of the two detectives asked the cop.

Gallagher gave him a rundown, ending with Danaker's request to go to the hospital. The detectives asked to see his ID, too. Then one of them inquired, "Say, are you the Danaker that runs that antique-arms business?"

Quinn smiled. "You must have seen the percussion lock cavalry pistol that the police chief's got encased in glass behind his desk."

The detectives grinned and nodded.

"Yeah. Okay. We'll catch up with you at the hospital," the big one said.

They'd heard of him. He wasn't likely to run to ground. And he had a reputation for being some sort of retired private troubleshooter, hush-hush stuff, a kind of corporate intelligence agent.

"Thanks," Quinn said.

He turned back up the cobblestone hill to his car, wondering grimly how the courier was doing. By the time he arrived at the emergency room entrance at Alexandria Hospital, the outcome had been decided.

"Sorry. He didn't make it," the emergency room physician said quietly.

"Dead on arrival?" Quinn asked.

The physician nodded. "Yes."

Grim-faced, Quinn nodded, then found a convenient wall to lean on until the detectives showed up. When they did, he was close enough to hear what the hospital staff told them. Someone in green hospital garb handed one of them the dead man's driver's license, saying, "His name was Connor Jamison. He lives in Springfield. Here's the address.... Uh, is one of you going to notify the next of kin?"

"Yeah," they said in weary unison.

"We'll take care of that next," one added. The two detectives looked a little pained. They obviously hated this part of their job.

They turned to Danaker. "We have a couple of questions for you...."

He smiled grimly. "I thought you might."

They walked him over to a small cubicle off the main waiting room.

"What were you doing in the vicinity, Mr. Danaker?" one of them asked.

"I was waiting to meet a man in a tam-o'-shanter and a beige jacket. He was supposed to have been at that corner at nine-thirty. I stuck around, but by eleven o'clock I figured he wasn't going to make it, so I was getting ready to drive home. Then I saw the man running, heard the gunfire, tried to help."

The detectives stared at him. They hadn't seen the man's body yet and had no idea what he'd been wearing. The victim had been taken away by the ambulance before they'd arrived. "Were you waiting for the deceased?" the bigger man asked.

"It looks that way. He was wearing the right clothes. He was at the right place. Unfortunately, it was sure as hell the wrong time for him."

"Why were you meeting him?"

"Assuming he was the man I was to meet," Danaker pointed out.

"Assuming that."

"He was bringing me something from an old business associate in Eastern Europe. I was expecting a message or an item that would convey a message."

"What kind of message?"

Quinn laughed without a drop of mirth. "I wish to hell I knew. If he'd sent me a wire, I'd know. Apparently he preferred the privacy of using a courier."

"I suppose that makes sense." The detectives looked unconvinced, though.

"I'd appreciate it if you kept my name out of this as long as possible," Quinn said. "There is no way of knowing at this point whether my connection with the courier has anything to do with the man's death. I'd prefer to be left out of the limelight, if you wouldn't object."

The detectives looked at him a little harder. Then they looked at each other.

"You will cooperate with an investigation, however?" the bigger one asked rather pointedly.

"Sure. I'll cooperate fully. I intend to keep involved, as a matter of fact. For personal reasons."

"Personal reasons?" the younger, smaller detective asked curiously.

Quinn's face hardened. "I was there at the man's assassination," he said in a deadly soft voice. "I'd like to see the bastards that did it nailed."

"You *have* taken it personally," the big detective observed.

Danaker clamped down the memories that welled up. Yeah. He took it personally when someone was shot to death in front of him. Whether it was a stranger—or his wife.

The two detectives thought it over, conferred privately for a moment and finally gave qualified agreement to Danaker's request.

"Okay. Until there is evidence linking your rendezvous with the victim's death, we'll bill you simply as a citizen rendering help at the scene of a shooting. We can keep you anonymous for the time being. Someone in the police files, but out of the newspapers. That okay?"

"Thanks, Detective . . . ?" Quinn's note of question produced the detectives' names.

"I'm Lt. Yarbro," the big one said. "This is Sgt. Foley."

"Pleasure to meet you."

The men shook hands.

Lt. Yarbro added, "We're going along with you at this time for three reasons, Mr. Danaker. One, you've got a reputation as a reputable businessman. Two, we heard the scuttlebutt about you being some kind of retired international corporate troubleshooter. And three, if the message you were expecting at this rendezvous was related to the murder, you might be in danger yourself. All three are good reasons to give you a little short-term anonymity in this case while you're giving us some quiet, backdoor assistance." Yarbro cleared his throat. "You had thought about the possibility of being their next target, I presume?"

Quinn nodded. "That thought had crossed my mind, Lieutenant. But I think it's pretty unlikely. I'm in the antique-arms business. No threat to anybody." Changing the subject, Quinn asked, "Are you going to tell the family tonight?"

The detectives nodded.

"Mind if I wait?" He wasn't relishing the prospect of seeing the dead man's family walk through this nightmare, but the sooner he figured out what was going on, the better.

The detectives thought about it for a minute. Then they looked at one another and shrugged.

"I don't see that it would be a problem," Yarbro said. "Do you know Jamison or his family?"

"No. I never heard of them before today."

"This is not a great way to get acquainted."

"No. It's not."

"If they want to ask you what happened, are you willing to talk to them?"

Danaker nodded. "Sure. Maybe knowing that someone was with him when he went down will be some small consolation to them," he suggested somberly. It had been to him, he recalled bitterly, when his wife had been killed. Unfortunately, *he* had been that someone *then,* too.

Yarbro looked at him curiously, as if wondering what was going through Danaker's mind. Quinn forced the bitterness and anger out of his thoughts and erased the telltale expression from his face.

"I'm sure it did Jamison some good, Danaker, having you there," Yarbro said softly. "Well, after we bring back a member of the family to ID the body, we'll look for you."

"Okay. I'm going to get some coffee, but I'll be here when you're ready."

"Good."

He glanced at the date on the newspaper at the cashier's register and suddenly he realized that it was his birthday. What a hell of a way to celebrate, he thought darkly. Certainly not what he would have chosen.

Danaker was sprawled in the waiting room chair, his long legs thrust out and crossed at the ankles, his eyes half closed as he dozed at the edge of unconsciousness, when Yarbro and Foley returned an hour and forty-five minutes later. Even half asleep, he picked out the brisk, flat-footed walk of the lieutenant and the soft, sliding shuffle of the sergeant. He opened his eyes and saw them walking down the hallway in his direction. They had a woman with them, and they were coming from the general vicinity of the hospital morgue.

Quinn rolled to his feet and flexed his sore shoulder and neck muscles. They'd been bruised and stretched when he'd had to dive and roll to avoid the gunfire several hours ago, and now the pain was beginning to set in. He was definitely getting a little old for this kind of action, he thought wryly, as the three people joined him.

Yarbro and Foley kept sliding concerned looks at the black-haired woman walking between them, as if they were afraid she

might keel over without warning. Danaker took a closer look
at her and understood their worry. She was as pale as alabas-
ter. There were dark smudges under her eyes, and she was
walking like a zombie, with her gaze fixed, eyes unseeing.
Blindly, she allowed them to shepherd her to stand in front of
him.

"Uh, I guess this is as good a place as any to talk, Mrs.
Jamison," Yarbro suggested uncomfortably, giving the empty
waiting room a cursory perusal. "All the cubicles back in the
emergency area are being used. And I don't suppose any of us
wants to waste time searching for an office...." His voice trailed
off, as if he were uncomfortable with his rambling. He cleared
his throat and leaned solicitously close to the woman at his side.
"Why don't you sit down, ma'am?" he suggested gently.

She frowned, as if she were concentrating hard to hear his
words and make out their meaning. Then she tilted her head a
little to be able to see the lieutenant's face. "Sit down?" she
questioned in a husky voice. She blinked at him, confused.

He put a big hand on her shoulder and gently eased her into
the seat next to Danaker.

She sat, still looking dazed.

Danaker half expected to see her slump face down into a
dead faint. She looked as if she'd been hit by a car and had the
breath knocked out of her. He sat down and shifted in his seat,
preparing to catch her if she passed out. The poor woman, he
thought. It was a hell of a thing to have to go through. She had
probably been sound asleep in a warm bed when the detectives
had rapped on her door. Then, boom, in the length of time it
had taken for them to explain what had happened, she'd gone
from being married to being a widow. She had his sympathy.
He knew what that kind of sudden loss felt like. He wished to
hell he didn't.

He couldn't help but notice that she was an attractive widow,
too. Even without makeup, exhausted, in shock, barely aware
of what was going on, she was a good-looking woman. She
looked like the kind of girl who'd been a cheerleader in high
school, he thought, a girl with lots of smiles and enthusiasm
and zest. She had good-looking legs. Pretty face. Good bone
structure.

Poor Jamison. He should have had a lot of happy years with
her. Now he never would. Danaker watched her slide back a
little in her seat and eased his own position. At least she no

longer looked like she would keel over onto the floor, he thought grimly.

Yarbro cleared his throat and said, "Uh, Mrs. Jamison, this is the man who reached your husband's side first."

She lifted her eyes to his and stared at him, seeing him for the first time. For a moment Quinn could only stare back at her. Her eyes were a deep, violet-blue. They were beautiful eyes. Filled with pain now, but gentle and searching. Her lashes looked wet, but he saw no tears, no redness from crying, just that incredible color. And the empty, startled look. It made him want to reassure her. He wanted to tell her that it wouldn't get any worse than it was now. But who was he to say that? Maybe it could get worse. That would depend on who had killed her husband and why, among other things.

Yarbro continued the introductions. "Uh, Mrs. Jamison . . . this is Quinn Danaker."

Quinn quietly extended his hand, and she automatically put hers in it. She felt as cold as ice, he thought. The bones in her hands were fine but strong. He was surprised when she squeezed his hand. Granted, it was a trembling hold, but she was trying, and he admired that, under the circumstances. After a brief, shaking clasp, she withdrew. He watched her as she swallowed and struggled to compose a coherent sentence. He wished there were some way to make it easier for her, although he knew there wasn't. She would have to walk this road herself. As he had.

"Thank you for going to Connor's assistance, Mr. Danaker," she said huskily.

Her voice was rusty and mechanical. It reminded Quinn a little bit of a tape recording. She was running on automatic, he decided. Much of her had simply shut down while she absorbed the enormity of the awful situation.

"I'm sorry I couldn't do anything to save him," he told her quietly.

"The doctor said there was nothing anyone could have done, but I'm glad there was someone there with him at the last . . . that he wasn't alone." Pain etched her delicate features. She moved her head, and her black hair, still mussed from sleep, swung around her pale face. "Thank you for staying so late to see me. The policemen told me you'd volunteered to be here when . . ." Her voice trailed off. Then, forcing herself to finish the sentence, she went on. "When I came to identify Connor's body . . ." Her voice trailed off to a whisper.

"I'm sorry you had to be the one to do it." He looked up at the two detectives, tempted to blame them for not searching for someone else. They shrugged helplessly and shook their heads. Apparently there had been no one else to ask. Not in the area, anyway.

"There was no one else who could do it," she explained, bowing her head. Her shoulders slumped a little beneath the impact of the tragedy. She seemed fragile in the summer cotton shirt and blue jeans. She looked down at her hands, clasped tightly in her lap, and murmured, "Besides, it was the last thing I could do for him, I guess." She closed her eyes as if she were shutting out the memory of seeing him in the morgue. Her breath caught in her throat; then she added brokenly, "Nobody ever said life would be easy."

"No," Quinn agreed softly. "They didn't."

She drew herself up then, stiffening her spine and straightening her shoulders. She looked directly at Quinn, trying to claw her way past the shock and really see him. "The police say that the people who shot him were driving in a car and that they got away."

"Yes," Quinn confirmed, watching the color slowly return to her face. Good. Some of the initial shock was beginning to wear off. He was tempted to ask her if she'd like a stiff drink, but since it was nearly three in the morning, there was no public place where they could get one. And having never met the woman, he didn't think she'd appreciate his inviting her to go back to his place or hers, under the circumstances. He doubted that the detectives would care for it much, either. They were hovering over her like a mismatched pair of Dutch uncles.

She looked puzzled and waved one hand in a gesture of helpless dismay. "I don't understand why this happened. Connor was a *businessman*. Why would someone have been chasing him? He didn't have any enemies. We're just middle-class people living in the suburbs of Washington. Why would someone do this?" She gave an anguished look to each of them in turn. "The hospital gave me his things. He wasn't robbed...." She shook her head and reached out as if asking for help. "Why?"

Before attempting an answer, Danaker glanced sharply at the two detectives, wondering what they had already told her. Cautiously, he said, "I don't know why he was shot, Mrs. Jamison, but I'm sure that the police will do everything they can to find out."

Yarbro nodded. "You can count on that, Mrs. Jamison. I, uh, know we asked you a few questions as we drove you up from Springfield, but it's pretty late now to ask you any more. You've had quite a shock, and I imagine you could use some rest."

She sighed and slumped back against the chair. "Rest? Yes. I suppose you're right." She put her head in her hands briefly, then drew a long, steadying breath and pulled them away again. "I'll have to make funeral arrangements...." She looked at the three men. "I've never done that..." She stared into the empty waiting room, realizing the finality of her husband's death. "As you say, I can't do any more tonight," she agreed huskily.

"A good night's rest will help," Yarbro said encouragingly.

"Yeah. That's it, ma'am," added his partner solicitously.

She stood up and looked at Quinn, who had risen along with her. "Perhaps I could talk to you some other time, too... Mr. Danaker?" she asked hesitantly. "I have the feeling that eventually I'll want to. There will be questions.... But, right now..." She bit her lip and shook her head. "I can't think straight enough to know what to ask," she admitted unhappily.

Danaker nodded. "I understand. Call me whenever you like, Mrs. Jamison." He pulled his wallet out of his pocket and removed a business card. Handing it to her, he repeated, "Anytime."

Her hand was trembling slightly as she took the card from him. She looked at it and raised her eyes to his. "That's ironic," she murmured.

"What is?" he asked, raising an eyebrow questioningly.

"That you're in the firearms business," she explained. She managed a wan smile. "I don't mean it badly, Mr. Danaker."

"I didn't take it that way," he assured her softly. "It's *antique* firearms and weaponry," he pointed out. It hadn't always been, but at the moment, he was glad he could distance himself a little from modern weapons. He found that he didn't want her to link him with the violence that had just ripped her life to shreds. "And I meant what I said about calling," he added. "Even if it's just to talk."

Their eyes met. Hers were clouded with ambivalence about taking him up on his offer. His were clear with the message that he would help her if he could. Gradually, he sensed her relinquishing the doubt and letting herself accept his genuine offer of support.

"Thank you, Mr. Danaker." She put his card in the canvas summer purse slung over her shoulder.

He debated whether he should say what he had been thinking. What the hell. It couldn't hurt. "I've been in your situation," he said quietly. "Sometimes, talk helps." He was a little surprised to hear himself admit that. It wasn't something he mentioned often. Not to anyone. But there was something fragile and warm and needy about this woman. She aroused his protective instincts, he thought, with a twinge of unease.

"You've been in my situation?" she asked, surprised and curious in spite of her own recent shock.

He nodded. Ignoring the inquisitive stares of the police detectives, he said, "When you're feeling up to it, we can talk about it, if you want."

"I think I would like that, Mr. Danaker." Her eyes clung to his. She needed to believe that it was possible to get through this and come out whole on the other side.

He smiled and took her hand comfortingly in his. It was small and soft and cool as they began walking toward the exit. He could sense her relaxing a little, responding to the warmth and support implicit in his human touch. Even a simple holding of hands could offer strength and reassurance, he thought, lacing his fingers with hers, bringing her hand up so he could wrap his other over it.

They were total strangers linked only by a sudden, violent tragedy, but she accepted his touch in the spirit it was offered: as a healing balm, a connection with life, an apology for the blow that fate had dealt her. Danaker gave her a half smile of encouragement. *You'll make it,* he told her wordlessly.

She glanced at the detectives who were trailing along, murmuring to one another. "Could you give me a ride back home now?" she asked them tentatively.

"Certainly, ma'am," Foley said, beating Yarbro to the punch.

Together, the four of them walked out to the emergency room parking lot. Quinn stood by, his hand still laced with hers, as the detectives opened a back door of their vehicle to let her slide in. She looked up at Danaker as they slowly unclasped their hold. There was sadness in her eyes, but there was something else, too.

He would have bet his best flintlock that there was guilt there, hovering barely within sight. Now why would that be? he wondered. Sometimes survivors felt guilty, instinctively feeling they shouldn't be left behind alive. Perhaps that was it. And yet . . . it didn't quite seem like that, somehow. That wasn't the kind of guilt that he had glimpsed in her eyes.

Yarbro and Foley were getting in the car and talking quietly with one another, leaving Danaker alone with her. He held the door for her, but she hesitated, not moving to get into the car.

She raised her eyes to his, ran her tongue nervously over her lip, as if bracing herself, and asked, "Did he...did Connor say anything?"

That was a normal thing to ask, and yet she seemed so nervous. He wondered why. Hell, he must be getting paranoid as he reached midlife. She just wanted to know her husband's dying words. Who wouldn't? Danaker's eyes softened, and he hoped that his answer would bring her some comfort.

"Yes. He did say something. A name."

She looked surprised. "A name?"

"Christina."

Her expression went completely blank. She blinked like a doe suddenly blinded by piercing headlights on a pitch-dark night. "What did you say?" she asked faintly.

"He said 'Christina.' That's your name, I assume." Danaker frowned, puzzled by her strange reaction.

She looked away, but he saw her bite her lower lip. "Are you sure? There must be some mistake. . . ." she murmured.

His frown deepened. "No. I was leaning over him. I heard it clearly. What's the matter?"

Her rich, violet-blue eyes met his, and there was no mistaking the deep hurt and utter bewilderment there. She lifted her chin in a gesture of feminine pride. "My name is Daphne," she said with as much dignity as she could manage. "As far as I know, we don't know anyone named Christina."

Chapter 2

Quinn called himself sixteen kinds of a fool. Why in the hell had he told her without finding out more about her? Well, it was too late now, he thought grimly. And who would have thought it a problem? Daphne Jamison struck him as the kind of woman whose name surely should have been on her dying husband's lips. He watched her settle into the car, buckle her seat belt and sit, hands folded, the pain carefully under control now.

"I am sure there's a simple explanation," he said, trying to reassure her. Hell. Why couldn't they invent something that took away the pain and suffering at times like this?

"Of course," she murmured, without a trace of conviction.

He closed the car door, and she looked at him through the window, a haunted expression on her face. Damn it, he thought. Daphne Jamison was going to be another complication. He could feel it in his bones already. He stood back and watched the detectives' car back up and pull out of the lot. Then he walked over to his own car and got in behind the wheel.

So who had killed Jamison? And why had his widow looked haunted by guilt? Where was the item that Jamison was to have delivered to him? And who was Jamison talking about in his dying breath as he'd murmured the name Christina?

All the way home Danaker turned the questions over in his mind. He never found an answer. But as he checked the locks and security system in his home before turning in, he was haunted by something else, something disturbing in a different way.

The memory of Daphne Jamison's violet-blue eyes.

Daphne fingered the business card thoughtfully. The name, Quinn Danaker, was boldly engraved in black letters on the plain, off-white paper. It gave the impression of solid strength. It was as formidable looking as the man himself had been on the soul-numbing night that Connor had been killed.

Connor. His death had been totally unexpected. However, once she got past the initial shock, she found that she couldn't grieve for him, even though she wished that she could.

Their marriage had been disintegrating for years, but the violence of his death had wiped away that memory at first. After all, she had married him. He was the father of her child. But when Danaker had said the name Christina, anger and dismay and an icy sense of betrayal had overwhelmed her grief.

In spite of their estrangement, it hurt her to think that Connor might have been involved with another woman, so involved that he would say her name in his dying breath. That was the final blow to whatever had been left of their marriage. If she had discovered that when Connor had been alive, she probably would have divorced him. Now it was too late. She would never have the chance.

Daphne was so distraught that she wasn't sure what she felt anymore. Betrayed. Grief stricken. Angry. Frustrated. Worst of all, she had nowhere to direct her anger and outrage. With their natural target now dead, her emotions swirled and whipped around her like a desert sandstorm.

Daphne stared at Danaker's phone number, trying to decide what to do. Should she call him? *I've been in your situation,* he had said. *Sometimes, talk helps. When you're feeling up to it, we can talk about it, if you want.* That was a very tempting offer. She did need someone to talk to. Preferably someone who could be objective, but who really knew what she was facing.

Sometimes she thought she could still feel the warm strength of his hands holding hers, comforting her. He had been very perceptive that night. Done the right things. Said the words she needed to hear. And those clear, confident, warm eyes of his...

Daphne pensively flicked the card with her thumbnail. What had he meant when he had referred to a similar tragedy in his own life? How had he gotten through it? Could he tell her when she could expect to feel alive again? Whole and healed? She smiled sadly. That would probably be too much to ask.

Besides, her recovery was probably going to be different than his had been. After all, she hadn't really loved her husband for a long time, and Connor hadn't loved her, not with any depth, anyway. She was sure of that. She bitterly regretted that she'd been too naive to realize he was incapable of any genuine depth of feeling until after they'd married. It had taken her several years to admit that Connor wasn't nurturing a deep and abiding love for her. He had been charming and manipulative and had given a good imitation of love, of course. That had been her downfall. She'd believed the imitation was the real thing. But she had been wrong.

Daphne shook off the sense of defeat that always plagued her when she thought of her failed marriage. There was no point in going over all that again. She had to look forward now. That part of her life was behind her.

Since Connor's death, people had tried to be helpful, but they'd been doing as much harm as they had good. Their clucking sympathy depressed Daphne. She appreciated their concern, but she couldn't bring herself to confess that she hadn't loved her husband when he died. That made it difficult to accept people's heartfelt condolences. If she had to listen to much more of their murmurings, she thought she might go out of her mind, babbling all the things she didn't want to say aloud about Connor and the double life she now suspected he might have lived.

She was determined to avoid that. Not for her own sake, but for her son's. He shouldn't have to hear the neighbors whisper behind their hands about his father, or see the sly looks that gossips would give him if the truth were known. No. She would bear the solicitude and condolences as best she could. Somehow.

Determined not to go crazy, she had dragged herself into the offices of the local community paper, where she usually worked two afternoons a week, hoping for a little normalcy in her upturned life. Unfortunately, when she walked through the door, she was greeted by a melodramatic silence. It was soon followed by a rippling murmur of condolences and the awkwardly averted eyes of her coworkers for the entire time that she was there. It was as if she had the plague and her colleagues were all desperately afraid that they might catch it. It didn't help at all.

Then guilt reappeared, adding to her problems. She felt guilty for letting her friends believe a lie. And she felt guilty about Connor's death. She had felt that way since the night in the emergency room when she realized that his life had actually ended. She remembered thinking that if she hadn't argued with him earlier that evening, perhaps he wouldn't have gone out when he did, perhaps he wouldn't have been at the wrong place at the wrong time, perhaps... She shook her head, trying to stop her thoughts.

She needed to discover the truth about Connor's death...and about his life. Then she needed to pick up the pieces of her own shattered life. After all, it wasn't just *her* life. She had a son who was depending on her. A son whom she loved with all her heart. For his sake, she would find a way to get through this disaster.

So, first, she would try to find out what had really happened. That brought her back to the night her husband had been gunned down. And Quinn Danaker.

He was a natural starting point. Granted, he made her feel uneasy, but she would be foolish not to see him again. If for no other reason, she wanted to see him because of that name. *Christina.* Who could she have been? Why would Connor have died with her name on his lips? And why on earth had he been killed? Had it been a robbery gone awry, or a case of mistaken identity? Daphne still found it very hard to believe that her late husband's death could have been intentional. Whatever his personal life might have been, he had simply been a businessman! He had never seemed concerned that his work might make him a target.

What really drove her to see Danaker again was the thought that he might know more than he realized. Perhaps Connor had said something else before he died, some small scrap of a sound that might help make the pieces of the puzzle fall into place. Daphne wanted to ask Danaker that, even if the answer resulted in additional humiliation for her. At this point, that was a price she was willing to pay in order to discover the truth about her late husband's life. And death.

She recalled wondering once or twice if Connor might have been seeing other women, but he had always assured her that in spite of their marital differences, he would respect his marriage vows. She had accepted his word and had never had any reason to suspect him of breaking his promise. Obviously she'd been a naive fool, she thought bitterly. Whoever this Christina was, Daphne was now braced for the possibility that she might not have been the only "other woman" in her late husband's life.

If she *had* been betrayed, she wanted to know about it, she thought stoically. The idea of some woman walking around, smiling secretly, knowing that she had been with her husband, was as galling as the thought of Connor's possible infidelity. Daphne's anger flared. He had no right to treat her like that! She had kept her end of the bargain. She had been faithful, even though they had not slept together since Kyle was born. Years ago.

Her anger and anguish were quickly doused by a heavy shower of guilt. She had no real *proof* that Connor had been unfaithful. And he certainly couldn't defend himself now.

"What happened, Connor?" she whispered, feeling confused, miserable and a little bit afraid, as the violence of his death came back to haunt her again. Why?

Daphne sighed. Wallowing in her marital problems would get her nowhere. She would have to concentrate on the living if she wanted to discover the truth about her late husband. That brought her back to Quinn Danaker.

The police hadn't appeared concerned about him, she recalled thoughtfully. So he ought to be safe enough to talk to. She had no reason to think that he would be threatening to her in any way, from the way he had spoken to her at the hospital. He had seemed trustworthy enough. Of course, her judgment hadn't proved to be too great with Connor, a man she had lived with for twelve years and never really known, apparently.

Then there was the vague sense of uneasiness that she felt about contacting Danaker. There was something about him that bothered her, and she didn't think it had anything to do with the violent circumstances under which they'd met. Every time she thought of Quinn Danaker, all her caution signals came on, and she wasn't sure why. Even numbed with shock and half asleep on her feet the night they had met, she remembered him quite vividly.

She responded to him at a visceral level, every instinct crying, *Be very careful, Daphne. He is no ordinary man.* She thought it was something in his eyes that did it. She had glimpsed a feral gleam behind the clear brown color. A shiver went down her spine. Thinking of him made her feel like some animal's prey.

Daphne bit her lip and forced herself to think logically. She had to prioritize her options. There was always a way out of trouble if you kept a clear head, didn't panic and didn't give up. That philosophy had helped her manage the chaos so far, and she was counting on leaning on it some more. She had stoically tackled each new problem and decision as it had been thrown at her, and there was a tidy pile of them successfully resolved and behind her to show for it. That thought made her feel better. It shored up her confidence.

It had been three *days* since she'd seen the steady-eyed Mr. Danaker in that hospital emergency room, but it felt like three *years*. There had been an endless number of phone calls to make, tearful explanations to Connor's boss and the family and the neighbors. She'd signed insurance papers and legal papers and police papers. She'd told Yarbro and Foley that she'd see them in a few days, and she'd numbly listened to funeral directors as they patiently explained the high cost of burial arrangements to her. She had written checks and filled out forms until her fingers ached and her bank account had been drawn nearly dry.

All that had to be counted as progress, she told herself stoutly, clinging to the thought like a lifeline.

Then there was Kyle. A tender smile curved her lips as she thought of her eleven-year-old son. He was holding up incredibly well, and for that she was profoundly grateful. Thinking about her cocky young son always made Daphne feel better—even now. He had tried hard to keep a stiff upper lip in spite of the shock of losing his father so suddenly, and Daphne knew he was doing it for her. He didn't want to act like a little kid. At his age, it was important to avoid that. She'd practically driven him away with a stick to get him to stay with his grandparents for a few days. He had argued quite loudly that he should remain to help her. The memory of his earnest face as he had pleaded his case made her heart nearly burst with pride in him. He was trying to be a young man, even if he was only eleven years old.

Kyle was the one good thing that had come from her marriage to Connor Jamison, Daphne thought sadly. *Kyle. My little love.*

The ornate, white-and-gold porcelain clock that squatted on the antique highboy in the living room chimed seven o'clock.

It reminded her that time was passing, and she still hadn't decided where to place Mr. Danaker on her list of things to do.

Daphne frowned. Okay. She'd see him. *Get it over with, Daphne.* But when? She could call him now, but she might interrupt his dinner, and she hated to do that to people. Besides, if he was working late, he might be with a customer. She didn't want to interfere with his business or sit around waiting for him to be free.

She rechecked the information on his business card, although she'd long since memorized what it said. *Hours by appointment.* Well, who knew what appointment hours were normal, in the antique-firearms business, anyway? she wondered in frustration. He sounded as if he enjoyed being his own man, keeping his own hours. That had a familiar ring to it, and her disposition became a little prickly. Connor had always insisted on naming his own hours for everything.

Daphne touched the cool, smooth plastic phone, then decided against calling. If she called, he might take charge of the discussion. He might invite her to dinner or offer to come by her house. She preferred to keep him a little farther away from her than that. Calling was not the right approach here.

She could drive by his place of business, she thought. If he were there, and not busy, perhaps she could talk to him a short while. Daphne mulled it over and began to smile a little. Yes. That approach appealed to her. It would give her more control over the situation. She could see him if he was available, and she could leave whenever she wished. If her nervous vibrations about the man started up again, she would simply back out his door at the earliest opportunity and come home. And if he were busy, she could drive by without stopping at all. Daphne grinned, feeling as if a load had just been removed from her shoulders now that she'd decided what to do.

She grabbed her canvas purse and thick ring of keys and headed for her front door. "Just *do* it, Daphne," she exhorted herself, mimicking the phrase that Kyle and his friends were always using when they needed to bolster their courage with a noisy show of bravado. "Just *do* it!"

She was a little surprised to see what Danaker's business address looked like. Once she had pulled into his gravel drive and put her ten-year-old car in park, she just sat there and stared at it.

It was a large, two-story house built of big gray stones, and it had a wraparound porch on the front and two sides, as many southern houses did. Fifty years ago it must have been a farmhouse, she decided. Remnants of a barn were probably hidden among the trees out in back. The house would have been considered out in the country back when it was built.

Things had changed a lot around here over the years, and now the house was surrounded by creeping suburban developments, new roads and sprawling shopping malls. Fortunately, the property was secluded enough that it was still possible to forget about those things until you were about five hundred feet down the road that passed in front of his winding drive. Unless he owned the surrounding land, that solitude probably wouldn't last for long, she thought.

The lights were on, but she didn't see any cars. It didn't look as if he had company or was entertaining or seeing someone who'd come shopping for antique weapons. She noticed a brick garage not far from the house. If he were home, his car could be parked there, she decided. Of course, to find out, she'd have to go knock on his front door.

She turned off the car engine, took a deep breath and muttered, "Just *do* it, Daphne."

The minute she opened her car door, she heard the sound. In the ivy covering the ground next to the graveled drive, something rustled like a mouse running through dry leaves. She shut the car door and gingerly scampered up to his front porch, glancing here and there, looking for the source of the sound.

"I hate rodents," she whispered fiercely, clutching her purse.

She raised her hand to knock and heard the peculiar rustling again. This time it was over her head, in the huge oak overhanging the porch. She saw a shadow flitting through the branches. Some sort of bird, she thought. There was something odd about the way it flew, though. She peered at it, her fist still poised to knock. Then she realized what the creature was.

"A bat!" she exclaimed in horror.

"Sometimes we get them at this time in the evening," said a slightly amused male voice immediately behind her.

Daphne jumped and swiveled her head to see Quinn Danaker standing in his now-open doorway, his hand resting on the frame, his feet bare, his chest bare, and jeans shaping his muscular body like an ad for a male adventure series.

"You scared me to death!" she said indignantly. She noticed her fist still upraised to knock on the door and quickly lowered it.

"Sorry," he said, unrepentant and grinning. He stepped back, opening the door more fully. "Come in."

Daphne glared in the direction that the bat had flown and followed Danaker inside.

"I'm sorry I didn't call first.... I hope this isn't a bad time," she said. She gave his bare chest an uncertain glance.

Danaker shook his head. "No. As a matter of fact, I've been wondering about you." He gave her a steady look. "I saw the small notice about the shooting in the *Journal*."

Daphne smiled wanly. "The reporters were persistent, but they finally realized I didn't want to talk to them."

"That's what I thought. The article had the bureaucratic ring of a police report," he observed wryly.

"I think they cornered poor Lt. Yarbro after they gave up on me," she admitted a little sheepishly.

"Probably." He grinned again. "Although I bet you're the only person who's ever described Lt. Yarbro as a *poor* or cornered man." Danaker hesitated. "I didn't see anything about a funeral."

"The service was private. He was buried in the family plot near his parents' home. They live farther south in Virginia," she explained, trying not to think about it. Her mother-in-law had been prostrate with grief at the graveside. "We kept the notice out of the paper, though." Daphne's voice caught, and it took an effort for her to go on. "The police thought it might be a good idea, under the circumstances."

"The circumstances being that they don't know who killed your husband, or why?" he probed.

"Yes. They told me they thought it would be... how did the lieutenant put it? 'A prudent measure.'"

"Has anyone bothered you?" he asked, frowning.

"No." She laughed, although rather uneasily. "I don't think they believe we're in imminent danger of being attacked. I think Lt. Yarbro and Sgt. Foley were just being cautious."

"Hmm."

Daphne felt a chill just thinking about Connor's murder. She watched Danaker, hoping that he would calmly nod his head, agreeing with her that the police were just being overly concerned about her safety. He didn't. He was still frowning pensively, and she thought that his "hmm" had a very non-committal ring to it. Her heart sank.

"I guess you could say so far so good," he conceded. With a slightly lopsided grin, he added, "Anyway, caution is usually the better part of valor. I'm glad Yarbro and Foley kept that in mind."

Danaker walked across the polished wooden floors, his tread soundless but for the occasional creaking of a board beneath his bare feet. "Come on," he called back to her casually. "We can continue the conversation in here."

Daphne smelled the aroma of food as she followed him to the entrance of his kitchen. "Uh...am I interrupting your dinner...or...anything?" she asked hesitantly.

She hovered in the doorway, trying to seem at ease but failing miserably. His bare back was unsettling. She hadn't had a conversation with a bare-chested man outside of a swimming pool since she was twenty years old. Of course, when she'd been in college or at the beach, there had been a lot of that, but it had been normal then, and no one thought much about it. This wasn't the same thing at all.

Danaker sat down at a cluttered kitchen table and absent-mindedly motioned for Daphne to join him. Judging by the reports and magazines spread all over, she assumed he must have been working while he ate. He stacked the reports and looked up to see what was keeping her. He looked perplexed to find her glued to his kitchen entryway.

"Come in," he suggested. "Have a seat. Would you like a glass of wine? Or a cup of coffee?"

"No. Thank you," she murmured.

He looked at the remains of his dinner. "How about some dinner? I've got another steak, if you're interested." He grinned slightly, and added, "I can guarantee you a good one."

She smiled. "I'll take a rain check."

"Okay," he agreed, turning his attention to cutting the last pieces of steak on his plate with the precision of a die-maker.

Reluctantly, Daphne joined him at the table and sat down. The unexpected intimacy of the situation was making her feel very uncomfortable. Maybe if he had his shirt on... "Perhaps I should come back another time...." she suggested lamely.

"No. Tonight's good," he was swift to assure her. He took a critical look at her. "You look a little pale. Are you sure you wouldn't like anything? Maybe something stronger than wine?"

"Well, maybe I *will* take a cup of coffee," she conceded. It would give her something to do with her hands, she thought nervously. She sternly tried to prevent her gaze from sliding back to his bare chest and its generous dusting of golden brown hair.

Danaker didn't notice her gaze as he reached for the automatic coffeepot on the counter next to him. He grabbed a mug from a hook on the wall and poured her a cup. As he handed it to her, however, he noticed the color blooming in her cheeks and the way she averted her gaze from his chest. He leaned back in his chair, looking faintly amused as she lifted the mug to her lips.

"Have I embarrassed you, Mrs. Jamison?" he asked softly, beginning to grin. "Would you feel more at ease if I put on my shirt?"

Daphne nearly choked on her first swallow of coffee. Her eyes watered, and she cleared her throat a few times. Finally, shaking her head, she managed to say, "No! Of course not. This is your home. You can wear whatever you want, for heaven's sake!"

His grin became a little broader. "You're right, but I hate to embarrass a guest," he pointed out. He reached behind him, grabbed a dark red polo shirt off a knife-scarred butcher-block table and put it on.

"Is that better?" he asked, amusement still gleaming in his eyes.

"Yes. I guess it is," she admitted, blushing a little more in embarrassment. She felt like an idiot. Or an inexperienced young girl. For heaven's sake, she was thirty-six. The mother of an eleven-year-old.

He shrugged it off. "No problem. I should have thought of it myself. I must be too used to living alone. I'm forgetting basic manners. Speaking of which . . . are you sure you aren't hungry? I'd be glad to broil you a steak, if you'd care to join me." Ruefully, he indicated the few remaining scraps of food on his plate, admitting, "To tell you the truth, I feel a little rude eating in front of you like this. My great-aunt Mehitabel would be after me with her rolling pin if she were here. She was very strict about good manners." He shook his head mournfully, as if rueing the bad end he had come to.

Daphne smiled until she laughed. "You don't *really* have an aunt named Mehitabel, do you?" she demanded dubiously.

He raised his brows as if shocked that she could doubt him. "I most certainly do. And she's my *great*-aunt," he corrected.

Daphne eyed him askance, trying to decide if he was teasing. Maybe he had a great-aunt Mehitabel and maybe he didn't, but he had certainly made her feel better. She shook her head in reply to his repeated offer of a quick supper, though.

"I've already had dinner," she explained. It had been coffee and a slice of bread, but since she didn't have much appetite, it had been more than enough. "Thank you, though. Please . . . go right ahead and finish your own." She smiled. "And don't worry about Great-aunt Mehitabel. I won't tell." She cleared her throat. "Actually, I had been hoping not to interrupt your dinner when I came here. I should have called, but . . ."

When her voice trailed off, he prompted her softly. "But?"

She tried to be honest without telling him everything. "I wanted to get out of the house, and I thought I'd take a chance that you were doing some business this evening." She gave him a slightly confused look. "This *is* where you work, isn't it? I mean, I didn't see any guns or anything in the other room. . . ." She peered around behind her and looked back into the hall. "This looks like your home, but it was the address on the business card. . . ."

"It is. I keep the business in an underground addition that I can enter through the house," he explained casually.

"You keep your business underground?" she repeated, surprised.

"Yeah. For safety, security and general appearances."

"General appearances?" She was fairly certain what he meant by *safety* and *security* but *general appearances?*

He grinned. "I like to see the grass and the flowers, so I put the building under them."

"Oh. I see."

She watched as he turned to his meal and forked the last piece of steak into his mouth. Whatever discomfort he might have felt at eating alone in front of her had pretty much evaporated, she thought. As he finished, Daphne glanced around his eclectically decorated kitchen.

Decorated probably wasn't the right word. It looked as if all his female relatives had been giving him their cast-off kitchen equipment for years. Nothing matched and little was modern, and yet it still managed to seem cozy, in a disheveled sort of way. The blue-and-white checked curtains swagged across the window were homey enough, but the white porcelain sink was half filled with what looked like a whole day's worth of dishes. There was no dishwasher in sight.

"Would you like to talk now?" he asked, leaning back in his chair.

"Talk?" Daphne blinked and dragged her attention away from the eclectic decor. "Oh, yes. It was generous of you to invite me to come and see you. I was too shocked at the hospital, but now, well, there *are* some things I'd like to ask you, if you don't mind...."

"I wouldn't mind at all," he assured her. His eyes crinkled in a kindly way. "Talking can help. So can listening."

He swung off his chair, slid his dinner dishes in with the others in the sink and filled the basin with soap and water, letting them soak. Then he grabbed a half-empty fifth of Irish whiskey from the counter and came back to sit down across from her.

"How about a shot of this in your coffee, Mrs. Jamison?" he suggested with a wry grin. When she shook her head, he poured some into his own mug and capped the bottle. "I thought you held up very well that night at the hospital," he told her seriously. "That was a hell of a thing to have to face, especially alone." He lifted his cup in a sober toast. "Here's to recovery. May it be a short trip on a smooth road."

"To recovery," Daphne concurred. She clinked her mug to his and drank somberly. Her eyes went a little out of focus as she murmured, "How long does it take?"

"Recovery?"

"Yes."

He shrugged noncommittally. "It varies, but I'd say that the worst part is probably already behind you. Every day brings its own form of pain, of course, but the more distance between you and that night, the duller the ache is. It will fade a little every day."

She studied him, seeing the finely etched crow's feet at the corners of his eyes, the depth of experience in the steadiness of his gaze, the weathered texture of his skin, the conviction in his expressions. He looked like a man who knew what he was talking about.

"You said you'd been through this yourself," she murmured cautiously. "I don't want to pry into something you don't want to discuss, but..."

"Ask whatever you want," he told her with a reassuring smile. "If I didn't want to tell you about it, I certainly wouldn't have mentioned it that night at the hospital," he pointed out.

Daphne hesitated, then repeated, "You've been through something like this?"

"My wife was shot to death," he explained. His voice was calm and nearly devoid of emotion, but he couldn't keep the anger from his eyes.

"Oh, no! I'm so sorry." She hesitated awkwardly. "I wish I could think of something to say that would..." Help? What words could?

"You're right. No one should have to face it, and when you do, there aren't words to comfort you."

There was a prolonged silence while Daphne absorbed his admission and grappled with how to proceed. "Did she suffer very much?" Daphne inquired gently.

He wrapped both hands around the mug and stared into it for a moment. Then he nodded. His mouth was grim and his face hard with the memories of his loss.

"Yes," he answered in a soft, deadly voice. "She suffered. Help was too far away to do her any good. She bled to death in my arms."

"You were with her?" Daphne exclaimed, horrified at what he must have gone through. She hated thinking of Connor being shot down in the street, but the thought of witnessing it, of holding his dying body in her arms, was awful.

"Yes. I was there." He took a long drink and then looked at Daphne.

"Living with that memory must be terrible," she murmured sympathetically. She reached out and covered his hand in a gesture of comfort, as he had reached out to her that night at the hospital.

His gaze dropped to their hands, and something slowly changed between them. It was like warm static electricity, muffled and buried deep.

Daphne quickly withdrew her touch and swallowed nervously.

"You have to give yourself time to grieve," he said neutrally, raising his eyes to hers. "It takes a while to say goodbye to someone you loved."

Daphne heard the tenderness beneath his even words. "You must have loved her very much," she said quietly.

"Yeah. I did."

She envied him that. She wished she could have said the same of Connor and herself.

He had heard the wistful envy in her voice and wondered what it meant. He'd been trained to pick up on cues like that, and, automatically, he did it now. If she envied his lost marriage with his late wife, perhaps she hadn't been happy in her marriage to Connor Jamison. He remembered the night in the hospital, when he thought he'd seen guilt in her eyes and wondered why it was there.

"Were you and your husband happily married?" he probed carefully.

"Reasonably." She looked away from him. "At least, I thought we were reasonably happy...."

He raised his brows. "That's not a very convincing answer," he pointed out.

"It really isn't any of your business, is it?" she retorted sharply. She immediately regretted her words. They revealed too much.

"I suppose not," he conceded with a shrug. "However, if you want to talk about getting through this, it would help if I knew the truth. If there were problems with the marriage, you might be even more inclined to feel guilty than people usually are."

"Guilty?" she asked, surprised. Well, she had felt guilty, she thought, but it was odd he would think that was a normal reaction.

He took another long swallow of his liquored coffee and leaned back in his chair, balancing it on the two back legs. "Yeah. Guilty. It's a common reaction. When you're angry or dislike the person who died, you tend to feel guilty about that. We get raised to be 'nice' to people, and it's the ultimate in 'not nice' to be at odds with someone who's just lost everything to the Grim Reaper."

Daphne frowned. "That sounds like pop psychology."

"It's not pop psychology," he argued firmly. "Survivors often do feel guilty that they are still alive when their loved one—or their buddy or their fellow passengers—didn't make it out alive from some catastrophe. It's just human nature."

"I...was angry with him," she admitted with a sigh. "You're right, I think, about the guilt. I did feel guilty...but not because I was still alive.... It was because we had had another fight that night, and I was glad to see Connor go out. Then, when the police came and told me that he'd been gunned down, well, I felt awful, as if it were my fault. If I hadn't argued with him, maybe he wouldn't have left, and maybe he'd still be alive. He really had nothing to go out for. No one to meet."

Danaker frowned. That wasn't quite true. But she didn't know it.

Daphne leaned her elbows on the table and buried her face in her hands, trying not to give in to the tears that threatened.

"Later, when I realized the financial situation he'd left us in, I really became furious. The bills keep coming from all over.... He must have eaten at every fancy restaurant and shopped at every expensive store in Eastern Europe!" she complained bitterly. "I never opened the bills before. They just collected until he flew into town and took care of them. Now I'm going through a backlog of two weeks' worth of credit card bills and—" she shook her head in dismay "—I can't believe it! He was living like an oil sheikh. I didn't even know Eastern Europe *had* luxury establishments!"

Embarrassed by her candor, she got a firmer grip on herself and finished her coffee.

"Go ahead and be angry," Danaker told her softly. "It helps to let it out." He hesitated, then added in a low voice, "If you were very much in love, sometimes you're also furious that you got left behind. That can be tough to admit, too."

Daphne blinked away the moisture blurring her vision and stared at him. "That's the way it was for you, wasn't it?"

"Yeah. I was mad as hell that she left me. And boy, did I feel guilty about being mad!" He'd also felt responsible. If it hadn't been for his work, she never would have been a target. That guilt would go with him to his grave, he thought bitterly.

"Not many men would admit what you've been admitting to me," she told him softly.

He laughed. "Don't be too sure, Mrs. Jamison. You bring out the protective instincts in the male of the species. I bet I could line up some other testimonies for you, if you think it would help."

She shook her head. "No. I don't think you need to do that. You've been a great help, Mr. Danaker."

"Just Danaker," he corrected her with a grin.

"Danaker, then," she agreed shyly. More soberly, she brought the conversation around to the original purpose of her visit. "I, uh, wanted to ask you about what happened the night that Connor died. If you wouldn't mind?"

"Of course not. What would you like to know?"

She lowered her eyes and drew an imaginary pattern on the bare wood table with her fingernail. "You told me that he said a name...."

"Christina."

She winced. "Yes. Did he ... Was there anything else? A fragment of anything?"

He frowned and mentally reviewed his memory of that night. "No. Not while I was with him. And he was unconscious by the time the paramedics got to him."

Daphne couldn't hide her disappointment. "I see." She swallowed. "The doctor who ... pronounced Connor dead ... said the same thing. He was unconscious when he was wheeled in."

"What were you hoping to hear?"

Daphne was at a loss to explain. "I don't know. Something ... anything ... to suggest that he was thinking of Kyle and me." She bit her lip thoughtfully. "Or something that could help explain what happened that night, why he was killed."

"Kyle?" Danaker zeroed in on the new name. His eyes narrowed, and his voice became more alert.

"My son."

Danaker remained silent. He could tell a lot just from the way she said the kid's name. She loved him, was proud of him. Emotions that never came into being when she mentioned her husband's name. Daphne Jamison's marriage had been troubled. Although he wasn't certain yet just how profound the rift between them had been, his instincts said that the estrangement had run deep.

Unfortunately, he found himself wanting to believe it. That was dangerous. He needed his objectivity. However, sitting here with Daphne was slowly eating that objectivity away.

Those vivid eyes of hers were as haunting as he recalled. They made him think of long walks in warm summer sunlight. Her soft voice was a slow, inviting caress across the ache of his inner loneliness.

She didn't seem to notice the effect she had on him, either. That had an enticing charm all its own. He let his eyes glide over her in a light, impersonal way, intending that she not see the intensity of his interest yet. Amend that last bit about the appeal of her ingenuousness, he thought dryly. Her body projected a seductiveness all its own.

Their eyes met, and Daphne felt that old uneasiness slide down her spine. Her caution signals began flashing yellow, and she hastily got to her feet.

Danaker rose automatically.

"Uh...well, I think I'd better be going...." she said awkwardly. She turned away, tightly clutching her canvas purse.

"We've barely begun to talk," he pointed out, going with her to the front door.

"Yes, but it's getting late. I've really got a lot to do. And I'm sure you do, too." She knew she was beginning to sound like she was babbling, so she abruptly stopped talking.

"Perhaps another time?" He followed her out onto his front porch and down the steps to the gravel drive.

"Yes," she murmured. "Another time." Not if she could help it, though. He had told her all that he knew. If he didn't know anything else, she certainly didn't intend to put herself in this nerve-racking situation again.

Danaker thought her *yes* had sounded a lot like *no,* and he had no intention of letting her escape so easily. "Would you mind if I stopped by to see you sometime?" he asked casually.

She was sliding into the front seat of the car, but her head jerked up in alarm at his words. She couldn't just say no. It would sound defensive and fearful. That wasn't surprising. She *felt* defensive, and she *was* a little alarmed. Of course, she wasn't about to let *him* know that.

"No, of course I wouldn't mind," she lied bravely. Before he could ask for her address, though, she turned on the engine and started to leave, a farewell smile plastered firmly on her face.

Danaker watched as she departed. She looked like a fleeing rabbit. Obviously the lady wasn't eager to have him drop in for tea, he thought, irritated.

"You're a lousy liar, Daphne Jamison," he murmured. "We make each other nervous, and you don't know what to do about it, but you're too proud and well mannered to come out and tell me to keep away." He grinned. "That's good. Because I need to find out what your late husband was bringing to me. The cops didn't have a clue. So, sweetheart, that means I've gotta get a look at his things ... *with* your knowledge or *without* it."

He hoped she continued to find it difficult to reject his social advances. It would buy him some time. He would prefer a discreet examination, in Daphne's full view but without her being aware of exactly what he was doing. That wasn't going to be easy.

And then there was the issue of safety. He hoped that she didn't get dragged into anything deadly because of her husband's undercover sideline. It wouldn't be the first time that innocent family members had gotten caught in the clandestine cross fire. She was potentially at risk.

Grimly, he remembered what had happened to his wife when she'd been connected with him by men willing to use anyone as a pawn in their dangerous games.

That wasn't going to happen again, he vowed grimly. Not if he could help it.

Chapter 3

The following day, Danaker decided to check on the progress of the police investigation.

"Yarbro?"

The police detective looked up from the paperwork sprawled over his city-issued metal desk, frowning ferociously at the interruption. As he recognized Danaker, he leaned back in his chair and laced his hands behind his head, grinning slightly.

"Good afternoon, Danaker. I wondered when you'd be dropping in on us," Yarbro said congenially. Indicating a straight-backed chair nearby, he added, "Have a seat."

"Thanks," Danaker said as he sat down in it. "You've been expecting me?"

Yarbro nodded. "I figured your old investigatory instincts would force you into town sooner or later."

"That's very perceptive of you, Lieutenant."

"Tell that to my boss," Yarbro suggested, grinning. "So, what's on your mind?"

"I wanted to know if you've got a suspect in the murder of Connor Jamison."

"Not yet," Yarbro conceded. He gave Quinn a speculative look. "Do you have any suggestions? Want to add any information to your previous statement?"

"No. I told you everything I saw that night." Quinn hesitated. "Remember my telling you I was expecting a message from an old business associate in Eastern Europe, and that I think Jamison was the courier delivering it?"

"Yeah."

"I've been trying to reach my associate for the last four days without luck."

Yarbro turned the swivel chair around, opened a drawer from the filing cabinet behind him and pulled out a thick manila folder. Thumbing through it, he found the information that Quinn had given them the day after the murder.

"Janisch Kopek?" the detective asked.

"Yeah. I assume you've tried to find him?"

"We made a few calls. We asked the police in Vienna to look into it, but they're a little backlogged, so I don't have their response yet. He wasn't answering his phone, though."

Quinn frowned. "Yeah."

"You still have no idea what the message or information could have been?"

Quinn laughed humorlessly. "It could have been anything. Janisch and I go way back. He could have been sending me a message about someone we worked with years ago. Or he could have seen a great buy in the antique-arms business and wanted to steer me toward it without letting word get out."

"Why didn't he just use the phone?" the detective asked sceptically.

"Too many listening ears."

The detective shook his head, as if he couldn't believe people would actually eavesdrop to snatch a musket or a pistol. "Are you sure there isn't something else that could have been involved here? What kind of business were you involved in with this Kopek?"

"International arms sales and shipments."

"Could Jamison's death have something to do with that?" the detective asked bluntly.

Quinn had been wondering that himself for days now. "It could, but I can't imagine how. I've been out of that for some time. Whatever I know about international arms sales is old information. It couldn't be worth anything."

The detective didn't look as if he had any counterargument for that.

Quinn shifted the conversation to the other question that had been bothering him. "Did you send someone to shadow Jamison's funeral in case the killers decided to check it out?"

Yarbro nodded. "Yeah. It was private. In Culpeper, where Jamison's family has lived since Reconstruction. You know, old Virginia money, family vault inside a wrought-iron fence. The whole nine yards."

"Did anyone suspicious show up?" Quinn asked sharply.

"Nope. It was strictly old Virginia society and small-town friends. But, hell, this isn't the movies!" Yarbro exclaimed sarcastically. "I'd have been surprised if anyone suspicious had driven halfway down the state to their victim's funeral, but we kept an eye on it just as a precaution."

"I'm glad you're a prudent man, Lieutenant," Danaker said, frowning. "Too bad you didn't see anyone worth trailing, though."

Yarbro's bushy eyebrows lowered, he rolled the pen on his desk with the flat of his palm and chose his words carefully. "Danaker, I've conducted a few murder investigations," he said with obvious understatement. "And, as a rule, I don't tell members of the public—or possible accessories—exactly what I am or am not doing."

Danaker wasn't intimidated. "I'm not an accessory, Yarbro, and you know it. By now you've probably checked my background and know I'm not a good candidate for that at all."

Yarbro smiled enigmatically. "A background check on you yields rather ambiguous information, Danaker. It proves that you are capable of killing someone if you have to. You've had weapons training and substantial experience with firearms, including using them on armed attackers. On the other hand, some people won't admit whether they know you or not. People like U.S. Customs, the State Department and some of the intelligence agencies."

"I find it hard to believe that Customs and State don't have a file on me," Danaker said drily. "I've been in and out of the country often enough. And I recall reading a lot of customs regulations when I was in the arms trade."

"Oh, they admit you exist. You've got a passport and know how to pass muster with Customs, all right," Yarbro conceded. "But I got the distinct impression that there was a lot left out of those files. You're the kind of man who could get on the wrong side of the law, and it wouldn't necessarily be known. Not for a long time."

"Does that mean that I'm a suspect after all, Lieutenant?" Danaker asked, amused.

Yarbro's face screwed up into a grimace. "No. It just means I hate mysteries." He began doodling on the pad in front of him. "I don't suppose you'd care to expand your biography a little? For the sake of my peace of mind?"

Danaker grinned without humor. "No. And I don't think your peace of mind is going to suffer that much."

"Hmm," the detective snorted in disgust.

"I'd like to keep in touch with you, Lieutenant, if that's still all right with you?"

Yarbro shrugged philosophically. "Sure. Just don't expect me to tell you my secrets if you won't tell me yours."

"I have no secrets, Lieutenant."

The detective didn't look convinced. "Danaker?"

"Yes?"

"If you hear from that business associate of yours, you'll let us know. Right?"

"You have my word on it, Lieutenant."

Danaker waited a few days before he went looking for Daphne. He debated long and hard with himself whether it was a good idea to keep his distance. If the men who had assassinated her husband came after her, she would be an easy target. Although Yarbro hadn't admitted it, Danaker thought the police were probably keeping an eye on her. Not a twenty-four-hour-a-day stakeout. More likely occasional surveillance, just in case someone suspicious started prowling about.

In the end, he decided to wait a while before seeing her, because he didn't want his pursuit to frighten her away. He didn't want her to get suspicious and refuse to see him. After her rabbitlike escape from his house, that was what he fully expected her to do.

It was a Friday afternoon when he finally went after her. It wasn't difficult to find out where she lived. He simply looked her up in the telephone book.

He was surprised it was that easy. If Jamison had been involved in some sort of clandestine work, it might have been an advantage to keep his telephone number and address unlisted. That wouldn't have provided his family with complete protection, but it certainly would have made it more difficult for anyone who was after Jamison to use Daphne and Kyle as hostages. Perhaps Jamison had hoped that by letting his family's residence be published, he would make his cover more credible, saying, in effect, that he had nothing to hide. Whatever Jamison's thinking had been, anyone who wanted to locate Daphne Jamison would have no problem at all.

Daphne lived in Springfield, a suburban residential area known for its shopping malls, family atmosphere and close location to Interstate 95. Danaker had just pulled onto her street when he heard a terrible screech emanating from the house halfway down the block. He frowned, checking house numbers. Damn. The howling scream sounded like it was coming from Daphne Jamison's home. Danaker accelerated to the curbside, braked and jumped out of his car, alert for trouble.

A middle-aged lady in the house next door peered out of her living room window as Danaker walked quickly around the side of Daphne's home. Then another bloodcurdling wail arose.

Danaker, a deadly expression on his face, broke into a run just as a boy and two furious animals tore around the corner of the house, yelling and hissing and howling. The shrieking threesome were coming so fast that they didn't notice Danaker until it was too late. As they collided, Danaker grabbed the boy's shoulders and turned on one foot, swinging the youth around him in an arc. Only Danaker's firm grip kept the boy from crashing to the ground. At his ankles, Danaker felt teeth.

He swore under his breath. "Don't bite!" he ordered harshly. He released the boy, letting him stand on trembling legs, and turned his attention to brushing away the two balls of fur busily attacking his feet and legs.

The boy stumbled and looked up at Danaker in complete surprise. "Who're you?" the boy demanded, his chin jutting out defensively, struggling to catch his breath.

Danaker grabbed the mutt—there was no other way to describe him—and held him by the throat at arm's length. "Down!" he ordered.

The ring of authority in his voice and the dominant light in his eyes got through to the dog, who could see that his young master was perfectly all right and not a bit afraid. The dog stopped his attack and began squirming hard in an attempt to get away.

Danaker released the dog and repeated sternly, "Down!"

The dog looked a little confused, whimpered and began to lower his body slowly to the ground.

Danaker looked at the startled dog and the irritated boy with a feeling of discouragement. He hadn't meant to start the acquaintance like this. Then he noticed the needlelike pain points still hanging on to his leg. He looked down to see a ferocious kitten dug in and spitting at him defiantly. Its claws were biting through his trousers, like miniature stilettos. He shook his leg and said warningly, "Get off!"

The cat arched its back, bared its fangs and hissed. With its hair sticking straight out all over, it looked three times bigger than it actually was.

"I don't care how much you puff yourself up, Tiger," Danaker told it, irritated and somewhat amused. "I'm still bigger than you are, and you're gonna lose in the end if you pick a fight with me. Now, why don't you just jump down on the ground and find something else to chew on?"

The attacking kitten had listened to every word, its back relaxing a little, its fur gradually falling back closer to its body. With a flick of its tail, it jumped off Danaker's leg and padded over to its pal, the dog. The disdainful look it gave Danaker made it clear that the kitten thought that it had won the battle, hands down.

Then Quinn turned his attention to the boy staring at him suspiciously. "My name's Quinn Danaker. I'm looking for Daphne Jamison. This is her house, isn't it?"

The boy took a step back and frowned. He chewed on his lip, as though trying to decide what he would be expected to say to the big stranger facing him. The mutt hopped to his feet and plopped down next to him, sensing the boy's uncertainty.

Danaker smiled gently. "I met Daphne recently. I don't think she'll mind if you tell me if I'm at the right house."

The boy's face took on an even more stubborn set. "I don't know you," he blurted out. "I'm not supposed to talk to strangers. Especially now..." His voice trailed off, and the distrust in his expression became clouded by sadness.

"That's good advice," Danaker agreed quietly. *Especially now.* Had he been warned to be more cautious than usual? By his mother?

He was sure this was Kyle. He had his mother's dark hair and steady gaze. Since the kid refused to admit it was Daphne's house, he didn't bother to ask Kyle his name. He wanted the boy to continue to avoid talking to any strangers who might come asking about Daphne. Someday, someone dangerous might ask the same question that he just had.

He looked the boy over, checking to see if he was hurt, and changed the subject. "Are you okay?" Danaker asked. "I grabbed you pretty hard when you came sailing around that corner."

"Yeah." The boy shrugged his shoulders nonchalantly. "I'm okay. No big deal."

"Well, that's good." Danaker headed toward the front door.

The boy followed, mutt and kitten trailing along behind.

Danaker pressed the doorbell, waited, then pressed it again when there was no reply.

"She can't come to the door right now," the boy offered in a hurried, high-pitched voice. "I'll tell her you stopped by, if you want."

Danaker turned around. That sounded like a child's way of saying that his mother wasn't home and that he didn't want the stranger on his doorstep to know it. He sat down on the front step, rested his forearms on his knees and laced his hands.

"I don't mind waiting," Danaker pointed out.

The boy chewed on his lip and frowned unhappily. "It might be a long time," he warned.

Danaker shrugged. "I don't mind."

The dog sat down and stared at him. The kitten began stalking his pants leg, cautiously batting it with one paw, crouching, then gingerly slapping it with the other.

The boy shifted his weight and slouched into a "cool" posture, trying to decide what to do with the man hunkering down in front of him.

"Daphne has a son named Kyle," Danaker said casually. "He should be about your age...."

The boy thought for a moment, taking the measure of the man in front of him. The worry faded a little, and, having decided Danaker didn't pose any immediate threat, he blurted out the admission that Danaker had been fishing for. "I'm Kyle."

Danaker raised his eyebrows, trying to look at least a little surprised, for the boy's sake. "Is that so?"

"Yeah. When did you say you met my mom?"

"Recently."

"Oh. She didn't tell me someone would come by...."

"She isn't exactly expecting me," Danaker admitted easily. "She came to talk to me last week, and I told her I'd come and see her one day."

"Oh." Kyle still looked a little perplexed. "What did you say your name was, mister?"

"Danaker."

"Mr. Danaker."

"Yes."

"Well, I guess it's okay, then."

"For me to sit here?" Danaker asked solemnly.

"Yeah." Kyle relaxed a little.

"Thanks," Danaker said.

From the corner of his eye, he could see the neighbor who'd peered at him through her window. She was coming outside and heading in their direction. Great. The neighborhood busybody. She looked as if she'd been typecast: rotund body, chubby legs, anxious but smiling face and very fast on her feet in spite of her football-player build.

Kyle, still a little wary of getting too chummy with a virtual stranger, sat on the grass. His dog bounded into his open arms, licking his face and generally behaving like a bundle of joy. They rolled over until Kyle was on his back and the dog was stretched out alongside him, growling playfully and tugging at Kyle's T-shirt. The shirt was emblazoned with a famous cartoon character making a face at the world. There were raggedy holes fashionably cut in his jeans. Kyle was a good kid, Danaker thought.

He felt a small twinge of envy, watching the boy play with his dog in the grass. He would have liked a kid. And a dog. A home filled with laughter and hoots and the outrageous things that children did growing up. It hadn't been in the cards, though. Well, hell. There were worse things that could happen to you. Much worse.

"Yoo-hoo," called out the breathless neighbor as she sailed up the drive. "Hello there."

Kyle glanced up between tussles with his dog, which had now been joined by the kitten, which was ferociously attacking the tip of the dog's tail.

"I'm Millicent Corrigan," she gushed, beaming. "Are you a friend of the family?"

"Yes," Danaker replied. It was a whale of a stretch of the truth, but he wasn't going to quibble over words with this woman. From the way she kept glancing around, looking protectively at Kyle, checking the front door, he assumed she was just interested in making sure everything was all right. "I'm Quinn Danaker. Kyle tells me Daphne will be back soon."

"Yes," the woman prattled on, blissfully content to talk away. "She had some errands to do. Poor dear," she clucked, her eyes narrowed, and she studied him more closely. "I don't believe I've heard Daphne mention you. Have you known the family long?"

"Long enough," he said, giving her a disarming smile.

His unexpected answer took the conversational wind out of her sails, and she gaped at him, trying to regroup. "Well . . . Daphne didn't tell me she was expecting anyone. . . ."

Kyle wriggled out from under the frantic pile of fur long enough to crane his head up to announce, "Mom isn't expecting him. He just dropped in!"

Mrs. Corrigan drew herself up and looked at Danaker a little more sternly. "Kyle, why don't you go over to my house now? There are some freshly baked cookies in the big jar on the kitchen table."

Kyle scrambled to his feet and brushed himself off. "I just ate. . . ." he complained.

Mrs. Corrigan gave him a platoon-sergeant stare. "Kyle," she warned. "Go."

"Yes, ma'am," he said dejectedly. He scooped up the kitten and perched it on his shoulder. "Come on, Pooch," he muttered. His dog cheerfully flopped along behind him as he trudged across the lawn toward Mrs. Corrigan's back door.

Danaker braced himself for a verbal frontal assault. Mrs. Corrigan put her hands on her ample hips and faced him like a bulldog protecting its bone.

"Now," she said, when Kyle and his furry friends had moved beyond earshot, "why don't you tell me why you're here, and I'll give Daphne the message. That way you won't have to wait around." She gave him an encouraging but warning smile, like one might give a child when trying to get him to confess.

"I don't mind waiting," Danaker said, shrugging off her comment. Her cheeks rosied with annoyance, and he couldn't help grinning a little. She reminded him of his third-grade teacher, a woman totally unaccustomed to being refused what she requested. He began to sit down again on the front step. "Why don't you go see if Kyle found those cookies yet?" he suggested.

Mrs. Corrigan was opening her mouth to object when a ten-year-old station wagon pulled into the driveway. It was Daphne. And she looked completely nonplussed, seeing him.

"I think our waiting is over," Danaker said softly, rising to his feet.

Mrs. Corrigan hurried over to the car, meeting Daphne as she opened the door. There was a strained, surprised look on Daphne's face, and a doubtful, questioning one on Mrs. Corrigan's. Daphne shrugged her shoulders helplessly and nodded, as if admitting knowing Danaker. Still looking uncertain about the situation, Mrs. Corrigan nodded and took her leave. She walked back across Daphne's front lawn toward her own house, tilting her head politely and giving a small wave of goodbye to Danaker as she went.

"Nice meeting you, Mr. Danaker," she sang out in her best church soprano voice.

Danaker smiled diplomatically. Then he went to Daphne's car.

"Hello again," he said, feeling more relaxed now that he could actually see her again, whole and safe.

Daphne smiled unconvincingly. "Hello. I wasn't expecting to see you again.... Not so soon, anyway."

Not ever, he thought sardonically. Well, too bad, Daphne. I'm here, like it or not.

"Excuse me, but I've got some things from work...." She opened the trunk and began tugging on a large, corrugated cardboard box.

"Can I help you carry anything inside?" he offered.

Daphne gave him a strange look. "I thought we said goodbye."

"No. Just good night." He smiled slightly.

Daphne bit her lip and tried to get a solid grip on the box. She looked unhappy.

"That box looks pretty heavy," he pointed out reasonably. "Why don't you let me carry it inside?" His smile faded, and his voice lowered. "I promise I'll leave if you ask me to. This isn't a ploy to get involved with you, Daphne."

She gave him a sharp look. "I didn't think it was," she admitted tensely. She bit her lip. "It's just..."

"What?"

"We don't have anything to talk about."

"No?"

She stared at him. "No. We don't. Unless you've remembered something else that happened the night Connor was shot."

He ignored her comment and removed the box from her hands. "Where do you want this?" he asked.

Unhappy, she slammed the trunk closed and walked up to the garage, opening it stiffly. She fumbled with opening the door to the house, then she stalked inside, letting him follow her to a family room in the basement. If he wanted to carry the darned box, he was welcome to it, she thought irritably.

"Would you put it down there, please?" she asked.

He put the box in the corner where she wanted it. When he straightened, she was already holding the door for him. Her black hair swung around her face, framing it dramatically. The violet-blue of her eyes flashed with emotion. Defiance? Anger? Fear? Frustration? He didn't know what it was, but it made her even more attractive than ever.

"I'm sorry, Mr. Danaker, but this is really a bad time for me," she said crisply. "Could we get together some other day?" In my next lifetime?

Their eyes locked.

The charge of electricity coursed through the air between them and sizzled across their skin.

Daphne trembled.

Danaker's eyes narrowed.

"No," he said softly. "I'm sorry if this is a bad time, but I wanted to see you again."

She moved to go, but he was too quick for her, grabbing her arm before she could escape.

"Daphne," he said softly, moving into the exit so that she could no longer leave unless she went through him.

She jerked free and stared at him angrily. "How dare you! Get out of my house!" She rubbed her elbow, glaring at him defiantly.

Perplexed, he held up his hands. "I'm not a threat to you," he assured her calmly. "I give you my word."

She flinched, but lifted her chin, trying to cover her initial reaction. "Your word? How do I know that your word is worth anything?"

"You don't," he told her softly. "You're just going to have to trust me."

Her eyes flashed. "Trust you? I barely know you! Give me one single reason why I should trust you, Mr. Danaker."

Chapter 4

The air sizzled between them.

Danaker's eyes narrowed, and he clenched his fist against the door frame.

Daphne stood her ground and tilted her chin upward in determination. As the seconds ticked by, she found it harder and harder to face his unrelenting gaze.

"There are a number of reasons why you should trust me," he told her evenly. "But I don't think you'd believe me, even if I told you, would you?"

Daphne's gaze wavered. His comment had hit a nerve.

He moved toward her a little.

She held her ground in spite of the rush of adrenaline that swirled through her like a cold river. "I asked you to give me a reason," she repeated, trying hard to sound unshaken and strong. "Is that the best you can do? Tell me it would be a waste of time?"

He shook his head and kept coming toward her in slow, measured steps. "No. It's not the best I can do," he said softly.

The room around Daphne dissolved, and all of her senses focused on Quinn Danaker: his muscular male presence, his piercing eyes, his enigmatic expression. Primitive alarms sounded loudly in her heart, and in spite of her determination to stand up to him and chase him off, she began backing away from him. Age-old instincts of feminine survival overrode her brave and noble plan. Maybe she shouldn't have asked if that was the best he could do, she thought nervously.

Her heel and back bumped against the wall behind her, and her pulse quickened.

Danaker stopped barely a foot away from her. The expression on his face was hard to read. One thing was certain. He was very intent.

"Trust me because your instincts tell you to," he suggested in a low, compelling voice. His gaze held hers. "Follow your instincts, Daphne."

She pressed back, flattening her shoulder blades against the wall. "My instincts got me into a lot of trouble once before," she retorted unsteadily.

She looked frightened and brave and defiant all at the same time, he thought. He wasn't touching her, but the tension between them was so palpable that he felt as if they were in physical contact. Her breathing, her heartbeat, her anxiety, were as real to him as if they were his own. He lifted his hand slightly, but made no immediate move to touch her. Wait, he told himself. Don't rush this. Don't frighten her away.

"How did your instincts get you into trouble?" he asked huskily.

Daphne swallowed and closed her eyes, trying to shut out the warmth and strength that he projected so effortlessly. It wasn't fair, she thought unhappily. It wasn't fair that he could mesmerize her like this. For that must be what it was. That was what it felt like.

"Daphne?" he prodded her gently. "How?"

She looked away from him, wrapping her arms around her middle protectively. "My instincts failed when it came to Connor," she admitted, barely above a whisper.

He leaned closer, just able to hear her tortured words. "In other words, your husband wasn't the man you thought he was?"

She gave a short, bitter laugh that ended on a choked sob. Turning to stare into his unwavering gaze, she said, "That's right. I thought we would be happy. We weren't. Then I thought that even if he wasn't wild about being a husband, he could learn to be a good father. He couldn't. Finally..." Her expression became even more pained for a moment. "Finally I thought that we would just make the best of it, be a family even though Connor and I weren't..."

He raised an eyebrow questioningly. His probing gaze was impossible to ignore.

Daphne swallowed her pride and forced the words out. "Even though Connor and I knew we weren't really in love anymore and that the marriage was not working out."

Danaker sighed and shook his head. "And because of that, you won't trust your instincts about me?" he demanded incredulously.

Daphne shot him a thoroughly irritated look. "I think that's an excellent reason. My instincts obviously aren't worth a wooden nickel!"

Danaker muttered an explicit opinion. "That's ridiculous. You can't tar me for the crimes of your late husband. Hell, it's not as though I'm proposing marriage, Daphne."

Her head shot up, and her eyes went wide. Her cheeks were pink with anger and embarrassment. "That's an awful thing to say at a time like this!" she exclaimed angrily.

Danaker grimaced and took a step back, holding his hands up apologetically. "I'm sorry. Frankly, it's tough finding a way to get through your defenses. And I don't have the time to work on it slowly."

"Get through my defenses?" she asked warily. "What are you talking about?" She rubbed her arms, trying to warm herself. Nerves were making her cold.

He gave her a slightly lopsided smile. "I'm worried about you. And I'd like to help you. I used to work with security arrangements for an international company, and I still have some contacts in Europe. If the police haven't come up with anything helpful, I thought I'd volunteer my services." He hesitated. "For example, you told me you want to know who this 'Christina' was that your husband mentioned. If you'd like, I could ask a friend of mine in Austria if he could help us out."

Daphne stared at him, completely shocked.

"Hey, don't faint." He firmly grasped her arms and led her the few steps to an old couch where he pushed her into sitting down. "Come on, Daphne, don't pass out."

She shook her head. "No. I'm all right. It's just..." She searched his face. "How could you do something like that? And why?"

He squatted in front of her and took hold of her cold, trembling hands. "Just believe me when I say that I can."

She looked bewildered. "But why? We're strangers."

He smiled engagingly. "My great-aunt Mehitabel made me swear never to abandon a lady in distress," he teased.

Daphne gave him a doubtful look, and the color returned to her cheeks. "All my instincts are shouting that you've just handed me a big excuse!"

Danaker laughed. "Your instincts are in perfect working order."

Regaining her composure, Daphne straightened and sat a little primly. "I still want a good reason why I should trust you, Mr. Danaker." She didn't know which she feared more, that he would come up with a reason, or that he wouldn't. A lock of hair had fallen across his forehead, giving him a boyish look, but she resisted the temptation to trust him too easily. After all, looks often deceived.

Danaker stood up and walked a few feet away, shoving his hands into his trouser pockets. He stared at the herringbone pattern on the brown tile floor, trying to decide what to say to her. Where did trust come from, anyway? Why did you trust someone that first time?

"I could give you some references," he said dryly. "But that wouldn't really be much help. After all, I would hardly send you to people who might say uncomplimentary things about me."

Daphne frowned. "No. I don't suppose you would."

"You could ask the police about me," he conceded with a shrug. "But all they could tell you is whether or not I'm a convicted criminal or have been charged with a crime." He gave a short, rude laugh. "I'm sure that Lt. Yarbro and Sgt. Foley would have warned you away already, if they suspected me of being a felon."

The two detectives *had* been very protective of her, she had to admit. Danaker had called them her "Dutch uncles." He was right. They hadn't seemed worried about him. If anything, they had treated him like a colleague.

"I suppose you're right," she agreed slowly. Then, trying stubbornly to resist his persuasion, she repeated fiercely, "But you still haven't given me a single convincing reason why I should trust you."

Danaker's temper began to fray. He wanted to tell her that she'd never meet anyone whom she could trust more than she could trust him. He was sorely tempted to shout it, damn it all. That wasn't like him. He rarely lost his temper. He concentrated hard on cooling it down a notch. Getting a good leash on his irritation, he gave her the most honest advice he could offer her under the circumstances.

"Trust me because you have no reason not to," he suggested flatly.

Daphne rolled her eyes. "That sounds a lot like 'Trust me because your instincts tell you to,'" she argued.

"Perhaps. In the end, that's the only reason that anyone ever gives their trust to another. They're trusting their gut, their instincts." He shrugged philosophically. "The reasons that people give for why they trust someone are just rationalizations. The reasons are window dressing, added to make an instinctual choice seem like carefully measured assessment. Trust is irrational, Daphne. It's a gut instinct."

Daphne stared at him in surprise. She'd never heard it put like that. At first she wasn't certain that he meant it. It was quickly clear, however, that he was deadly serious. Have faith in gut instinct? Trust him because she had no reason not to?

"Sort of like you're innocent until proven guilty?" she asked, feeling a sense of fatalism begin to encompass her.

"Exactly like that."

Daphne paced across the family room, anxiously wondering what she would be risking if she gave Danaker the trust that he wanted. What could he do? Surely nothing to her. It wasn't as if she were inviting him to move into her home! He couldn't do anything to Kyle, either. She'd make sure that Kyle wasn't left alone with Danaker. She could arrange that neither she nor Kyle was left in vulnerable circumstances with Danaker until she knew a great deal more about him.

She chewed on her lip, trying to consider every angle of their safety. Perhaps it was worth taking the chance. Her instincts—for whatever they were worth—weren't concerned about Kyle or herself being in any physical danger around Danaker. It was another kind of danger that was bothering her early warning system. Unfortunately, she wasn't clear what that danger was. She could live with that worry for the time being, though. She'd deal with it later.

The real question, then, was: Could Danaker be of enough help to her to make it worth any risk that she and Kyle might be taking by trusting him because she had "no reason not to," as he so charmingly put it. If he *could* help her discover who Christina was and whether she had anything to do with Connor's death, it would be worth a great deal to her, Daphne thought.

Her heart ached with the anguish of not knowing. She did indeed want an end to that nightmare. The police were getting nowhere. With the rising homicide rate in the area, Foley and Yarbro were being kept very busy. They couldn't spend all their time working on Connor's death. She wanted to speed the investigation along a little if she could. She wanted an end to not knowing.

Daphne stopped her pacing in the middle of the room and turned to face Danaker. He was watching her, looking relentlessly patient and strangely intent. A coolness slithered across her skin, a foreboding of things to come, she thought uneasily. Darn him. Why did he always have to set her nerves on edge? Her head tended to agree that he should be considered trustworthy until proven otherwise, but her instincts were protesting very insistently. She simply could not shake the vague feeling that Danaker posed some sort of threat to her.

Danaker saw the conflicting emotions in her face and silently swore in frustration. She was tempted, but she hadn't completely swallowed the bait. If he could just nudge her a little more, maybe she'd open up. He needed a bridge to her; he needed a common ground for them to work together. Offering to help solve the mystery surrounding her husband's murder had turned the handle on a door, but now he needed to push it open. That had to be done carefully. He didn't want her to feel threatened. At least, not threatened by him.

He noticed a photo album on a pine end table and casually walked over to pick it up. It was thick and well thumbed and bore the crayon marks of a childish hand that had once tried to decorate it. Kyle's handiwork, no doubt, Quinn thought with a slight smile.

"Family pictures?" he asked, making no immediate move to open the album.

"Yes." She looked a little puzzled.

"Would you mind if I looked at them?"

Their eyes locked. He wasn't just asking to look at the family photos. He was asking to walk into their lives, for a while, at least. Daphne understood that. She clasped her hands tightly in front of her, raised them to her mouth and uttered a silent prayer that she was making the right choice. Then she unclasped her hands and let them fall back to her sides.

"No. I don't mind if you look at the album," she said stoically, praying that this wouldn't be another big mistake.

He smiled slowly. His eyes still held hers, and she met his gaze without flinching. She felt the strange sizzle between them, as if they were on the same radar wavelength. Not by choice, but by fate. The hissing warmth enveloped her like a protective net. Or a finely woven trap.

Resolutely, Daphne lifted her chin. She had made her choice. And she would stick by it.

Danaker watched her stiffen her resolve and wondered if she felt the attraction between them as clearly as he did. He tended to doubt it. Otherwise, the look in her eyes would be less wary and more welcoming. He felt heat course across his skin like a desert wind. While he began to sweat, she stood there looking cool and resigned to a plan she didn't really want. He couldn't look away from her, though. In spite of her prickly ways, he was being mesmerized by her. There was no other word for it.

She had the damnedest color eyes. Like wild violets in the rain.

In an act of sheer discipline, Danaker forced his attention back to the photo album.

The first pictures made Danaker smile.

Daphne bristled. "What's funny?"

He turned the album so she could see what he was looking at. It was a picture of Daphne as a high school senior, wearing boots with pom-poms and a colorful leotard, tossing a baton into the air.

"I kind of envisioned you like this as a teenager," he explained, still amused.

Daphne frowned. "Like what?"

He turned the pages, scanning the snapshots. "Popular. Vivacious. Pretty. The girl every guy wants to take to the prom. Not the school beauty queen...the pretty girl with a kind heart and a zest for living."

She sat down on the arm of an overstuffed chair that had seen better days. "You see me like that?" she asked in surprise.

He nodded. "From these pictures, it seems I was right."

Daphne didn't know what to say. She'd never thought of herself in those terms, and she wasn't sure that she completely agreed with his description. However, she was very surprised that he had come to this conclusion based solely on meeting her at the hospital and at his home. He was obviously accustomed to doing quick assessments of people in his line of work.

"Was your husband your high school steady?" Danaker asked.

Daphne smiled and shook her head. "No, but we knew each other. He was two years older. Class president. Voted most likely to do big things in life. Popular and well liked by his teachers and his peers." Her eyes grew soft as she recalled those innocent bygone days. "The boys used to run a betting pool on who the prom queen would be each year. They quit doing it until Connor graduated, though, because the girl he took always won." She ran her fingers through her black hair, sweeping it away from her face. "He went for the beautiful girls. His 'little black book' was the envy of every boy in the county. That's why I was so surprised when he finally asked me out. I was very flattered. He could have dated anyone, but he chose me."

"You shouldn't have been surprised," he said softly. "You're a very attractive woman."

His steady gaze made her feel strange. A peculiar sensation spread like warm cognac through her veins. Daphne blushed and swallowed uncomfortably. "Mr. Danaker, I'd rather you kept that kind of comment to yourself."

He raised his eyebrows in mild surprise. "I meant it as a compliment."

Daphne frowned. "Thank you, but, I'd rather not let this conversation get . . ."

He waited for her to find the words, making no effort to help her out.

"Too personal," she finished, feeling even more awkward.

He nodded, but his expression was enigmatic. "I'll keep that in mind."

"Thank you," she said stiffly. She wondered if she sounded like a Victorian prude. After all, the compliment had been perfectly polite. Perhaps it was the way he had looked at her, that steady, unwavering gaze. Something had bothered her. Well, Danaker had told her to trust her instincts. So she would, she thought stubbornly.

Danaker flipped through the next pages of the album. There were pictures of the college that Daphne had attended. A laughing party of coeds with their hair in curlers and wearing floppy pink slippers and baggy terry cloth robes.

"When did you start dating Jamison?" he asked.

"When I was home from college. It was the summer between my junior and senior years."

"He'd already graduated by then?"

"Yes. He was in Washington, working for an import-export company and taking night classes at a university."

"Oh?"

"He said he needed a master's in Business Administration to rise through the ranks."

"You didn't have much time to see each other, then."

"No."

"When did you get married?"

"A couple of years after that." Daphne frowned. "Does this really matter? I mean, what bearing does our marriage have on his murder?"

"It may or may not matter. It certainly can't hurt for me to have an accurate picture of Jamison's private life. It might help us understand what he's been doing recently."

Daphne lowered her eyes. "But it's so personal. . . ."

"Yes," he agreed softly. "It's damned personal. And I know exactly how you feel, talking to me about it. When Cherie was kidnapped, I had investigators grilling me and going through our life with fine-tooth combs."

Her head jerked up, and she looked at him again, her eyes dark with pain. "Then you know why I'd rather you not ask any more about my marriage."

"Yes," he conceded neutrally. Then, in a less even tone, he added, "And I also know that it's important to dig through all of this for any clue, however innocuous."

"Did any of these conversations help find your wife?" Daphne challenged angrily.

Danaker flinched, and a muscle worked angrily in his jaw. "Yes. Indirectly. Eventually we were able to figure out where she was being held and who her captors were. We identified a woman standing in the background of a photo of Cherie. The woman was connected with someone known to have links with the group that had kidnapped my wife." His expression hardened stoically. "Unfortunately," he added, his voice devoid of emotion, "that wasn't enough to save her."

A painful silence stretched between them.

Daphne's heart ached. Danaker was tough, but he'd been badly wounded by his wife's loss. A blind woman could have seen it. She couldn't help feeling some remorse for the challenging question she had put to him.

"I'm sorry I asked, Danaker," she said quietly. With a sense of resignation, she capitulated. "Go ahead. What else do you want to know?"

He gazed at her for a long moment, and Daphne had the feeling that a bond was being forged between them. They were two battle-scarred victims, she thought whimsically. But at the moment, she was the more freshly wounded of the two, and he was eye offering her some of his own strength. Then he broke their eye contact, looking back down at the photo album. Daphne was surprised at the sense of loss she felt. Silly. She was being overly emotional. It had to be the result of Connor's murder. Nothing else.

Danaker was beginning to get an interesting portrait of Daphne's life. She'd married Jamison in a traditional wedding—white gown, church ceremony, catered dinner reception. They'd honeymooned in Bermuda. There was a stunning shot of Daphne standing thigh-deep in clear blue water, smiling happily and waving at the person taking her picture. She was wearing a bikini of silver, jade and sunset red. She was a knockout.

There were a few photos of family get-togethers at holidays. Then Kyle put in his first appearance. He was swaddled in blankets and staring in an unfocused way in the general direction of the camera, while Daphne held him in her arms and looked on adoringly. The radiance in her face made Danaker realize why the Madonna had been a favorite subject of artists for centuries. Her warmth and love and happiness reached out to him.

"Was your husband happy about Kyle?"

Daphne's head snapped up. She'd been daydreaming, but his question brought her back to attention.

"What do you mean by that?" she asked defensively.

Danaker held up his hand. "Easy, Daphne. Remember, I'm on your side." He tried again. "Did your husband want a child? Was he happy when Kyle was born?"

Daphne stood up. "Yes. As far as I know."

"As far as you know?" His eyes narrowed. "Is there some reason why you wouldn't know how he felt about Kyle's arrival?"

Daphne bit her lip. "Not exactly. The simple answer is yes. I told Connor I wanted a baby. He knew that. He kept trying to put off starting a family, saying he needed to be more secure in his work. But when I got pregnant, he was very excited. He started talking about the great things the baby would be able to have when business really became good."

"But?"

Daphne lowered her eyes.

"Daphne?" he probed softly. "Something bothered you about his reaction to Kyle, didn't it?"

She swallowed her pride. She might as well admit it, if she were going to go along with him. And she had decided to do that.

"Connor started traveling more. I know that many men do travel more as their careers progress, but he seemed relieved every time he walked out the door—as if he were escaping from a burden. I don't think it was Kyle that bothered him, though. I think it was the sense of responsibility. Here we were, a wife and a child, depending on him." She shook her head. "There were times when I wondered whether he regretted having to consider us."

The fool, Danaker thought.

Daphne looked at him and saw the anger in his face. "What's the matter?"

"Never mind," Danaker muttered.

He flipped through a few more pages. There weren't many pictures of Jamison in recent years. When Kyle was standing at the plate, baseball bat at the ready, waiting for a pitch, it was Daphne who had taken the picture. And all the pictures were of Kyle doing one thing or another. Soccer games, baseball games, school musicals, scouting events. It was as if Daphne's life had ended. Everything she did revolved around Kyle.

The last photograph was different, though. It was a picture of Kyle, Connor and Daphne at a family picnic. From the family resemblance, he picked out Jamison's father and mother. They were all sitting on a blanket spread out on a grassy rise overlooking a river. It was the expression on their faces that drew his attention, however.

Daphne looked tense and rather tired. Kyle was chattering away and looking up at his father as if he couldn't get enough of him. But Jamison looked as if he had very little to do with either his wife or his son. He was smiling like an ad in a magazine. Smooth, unruffled, confident. And yet there was a preoccupied air about him. He was checking his watch, as if counting down the minutes until he caught a train to somewhere more important. The family picnic was just an obligatory whistle-stop on his larger political tour.

Danaker turned the album and showed it to Daphne. "Daphne? Do you remember where Jamison was going after the picnic?"

She had to come over to see the picture clearly. Then she had to think about it for several minutes. "Let's see," she mused, trying to remember. Then her puzzled expression cleared. "Oh, yes. He was going to Europe on a special assignment from his new boss. He'd gotten a promotion about six months earlier, and he had just received an excellent evaluation, so he was being given a freer hand to conduct some negotiations."

That was interesting, Danaker thought.

Daphne concentrated. "He was going to Dulles Airport, then to Paris. From Paris to a couple of places in Germany. Then Austria . . . Vienna and someplace else, I think." She looked at the photo and shook her head. "I can't imagine how that picture is going to help solve the mystery of his death, though."

Danaker shrugged. "Maybe not. But I've got a clearer idea of what kind of man Jamison was, and I also have a long list of people I could contact to try to flesh out the more recent details."

Daphne looked at him. "That would take time."

"Absolutely."

"You aren't thinking of becoming a private detective, are you?"

Danaker laughed. "Naw. This is going to be slicker and faster than any P.I. investigation."

Daphne was dubious about that, but before she could voice her opinion, a loud bang and the sound of glass shattering wiped every thought from her mind.

Chapter 5

"Get down," Danaker shouted. And to make sure she did, he dove in her direction, taking her down onto the tile floor behind the nearest piece of furniture.

Daphne couldn't breathe. All the air had been pushed from her lungs when Danaker fell on her. Desperate for oxygen, she tried to gasp, but his weight was pressing down hard, and she couldn't inhale at all. With the last ounce of her fast-fading strength, she tried to shove him off. It was like trying to push a mountain of lead. When he didn't move but kept covering her, her efforts became frantic. Just when she thought she would pass out from lack of air, he realized she was in dire straits and quickly rolled to one side. Sweet relief rushed in. She took it in deep gulps, one long, life-giving breath after another.

Danaker continued to half sprawl across her, straining hard to hear any telltale sounds, tensed to be ready for anything. Seconds seemed like minutes. There was nothing out of the usual to be heard. Children chanting a jump-rope song...boys chasing each other while shouting starship commands...a car engine being turned off...the jingling of an ice-cream truck's bell fading away in the distance.

He looked down at Daphne. "Are you okay?" His voice was a harsh whisper.

She nodded. "Yes. But for a minute I thought I was going to suffocate on my family room floor," she whispered back tremulously.

His eyes softened a little. "Sorry." His gaze dropped to her lips, then to her chest. "I was trying to *keep* you breathing."

"I know," she whispered unsteadily. "Thank you." When their eyes met, the sizzle returned in force. Daphne swallowed nervously. Breathing was still a problem, but not for the same reason.

Danaker lifted his head and listened intently. There was no sound of footsteps. Although he was reluctant to leave her side, he needed to find out what had shattered the peace. And whether it would do it again. He pushed himself up into a crouch and prepared to do a little reconnaissance.

"Stay down," he whispered tersely.

Round-eyed with apprehension, Daphne nodded and flattened herself against the side of the couch.

Danaker rapidly crawled away from her. He didn't pause until he reached the large stuffed chair by the window. Cautiously, he raised his head to look around, keeping as close to the dark-print curtain as possible.

There was no sign of anyone outside the window. Nor did he hear the telltale sound of anyone running away.

He took a closer look at the hole in the windowpane and grimly visualized the trajectory to the shattered lamp. Its glass and bronze figure had stood in a line midway between Daphne and him at the time the incident had occurred. Either of them could have been the target, but since it was Daphne's house, he had to assume she had been in the cross hairs. It was too far to see, but he guessed they would find a small-bore bullet lodged somewhere in the wall. Looking for it would have to wait. Right now, he wanted to make sure that a second bullet didn't arrive. They might not be so lucky a second time.

He arched his back and carefully peered through the corner of the window again. He still saw no one lurking around, but two people were now coming into sight in the yard next door. They appeared to be cheerfully oblivious to any potential dangers as they meandered across the grass. They were heading for the front of Daphne's house, and they were being followed by two small scampering animals.

"Kyle and Mrs. Corrigan are on their way here," he told Daphne. He stood up and walked to the telephone. It was time to call for reinforcements. "Why don't you get them into an inside room upstairs? Keep the curtains drawn. I'll call the local gendarmes."

Daphne stumbled to her feet and looked at the broken lamp in dismay as she rushed to the door. Fear chilled her to the bone. "What on earth can I tell Kyle?"

Then, as she thought of what might have been, she whispered raggedly, "Kyle! Thank God he wasn't here."

She heard Mrs. Corrigan's generalissimo voice and Kyle's whoop of laughter. They had reached the front steps. For the time being, Daphne swallowed all the questions that she wanted to ask. Danaker was right. Until they figured out what was going on, Kyle and Mrs. Corrigan needed to be put in as safe a place as possible. She was surprised by how much her legs and arms were shaking as she hurried out to the two.

"Close the garage door and lock it," Danaker shouted after her.

He didn't have to tell her twice. She'd already thought of it herself.

After tending to the garage she ran up the outdoor steps two at a time, trembling so hard that she wouldn't have been surprised if she had fallen flat on her face. Miraculously, she didn't.

Mrs. Corrigan, who had been about to knock on the front door, turned and beamed at her. "Oh, there you are, Daphne! I wondered what happened to you and Mr. Danaker."

Daphne, glancing nervously all around the street, yanked open her front door and urged them inside. "We've been talking...." she explained vaguely.

Mrs. Corrigan gave her an expectant look. "Oh?"

Daphne didn't bother to elaborate. Instead she rushed to close the living room drapes, murmuring, "It's a little bright in here, don't you think?" The drapery fabric snapped shut, swaying from the force of her actions.

Mrs. Corrigan looked puzzled. "Bright? Not that I had noticed...."

Kyle made a beeline for his computer. "Thanks, Mom. It's hard to see the screen with a lot of sunlight on it."

Daphne grimaced. She hadn't intended to encourage more electronic game playing. "Why don't you go read a book, Kyle?" she suggested, glancing uneasily toward the light streaming through the dining room window.

Hypnotic electronic music and the bouncing, elastic sounds of small images being zapped by make-believe weapons on the game monitor were the only reply.

"Where is Mr. Danaker, Daphne?" Mrs. Corrigan asked, looking a little perplexed. "His car is still out in front, so I just assumed he was—"

"He's downstairs. He'll join us in a few minutes," Daphne explained. She didn't want to get into any details before she had to. She concentrated on stalling. And shielding them from any further attacks. Forcing cheeriness into her voice, she asked, "Would you like a cup of tea, Mrs. Corrigan?" To Daphne's knowledge, Mrs. Corrigan never turned down a cup of tea, and today was no exception.

" 'Never turn down a cup of tea. It makes life's problems all seem wee,' " Mrs. Corrigan said blithely, quoting the little ditty that her mother had taught her as a child.

Daphne managed a strained smile, then concentrated on pulling the dining room shades closed on her way to the kitchen. Within moments she was filling a kettle with water with one hand and pulling the frilly white kitchen curtains closed with the other.

Mrs. Corrigan blinked in consternation. "You *do* like it dark inside, don't you, my dear?" She tilted her head to one side, her pudgy face furrowing in deep thought. "You know...I never noticed that about you before. And I don't think I've ever seen the kitchen curtains closed here."

Daphne smiled weakly. "Sugar?"

The police arrived a short time later in two marked patrol cars. With all the curtains closed, Daphne and her two charges were unaware of it until Danaker brought the officers upstairs.

"Mom! Mom! The police are here!" blared the early warning system sitting on the floor playing on his computer.

Mrs. Corrigan spilled her tea. "Police?"

Daphne managed another lightweight smile of semireassurance. "We had a little problem...."

"What kind of a little problem, my dear?"

Danaker walked into the dining room. "Daphne, could you go downstairs and give them a statement? I'll keep Mrs. Corrigan and Kyle company."

He looked a lot more relaxed than he had the last time she'd seen him, and that made Daphne feel better. Things must not be as bad as they seemed. Maybe it had been some sort of teenage prank gone awry. She got up from the table and joined him. "Do you think it could have been some weird accident?" she ventured hopefully. "I've read about people loading a gun and shooting it in the air, thinking they were having some harmless fun, but the bullet ended up doing some damage...."

"Anything is possible." He didn't look like he believed it for a minute.

"But you don't think that's what happened," she guessed, her heart sinking.

"I certainly wouldn't bet my life on it," he murmured, smiling over Daphne's head at the obviously curious Mrs. Corrigan. "Did you tell her what's going on?"

"Not yet. I was going to let you explain."

"Terrific," he muttered sarcastically.

Daphne had a sense of déjà vu as she answered the policeman's questions. She'd talked to more police officers in the past month than she'd spoken with in her entire life.

She was surprised and relieved at the way that Kyle and Mrs. Corrigan had taken the news. After recovering from her initial astonishment, Mrs. Corrigan declared that it was probably just some potshot taken by a child with a new BB gun and no parents at home to keep an eye on him. Kyle's excitement quickly gave way to a consuming interest in getting a close-up look at the officers' holstered weapons and the bullet hole and its trail of disaster in the family room.

"Wow! What a mess!" he exclaimed with boyish admiration. "I bet I can find the bullet!" And with that he dashed toward the broken glass.

Daphne grabbed him by the flying shirttails. "Oh, no, you don't!" she told him severely. "Go upstairs and feed your dog and cat, Kyle Jamison!"

"Aw, Mom!" he wailed in protest.

"The police don't want any of us walking around there," Danaker pointed out. "We might destroy evidence."

The police didn't look too certain that much more could be done to the scene of the crime, but they chorused agreement and added that Kyle should listen to his mother.

Disappointed that his magnificent plan had been torpedoed, Kyle stomped up the stairs muttering about the unfairness of it all.

It took a while for the authorities to examine the room and locate the bullet. Danaker looked at it as they dropped it in a plastic bag for labeling.

By the time the police left, Mrs. Corrigan had gone home and night was beginning to fall. Kyle chased Pooch and Cleo, the kitten, around the living room furniture and put them downstairs in the laundry room where their beds were. Then he blasted up the stairs back into the living room, where his mother and Danaker were standing.

"I'm starved," he announced loudly. "What's for dinner?"

"Dinner!" Daphne groaned. "I should have put the meat loaf in the oven hours ago."

"Aw, Mom," the boy complained. "I can't wait hours and hours for dinner. I'll die of starvation."

"I doubt that," his mother said tartly. "Look, why don't you wash your hands and face? And put on a clean pair of jeans," she added, taking a good look at the state of his knees. "We'll come up with something else." She gave her son an affectionate look.

"Sammy Wong's!" he yelped, registering his preference in restaurant dining with his usual exuberance. As if that settled everything, Kyle zoomed up the stairs and slammed the bathroom door shut.

Daphne turned to the man standing in her living room to find him watching the domestic interchange with a strange expression on his face.

"Danaker?"

Whatever it was cleared immediately. He was his usual calm, competent self.

"So...Sammy Wong's is replacing meat loaf on the menu tonight," he observed wryly.

Daphne smiled. "I'm sure Kyle will be praying for bullet holes every day now. He loves that restaurant."

"Sammy serves good food."

She was startled to hear that. "Do you go there?"

Danaker grinned. "Sure."

She didn't believe him. "I've never seen you there. We go at least once a month. Are you kidding me, Danaker?"

"I wouldn't kid you." He chuckled. "I keep late hours sometimes. Sammy lets me eat with the family after the restaurant closes up. Sometimes they drop off an order for me. One of the cooks drives by my neighborhood on his way home.''

Daphne sat down and stared at him in surprise. "You know the cooks? And Sammy?"

"Sure," he said with a shrug. "I used to do some business with his cousins in Singapore and a friend of his in the Philippines."

"It's a small world," she murmured, then frowned. "Sammy and his cousins and his friends are your customers? They buy antique firearms and weapons?" That didn't sound like the Sammy that she knew...built like a Buddha, jovial, hardworking, a family man.

"You'd be surprised what people want to buy." Danaker had no intention of giving her any details, however, and he steered the conversation back to the present. "Are you sure you want to go out tonight?" he asked.

Daphne shrugged. "Why not?" She glanced toward the darkened stairs that led down into the family room. "I wouldn't mind getting away from that for a couple of hours."

He remained silent.

Daphne glanced at him. "Don't you think that's a good idea?"

He frowned. "I don't want to scare you...." he said slowly.

"But?" Daphne prompted him, bracing herself for more bad news.

His gaze intercepted hers. "But I think you'd be safer inside the house. It's locked up. The police have checked the grounds. They'll make another turn around the neighborhood in a few hours. But if you get in your car and drive around..."

"Go on," she murmured, trying to keep the fear at bay.

"If you drive around, you'd be easier to target. You can't draw the curtains in a car," he pointed out softly. His eyes were steady and his voice was even as he finished his thought.

"You think *I* was the target?" she asked, shocked. "You think someone wanted to shoot *me?*"

He sighed. "I don't know what to think yet. We don't have enough information. But it's a damned peculiar coincidence that your husband was shot to death and, a week later, a bullet flies into your family room." He saw the pallor creeping into her cheeks and moved closer to her. "Hey," he said softly, putting a comforting hand on her shoulder. "I don't want to scare you."

"No?" She laughed nervously. "You're doing a very good job of it, whether you want to or not."

The sound of an eleven-year-old voice singing a popular song, slightly off-key, floated through the air. Even the closed bathroom door and lots of running water couldn't dampen the volume.

Danaker put his hands on Daphne's shoulders and waited until he had her full attention.

"Why don't you call in the order and I'll go pick it up and bring it back for you? That way, Kyle can have his favorite dinner, and I won't worry about you being out of your 'safe house' for a while. How does that sound?"

"It sounds like something your great-aunt Mehitabel would be happy you're offering to do," Daphne admitted.

"You're right about that," he said with a grin.

He turned to go, but her voice made him hesitate.

"Could I order something for you, too, Mr. Danaker?"

He looked at her seriously. "I don't want to hang around if my welcome's worn-out. Maybe you and Kyle could use a little time alone."

Kyle piped up from the top of the stairs, "Why would we need that?"

Daphne laughed at Danaker's pained look. "Kyle has radar for ears whenever his name is mentioned." Then, a little more shyly, she added, "Your welcome's not worn-out, Danaker. We'd like to have you stay. After all you've done, it's the least I can do."

"In that case, why don't you add an order of whatever you like for me?"

"Ah...an eater who's not picky!" she exclaimed in delight. "You have no idea how rare that is!" She lifted the receiver, a rapturous look on her face, and began to dial.

Danaker left, feeling mildly annoyed. He found it irritating that she tried to use gratitude and a sense of obligation as the reasons for inviting him to dinner. He would have preferred an honest willingness to share his company.

That was expecting too much, he told himself unsympathetically. Besides, what was he complaining about? He wanted closer access to her so that he could go through her husband's things and try to discover what the man had been attempting to deliver. It shouldn't matter what reason she offered for letting him stay.

It shouldn't matter, but it did.

* * *

Sammy Wong's face was comical to behold.

"You're picking up food for Mrs. Jamison? I didn't know you know her! How come I've known you all these years, Danaker, and I didn't know that? Huh? How come?"

Danaker held up both hands to stem the tide of questions. "I just met the lady, Sammy."

Sammy blinked. "Oh. Well, I see." He grinned broadly, and a gold-plated tooth glittered in the mellow light. "She's a very nice lady. You're a very nice man. Have a nice dinner."

Danaker took out his wallet and paid the bill. While Sammy rang the cash register, Danaker casually put a question to him.

"Sammy, did you know Mrs. Jamison's husband, too?"

Sammy nodded.

"Yeah. But not so good as I know Mrs. Jamison and her boy." Sammy shook his head sadly. "I don't think Mr. and Mrs. Jamison were very happy. Too bad about Mr. Jamison, though."

"Why don't you think they were happy?"

"They didn't smile at each other. Their mouths smiled, but their eyes didn't. You know what I mean, Danaker?"

"Yeah." And he wasn't surprised to hear it. It was interesting that it had been obvious to Sammy Wong, though. Apparently they hadn't made a big effort to hide their estrangement. Or, if they had, they hadn't been successful. Other people were probably aware of it, too, then. And some of them might be more connected with Jamison's freewheeling life in Europe. Perhaps Sammy could point him in the right direction. It never hurt to ask. "Do you know whether Mr. Jamison had some favorite night spots around here? Other restaurants or meeting places?"

Sammy's face screwed up into a good imitation of a prune as he tried hard to search his memory for any fragment of information that might be helpful. "No..." Then his face lit up like a Chinese firecracker. "Wait a minute! I do know one place. The family was here on a Saturday night...oh, maybe three or four months ago. Kyle, the boy, he didn't feel too good, so Mrs. Jamison wanted to go home before they finished eating. Mr. Jamison said she could go, but he was gonna stay. He was hungry. And besides, he had some work to do later."

"You've got a good memory," Danaker pointed out dryly.

Sammy chuckled. "I remember because it was raining hard and I felt sorry for her having to go home alone with the sick boy like that, without even eating her dinner. My wife was at the cash register, and she complained about it for a week! Said I should have told the man to take the food home and help his wife!'' Sammy laughed. ''My wife has a very soft heart, especially for Mrs. Jamison. She like her very much.''

''I can understand why,'' Danaker muttered. ''You said you knew of some other place that Jamison went to?''

''Yeah, yeah. After Mrs. Jamison left with the boy, Mr. Jamison finished eating, and then he made a phone call for a cab. I thought he was going home, so I came closer to him, meaning to offer him a ride. After all, he's been our customer for a long time, and it was almost time to close,'' Sammy explained. His face grew sad and a little angry. ''But I heard him tell the taxi company that he wanted to go to the wharf over in Washington. He was going to The Blue Fin.''

''The Blue Fin,'' Danaker said thoughtfully. ''That's hardly a place for him to catch up on his work.''

Sammy shook his head. ''No. Unless his work is trading deals under the table and buying drinks for pretty girls.''

Danaker nodded grimly. ''Yeah.'' Maybe that was exactly what his business had been. ''Thanks, Sammy.'' He grinned. ''Say hi to your brother and your wife, huh?''

''Sure, sure. Next time you gotta say it yourself, though!''

Danaker smiled. ''I will, Sammy. And thanks for the information. I appreciate it.''

When Danaker arrived at Daphne's house with the Chinese food, he was greeted with the exuberance that only an eleven-year-old boy can produce. As the food was unpacked, Kyle enthusiastically peeked in boxes and containers and pleaded for helpings of this item or that. Quinn found the scene quite a contrast to the stoic silence that usually filled his evening meals.

''You look a little overwhelmed,'' Daphne observed in amusement as she poured boiling water into a large teapot and carried it to the dining room table.

''I'm not used to being welcomed like a victorious hunter,'' he admitted wryly. ''My bosses were always pretty low-key about success, and since I've been my own boss, even that's gone.''

Daphne laughed. ''Kyle doesn't hold anything back. And you *did* bring his favorite food. Like armies, eleven-year-old boys march on their stomachs.''

"Yeah," Kyle said eagerly, reaching for the sautéed noo-
les. "You saved me from starving!"

Danaker had his doubts about that, but he grinned and said,
"It was my pleasure. Call me any time there's a famine."

Kyle, mouth stuffed with food, vigorously nodded his head
hat he would.

Once he'd satisfied his stomach, Kyle began chattering.
Danaker soon noticed that neither he nor Daphne had to do
nything but respond to Kyle's meandering thoughts and un-
xpected questions. From the way Daphne was sitting—her legs
rossed tightly, her look aloof—Danaker wondered if she were
ntentionally letting Kyle be the focus of attention. In the midst
f the boy's ramblings, Danaker glanced across the table at
Daphne, but could tell nothing from her expression. She was
aughing at something Kyle had said, and when she lifted her
yes to look at Danaker, she was careful not to let him see too
eeply inside her mind.

Once his belly had been filled, however, Kyle began to wind
own noticeably. He started to yawn, and his eyelids began to
ook a little heavy. His conversation slowed and eventually
topped altogether.

Danaker helped stack the dishes and throw away the garage, doing it as naturally as he had in his own kitchen, Daphne
ealized. She liked that. Connor had never lifted a finger
round the kitchen. That was her "little kingdom," he used to
ay. She'd offered half of it to him on numerous occasions, but
e'd always smiled and declined.

"What put that scowl on your face?" Danaker asked in
musement. "Did I say the wrong thing?"

"No," she assured him, feeling embarrassed. "I didn't know
hat my face was such a window to my thoughts."

"Sometimes it is. Sometimes it isn't."

"You sound as if you wished you always knew what I was
hinking," she said in surprise.

He smiled slightly. "What man wouldn't wish he knew what
omen thought?"

Her eyes narrowed. "You're sidestepping, Danaker."

His smile broadened. "Obviously I'm not doing it very well."

"Do you always tease people away from pinning you
own?" she asked, laughing a little in spite of herself.

His eyes locked with hers, and the warmth in his expression
nade her feel mellow and languorous, eager to lie back and re-
ax, to know him better . . . and to let him know her better.

"No. I don't always try to distract an interrogator by teasing. But in your case, it seemed very appropriate."

Lulled by the masculine tenor of his voice and held in the warm gaze of his eyes, Daphne lost all sense of time and space. The room dissolved around her, and she and Danaker were alone. Something simmered inside her heart, shimmered across her flesh. Awareness. Intimate physical awareness. She felt deeply feminine again, something she hadn't experienced in a long time. Primitive urges were reawakening. Delicately though. She wanted to reach out and touch him. She wanted him to touch her.

If they had been someplace where music was being played, he might have asked her to dance, and she would have said yes. Not to dance, but to be close, to feel his arms around her body, to be within the circle of his strength.

The silence was so prolonged that Daphne finally became aware of it. It snapped her out of her reverie and slammed her back into reality. With reality came confusion and a sense of shame. She was embarrassed by the direction of her thoughts. She was shocked at the elemental feelings welling up inside her for a man who was a virtual stranger. Worse still, she felt horribly guilty that she could be thinking and feeling such things when Connor had so recently died. What was the matter with her? Had she lost all her values? Her sense of decency? She was the mother of a young boy and needed to set a good example!

Heat flooded her cheeks. Her palms felt damp and her thighs trembled. The sizzle that had electrified the room was a vivid tactile memory. She felt it burn across her skin, tightening her, tingling her. She wanted to deny it, but she was old enough to recognize the feelings for what they were: the stirrings of desire.

She was a healthy young woman, but she'd ignored that for years. Connor had let her ignore it. With him, she'd repressed that part of her nature. She'd bottled it up before she had ever really explored it. Now, like a genie, it was pushing the cork trying to escape.

She clenched her fists, digging her nails into her palms in an effort to drive the sensations away with pain. The saints used to have great success with hair shirts, didn't they? She wasn't sure she could go quite that far. Pain wasn't helping. She needed to escape.

"I'd better get Kyle heading toward bed," she said, sounding breathless as she made a hasty retreat to the living room.

Bed. The word brought a waterfall of images cascading through her inner mind. Warm bodies closely entwined. Moving. Stroking. Hot words muttered in hoarse, breathless voices. Laughter filled with tenderness. Deep physical and emotional intimacy. Cries of pleasure that spiraled down into the darkest wellsprings of life. *Bed.* Why had she used that word? she thought despairingly.

She stared at her unconscious son, sprawled across the living room couch, limp as a sleeping baby.

"Oh, Kyle," she murmured. Her chaperon had fallen asleep.

"Want me to carry him upstairs for you?"

Daphne started at his voice.

"Uh...well...if you wouldn't mind. He's too big for me to carry up the stairs."

He wasn't too big for Danaker. Within a short time Kyle had been carried upstairs and gently laid down on his bed. Daphne turned out his lights and quietly closed his door.

Which left her alone with Danaker.

Chapter 6

The hall was dark, illuminated only by a small night-light in a wall socket. For a moment they stood outside Kyle's bedroom door, each waiting for the other to speak.

"I . . ."

"Maybe . . ."

Neither of them had a chance to say what was on their minds. They were interrupted first.

The phone rang.

Daphne flattened herself parallel to the wall and gingerly passed by Danaker. "Uh . . . I'll get it," she murmured. As soon as she was past him, she picked up speed.

"Yes. I can see that," he conceded, brows raised in mild surprise at her reluctance to be anywhere close to him. Silently he followed her downstairs and watched as she snatched up the receiver.

"Hello?" she said nervously.

As she listened to the caller's voice, she became quite still. Then she turned her head so that she could see Danaker. There was surprise in her eyes.

"Oh, hello, Lieutenant!" she exclaimed, relaxing. "I wasn't expecting to hear from you. . . . No. It's not too late at all. Go right ahead. . . . Yes . . . that's right. . . . When they left they promised they'd get in touch with you and let you know. I hope that was all right.... Do you think there's any connection between the gun fired here and my husband's murder?''

There was a pause as Lt. Yarbro gave his assessment. Daphne raised her eyes to Danaker's and shook her head. Apparently Yarbro had no proof of a link.

That didn't surprise Danaker. The only physical evidence they'd found in or around Daphne's house had been that one small bullet. It would be hard to make any connection between the two crimes without more to work with than that. Car tracks or witnesses who could help identify a suspect, for example. With the bullet, the only hope would have been a ballistics test matching it with the bullets that had killed Connor Jamison. Danaker could rule that out himself, however. Jamison had been killed by a higher caliber bullet than the one he'd seen in Daphne's family room. The bullets must have been fired from different weapons. Of course, the same finger could have pulled both triggers, but they needed evidence to prove that, evidence that they didn't have.

Daphne was listening intently and saying ''Uh-huh'' and ''I see'' with great seriousness, and Danaker frowned, trying to guess what the lieutenant might be saying.

''Thank you, Lieutenant. Yes, I'd appreciate it if someone would drive by every once in a while to check on the neighborhood. We'll call you if anything else happens....'' Daphne's cheeks began to redden in embarrassment, and she nervously twirled the telephone cord around her finger. ''Yes. He's still here.... Thank you, Lieutenant. Goodbye.''

Daphne hung up the phone.

''I see your Dutch uncle is still keeping an eye on you,'' Danaker observed drily.

''I think it's very nice that he is,'' she said, bristling defensively and regretting it immediately.

''Nice?'' he repeated, amused by her choice of words. ''I'll bet you're the only person other than Yarbro's mother who applies that word to anything he does.''

''What word would *you* use?'' she demanded.

''Professional.''

''Oh, I *see!*'' Daphne nodded her head knowingly and gripped her hands behind her back. ''You don't think it's possible to mix business with pleasure. If he's being professional, he can't also be reacting like a human being!''

Danaker could hardly agree with that. He was mixing professional interests with his own human interests, too, every time he had any contact with her.

"I didn't say that," he pointed out tersely. "Look, let's not get into a fight over semantics."

"I'm *not* fighting!" she exclaimed. Shocked at how vehemently she had denied it, she repeated in a calmer, but strained, voice, "I'm *not* fighting with you, Danaker."

He looked unconvinced.

She sank her hands into her hair and pressed her fingertips hard against her head. "How did we get into this?" she murmured unhappily. "I don't usually sound this irrational."

Danaker crossed the room, stopping directly in front of her. "Why don't you sit down?" he suggested, concerned. "You look like you'll keel over any minute."

Her eyes snapped open, and she stared at him uneasily. The air between them crackled softly. There went that electricity again, she thought wildly. It filled the room with possibilities. Possibilities that she didn't want to think about.

Danaker's expression hardened. He took her gently by the shoulders and then firmly pushed her down into the nearest upholstered chair. "I've got a great cure for a headache," he muttered. "If that's what's bothering you."

A headache? She wished that were it. Daphne felt his hands on her and forced herself not to flinch.

"You're as tense as steel wire," he muttered. "Relax."

Relax? What a hysterically funny command! She tried anyway. Instead of loosening up, she began to tremble again. Maybe she needed some sugar.

"You're shaking," he said, surprised. His hands stilled on her shoulders.

"It's probably just a reaction to stress," she said quickly, wishing she could believe it. "I've had a lot of that lately," she added with a defeated sigh.

"True," he agreed huskily.

He could feel the delicate shape of her shoulders and neck, the line of her vertebrae, the fine layer of silky smooth skin, and he was tempted to slide his hands down over her. He could vividly imagine the sensation of her body fitting against his palms.

It was very tempting. Somewhere in the back of his mind, though, reason managed to make itself heard. Keep it honest, Danaker. She doesn't know the whole truth. You haven't told her why you were there the night her husband was shot. I would be taking advantage of her to pursue this attraction now. She's vulnerable. And she wouldn't be giving informed consent.

But damn if he wasn't tempted, he thought in frustration. Hell. Great-aunt Mehitabel had better give him a purple heart for this one.

Daphne felt his hesitation and wondered what was going through his mind. She sensed a change when he began to move his hands. His touch became more impersonal, as if he had withdrawn from her. She thought that was odd.

Even so, she soon realized he knew how to give a very skillful massage. Light, smooth, circular strokes. Rolling motions and feathery pressure. Turn her head this way. Bend her neck gently that way. Walk up her spine with firm little finger pads. Gently tattoo her neck and head and forehead with intricate patterns on her pressure points.

She closed her eyes and let her head and neck roll with each deft motion. In spite of her nervousness at being so physically close to him, she found herself being soothed. Tension unraveled like yarn from a skein.

The time when she could have said "no" had passed the moment that his hypnotic touch had begun its magic. Much as she tried to be dignified about it, she couldn't help murmuring sounds of pleasure from time to time. She did her best to keep those sounds deeply buried, though. She didn't want him to misinterpret them, take them as some sort of invitation and pursue greater intimacy. Instinctively, she tried to maintain some kind of distance between them.

But it *did* feel good. And in spite of herself, she finally succumbed. She moaned aloud.

"Feeling better?" he asked softly, running his thumbs up the muscles paralleling her spine.

"Yes," she murmured, trying to find the strength not to sound blissful. "Were you a professional masseur in some past life?" she asked on a sigh.

He laughed softly. "Not that I'm aware of." He began a rapid pattern of light slaps across her skin, making her feel invigorated.

"That has the same effect as a cool shower," she murmured in surprise.

"Not on me," he muttered. He was feeling warmer by the minute.

She opened her eyes and leaned back to look at him. He stopped massaging her as soon as their eyes met.

His eyes were darker than she remembered. And there was a fine line of tension in his expression she was certain hadn't been there before. She suddenly became very much aware of him as a man of flesh and blood with needs and human reactions just as normal as hers.

She blinked. "Danaker . . . I think you'd better go."

Reluctantly he removed his hands. His mouth tightened. "Firing your masseur, Daphne?" he asked sardonically, a gleam of amusement in his eyes.

"Not exactly," she muttered, getting up and moving away from him.

He followed her, allowing a little distance to remain between them, but shadowing her all the same. It wasn't a threatening move on his part, but it ensured that she couldn't just cut and run. He wasn't going to let her disengage just yet.

Daphne lifted her chin and tried to appear calm and cool. She hoped it looked convincing to him. However, she was shocked at how far from cool she felt. Putting a little distance between them hadn't helped at all. She was as aware of him as she had been when his hands were on her. It was as if they were connected by an invisible force. Was she losing her grip on reality? she wondered desperately.

Danaker made no move toward the door.

"Well, good night, Danaker," she said firmly. To underscore her determination, she hurried to the front door and opened it for him. She waited, a strained but gracious smile on her face, her delicate brows raised expectantly.

"Here's your hat. What's your hurry?" he quipped in amusement as he agreeably did as he was being asked and ambled toward the exit.

Daphne shrugged innocently. "I guess you could put it that way," she conceded. The ornate porcelain clock that squatted on the highboy came to her aid by chiming the hour. "It's getting late," she pointed out quickly. Well, not *very* late. But it would have to do, she thought.

Danaker stopped when he reached the door. He looked at her, as if trying to decide what to say . . . and what not to say.

Daphne held her ground and bravely looked him straight in the eye, trying to convince herself that the attraction she was feeling was of no real significance. It was merely a biological attraction in a stressful environment, she told herself. As soon as the stress cleared up—or Danaker cleared out—she'd be better. She'd be her normal self again. Everything would be fine.

So why didn't he leave, darn it, and let her get back to normal? She tapped her toe impatiently.

"There are a few questions I would still like to ask you," Danaker said evenly. Then, smiling faintly, he explained, "I seem to have forgotten them for the past several hours. Put it down to the unexpected events... and a dinner that I wasn't planning on."

Daphne frowned in confusion. She understood that the "unexpected events" were the shooting and the arrival of the police. She was a little uncertain how to take his reference to dinner, though. Was he sorry he'd had to endure it?

"I'm sorry if we interrupted your plans for the evening," she said, a little at a loss. She bit her lip. It had never occurred to her that he might have had something to do. Maybe someone had been expecting him. A business contact. Friends. A woman. Her face reddened.

"Daphne," he said softly, seeing the confusion in her face. "You have nothing to apologize for. I enjoyed the evening."

She searched his eyes, wondering if she could believe him. He seemed to be speaking with complete honesty. She wanted to believe him. As he had pointed out, she had no reason *not* to believe him.

He was staring at her intently, appearing to want her to accept his reassurance. The kindness of his words, the touch of humor in his eyes, the honesty in his voice, all eased her fears. She relaxed a little and smiled back shyly.

"I'm glad you did." She hesitated. "I think it was good for Kyle, too. He had a wonderful time talking with you. It took his mind off of... a lot of worries."

Danaker was glad to hear that, but he wondered if his staying had been good for her, as well. He was shrewd enough not to press her on that point. *Slowly, Danaker. Don't push her too fast.*

"He's a good kid."

Daphne's smile blossomed. "Yes." Her cheeks dimpled a little as the smile deepened. "Of course, you're carrying coals to Newcastle telling me that."

He grinned lazily. "I guess I am." Building on her good mood, he returned to the point that he wanted to make before he left. "Daphne, if you wouldn't mind, I'd like to ask you those questions I didn't get to. Not tonight. It's too late. You're tired, and I've got to get home and take care of some other matters."

Daphne's smile faded. "What kind of questions did you want to ask?"

"What did Jamison talk about before he left you the night he was killed? Who are his business associates and friends? Where was he during the weeks before he was murdered?"

"That sounds like the police investigation," Daphne pointed out, uncertain whether the risk of spending more time with Danaker was worth the chance of solving the mystery. "Why do you think you can do any more than they can?"

Danaker shrugged. "I don't know that I can," he admitted. "But I have some friends in Europe. They aren't police, but they have an intimate knowledge of several business networks, and they may be able to help us shed some light on what happened." He saw the ambivalence in her eyes and moved in for the kill. "You wouldn't have anything to lose by giving me the information. It wouldn't hurt, and it might help."

She wouldn't have anything to lose? Perhaps. Perhaps not, she thought. She *did* want to find out who Christina was. And she wanted to discover what her husband had been up to.

She knew that Yarbro and Foley were concentrating their investigation in the local area, and their overseas connections were slow. Connor's murder wasn't of great immediate worry to the international police community. Also, Yarbro and Foley had other cases to work on, so there were limits to how quickly they could accomplish much.

If Danaker could help discover some of the answers by making a few phone calls, wasn't that worth a few hours of her time? Surely she could consent to answer his questions without any great harm coming of it. Couldn't she?

"All right," she finally agreed. "But I can't answer your questions tomorrow. Kyle has a soccer game, and I'm providing the oranges and transportation for three of his friends." She was trying to keep things as normal as possible for them. Keeping to their routines was supposed to help them weather the crisis, her pediatrician had told her.

"How about Sunday, then?" he suggested. His eyes were steady, and there was no trace of pressure in the question. Just a straightforward offer of an alternative.

"Well, Kyle is spending the day with his scout troop...."
Which would leave her alone with Danaker. That wasn't great.

On the other hand, she wouldn't have to worry about Kyle stumbling onto their conversation. Which was good. She didn't want Kyle to hear what Connor had been doing. Driven by a surge of fiercely maternal protectiveness, she declared, "Sunday would be fine."

A slow grin spread across Danaker's face, and the warmth in his eyes became a gleam of satisfaction.

"Sunday afternoon it is. See you then, Daphne."

Daphne felt a renewed chill of apprehension as she watched him turn to leave. There had been something vaguely predatory in his smile, a hint of the hunter closing in on his prey.

She closed the door and leaned on it, shutting her eyes against her fears.

"Sunday afternoon," she murmured to herself. "Just get through that, Daphne, and you're home free. What can happen?"

But as she drifted off to sleep, she heard the echo of his voice promising, *See you then, Daphne.* And in her dreams it sounded like a threat.

Forty minutes later Danaker reached for the telephone in his underground office. He dialed Janisch Kopek's phone number in Vienna. As he had before, he got the answering machine. There was a very long tone while the machine fast-forwarded to the section of the tape where he could leave a message. That meant that there were a lot of messages on the tape. It also meant that Janisch wasn't checking his answering machine. Or, if he was, he wasn't erasing the messages, which could mean he didn't want people to know he was around.

"Janisch, this is Danaker. Reach me when you can."

He hung up, frowning. Was Janisch dead?

He'd been avoiding thinking about that possibility. But this was a long time for Janisch to be out of touch. And his courier had most definitely been killed.

What in the hell was going on?

Danaker moved a heavy cabinet and peeled back the carpet. Using a thin-bladed pocket knife, he slid loose a square of wooden parquet flooring, exposing a safe that had been built into the poured cement floor. With a few deft twists, he released the combination lock and opened the door.

There were a number of items inside, but he wanted just one: a small, red morocco book with carefully noted names, ad-

dresses and phone numbers listed in code. He had hoped that
this part of his life was behind him forever.

Grimly, he faced the fact that it was not.

"Would you like a cup of tea?"

Danaker looked over his reading glasses to see Daphne
standing in the middle of her kitchen, holding a pale blue tea-
kettle in one hand. She was wearing khaki slacks and a russet-
and-brown cotton madras shirt with the sleeves rolled up to her
elbows. Her black hair was swept up on one side with a tor-
toiseshell comb, and her lips were very temptingly glossed an
attractive shade of peach. With her willowy build and healthy
good looks, she certainly made casual clothes look terrific.

"Danaker?" She smiled until her dimples showed. "You
look like your mind is blank! I told you going through that pile
of receipts would be a numbing experience."

He cleared his throat. He didn't feel numb. He rather wished
he did. It would make their relationship less complicated. But,
hell, there wasn't anything that could be done about that now.

"Yes, I'd like a cup of tea," he said, replying to her first
question and ignoring her teasing for the time being.
"Thanks."

He watched her walk back into the kitchen and put the kettle on to boil. She reached into a cabinet and pulled out some
china cups and saucers, then knelt to pull a large wooden case
containing silverware out of another one. The kitchen, like the
rest of the house, was clean and neat, warm and welcoming.

"Have you seen anything interesting in those credit-card
bills?" she asked. She called out the question a little more
firmly than necessary, because she hadn't turned toward him
when she spoke. She was standing at the kitchen counter, head
bowed, intent on slicing apples and cheddar cheese and layer-
ing them on a handpainted, stoneware dish.

Danaker barely heard what she said. He found it hypnotiz-
ing to watch her. Her graceful walk. Her well-balanced car-
riage. She probably hummed to herself when she worked
around here alone, he thought. He wasn't used to seeing a
woman like this. It had been a long time.

She brought in the plate of cheese and apples and a small,
cloth-lined basket of freshly baked French rolls, and placed
them on the table. Then she looked at Danaker, who still hadn't
answered her question. Seeing the out-of-focus expression in his

eyes, she put her hands on her hips and lifted her brows questioningly.

"Danaker! You look like you've been hit with a sledgehammer! What have you found?"

He was still staring at her over the top of his glasses. What had he found? That he enjoyed her company. That this domestic setting, with its warmth and aromas, was a tempting pleasure. That he'd like to ask her out on a date. That he'd like a lot more than that. More than he'd let himself want from a woman in a very long time.

"Danaker?" This time she was less self-assured, and a frown appeared on her brow. "Is something wrong?" She put a small china plate in front of him, and glanced down at the material he had been reading, as if she would find the answer to her question there.

Danaker removed his glasses, folded them and slipped them into the case on the table. He looked at her seriously and considered whether to tell her the truth.

"Yes. There is something wrong."

Daphne sat down in the chair nearest him. She ignored her tea and the food arrayed between them.

"What is it?" She looked at the bills. "Do you think you've found a clue?"

"I'm talking about something else, Daphne."

She was perplexed. He seemed reluctant to explain what was on his mind, and yet it was clear that it was something fairly serious. Perhaps he thought it would hurt her. Well, she could lay that to rest. She'd already been disillusioned and wounded. More bad news surely couldn't be that hard to handle, she reasoned.

She held out her hand expressively and said, "Danaker, whatever it is, it can't be worse than what I've already been through, and it can't be worse than not knowing the whole truth. If you'll remember, that's why I agreed to let you look at these things and to answer your questions . . . so I could discover the truth." She braced herself to hear some astounding—and probably revolting—fact about her late husband's life. "Now . . . what's wrong?"

He smiled wryly. "You don't need to prepare for a direct hit," he said, noting her I'm-ready-to-take-it-on-the-chin posture. "I'm not talking about Jamison. I'll get to him later." He paused.

Daphne went from perplexed to completely lost. "Then what *are* you talking about?"

"Meeting you in this...situation...is what's bothering me," he said slowly.

"What?" It took her a moment to switch gears. She hadn't been expecting this.

"I wish that we had met under different circumstances," Danaker explained patiently. He sighed and leaned back in his chair, steepling his fingertips in front of him and carefully choosing his next words. "It's difficult to ask a woman who's just been widowed to go out to dinner." He looked at her startled expression and said ruefully, "If you could see your face right now, you'd know what I'm talking about." He swore softly. "I'm sorry, Daphne. I guess I shouldn't have admitted it. I thought that since you weren't deeply in love with Jamison and hadn't been for a while, it wouldn't offend you to hear that. Was I wrong?"

"You want to ask me out to dinner?" She stared at him, wide-eyed.

He lifted a brow, and his grin became charmingly lopsided. "Yes."

She tore her eyes away from him and lifted the lid on the sugar bowl. Her hand trembled as she spooned some sugar into her tea.

"Daphne?" he said softly. "After this is over... and you've had time to get your bearings in life again...I'd like to take you out."

She swallowed her tea, nearly choking on it, and cleared her throat. "On a date?"

She wasn't being obtuse. She was stalling for time, trying to gather her wits and hold her emotions together. She had felt an elemental pull toward *him,* but she hadn't expected him to admit an interest in *her.* Now what did she do?

"Yes, Daphne," he said softly. "I'd like to get to know you better, spend time with you."

He didn't want to call it a date, though, because it was more than that. To him, "dating" was what he'd done twenty years ago: the casual pursuit of a variety of appealing women. No strings. No promises. Just a mutually good time and no hurt feelings when it was time to move on. Then he'd fallen for Cherie and retired from the world of singles with no regrets. After she died, he hadn't gone back to it. He'd never wanted to.

He had learned what genuine intimacy with a woman could mean, and it had spoiled him. He wasn't interested in anything less. He was reasonably self-sufficient; he didn't need to go hunting for a woman to fill some void in his life.

But this was different. Daphne intrigued him, and he was damned if he could explain it. What he wanted from Daphne wasn't going to be satisfied by anything casual or superficial. It went deeper than that. He could feel it in his bones.

Just then Daphne lifted her head and caught his unguarded expression. Heat flowed through her, and her breath caught. No woman could mistake the look in his face. He wanted her. She felt an answering surge of desire that drenched her in fire as it coursed through her body. She saw something flicker in the back of his pale brown eyes, as if he knew how he affected her.

He mustn't touch me, she thought desperately. No holding hands, no dancing, and most certainly nothing else! She was responding to him as she had never responded to any man before in her life, and they were barely acquainted! Was it the stress she was under? A reaction to Connor's probable infidelity? Middle-age craziness?

His eyes were warm and strong and hypnotic, and Daphne felt herself falling into enchantment in spite of herself.

Danaker had seen the recognition in her eyes. And the fear.

He badly wanted to reach out and touch her, to tilt her face toward him, to lean forward and brush a light and tender kiss on her trembling lips. But it was too soon for that. She was too fragile to handle it. Their relationship was in a delicate state of balance, and he didn't want to rock the boat.

His gaze dropped to her lips.

Daphne's mouth tingled. Was it wrong to ache for a kiss, she wondered? It had been so long....

He lifted his eyes and saw the longing, the sadness, the desire, the guilt.

"I promise you," he said softly. "There will be a time when you won't mind being kissed again."

She blushed. "Am I that obvious?" she whispered unhappily.

His eyes grew tender. "No. I'm paying damn close attention."

In the living room, Pooch and Cleo began yowling and tugging on the same toy, breaking the spell.

Daphne moved her chair a little away and made a very determined effort to fight the disturbing affect that Quinn Danaker was having on her.

"How long did it take you?" she asked, trying to redirect his interest away from her.

"'Til now."

Daphne recoiled in surprise. He was telling her that she was the first woman who had interested him since his wife's death. His eyes hadn't wavered, and there was a steadiness about him that made it very hard to disbelieve him.

"That's been a while, hasn't it?" Daphne said cautiously.

"Seven years."

Daphne swallowed. "Are you telling me you haven't kissed a woman in the past seven years?" she asked incredulously.

He laughed softly. "Yes. But I'd appreciate it if you could tone down your dismay. I promise you, it was a matter of personal choice." His eyes darkened to the color of warm cognac. "I haven't forgotten how, Daphne."

She felt her cheeks heat. "Well, *I* probably have," she muttered.

He grinned. "Would you like to find out?"

"No!"

He laughed again. "Let me know if you change your mind."

"Are you teasing me, Danaker?" She eyed him suspiciously.

He leaned toward her, sobering. "Yes. But I meant everything I said."

From the way he was looking at her, she had no doubt that he did. Nervously, she reached for the dish of food and offered it to him. Her mother had always told her the best way to keep a conversation moving was to keep the food coming. *Mother, I hope you were right,* she thought fervently.

He went along with her, taking some apple and cheese without argument.

"Now," she declared firmly, "getting back to the reason you're here . . ."

Danaker restrained himself from pointing out that *she* was the reason he was here and took a solid bite out of the apple and cheese instead. Let her take charge for a while, he reasoned. It would help build up her confidence, something marriage to Jamison had apparently torpedoed. Then, the next time he brought up the subject of kissing, she might not act like that held about as much appeal for her as a stiff drink of hemlock.

"What have we learned so far?" Daphne looked at him, trying to don a businesslike attitude and finding it difficult. Danaker was looking at her in a decidedly unbusinesslike way. She frowned. "Danaker!"

He finished munching on the food, drank some of the tea and tried not to let his fantasies about her show on his face.

"All right," he said. He put on his glasses and opened the notebook he'd brought in which to organize information about Connor Jamison. "Here's what I've got so far...."

Chapter 7

"For most of the three months before he died, Connor Jamison was in Europe working on several different projects for his employer, Corday International. He came home every two or three weeks for a few days, went into Corday's Washington office when he was here and told you very little about what he was doing."

Danaker glanced over his reading glasses at her and paused significantly.

Daphne nodded. "Connor hadn't talked in much detail about what he was doing for several years, ever since he started working for John Sarmien. When Sarmien moved his division to Salzburg, he took Connor with him, and everything got even more secretive. Connor said if their competitors knew what they were working on, it would make it more difficult for them to win contracts." She ran her fingertip around the rim of her teacup, wondering how many lies had been hidden under that broad canopy. "I had no reason not to believe him."

Danaker nodded. "He was probably telling you the truth."

Her head snapped up, and she looked at him in surprise.

"He just wasn't telling you the *whole* truth." He went back to the notes he'd jotted down. "Now...he'd mentioned that the three projects were taking up a lot of travel time. And, from looking through the bills you've gotten, it's possible to get a rough idea of where he was going." Danaker flipped the page and read on. "He seems to have covered a pretty broad territory. Most of his time was spent in Salzburg and Vienna. But he was also in Hamburg and Bremen several days each month. The same is true of Copenhagen, Rotterdam, Zurich, Monte Carlo, Naples, Nicosia and Istanbul. Then there are the two one-day trips to Basel that don't seem connected to anything." Danaker frowned and looked up at Daphne again. "Did he mention anything about arranging shipments from Basel? Or Rotterdam?"

Daphne thought hard but came up with no more than she'd already given him. Regretfully, she shook her head. "I'm sorry, Danaker. I really have no idea what he did in all those cities. He'd say things that I didn't understand and he didn't want to explain. He'd mention a name, but when I'd try to pursue it, he'd change the subject, so I don't remember them. Although . . ."

"What?"

"I might recognize them if I saw them again. Or heard them."

That wouldn't do them much good at the moment, but Danaker nodded his head and went to the next page of items. He smiled cynically. It was the summary of Jamison's hotel and restaurant bills that had been charged to his credit-card accounts.

"He entertained a lot. Some of the bills don't match the business-trip locations. It appears that he spent Thursdays in an Austrian luxury hotel when he was in Salzburg. We might be able to get some information from them about anyone who might have been with him."

Daphne stiffened. "Yes."

He looked up sharply. "Do you want me to stop?"

"No," she said grimly. "Go on."

He went back to his notes and flipped through several more pages.

"I have the names, phone numbers and addresses of Jamison's business associates that you knew about. I'll mention their names to some friends of mine who work in Austria and other parts of Europe." Quinn rolled his gold mechanical pencil between his fingertips and tapped it on the blank page in front of him. "That's a general summary of what I've gotten from listening to you and examining the bills that have come in. It sheds light on two of the questions I had. First, where was

Jamison during the week before his death, and second, who are his business associates and friends?''

Daphne poured them each another cup of tea. Her hand was still trembling, but she tightened her grip, determined to overcome the shakiness. ''There was a third question.''

''Yes.'' He hesitated. ''What did he talk about during the last days of his life...and, specifically, on the night he was killed?''

''I've been trying to remember,'' she said seriously. ''The police asked, and you told me you were interested, so I've gone over everything I said to them.''

Danaker leaned back in his chair and laced his hands behind his head. The notebook and pencil lay abandoned. ''When did he come home?''

''The night before he was killed.''

''Was the trip a last-minute decision?''

''No. He called from Salzburg on the weekend...something he usually did...and he told me when to expect him.'' Daphne frowned. ''Well, I suppose you *could* call it a last-minute decision....''

''Why?''

''He'd been telling me that he wouldn't be back for another week and a half. When he called that Saturday, he was advancing his schedule. He didn't do that very often. And he was very rushed on the phone.'' She frowned. ''Do you think that could be significant?''

''Did his boss offer an explanation for the schedule change?''

Daphne shrugged her shoulders. ''No, but I haven't spoken to Sarmien since the funeral. We...didn't get into a discussion about work there.''

Danaker narrowed his eyes. ''Did anyone else from Corday attend? Or any other business associates of Jamison's?''

''No.''

Danaker wondered why the police had missed Sarmien. He distinctly recalled Lt. Yarbro assuring him that only the immediate family had attended. Was Yarbro's surveillance team sloppy? Or was the detective not telling him everything?

''Have you talked to anyone else at Corday since the funeral?''

''Yes, the personnel manager and his secretary. There was a lot of red tape to wade through...life insurance, pension-plan information, health-insurance arrangements....'' She didn't really want to go into all that.

Danaker wondered whether the police were going through any of those papers as part of their investigation, and if there were any irregularities there. Such as an unexpected beneficiary. Named Christina.

"Was everything in order?" he asked carefully.

Daphne hadn't the faintest idea what he could mean by that. What could be wrong? "Yes. They even helped me with the paperwork for Social Security. Why?"

"It's a routine question," he hedged. It was easy to see that rehashing the days immediately preceding her husband's murder was still difficult for her. He didn't want to make it any harder than necessary, so he picked up the pace of his questions. "You said Jamison flew in the night before he was killed."

"Yes."

"Did you pick him up?"

"No. He took a cab from Dulles."

"What time did he get home?"

"About nine-thirty, I think." She wrinkled her brow, thinking back. "Yes. Kyle was watching the beginning of a weekly television comedy that starts at nine-thirty when Connor walked through the door." Her eyes saddened. "Kyle was so thrilled to see his father again," she said wistfully.

Their eyes met.

All that could be heard was the faint ticking of the clock in the living room.

Danaker cleared his throat. "So what happened the first night? Did he talk about the flight? Mention anyone sitting next to him? Say anything about the meetings he'd come from?"

"It was evening and we were watching television...." Daphne tried to remember. If she concentrated really hard, she could see it as if it were happening now....

Time rolled back, and she saw Connor striding into the living room. Kyle leaped on him, wrapping his arms and legs around his father, yelling "Daddy!" and grinning from ear to ear. Connor had to drop his bags on the floor to catch his son. Big, soft leather bags. New. She didn't remember seeing them before. She wondered fleetingly why he'd needed new ones. His old luggage was barely a year old.

The mists of time swirled around the picture, and when they cleared it was later that night, in their bedroom. Or what had been their bedroom. Connor was stripped to the waist and searching through a small nylon dob kit that held his shaving supplies. He looked up, lazy smile lifting his expression as he saw her, standing in the doorway, wearing pajamas, a floor-length cotton robe and slippers on her feet. "You don't look like you're volunteering for duty in the marital bed," he'd teased.

And she'd laughed. It had always been hard not to laugh at his teasing. Connor must have been born knowing how to charm people. He'd certainly known how to charm her. But she hadn't been cajoled back into his bed that night. She'd ignored his teasing and asked what she thought was probably a normal question for a wife to ask her husband when he got back from an extended set of business negotiations. "Did you close the deals you've been working on so hard?"

To her surprise, his teasing had frozen over. He'd stared at her, and a frown had dented his charming smile. "Not quite," he'd muttered. That hadn't been like him. Connor had always been flamboyantly articulate. Then, when she'd gently pushed the issue again, he'd murmured, "Just one more telephone call from Lilli Marlene ought to put us over the edge."

"Lilli Marlene?" she'd asked, curious and a little skeptical. "Isn't that a song?"

"A song, a dream, a pot of gold," had been his enigmatic reply. He'd zipped shut his dob kit and buried it in his suitcase, which lay still packed but open on the floor beside the bed. "I'm tired, Daphne," he'd said curtly. "My body may be standing in our house, but I feel like I've time-warped from the future and gotten sling-shot into the past. Let me catch up on my sleep, huh? I'm getting too old to go through this many time zones without a long nap."

"Sure, Connor."

He'd given her a long, hard look, and then added, "You haven't seen any strangers around the neighborhood have you?"

She'd been startled, unprepared for that. "Strangers? No. Why?" she'd asked.

That charming grin slid into place, and he'd rolled back the covers on the bed. "Nothing. I guess I've been reading too many wild stories about how dangerous life is around the nation's capital." He had pointed to the broad, bare sheet. "Sure you won't join me?"

She'd shaken her head. It would have felt like sleeping with a stranger, she remembered thinking. And she'd gone down the hall to sleep in the guest room that had gradually become her room over the years.

". . . And I didn't see him again until late the following afternoon," Daphne finished explaining. "I went out before he woke up, and when I got home, he was gone. He came back just before dinner." She frowned. "He'd taken the bus. The nearest bus stop is only about six blocks from the house. It was a little odd, though. He never liked to do that. I wondered why he didn't take a cab, or wait for me to come back with the car. . . ."

"Do you know where he went?"

She shook her head. "No."

"Did he have anything with him?"

"No." She frowned. "Well . . . he took something out of the pocket of his jacket. . . ." She shook it off as being inconsequential. "I think it was a bus schedule or a flyer. Some papers about the size of a legal envelope. Probably nothing important."

"Where did he put them?"

"I don't know! For heaven's sake, Danaker. Who pays attention to stuff like that?"

"You're right," he conceded. "It seems trivial. It probably doesn't mean anything. But it won't hurt to try to take a closer look."

"Maybe . . ." She wondered why he was so determined to look into every tiny nook and cranny of Connor's recent behavior. It seemed to go beyond necessity. After all, he was just going to give the information to his old friends and business associates to see if any of them knew of any scuttlebutt that might explain the mystery.

"*Think,* Daphne," he said evenly. "Imagine him walking in that afternoon. He's standing in the middle of the room. He takes something out of his pocket. . . ." Danaker let the suggestions dangle encouragingly.

She bit her lip. "I think he went into the bedroom."

"Did he wear the jacket later in the evening? When he went out . . . before he was shot?"

"No." She blinked and looked at him, realizing what might have happened. "It must be in his bags or hung up in the closet."

"You haven't disposed of his things?"

"No." She lowered her eyes uncomfortably. "I wasn't ready to deal with that yet. I've been putting it off. The police looked through his stuff, but I didn't get involved. They brought me anything they had a question about."

There was a moment of silence.

"Would you be willing to go look through his things now? With me?" Danaker asked quietly.

Daphne bit her lip. "Danaker, something is bothering me about this whole conversation."

"Oh?" With steady eyes, he waited for her to explain.

"You're getting very deeply involved in this," she pointed out. Frowning, she said, "I know your great-aunt Mehitabel wouldn't have insisted you go to such lengths to help a lady in distress." She didn't want to sound ungrateful, though, and she hurried to add, "You've been a Good Samaritan, and I appreciate it, but . . ."

He raised his eyebrows. "But?"

"Exactly who are your friends in Europe? And why would they be able to help us sort any of this out? What kind of business were you in?"

She didn't believe it had been anything dishonorable. She couldn't be attracted to a man who was shady. At least, she sincerely *hoped* that she couldn't be. But . . . why was he going into such detail? He was treating this like a full-scale investigation, with him cast as the P.I. It didn't make sense. The man had a business, a life of his own. She stared at him, hoping he would say something that would erase her fears. Something better than the old *Trust your instincts, Daphne,* that he'd come up with last time. But could she tell the truth from a lie?

"Why are you going to so much trouble to help me, Danaker?" she whispered.

He didn't smile, and his eyes never left her face. "In the beginning, I got involved because a man had been murdered in front of me and I wanted to help find his killers, if I could."

That was true. Not the whole truth, he knew, but true. He hoped she wouldn't hold it against him later, when she found out the rest of it. And he was sure that she would, because he was damned if he would walk out of her life when this was over. That would have to wait for now, though. She had enough to

deal with; besides, some of his previous work was still classi-
fied as secret by either the government or the company he'd
worked for, or both, so he wasn't free to discuss it, in any event.

"That was the reason 'in the beginning'?" she repeated,
puzzled. "Is there another reason now?"

He smiled slightly and looked straight into her beautiful eyes.
"Yes. And you damn well know what it is," he said softly.

Daphne stared at him and struggled against an unexpected
wave of longing.

"I wish you wouldn't. . . ." she whispered unhappily.

"Be attracted to you—" he paused "—or admit it?"

Her head swung around, and her eyes cooled slightly. There
was a dangerous ring to his words that brought her partially
back to her senses. Danaker was not the kind of man to take no
for an answer. He would press for the answer he wanted with
every means of persuasion he had.

Connor had been like that. The thought hurt.

She told herself that the two men were very different. From
what little she knew about Danaker, she had no reason to cast
him in her late husband's mold. Still, his determination worried her.

"How can you be attracted to me? You hardly know me."
She stared at him warily.

He rose from his chair and, with great deliberation, came
around the table to her. He'd heard the distrust in her voice,
and it had angered him, even though he understood why it was
there.

Hell. She was right. They hardly knew each other. And yet,
in his bones, he knew she was wrong. When he looked at her,
he felt as if he'd known her forever. But he wasn't idiotic
enough to admit something like that to her. Understanding her
wariness was one thing, he thought grimly. Handling it with the
finesse that he would like, well, that was something else again.

Daphne lifted her face and jutted out her chin defiantly. She
wouldn't let his nearness bother her, she swore. So what if her
heart beat faster and her palms were getting damp and she
could hear the roaring of her own breathing? She'd ignore those
things, she vowed. She wasn't going to become ensnared by
another man's silvery words. She'd been vaccinated against that
particular virus in the long, empty years with Connor.

But as he rested one hand flat on the table in front of her and
leaned closer, her nerve faltered. She sank back in her chair and
prayed he wasn't going to kiss her.

He was a very impressive man, she thought faintly. Attractive. Determined. Articulate. Rugged looking. All man. And, at the moment, he was breathtakingly close. What would it be like to be the woman in his life? She had the feeling that it would be an experience without many equals. She wondered fleetingly what his mouth would feel like. Her eyes glazed over. His mouth. Hard, firm, smooth and warm. Strong and yet tender. Honest and somehow mysterious. Complex and tantalizing. Like the man.

"Daphne?" he said softly.

She blinked sharply and quickly gave her tantalizing thoughts the deep six. Thinking about how it would feel to kiss him would get her into acres of trouble. Surely she already had enough, she thought bitterly. She swallowed and tried to pull herself away from him a little more, physically and emotionally.

His eyes glittered with anger as he saw her determination to keep him at arm's length.

Daphne frowned. What did *he* have to be angry about? She found it difficult to think with the heat from his body sizzling her skin and the faint scent of his after-shave tantalizing the air she breathed. He was very close, and although he made no move to touch her, she felt enveloped by him. And protected. In spite of his anger.

The glitter of his pale brown eyes made her feel hot and cold at the same time. Goose bumps scampered across her skin. Her mouth felt dry. Her lips tingled. What was happening to her?

He slowly leaned down until scant inches separated his face from hers. With his other hand, he grasped the back of her chair, fencing her in. She was truly surrounded now.

Daphne swallowed and tried, without a great deal of success, not to look intimidated.

"Which is it, Daphne?" he asked softly. "You don't relish my being attracted to you? Or you just wish to hell I wouldn't be so crude as to admit it?"

There was a gravelly edge to his voice. He was frustrated. And a little bit hurt, she thought, surprised. He really did feel something for her. And it surprised him as much as it was surprising her. Daphne stared at him, searching his face for some hint that he might be lying. There was nothing. Just masculine impatience at her reluctance to admit there was something between them.

Something inside her softened. An ancient pull, tearing down a brick from her wall of resistance. She lowered her eyes, trying to gather her courage. When she raised them again to his, she admitted softly, "I don't mind your being attracted, Danaker."

He was surprised she was willing to say that, and he made no effort to conceal his satisfaction. He held her wide-eyed stare and said in a mildly sarcastic tone, "I'm glad to hear that. I was beginning to wonder if I'd completely lost my judgment where women are concerned."

"No. Your judgment is unimpaired," she conceded, a little crossly. What had she expected? For him to go down on bended knee and kiss her hand in appreciation? Obviously his frustration was still biting, but Daphne was feeling raw herself. She wasn't up to handling his ego delicately, and she exclaimed in exasperation, "Men! You're all alike! Always wanting *your* feelings considered, *your* needs met. You become attracted, and it's the first time since your wife died.... Well, maybe it is or maybe it isn't...." Her voice faltered. That was a nasty thing to say to him, she thought guiltily. But then, betrayal was hard to forget. And she most certainly had been betrayed. "I don't know if you're telling me the truth or not," she said wearily. "But I wish you'd keep your... inclinations... to yourself."

He lifted his hand from the back of the chair and reached out, intending to touch her hair. He stopped short, letting his hand hover above the back of her head, not quite touching her. He suddenly ached to touch her. He wanted badly to connect with her in some fashion. He still didn't really understand why, but he didn't give a damn at the moment.

"So. You don't want me to admit my attraction?"

"It's silly to have this conversation, Danaker. You've already let the cat out of the bag. There's no putting it back in. Whether I wish you would or not, you can't take back admitting your interest."

She looked away, frowning unhappily, then ventured another glance at his unyielding expression. His eyes were narrowed, his jaw clenched, his posture tenser than she'd ever seen him before. Leashed energy, she thought faintly. She hoped the tether that held it was a strong one. For both their sakes.

"You're right. I can hardly take it back. I'm attracted to you, all right," he growled. "But I'm not a boy, Daphne, playing at growing up, like Connor Jamison was. I'm a man. I know myself. And I know what's worth having in life." He laughed bitterly. "You said we hardly know each other. All right. How well did you know your late husband? Apparently not as well as you thought. So time doesn't necessarily help you get better acquainted."

"Yes, but..." She didn't know how to argue against that, and yet she felt she should, somehow. "It doesn't seem right to say you can know a person's soul from just a first meeting...."

He touched her chin gently with his hand, cupping the soft skin and delicate bone beneath it. His eyes darkened, and he looked down at her ripe, finely cut mouth.

"Sometimes that's exactly what happens," he muttered. He cleared his throat and withdrew his hand, as if touching her burned him. "I don't need to know what you like for breakfast or what your mother called you as a little girl or what you thought you wanted to be when you grew up. I'll enjoy hearing about it, but that isn't what draws a man to a woman. And you damn well know it." He challenged her to debate it.

She touched her cheek, still feeling the trail of simmering fire that his fingers had lit. His voice was hypnotic. As were his eyes. She felt herself letting go of her arguments again. It would be so easy to succumb. To let him persuade her. To accept his offer of male attention. Attention that would end up expressed in the most fundamental and possessive ways known to man. Every cell in her body was responding to him. She wanted him to pursue her, to conquer her, to bring her the ecstasy and the fire and the possessiveness that had been denied her all her life. It was a hunger she had never really felt before, and she didn't understand how she could feel it for him. But she did. It had to be some sort of trick. Didn't it?

She was afraid of him, but mostly she was afraid of herself. That showed in her eyes.

"I won't hurt you, Daphne," he promised her softly. His fierce expression gentled a little. "Hell. I'm going about this all wrong." He grinned wryly. "If I'd been chasing women for the past seven years, I'd be better at it than this, don't you think?"

She smiled and shyly caught her lip between her teeth. "Maybe."

"Look...I'm not Connor Jamison." With an effort, he straightened and stepped away from her. "Be irritated with me for speaking too soon," he suggested, the hint of a smile still playing across his hard mouth. "But don't brand me for the sins of another man, Okay? I've committed enough crimes to be hung on my own spurs.''

Daphne blushed, already regretting that particular accusation. "I'm sorry for that. It was . . . a low blow."

He smiled slightly. "And I'm sorry for scaring you."

"Does that make us even, then?"

"I'll call it even if you will." He lifted a brow questioningly. "Ready to finish our investigation?"

"All right." And she led him to the room where Connor had slept the night before he died.

The first thing that Danaker noticed was that there was no trace of Daphne in the room. No clothes, no personal items, no scents of perfume or lotions.

It might just as well have been a nicely kept room at a motel. Bland and used by a traveling salesman. Which pretty much described Connor Jamison.

And Quinn Danaker.

Chapter 8

They didn't find a thing.

It wasn't for a lack of trying, either. Danaker looked through every one of Connor Jamison's possessions in that bedroom. He even showed Daphne how to check for hidden pockets to try to speed things up. And to keep her occupied.

At first she'd stared at him in surprise, wondering out loud where he had learned such thoroughness and why it was needed here. She had reluctantly accepted his suggestion that Jamison might have routinely concealed information because of the secrecy surrounding his negotiations . . . and the strong possibility that he was romantically involved with another woman. Stoically, Daphne had examined the seams of his clothing, the linings of his coats, even the construction of his wallet.

But the police hadn't missed anything. There was nothing to find.

If there were any hidden messages in Connor Jamison's clothes and luggage, Danaker swore that he'd swallow the ceremonial rifle hung in his study. The place was clean. Jamison had perfected the art of carrying no incriminating evidence on his person. Which left Danaker wondering whether the message Jamison had been bringing him might have been memorized. If it was, it was lost forever.

Only one faint hope remained. The jacket that Jamison had worn on the night before he was killed was still unaccounted for.

It had not been among his things. Daphne had fretted and muttered and checked every place she could think of inside the house, but it was nowhere to be found. She had volunteered to check the laundry that they usually patronized, and on Monday, she'd done exactly that.

But Jamison hadn't dropped it off there, either. No one had seen him, and he was well-known by the laundry staff, so it was unlikely he had been overlooked. Of course, if he had used some other laundry for some reason, it would be very difficult to discover. The fact that they hadn't seen any laundry claim checks among his things made the task a formidable one. Without a claim check, there was no way of knowing which laundry to investigate. Going to all of them would be a big headache. The number of establishments within a fifteen- or twenty-mile radius of their home was huge. It could easily take weeks to visit them all. And if he'd gone farther than that, the task became even more daunting. Especially since they might be pursuing a red herring. They had no reason to believe he'd even gone to a laundry with the jacket.

Danaker's advice had been succinct. Leave it for Yarbro and Foley. "They'll get less resistance and fewer suspicious looks than you or I would," he'd pointed out. Besides, they had more manpower that they could draft into service than either Daphne or he did.

"You're probably right." She'd sounded discouraged. On the phone, it was difficult to tell.

"Daphne?"

Silence. Then, "What?"

"I may have some information from my European contacts by this weekend."

She hadn't responded. The phone line echoed with emptiness.

How should he interpret her silence? he wondered. Anxiety about what his news might turn out to be? Unhappiness about the situation she was in? Nervousness about him? "Daphne? Are you still there?"

"Yes."

"I'd like to see you sometime Saturday or Sunday. Would you be willing?" He had tried to keep it cool and professional sounding. It had been tough.

She had hesitated. "Couldn't you just tell me what you've learned, over the telephone?"

"Yeah. But, depending on what I find out, it may be easier if you're not worrying about Kyle crashing in on the middle of it."

He felt her distress, even though she simply murmured, "Oh."

"Look," he'd suggested, "why don't I take you and Kyle to dinner Saturday? I can tell you what I've learned, and Kyle won't have to hear anything."

"How do you plan to accomplish that?" she'd asked dryly. "Kyle's ears are as sharp as an elephant's memory when it comes to hearing things he's not supposed to."

That had made him grin. He'd had the same tendency himself as a kid. "Don't worry. I know just the place to keep his delicate hearing filled with other kinds of noise."

"Oh." Then, doubtfully, "I don't know, Danaker...."

"Daphne ... it's just a quiet dinner and an exchange of information ... with some loud entertainment to keep Kyle busy. We won't stay out late. You have my word on it."

"Do you think you'll know who—" she had stumbled over the name again "—who Christina is?"

He'd sighed. "Maybe. My contacts will do their best, but I don't have a crystal ball, Daphne. I won't know what they're going to say until they tell me. Give me until Saturday. Okay?"

The prolonged silence that met his request had seemed like an eternity to him. He had tried to fashion some more arguments to persuade her to meet with him, in case she chickened out. Damn it. If he'd only met her before all this had happened. Or long, long afterward...

"All right," she'd agreed at last. "But Kyle has a soccer game at three, and we won't be back until close to six...." She had sounded almost hopeful that that might make him alter his plans.

"No problem," he'd said easily. "You won't even have to change. The place I have in mind is a favorite weekend hangout for tired soccer players." He'd grinned as he heard her groan in recognition.

"You want to go to The Farmer's Mouse!" she had exclaimed.

"Can you think of a noisier place to go to?"

"National Airport at five o'clock any weekday?"

"Well, if you really prefer it...."

"No! But, Danaker, if you don't have anything to tell me, promise me you'll cancel, okay?"

"No."

"You won't promise?"

"No, I won't." He wanted to see her again, damn it, and he wasn't about to let her undermine his plan so easily. "But don't worry. I'll have news. Even if it's still sketchy."

"Your friends must work fast," she said doubtfully.

"Yeah." Sometimes lives depended on it. Besides, they owed him. And Janisch.

"Danaker?"

"Yeah?"

"Thank you . . . for trying to help."

Her voice had been so soft that it melted his bones. He'd cleared his throat, but his words sounded rough to his ears. "Don't mention it. See you Saturday."

"How'd the game go?" Danaker grinned at Kyle, who was standing in front of the car, looking as proud as a peacock with his first fan of long tail feathers.

"We dusted 'em! It was a slaughter! Boy, you should have seen me!" And he excitedly launched into an extended play-by-play of the game and a few memorable moments when he'd made the difference between victory and defeat.

They were halfway to The Farmer's Mouse before Kyle finally paused to take a breath.

"What position do you usually play?" Danaker asked, interested.

"Fullback. Sometimes halfback." He fell silent, and his expression saddened. "Daddy used to play with me sometimes. When he could. Well . . . once last summer, when he was in town. . . ."

Daphne, who was sitting next to Danaker in the front seat, turned around and reached back to catch Kyle's hand and squeeze it hard. "Those were good times, weren't they, honey?"

"Yeah," he muttered. He blinked hard, refusing to let himself cry. He was too old for that kind of stuff. But it hurt. And it showed. "I wish he could'a been there today. I really played good."

"He would've been proud of you," Daphne assured him, her own heart aching at her son's sense of loss. "He was always proud of you, Kyle."

Kyle snatched his hand away and glared at her. "Then why was he always gone?" he shouted. "Why didn't he come to any of the games this year? Other fathers come. Why couldn't he?"

Daphne didn't know what to say. "He...was the way he was, Kyle," she said unhappily, still looking into her young son's tortured face. "He loved you." As much as he could love anyone, she thought to herself.

Kyle screwed up his face into a portrait of boyish rebellion. "I don't think he really did," he declared stonily.

"Kyle..." Daphne murmured.

Danaker pulled smoothly into the large lot surrounding the restaurant and amusement center, and parked the car. After he'd turned off the ignition, he twisted in his seat to look from Daphne to Kyle and said, "Would you like to talk this out? I'm willing to sit here awhile."

Kyle frowned fiercely. "No! I don't want to talk about anything." He noticed people going into the restaurant and some of his anger eased. "Say, they're on my team! Let's see if we can sit near them, huh?"

Danaker looked at Daphne questioningly.

"It's all right," she said, sighing, as Kyle piled out of the back seat and ran around the car, making a beeline toward his friends. "It's going to take Kyle a while to get used to losing Connor."

Danaker nodded. "He's doing pretty well, I'd say. Considering."

She gave him a sharp look. "Considering what?"

"Considering how much of a disappointment Jamison must have been to both of you."

They got out of the car, but Daphne was bristling. "You have no right to criticize him," she said defensively.

"I'm not trying to be critical, Daphne."

"Yes, you are. You're jealous of a dead man."

He grabbed her by the shoulders and swung her around. His eyes were hard. "You're right. I'm jealous that he spurned what I would have cherished—a loving wife, a great kid, a home to go to. He threw it all away. The bastard didn't know what he had."

She started to shake. "Don't say such things," she whispered.

"Scared, Daphne?" he asked, sliding his hands down her arms a little, enjoying the contact, fascinated by her reaction. Wide pupils. Trembling body. Lips parted. "Don't be scared," he whispered. "I promised you, I meant no harm. Not to either of you. I swear it."

Their eyes locked, and Daphne felt the world swirl out of focus, as it had before with Danaker.

"I'm not scared," she lied, barely able to say the words.

"Good."

"We'd better catch up with Kyle." She pulled away from him, rubbing her arms where he'd held her.

He followed her, watching her hips sway in spite of her ramrod stiff back. He could imagine what she looked like naked in a shower...what it would feel like to run his hands over her silky skin.... An ache settled in his loins.

He had to tell her the truth about his own involvement in Connor Jamison's murder before he got any more involved with her. It wasn't fair to her to keep back the truth. And he fully intended to get more involved with her. So, when could he tell her? Timing was going to be important. Tell her too soon and she might shut the door in his face. Tell her too late and she might feel he'd betrayed her trust.

That was the problem. What could he do if she refused to see him again after he'd given her the facts? He didn't want her to turn away after she knew the truth, damn it.

Considering the risk he would take of alienating her, he was probably a fool to tell her. But, hell, he would rather be hung for the truth than for a deception. He'd just have to find the right moment. And find a way to win her trust all over again, if necessary.

They found Kyle leaning near the turnstile by the cashiers, waiting for them impatiently. Wild music blared from within the brightly painted interior of the building. Chartreuse polkadot purple and canary yellow. Just looking at it made Danaker feel like the older generation.

Daphne caught his expression and laughed. "This was *your* choice," she reminded him mercilessly.

"Yeah. Next time we'll go to the airport." He pulled out his wallet and paid their admission, politely shoving Daphne's money back into her purse when she tried to pay for Kyle and herself.

"*I* invited *you*. Remember?" he said.

"Yes. I didn't mean..."

He grinned. "I'm not opposed to women paying," he pointed out easily. "If *you* ask *me* out, you're welcome to pay."

Daphne blushed. She'd never asked a man to go out with her. She didn't want to seem out-of-date or completely inexperienced, though. "Fine."

He grinned. "When are you going to ask me?"

She stood in the middle of the crowd, her mouth agape. "Are you trying to maneuver me into asking you out?" she demanded.

"Would I do that?"

"Yes!"

He laughed. "I'll be damned if I say yes and damned if I say no."

Daphne was not particularly sympathetic.

Kyle, who had spotted his friends in one of the video arcades, dove into the crowd, blithely dismissing them with a shouted, "See you later, Mom!"

"Come on," Danaker said. "Let's see if we can find a quiet corner around here somewhere."

"People don't come here for the quiet," she pointed out, scanning the people flowing in and out of the maze of rooms. Kyle and his friends had found a large round table for ten. She could just make him out. He looked like he was having a ball.

Danaker took note of Kyle's location and looked for a table where they could see him if he were to wander. "I think I see the perfect spot," he murmured.

"What?" She frowned and tilted her head back to look into his face. She couldn't hear him over the music, which had gotten unaccountably louder. She pointed to her ear and shook her head.

Grinning, he bent close. So close, his lips brushed her cheek. "Come with me."

His breath warmed her ear. Right down to her toes. Daphne stared into the crowd and nodded stiffly, trying to convince herself she would have felt the sizzle with any man who'd whispered in her ear. Not true, Daphne, a small, rebellious voice hollered back. It's Danaker who does this to you. And he would have raised goose bumps on your skin and sizzled your innards any time you met. Past, present or future.

Danaker steered her toward an alcove not far from the room Kyle was in. The music throbbed, tortured and rhythmic. The lyrics were about love. And the pain of losing.

That seemed appropriate to Danaker.

He held a chair for her.

Their eyes met.

Held.

Daphne sat down. She felt the heat of his body behind her. And the coolness when he moved away.

He pulled the other chair around and sat down. Next to her.

Daphne looked at the bare table. She wondered what her neighbors would think if they saw her like this, sitting close to Danaker. It would look like . . . well, it would look like they were . . .

"Too close?" he murmured.

He didn't look amused. And he didn't look as if he were planning on moving an inch, either.

Daphne shook her head. "If you were farther away, we couldn't hear each other."

"That sounds reasonable," he said easily. He glanced around. "See anyone you know?"

She shook her head.

"If someone sees us, are you afraid they'll be shocked?"

"Shocked?"

"To see the widow sitting thigh to thigh with a new man."

Daphne laughed nervously. "That's a little overstated!" She resisted the urge to inch her chair away. "My thigh isn't near yours!"

"It was just a figure of speech," he said, grinning.

She flashed him a dangerous look. "No it wasn't! Now, could we stop talking about thighs and get down to business?"

He laughed and leaned back, draping his arm behind Daphne's chair. He stretched out his legs and crossed them casually at the ankle, enjoying the soft blush of color sliding over Daphne's cheeks and the determined tilt of her pretty chin. "Sure. But—" he nodded at the waitress bearing down on them "—I think we'd better stall a little until we've taken care of her."

The waitress was a nubile nineteen-year-old with long blond hair, which she wore in a beautiful plait that hung to her waist. She was wearing the mouse costume that the restaurant insisted on. The black mini skirt and gray nylons showed off her shapely legs, and the white fur trimming her well-filled bodice fluffed nervously as she bent to take their requests. She was politely attentive to both of them. But she only had eyes for Danaker.

"That will be two draft beers and two Reuben sandwiches," the waitress said, repeating their order. She smiled brilliantly. "It won't take long," she promised sweetly, and cast a shy, wistful look at Danaker as she left.

"You have quite an effect!" Daphne exclaimed, a little irritably.

Danaker just laughed. "At her age, it doesn't take much to be impressed."

"No? I don't think it was your age that was impressing her."

"Is that a backhanded compliment? Are you saying I'm not over the hill yet?" he asked, laughing.

His laughter was hearty and male. It vibrated in Daphne's body, down to the marrow of her bones, and formed an unexpectedly intimate bond, as warm and real a connection as the touch of his hand. Or a kiss on her lips.

She stared at him in fascination. Suddenly she wanted to know all about Quinn Danaker. Where had he come from? What had he done all his life? He hadn't talked about himself much, and she, trying to keep him out of her life, hadn't asked many questions.

She knew he had suffered at least one bitter loss, and she knew he hadn't let it cripple him. He'd risen from that tragedy a strong man, perhaps stronger than he'd been before. She wondered if she would ever meet anyone who had known him then. Someone who could tell her what he'd been like.

She found that she wanted to know.

The lights in the restaurant flashed in rhythm with the new song being played. It was an old ballad, a slow, mournful song about the pain of unrequited love. Colored lights flickered, casting faint shadows across Danaker's face, accentuating his features, drawing out his strengths. They painted his dark blond hair a silvery gold and made his brows look as fierce as a Viking raider's. His cheekbones gleamed in the light, broad and solid, and his coppery-hued chin looked like it had been cut by a stonemason. The faint crow's feet that marked the corners of his eyes almost disappeared next to the irridescent fire reflected in his pale, amber gaze.

Lambent eyes. Cat eyes. They caught her in their fire, wrapped her in their shimmering flames.

"Who *are* you, Danaker?" she asked softly, searching his face as if she would find the answer there.

He lifted one brow quizzically and bent his head slightly to one side. As he moved, the rainbow lights played across his face, making him look savage for a split second. Daphne felt a frisson of alarm. At that moment she would have sworn he had been a street fighter at some point in his life. The toughness that he usually masked with a courteous and easygoing manner was unmistakable.

Then, as quickly as it had come, the savage cast melted away. The lights flashed again, and new shadows fell across his face. Softer ones. Making him look like a statue of some ancient warrior king. Masculine strength of character was etched with a subtle sensuality. The icy frisson that had clambered down her back now felt like warm steam rising.

The lights shifted to a rainbow of soft yellow and peach. And then she saw the simmering heat in his eyes. A heat that hadn't been there moments before. He had been staring at her while she had been staring at him, she realized.

"Still trying to read my mind?" she asked uneasily.

He didn't smile. "Yeah." She would be shocked to read his. "You were asking who I was." He hesitated. He didn't want to get into too much detail yet. He'd play this one card at a time. Carefully. "I assume you didn't mean that literally," he added dryly.

"Literally?" She was perplexed. Then she realized what he must mean, and she laughed. "No. I believe that you're Quinn Danaker, owner of an antique weapons and firearms business and resident of Alexandria, Virginia." She watched him relax and reach for his sandwich, listening to her attentively at the same time. "I'd like to know more about you.... You know, things like where you were born and where did you grow up and do you have any family? Beyond Great-aunt Mehitabel, that is," she added with a grin. She watched him lick some sauce from his top lip. Blinking, she jerked her gaze back to his eyes. "How long have you lived here? Why did you choose Alexandria?"

"Whoa!" he objected good-humoredly. "One question at a time, okay?"

Daphne took a sip of her beer and pierced him with an uncompromising look. One question? All right. "Tell me the story of your life, Danaker."

He nearly choked on his food. After a quick swallow of his draft, he cleared his throat, blinked his tearing eyes and looked at her in amazement.

"That could take a while."

She took a bite of her sandwich and nodded her head serenely.

He pushed his plate away. "Why don't you take a rain check on the story of my life?" he suggested. "We may not have a lot of time before Kyle comes back, and I think you might prefer hearing the story of your late husband's life."

For a moment she didn't know what to think. He had changed the subject so abruptly, her first thought was that he was being evasive. He sounded like a man who preferred not to discuss his past. As if he were hiding something from her.

That was not the reaction she had expected at all, and she stared at him, her rich violet eyes wide and startled and more than a little perplexed.

Seeing her confusion, Danaker silently cursed his own ineptness. He'd have to smooth this over. Now wasn't the time, or the place, to tell her the story of his life. But he didn't want her to start wondering why. "We came here to discuss Connor's life, remember?" he explained. His voice was rich with persuasion, and he met her gaze and held it firmly with his own.

Her sandwich had lost all its flavor, and it required a concerted effort for Daphne to swallow it. She left the rest uneaten on the plate and took another sip of her beer in an effort to ease the ache in her throat. Her drink had also become peculiarly flat and flavorless. Like so many things in her life recently, she thought dispiritedly.

"Yes. That's why we're here," she murmured a moment later. "I had almost managed to forget...." She looked at him, searching his face for some hint of secrets held, but she found nothing. He was still the strong, lionlike warrior, bearing news for her.

His eyes darkened. He knew exactly what she meant. He'd nearly forgotten why they were here, too. And if he didn't get the discussion out of the way, he'd be tempted to drop it for the rest of the night and find something else to do. Something much more pleasurable. For both of them. The temptation to taste her lips, to feel her body in his arms, was growing stronger. He wasn't going to be able to keep his hands off her for the rest of the evening. He was dead sure of that now. But first he needed to get the talking done. Grimly, he forced himself to ignore his body's countermessage to shut up and find some way to get closer to her. Skin close. Mouth close.

"You found out something," Daphne said tonelessly.

"Yes."

She braced herself mentally. Whatever it was, it was history. It couldn't hurt her anymore. "What did your friends say?" she asked stoically.

"They said the new deal he was working on, the negotiations that were taking him all over Europe and down into Istanbul, involved under-the-table arms transfers."

Daphne looked completely blank. "Arms transfers? As in guns? Weapons?"

"Yes." He watched her bafflement become even more profound. Gently he asked, "Did Connor ever mention dealing in the sale of rifles, grenades, pistols, or other arms?"

Daphne shook her head. Her eyes pleaded with him to make sense of the accusation he had leveled against her late husband. "Your friends must be wrong," she argued, feeling helpless and bewildered. "Connor didn't discuss his business activities with me...at least, not in any detail...but he wasn't working for an arms dealer!" She laughed, but it was short and humorless. "For heaven's sake, everyone knows that Corday International provides educational consulting and technology transfer consulting for private businesses. They don't sell guns."

Danaker became grim. How could he tell her the truth without telling her how he knew? "Everyone I spoke with was in agreement, Daphne," he said slowly. "Corday's 'educational consulting' is a broad cover. So is their 'technology transfer consulting.' They keep a number of paying contracts with nonmilitary groups in order to maintain their offices and their network of warehouses and shipping conduits."

Daphne shook her head and laughed again, and her eyes searched his for reassurance. "No. There must be some mistake. I know the people there. At least . . . I've met some of them. They're just like any import-export group, with desks and phones and secretaries." She tried to remember everything she'd ever heard Connor mention about his work. "Connor didn't know anything about . . ."

"Weaponry?" Danaker supplied neutrally.

"Yes." She swallowed hard. Danaker looked so sure of his information. Could she be wrong? Could Connor have been involved in a business that she had known absolutely nothing about for all these years? It was a horrible thought. To have been lied to for so long . . .

Danaker saw her pale, saw the dismay and the hurt in her eyes. He reached out and enfolded her hand in his, warming it, trying to comfort her, and cursing Connor Jamison for a son of a bitch. How could the man have betrayed her? It was obvious he'd kept Daphne completely in the dark about the true nature of his business. Some of that might have been understandable. But not all of it. It was an open secret with every arms shipper in Europe and North America that Corday ran guns on the quiet to the highest bidder.

"A half-dozen governments have been watching Corday's activities for several years, trying to prevent weapons from getting into the wrong hands. Corday is quite adept at covering their trail, I've been told."

Daphne's fingers tightened around his. His strength flowed into her, and gratefully, she accepted it. She saw his desire to comfort her and thanked God he was here when she needed him: gratitude and trust and a strange mystical bond that coiled deep in her heart and soul.

"You're certain your friends are right?" she asked, instinctively trusting his judgment.

He nodded. "Yes. I'm sorry, Daphne. Sorry that he lied to you. And sorry that I had to be the one to tell you."

She leaned forward until their faces were so close she could inhale the intoxicating scent of his skin, see the finely grained color of his irises, taste the erotic flavor of his breath on her lips. "I wanted to know. I don't ever want to be kept in the dark again. I think I could forgive almost anything but being lied to by someone I trusted . . . or loved."

He slid his hand into her silky black hair, letting it spill over his knuckles, relishing the sweet pleasure of gently cradling her head in the palm of his hand. Her trust was a double-edged sword, bringing him pleasure and pain. He still hadn't been completely honest with her about his own involvement in her husband's death. His gaze dropped to her mouth. God, he wanted to kiss her. He wanted to ignite the fire that was simmering within him, that he sensed was lambent and simmering within her. He wanted it so badly that he could taste it.

"Daphne . . ." he whispered hoarsely.

Her lips tingled. She wanted him to kiss her. Learning about Connor no longer mattered, somehow. Whatever he had been doing, it was going to be something she wouldn't like and would be disgusted by. From the reticent way Danaker was approaching the whole subject, she sensed that Connor must have been up to his neck in all kinds of things she wouldn't have dreamed of.

"Maybe I shouldn't know...." she whispered. Chills were radiating down her spine from the warmth of his hand on the back of her head.

"I thought you wanted the truth," he murmured huskily. It was becoming hard to think, though, with the sweet scent of her filling his nostrils, her eyes soft and mysterious as a midnight fog. He closed the distance between their chairs, pressing the length of his leg against hers from hip to knee. Searing heat blended with the flashing colors all around them.

"The truth?" she said slowly, feeling as if the final nails were being driven into the coffin of her dead marriage. "The truth is that I never knew him. He was careful to keep his life compartmentalized, so that one part wouldn't mix with another part."

"That's a very accurate description of the way he was living." Danaker felt the heat rise in his body and his cheeks ruddied. "Do you have any idea how damn much I want to kiss you?" he whispered huskily.

His eyes glittered like amber diamonds.

Daphne felt the last of her inhibitions begin to unravel. "How much?" she whispered shyly.

He stood up, left just a tip since he'd already paid at the door, and led her rapidly through the crowd into a room jammed with dancers. It was brightly lit, but it was so crowded that they were quickly swallowed up by the gyrating bodies of laughing teenagers and young adults.

"Where are we going?" she asked, feeling her knees go weak. He was very determined, if the set of his shoulders and the look in his eye was any indication. She had glimpsed Kyle putting coins in a video game with one of his friends as Danaker had pulled her through the crowd. He'd be glued to it like an electronic babysitter for at least twenty minutes, she thought.

Danaker pushed open a door and pulled her outside. The cold air hit her hot skin like a shock wave. The door slammed closed behind them, and Danaker turned and pushed her back against the brick wall. They were behind the building. It was deserted. Except for them.

His hands were on her shoulders, and he leaned forward in one fluid movement, trapping her against the rough brick wall with his body as he lowered his head. His eyes were fixed on her lips. His fiercely intent expression made her feel hot and then cold and then hot again.

She raised her arms and encircled his neck. Nothing had ever felt so right to her. Years of loneliness fell away.

He pressed full length against her, swearing softly at his body's instantaneous response. "You feel so damn good," he murmured, touching his lips to her bare neck, running his hands over her waist and hips and up across her breasts. The nipples were tight. He could feel them against the cotton fabric of her blouse. That only served to make his own body respond in kind. He hadn't realized how long it had been until this moment. He could gladly have taken her standing against the wall. As often as she was willing. He wanted to possess her, to fill her, feel her body eager and yielding beneath him. "Hell. Daphne . . ."

He lifted his head and stared down into her dark eyes. He slid his hands into her soft hair, gripping her head gently but firmly, wanting her to know what she was doing and to want it as much as he did.

"I want you, Daphne," he whispered unsteadily. "But I don't want to hurt you." He brushed a kiss against her soft lips. And groaned. It was too light. Too little. He wanted more. He closed his eyes and rested his forehead against hers, sliding his hands around her head, down her shoulders. He stopped above her breasts. "Do you want me to stop?"

It was the hardest thing he'd ever done, asking her that. It gave her the chance to say no. And he didn't want her to say no. Every cell in his body was vibrating with the need to make her his. He could hold off for a while. At least, he thought he could. He lifted his head and gently tilted her face up.

She looked as dazed as he felt. He lowered his mouth to hers. Hesitated when their lips just began to touch. "Daphne?" he whispered.

Desire whispered across her lips, down into her soul. The ache was too strong. She wanted him to kiss her. Very badly.

"Don't stop," she murmured. Her lips skimmed his as she spoke.

She didn't know who groaned. Maybe both of them.

His lips were warm and firm as they teased hers with the lightest of caresses.

She moaned softly and wrapped her arms around his neck, lifting her lips to be kissed.

"Daphne . . ." he murmured.

And he lowered his head, finding her mouth fully with his.

Chapter 9

His kiss was the sweet, forbidden fruit that she had feared it would be. Tempting. Succulent. And utterly irresistible.

The sizzle came back with a vengeance, racing haphazardly across her skin and burrowing intimately into her body, electrifying every nerve along the way. They were nerves that had been sleeping a very long time. Nerves she had never known existed before. Nerves that had never been truly awakened. Until Quinn Danaker had walked into her life. And kissed her.

The enveloping pleasure numbed her last, hesitant fears. It had been a long time since she had felt real pleasure. She hadn't realized just how long. Not until now. Until she'd tasted his mouth, moving warmly and persuasively on hers. He tasted faintly of beer and deliciously of himself. It was addictive, the flavor of Quinn Danaker.

Daphne's half-closed eyes slid all the way shut, and sensations poured in from every part of her body. She relaxed into his embrace, hungering for each and every feeling. The haunting, clean scent of his skin . . . the rich warm taste of his mouth . . . the muscular strength of his arms encircling her . . . the angular male contours of his body pressing against hers. Everything was new and fresh and exciting.

Desire flooded her, heating her skin and making her blood pound until she ached. Her body tightened, and she moaned against his lips. She felt him draw her more tightly into his embrace, lifting her up until her toes brushed the ground. Then he let her slowly slide back down, their bodies gliding in full, exhilarating contact.

He slanted his mouth, securing a new and equally delightful fit, and the tight bud of passion relaxed a little inside her, allowing the first delicate petal to open. She could have purred like a satisfied cat as his hands slowly caressed her back, her waist, her hips, in long, smooth, knowing strokes. Another sweet bite of the apple.

He gently broke off the kiss. When she would have opened her eyes to discover why, she felt his lips on her cheek. She tilted her head back and smiled, savoring the fiery trail of kisses he laid across her jaw, her neck and the delicate folds of her ear.

Lightning struck, and sparks showered her body with the fallout. She gasped and arched against him in surprise and delight as he proceeded to kiss her other ear and caress it with his tongue in the same deeply intimate way. She clutched him tightly and sensed his satisfied smile.

"Do you like that?" he whispered against her ear.

She shuddered. His breath was as exciting as his tongue had been.

He traced the delicate pattern again. Slowly. Lightly. Provocatively. His touch was that of a man who wanted more than kisses. It was gentle and coaxing and exquisitely pleasurable. But it wasn't casual. There was something about the way he touched her.... It was a lover's touch. Marking her as his. Discovering her and savoring it and intending to take the voyage a whole lot further.

Her hands tightened on his shoulders, and she opened her eyes, wanting to see what was in his face. They were standing in the shadows, and he was heavily cloaked in darkness, but she could still make out his expression. His face was taut, and his eyes glittered and were narrowed intently.

She'd never been on the receiving end of a look like that before. It didn't matter. Her body responded and explained to her mind. He wanted her. As he had said. And seeing the intensity of his interest made her feel gloriously female. Utterly receptive.

He smiled, but with the sexual tension he was trying to control, it was strained.

"Lucky for you there isn't a bed around here," he teased her huskily. He tugged her blouse loose from the back of her slacks and slid his hands against her warm bare skin. Sighing, he lowered his face to her neck and inhaled the intoxicating scent of her. "God, but you smell good. I could strip you just for that. You're pure aphrodisiac."

She laughed. Not much of a laugh, but it was the best she could do. "Are you trying to scare me?" she shot back bravely.

Reluctantly he pulled his hands away from her and tucked her shirt back in. Then he cupped her face in his hands and lowered his mouth to hers, kissing her with great deliberation and unbelievable thoroughness. When he lifted his lips this time, she was clinging to him and breathing strangely.

"Yeah. I guess I am trying to scare you, Daffy," he murmured tenderly. He proceeded to open her blouse a couple of buttons in order to nuzzle her there while he caressed her breasts through the fabric. As his palm passed over her nipples, each one pouted a little more. And with each caress a small strand of pleasure twisted downward into her. "I'm trying to scare you, but I'm also hoping you don't scare easily." His hands went to her hips and pulled her up against him. This time, when he kissed her, he deepened the kiss, sliding his tongue between her lips, pulling her more deeply into a sea of desire. "Don't scare, Daffy," he whispered huskily. His lips touched hers. Electricity. And lights. And sound.

"I'm... not scared," she whispered, relaxing against his shoulder and burying her face against his neck. Not scared? Then why were her knees shaking and her legs growing weak? She was scared, all right. Of her own profound attraction to him. And the unexpected depth of her need for him. The juice of the apple was tartly sweet. Which was also the sensation in her abdomen at this point.

His hand on her back was soothing, and yet the ache inside kept getting worse. She wanted him. And she wanted him in exactly the way that he wanted her, she thought, dizzy with the realization. She splayed her hand out on his chest, fingering his shirtfront, wondering what it would be like to touch his bare flesh. The temptation to find out was just about overwhelming.

He put his hand under her chin and made her look at him. Solemnly he told her, "I want you to know that all this is new to me. I don't do this kind of thing."

"This kind of thing?" she repeated dubiously. She laughed tremulously and tried to find some residue of strength in her trembling knees. "You mean ... dragging women into restaurant alleys for a little kissing?"

"That wasn't exactly the way I was going to put it." His eyes darkened. "But it's true that I've never in my life dragged a woman into an alley to steal a kiss." A sardonic gleam lightened his eyes. "But then, I never went to a restaurant with *you* before, either."

"Are you blaming *me* for your—" she struggled for a suitable word "—your enthusiasm?" she demanded indignantly.

He ran his hand through her hair, letting it slide through his fingers, and his eyes roamed her face as if it were the most beautiful thing he had ever seen. "I plead guilty for my own, uh, enthusiasm ... as you call it." He smiled, but soon faded back into seriousness. "I'm not *blaming* you. I'm telling you how it is for me, in case it's escaped your notice ... or you don't want to see the obvious."

His gaze dropped to her mouth, and he traced her slightly parted lips with a fingertip.

She'd never felt so alive, she thought, as the tingling spiraled out from his touch, enveloping her in tender excitement. "I wish ..." she whispered. Then she caught herself and fell silent before the rest of the admission slipped out.

"What do you wish?" he murmured, watching her lips move. Fascinated by her. By everything about her.

"Nothing ..." She lowered her gaze, shielding her eyes from his behind a soft veil of black lashes.

I wish we had met before. That was what she'd been thinking. *Before Connor. Before life turned bitter. Before she'd learned the meaning of betrayal.* Why couldn't life be simple? Filled with happy endings. Like a fairy tale.

"Don't hide the truth from me, Daffy," he murmured.

"I can't just ..." She searched wildly for some explanation.

"Admit that you want me as much as I want you?" he suggested.

That wasn't exactly what she'd been thinking, but perhaps it got to the same point, in the end. She *did* want him. And, until now, she'd never really understood what *wanting* was. Searing heat. Flames that arose from nothing and burned until they were quenched. It was a willingness to seal off the rest of the world and forget about it and concentrate on one thing ... one person ... one man. The ache in her belly intensified. He was right. She did want him. And if he wanted her as much, they were in big-league trouble, she thought. Because there was only one way such intense longing could be eased.

Danaker tilted her head back with great gentleness. From the expression on her face, he could see she was still struggling with the enormity of their problem. That was good and bad, he supposed. If she weren't struggling, *he'd* have to be the one to slow down. And he wasn't all that confident he would be that noble. Because right now all he wanted was to find some quiet, private place with a soft bed and make love to her until they were both so exhausted they couldn't move. But she looked so vulnerable that he felt a twinge of conscience. She *was* vulnerable. He'd be a heel to press his advantage. But he'd also be a fool to let it pass.

He placed a lingering kiss on her lips, teasing her lightly with his tongue, withdrawing reluctantly as his own need for more became difficult to conceal. He stared down at her closed eyes and her kiss-swollen mouth. He had to swallow hard and concentrate on the brick wall behind her for a minute to keep from losing his resolve. *Time.* Just give her a little more time, he told himself. Then he'd pursue her with everything he had.

She leaned her forehead against his shoulder, drawing great comfort from his arms wrapped tightly around her, from his cheek resting comfortably against her head, from the warmth of his well-knit body shielding her from the autumn night's chill.

The silence was broken by the wind rustling a tin can through the parking lot and the brittle leaves of fall scurrying around their feet.

"Danaker?" she murmured.

"Hmm?" He pressed a kiss to her temple.

"You sure do remember how to kiss. . . ."

He laughed softly and tightened his hold on her. "Does that mean you won't mind if I do it again?"

She leaned back and looked at him solemnly. "I won't mind at all."

"In that case . . ." he murmured huskily. And he proceeded to lower his mouth to hers for a long, slow, deeply satisfying kiss.

Daphne softened against him. This was too good to be evil. Too right to be wrong or sinful. She yielded to him, thinking, *Yes.*

His entire body received the message, and it had an immediate and electrifying consequence. He broke off the kiss and held her by the shoulders, pulling her a little away from him. He hated losing touch with her body, but it was the only way he could cool himself down in a hurry.

The door to the restaurant was suddenly flung open, and Kyle stuck his head outside. With the light streaming over his shoulder, he was temporarily blinded. And since Daphne and Danaker were off in the shadows, he didn't see them at first.

"Mom? Are you out here? Someone said they saw you come this way."

Danaker let her go and leaned one hand on the cool brick wall. He shut his eyes and inhaled the cold air, trying to get hold of himself.

Daphne, trembling and frustrated, stepped closer to the light. She rubbed her arms and tried to straighten her hair a little.

"We're over here, Kyle." She was embarrassed by her tremulous voice. It was a good thing Kyle was too young to understand what passion was all about, she thought thankfully.

He peered around the door. "Are you out here to have some sort of important grown-up talk?" he demanded.

"Uh . . . you could say that," she hedged cautiously.

"Oh." He grinned mischievously. "Being grown-up isn't much fun. When the kids come out here it's 'cause they want to kiss."

Daphne blushed and straightened, trying to show a regally maternal appearance. "Kyle Jamison!"

He laughed and swung on the door. The rock-and-roll music blared out into the still night, breaking the peace with great finality.

"Didn't you know that, Mom?" The boy laughed again. "If you didn't see anyone it's because they saw you first and went somewhere else to kiss. To their cars, or something."

Daphne couldn't help looking around. Her cheeks grew even redder. Had they been so lost in their kissing and fondling that someone had seen them and she hadn't even noticed? She sent a pleading look at Danaker, who was still leaning against the building and looking rather unhappy about the whole situation. He shook his head.

"I didn't hear or see anyone," he said quietly. Then he grinned ruefully. "Of course, our, uh, conversation . . . might have drowned them out."

Daphne turned back to her door-swinging son. "Why did you come looking for us, Kyle? Did your friends leave?" She stepped into the light and pulled him gently but firmly off the door. "I don't think they'll appreciate the cold air inside. Why don't we close it?"

He shrugged and hopped down to the ground, letting the door slam shut behind him. "Naw. They didn't leave. They want me to spend the night. I came to ask you if it's okay."

Daphne froze. "It's all right, but—" she frowned thoughtfully "—we'll need to go home and get your pajamas and things. And you'll need to take a shower first." She pointed to his still-dusty knees and mud-spattered soccer uniform. "You came right from the game, remember, hotshot?"

Kyle gave a blasé shrug. "That's okay, Mom. I can take a shower at Crabby's house. His mom said she's got plenty of towels, and it'll be easier to get Crabby into the bathtub if he knows he's not the only kid who has to wash."

Daphne couldn't think of an argument to counter that. Getting the boys to clean up was a major battle. She knew just how Crabby's mother felt. "Well..." she said uncertainly. She glanced at Danaker. "Would you mind taking us home now?"

"No. I don't mind." As long as he had another minute of cold air before he had to walk to his car in front of any discerning eyes.

But Kyle had one other bombshell to drop. He pulled the house key up from its chain around his neck. "You don't have to go yet, Mom. I've got my key! Crabby's brother drove, and his mom said she'd keep an eye on me and make sure I brought my toothbrush and everything."

He looked very pleased with himself. "See. I'm a big kid now. You don't have to do everything for me. So can I go to Crabby's? Huh?"

Daphne stared at Kyle's winsome smile and watched the colored lights from inside the restaurant glint on his key.

Danaker straightened. "This Crabby... is he a long-time friend?"

Daphne nodded. "They live around the corner."

"Sounds reasonable." And safe, he added to himself. Then, softly, "Why don't you let him go, Daffy? He could use a good time."

And so could she. That was what he left unspoken, but she heard it quite vividly. She stared at him. She wanted to be with him. Alone. Without interruptions. And yet... maybe it would get completely out of hand.

His eyes glittered in the darkness. He wanted it to get out of hand, and he was willing to let her know it.

Heat flooded her. She felt like a teenager again. Wild and hot and eager for life and love and excitement. Wanting to be wanted. Needing to be close to someone who cared for her.

"Is it okay?" Kyle repeated, getting a little annoyed at the delay. As far as he could see, it was a terrific plan and there was no reason why any normal person, not even a weird person like a mother, could object.

Daphne swallowed. If she said yes, her chaperon would be gone. She'd be on her own. Oh, God, what should she say?

Crabby and his mother appeared in the doorway, squinting into the darkness. "Daphne? Is that you out there? Is it okay to take Kyle with us? Crabby's been begging for Kyle to spend the night. We'd be happy to have him." She smiled at the boys. "They always have a good time."

Everyone looked at Daphne. Waiting.

Daphne closed her eyes and nodded. "Sure. Kyle knows where everything is." She opened her eyes and gave her son a hug. "You be a good guest, okay?"

"Sure, Mom!" he exclaimed. Then, with a whoop, he tore back into the restaurant, chasing Crabby through the crowd toward the front door. "See you tomorrow." His words barely reached her over the din inside.

"We'll send him back around three or four, if that's all right with you, Daphne," Crabby's mother said.

"That's fine." Daphne felt a sense of anticipation settle over her.

Crabby's mother sent a curious glance at Danaker, who was still standing silently in the shadows. "This must be your friend, the man Kyle was telling us about...uh, Mr. Danaker?"

He stepped into the light. Crabby's mother's eyes opened a little in surprise. And admiration.

"This is Corina Floyd. Crabby's mom."

Danaker held out his hand. When Corina Floyd had finally stopped shaking it, she turned to Daphne and said, "Anytime you'd like Kyle to come and stay with us, you just let me know, Daphne." With a last appreciative look at Danaker, she followed the boys and tried to herd them in the direction of the car.

"It appears I have your neighbor's blessing," Danaker said dryly.

Daphne blushed furiously. She dropped her face into her hands. "I can't believe this is happening," she muttered.

"Do you want to go back inside?" he asked evenly.

"No."

"Good. Then let's go someplace where we can have a little more privacy." He draped an arm over her shoulders and walked her to his car. When they reached it, they saw the car with Kyle and his friends pulling out of the lot. Danaker stopped. He couldn't resist asking, "How in the devil did that kid end up with 'Crabby' for a moniker?"

Daphne laughed.

"Well?"

"The boys on our street had a contest to see who could eat the most crab apples from Mrs. Corrigan's tree."

Danaker shook his head and stared after the car with a certain respect. "And Crabby won?"

"No. But he was the crabbiest loser."

Danaker grinned and opened the car door for her. "I've got a lot to learn about family life in the suburbs," he said in amusement.

"Oh, that's straight out of Mark Twain," she argued, fastening her seat belt as he settled into the driver's seat. "Boys always come up with something wild and crazy like that." She glanced at him curiously. "But I've been wondering...."

He lifted a brow and started the engine.

"How in the world did you know about The Farmer's Mouse?"

He was pulling out onto the road, but he couldn't help grinning. "You don't think an old single man like me would know about a raunchy family-and-kids hangout like that?"

"In a word...no."

He laughed. "Your intuition's batting a thousand. I'd never heard of it until six months ago."

"What happened then?" she asked curiously.

"My brother-in-law was in town for a task-force meeting, and he brought my sister and nephew along with him. They stayed for a couple of weeks, and while they were here my nephew turned eight."

Daphne began to smile.

He glanced at her and grinned. "You guessed it. I had to come up with a place for a birthday party for him." He shrugged philosophically. "I wanted to take him downtown to the Watergate, but my sister said his manners weren't up to white-linen tablecloths."

She giggled. "Eight-year-old boys usually have manners better suited to eating at the zoo," she managed to say.

Danaker nodded. "At a trough."

She laughed, and when he reached for her hand and laid it on his thigh, she was too relaxed and feeling too close to him to think of resisting.

He looked in the rearview mirror to check traffic. "You'd like my sister," he said. Reflecting on that, he glanced over at Daphne. His eyes had turned the color of dark honey. "And she'd like you."

Their eyes clung.

He looked away first. From the tensing of his jaw and the gentle pressure of his fingers holding her captive hand on his thigh, Daphne sensed that he was frustrated that the need to watch the road took his attention away from her. As his fingers tightened, she flushed with pleasure.

"So," she said softly, her voice shaking a little as adrenaline pumped through her in response to him, "you needed to come up with the equivalent of a zoo for kids?"

"Yeah. That about sums it up. So I asked a couple of the boys who live in my neighborhood where to go, and they told me about The Farmer's Mouse."

"And the rest, as they say, is history," Daphne said, marveling at the image of big Quinn Danaker chasing down neighborhood ragamuffins to locate the current kids-and-teens hangout. Somehow she hadn't expected there to be any kids in his neighborhood. It had seemed so... out of the way. Of course, it had been dark the night she had gone to his home. And Danaker had seemed like a man who rarely came into contact with kids. But maybe she'd been wrong about that, too.

They stopped at a red light. A light rain had started to fall, and Danaker turned on the windshield wipers. Daphne watched them for a moment.

"Do your sister and her family live near here?"

"No. Not at the moment. They live in Massachusetts, but they'll be moving here next spring."

"It's a small world," Daphne murmured huskily. His thumb was moving slowly across her palm. She felt it all over her body. And it was wonderful. She tried to hold on to the fine thread of conversation. "Are you happy they'll be closer?"

"Yeah. I like them. Hell, I'd like them even if we weren't relatives. They're good people." He chuckled. "My brother-in-law coaches Little League baseball, and my nephew plays, and they've sworn to draft me as Milo's second-in-command."

"Milo's your brother-in-law?"

"The one and only."

She studied him thoughtfully, staring at him shyly from beneath her lashes.

"You don't see me coaching little kids?" He grinned at her and lifted her hand to his lips for a quick kiss. "Honey, you've got a lot to learn about me."

"I guess so," she said faintly. "It's funny, Danaker...."

He pulled into the semideserted parking lot of a shopping strip consisting of sixteen small stores and drove into a space in front of the drugstore. He put the car in park and turned on the radio. Low, sultry music filtered into the close atmosphere between them. He tightened his grip on her hand, sliding his fingers intimately between them.

"What's 'funny'?" he asked softly.

Daphne swallowed. She felt hot all over. Inside. Outside. The air around her. Deliciously, sinfully hot. "Funny?" She stared at him, dazed by the need to feel closer to him. What had she been trying to say? Oh, yes... "I was just thinking that it's funny that I hadn't imagined you having much to do with kids." She smiled at him, gentling the words, not wanting him to take them the wrong way. "Did you ever want children, Danaker?"

She saw the shadow darken his face. Like a memory of a long-forgotten pain. A thorn that had once hurt. And then the shadow was gone. She saw the toughness in him again, that and a fundamental acceptance of life and its infinite disappointments.

"Yes," he answered. He didn't look away. And he didn't flinch from the admission. "It wasn't in the cards."

Daphne wanted to ask more, wanted to discover the truth about his life, what had made him happy...what had inflicted pain and sadness. But she could see he wasn't encouraging her to talk about this particular disappointment. At least, not right now.

He leaned over, capturing her cheek and jaw with one warm hand, bending to kiss her warmly, intimately, on the mouth.

Daphne felt the jolt of pleasure from her mouth to her toes. As it arrowed through her middle, she grew hot and aching. When he reluctantly pulled away from her, she could barely see him, even though her eyes were open.

"I'll be right back," he promised, his gaze dropping to her still-parted lips.

She wondered vaguely what he was shopping for, but she was too lost in the haze of arousal to think about it. She felt as if she were connected to a new source of energy, every inch of her body alive in new and exciting ways.

She didn't say anything. She simply watched him go. . . .

. . . With those limpid violet eyes, he thought, his body clenching at the open desire he saw pooling in their deep blue depths. He'd told himself that this stop was prudent, just in case things got out of control. . . in case he couldn't stop, or *they* couldn't stop, once they were alone and skin was on skin and the flames burning them up went into blue-white heat. Stop? He could as easily stop breathing.

This purchase represented more than last-minute insurance in case they ended up needing protection from an unplanned pregnancy. It was the last tenuous thread connecting his rational thinking with his behavior before he went out of his mind with wanting and lost it all.

He had thought that he was beyond this kind of incendiary desire. This licking fire that burned clear to the bone. This unrelenting ache that would not ease. This fierce need that mercilessly strangled his conscience and unlocked primitive hungers much too elemental to be denied.

Well, he wasn't beyond them. He was being consumed by them. Hot. Eager. Willing to forget his promise to himself to wait. His unspoken promise to her to let her have time, let her know the truth first. All that was pushed back deep into his mind, locked away where it wouldn't interfere with the pleasure he hungered for now. The pleasure that her yielding body had also been so clearly eager for.

When he slid back into the driver's seat, she looked exactly like he felt. Ready. He clenched his teeth against the urge to pull her into his arms and pick up where they'd left off behind the restaurant. Hell. They were *adults!* This was a public parking lot. Not that far from her neighborhood, either. They'd been lucky so far, but he didn't want to create a scandal in her life. However, he was definitely feeling like breaking the bounds of propriety, and with a vengeance.

"Would you rather go to your house or to mine?" he asked in a voice made gravelly by desire.

Daphne blinked. "Um . . ." She blinked again, tried to focus, pressed her fingertips to her temples. His house? Her house? He wanted her to choose? Oh, God . . . did she have the courage to say? To take charge of a decision like that? This was all so new to her. She knew the message that she'd sent him earlier. *Yes. I want you.* Her body had spoken for her, loud and eloquently clear.

"Daffy?" he murmured, amused and husky sounding, waiting for her patiently, yet gently urging her to get on with it. "Where to, sweetheart?"

Sweetheart. The tenderness in his voice and the sultry heat she sensed beneath the word he had spoken ran over her like warm velvet. She stared into his eyes, hot and mysterious in the shadows of the car. Could she go to his place? Vaguely, she re- called there was some reason why she usually had to be at her house at night. In the sensuous fog in which she was drifting, it was an effort to try to dig out the memory why. The time . . . What time was it? The dial on the clock on the dashboard showed nine-thirty. "I usually take Pooch out before I go to bed. . . ." she said weakly.

His gaze drifted over her, and she knew he was thinking about the last word she had uttered. *Bed.* She blushed from her cheeks to her knees. When his eyes met hers again, he was smiling. Barely.

"Your house, then." He leaned over and gave her a quick kiss. Lightning fast. Anything lingering would have been tor- ture. Later, he promised himself. Later. He kept his hands on the wheel this time, too. He told himself it was just to get where they were going—as quickly and safely as possible.

Of course, the fact that his hands trembled just from his thinking about running them over her smooth, warm skin cer- tainly didn't help. He tightened his grip on the wheel until his knuckles paled. So...no kissing. No touching. Damn. It wasn't enough. Unfortunately, he couldn't stop breathing. And every time he took a breath, he inhaled her elusive, intoxicating scent, and his body throbbed and hardened in response.

By the time he pulled into her driveway, he was covered with a fine sheen of sweat and filled with the driving ache of need unsatisfied.

"I'll get the door," she said quickly, her voice sounding tense and high-pitched to her ears. Before he could say anything, she jumped out of the car. He'd barely killed the engine, just turned to look at her.

She raced ahead of him, fumbled in her purse for her house key. Moments later, her hand shaking on the knob, she finally managed to open the door and hurry inside. She heard his footsteps on the cement behind her, steady and purposeful, then stepping into the living room after her. The front door closed with great finality, and she heard the resounding clicks of the locks being thrown into place by his sure masculine hand.

She dropped her purse onto its hook in the living room closet and went downstairs to take care of Pooch and Cleo.

"Help yourself to a drink," she shouted up to him, hoping she sounded lighthearted, fearing she sounded nervous, because that was how she felt. Nervous. Excited. Frightened. Curious. All mixed-up, and yet still too hungry for him to back out now.

Pooch yowled happily as she opened the laundry room door. Cleo, looking mildly annoyed at having been rudely awakened, uncurled on her side and stretched out her legs, watching Daphne through slitted cat eyes.

Daphne unbolted the door and let Pooch out for a quick visit to the backyard. He scampered outside, tongue lolling happily. Used to the routine, he finished his business promptly and ran back, licking her hand and resting his head briefly on her knee, looking up at her with adoration in his doggy eyes.

"Go to bed, Pooch."

He wiggled his tail and trotted over to his pile of blankets, circling until he'd found just the perfect spot, plumped his bed just enough. Then he dropped down, curling his body until his nose rested over his legs. His tail beat softly against the bedding. His eyes were on her.

Daphne smiled. "Good dog."

His eyes shifted. To the doorway. Behind her. His tail hesitated in midwag. Then it beat the pillows a little faster, and he whined.

Daphne didn't have to turn around. She knew who was there. A chill of anticipation ran down her spine. She avoided looking at Danaker as she brushed by him, leaving the laundry room, closing the door after them.

She stood in the middle of the family room. It was where he had come that first day, carrying her box of work materials. Where the bullet had come so near them. Where he had fallen onto the floor, covering her body protectively with his.

She felt his hands on her shoulders and the heat of his body as he stood behind her. She leaned her head back against his shoulder, soaking up his strength, closing her eyes.

"I'm scared," she whispered.

His fingertips traced the fine muscles of her neck and shoulders, drawing out the tension in long, sweeping arcs. In gentle massage. In unhurried caresses.

"What are you scared of?" he asked, the words so close to her ear that his breath tickled. Delightfully.

"I've never done anything like this before...." she whispered, embarrassed and unsure of herself. But his hands were so inviting, so comforting that they drew the words straight from her heart.

"That's *my* line," he reminded her, smiling, enjoying the feel of her beginning to relax against him, feeling her soften a little beneath his touch.

"Your line?" she murmured, sinking into the warmth of his magic. Then she remembered his words behind The Farmer's Mouse. *I want you to know that all this is new to me. I don't do this kind of thing.*

She turned in his arms. He let them slide down around her as she moved, encircling her in that strange, sizzling net that she was beginning to adore.

"I've never... felt like this...."

He was looking at her mouth. "You were married," he pointed out quietly. "Even though it's been a while since you and your husband..."

"No!" She blurted it out sharply and shook her head. "I never felt this way about him... not even in the beginning...."

She looked bewildered and confused and a little desperate to understand what was happening to her. Danaker felt himself slowly losing the last of his good intentions as he drowned in the limpid violet eyes pleading with him to understand, not to hurt her, to be the comforter and lover she had always longed for but never found.

He released her and cupped her face in his hands, slowly tracing patterns on her flushed cheeks with his thumbs.

"Daphne..."

She stared up at him. Trusting.

"Until I met you, I hadn't considered getting seriously involved with a woman again." He slid his fingertips up across the delicate skin of her cheekbones, relishing the sweet softness. "But that night in the hospital, I discovered what it was to want a woman at first sight." He smiled slightly. "That's a first for me, baby. Never happened before. So I'd say we've both got a definite problem. And it's the same one."

She clung to the words, to the strained intensity of his voice as he spoke, to the slight tremble of his hands as he held her. But, most of all, to the burning truth in his eyes. Eyes like the hot desert sands. Promising fierce winds of change and the sweet mysteries of eternity.

Unable to wait for his kiss a minute longer, she reached up and drew his head down until their lips met. "Kiss me? Please, kiss me."

He groaned and slid his arms around her, lifting her against him, hungrily finding her mouth with his.

Chapter 10

The fierce kiss broke through her last barriers and shredded the tattered remains of her sense of propriety. The bitter memories of a man who had failed her were swept away in the relentless sea of desire that rolled through her. As their mouths fused in sweet desperation, her sorrowful past burned to ashes, a nightmare that would not have the power to destroy her again. Danaker's kiss did that. And more.

The world contracted until there was only the point where their mouths were so intimately joined. The kiss was as red-hot and life-affirming as the sun, and it burned and destroyed and gave her life new meaning.

Daphne felt the elemental need rising strongly within her and nearly sobbed in astonishment and gratitude. For it, and for the man igniting that need. Quinn Danaker. She was vividly aware of him, and only him, as his strong arms tightened around her possessively, as his hungry mouth searched hers, discovering her taste and feel as he skillfully plied her with sweet promises of ecstasy. Their rough-smooth tongues mated in a silken dance as irresistible as breathing and as hypnotic as the ageless rhythm of waves rolling thunderously onto the shore. Plundering and entreating. Sliding and caressing. Teasing and satisfying. He drew her out and he led her on. And she followed. Willingly. Eagerly.

The world tilted, and she dimly realized that it wasn't just her highly charged senses making her feel as if the earth had moved. She was being lifted up against his chest and swung around in a slow, sensuous semicircle, rocking to one side and then to the other, their mouths rolling with the pressure. It felt so good. How could anything feel this good? she wondered hazily. She gripped his shoulders, feeling lighthearted and alive for the first time in years. Her breath caught in her throat, a sob...revealing her happiness and her regret at so many empty years. She realized he'd sensed the change in her, because he changed, too. Something in the way his mouth moved against hers altered. And the subtle new texture of his lips on hers made her feel . . . cherished.

Regretfully, she broke off the kiss, smiling as he followed her up for a moment, not wanting to let her lips separate from his. Then he understood and remained still.

She lifted her head so that she could see directly into his eyes, and she searched for the truth within him. No more lies, she promised herself, drowning in sensation and barely coherent. She tried hard to focus on his eyes. There. She saw them. Looked into them. And her breath caught at what she saw.

Raw, masculine desire burned there plainly for her to see. It was deep and intense, and it was directed exclusively at her. Goose bumps rose on her skin, and her wits scattered for a split second.

"Too much for you, Daphne?" he asked, his voice a thick growl. He didn't want to alarm her, sounding like a bear in the mating season, but it wasn't easy holding himself back now, and the effort required to speak rationally was costing him what little charm he figured he had. Well, hell. He was doing his best, damn it. He hoped she could see that. And that she would realize she could control him. If she wanted to. "Am I going too fast for you, Daphne?" His voice was still a husky rumble.

Too fast for her? She nearly laughed. Or cried. Or maybe it would have come out a combination of both of them. She didn't know. She only knew he wasn't going too fast for her. She was as ready for this as he was, as crazy as that sounded, considering what a thoroughly tame and sexless life she'd led. She sank her fingers into his dark golden hair, delighting in the silky feel, sliding her hands through the strands in a tender caress. When he half closed his eyes and leaned into her palms, obviously enjoying her touch, she felt a rush of purely feminine pleasure. She liked petting him. Wanted to stroke him more. It made her blush to think about it. The images that were rushing at her were new to her. She'd never wanted to touch a man like this. But with Danaker...

Her breasts were pressed flat against his chest, and she finally became aware of a dull hurting in them. It took her a moment to realize what it was. *Aching for his touch.* She was aching to feel his hands on her, caressing and exploring and doing everything to her that she wanted to do to him. Too fast? Oh, no. Not too fast at all. It was a heady feeling for her, tinged with excitement and a little stage fright, and she stared into his hot, golden brown eyes, remembering the desire in his husky voice. Treasuring that endearing sound.

"No," she whispered, answering him at last. "You're not going too fast for me." She leaned down to press her lips against his hard cheek. Then she shifted and kissed the other, savoring his scent and taste and everything about him. She wrapped her arms tightly around his muscular shoulders and promised herself that she would remember this forever. It would be her special memory, the glow that would carry her through when she needed strength, when there was no one near to lean on, no one to share the burdens. She rested her cheek against his, surprised and exhilarated to feel the firecracker heat of his skin. "You're not going too fast for me," she repeated, her own voice shaking with need this time. "And it isn't too much." She rubbed her cheek against him. Just like Cleo rubbing against her catnip, Daphne thought, smiling. "I don't think it could ever be too much or too fast with you."

He wanted to groan aloud as her words reverberated throughout his body like a slow, intensely intimate caress. He swore softly and let her body slide down his until her feet were on the floor. He could feel the outline of her breasts against his chest, the curve of her hips and bottom as he let her glide through his hands. No longer needing to hold her up, he captured her head with both hands and scanned her face intently.

"That's a hell of a thing to tell a man who wants you as much as I do," he muttered. He punctuated the sentence with a hard, sizzling kiss.

When he released her lips, she smiled. She had no idea how seductive and come-hither the expression on her face appeared to him. "I'm not teasing you, you know," she murmured, hoping he didn't think that was what she was doing, when she was literally laying her heart open for him to see.

"I know you're not, honey," he managed to say. Speaking was becoming a definite effort. Every look she gave him, every touch of her hands, her every gesture and word, was catapulting his blood through his body like hot water through a high speed flume.

He ran his tongue over her lips in a caress that was both infinitely sweet and agonizingly arousing. He felt her hands on his shoulders, and when her slender fingers tightened against his muscles in response to the intimacy, he could have howled in sweet triumph. She responded like quicksilver. Fast. Sweet. Completely in tune with him. She was a dream he'd never had and now would never be able to forget.

He found her mouth with his and kissed her again. This time the intimacy and intensity made the first kiss pale in comparison.

Daphne whimpered and pressed herself against him, needing to be close. Closer. There was so much keeping them apart. Even though she could feel every muscular plane of his body through the clothing they were wearing, could feel the leashed tension coiling through him, she wanted more. Skin on skin. Nothing in between them at all.

He swore softly and kissed her over and over. On the mouth. On the cheek. The jaw. Her throat. And his hands ran over her, lightly at first and then more firmly. Sliding across the curve of her breast, lightly passing over the nipple puckered beneath layers of bra and blouse.

Daphne writhed against him. *Yes. Yes,* she said in every way she could. With her yielding body, with her delicate caresses, with her eager mouth. *Yes.*

The gates of temptation widened with every sweep of his tongue, every subtle increase in pressure of his fingertips, every shared moan, every intermingled breath. Each time he swung her up or let her slide erotically down was a step into the forbidden garden. So was each caress of his hand, every loosening of suddenly cumbersome clothing.

Wild sensations swirled over her, as irresistible as the pull of the ocean's endless tides. She felt his hands sliding over the bare skin of her shoulders and arms, down across her hips. Felt him further loosen her blouse until the fabric was completely pushed away and hanging about her hips. He found the warm, bare skin of her stomach, and "Yes," she moaned, pressing helplessly against his palms, against his muscular body. "Yes...."

His hand glided up, cupping her breast. Lean fingertips slid across the tightening nipple, bringing it to full attention. Back and forth. Each caress sending starlets of delight in all directions from the tautened peak. Over the nylon of her bra, then, after a twist of the metal catch at her back, beneath the filmy covering, on the delicately aroused bare skin.

She moaned against his lips as he kissed her mouth. He gently nipped her lower lip, then the upper one. At first he suckled gently, but gradually the suction became stronger, sending fresh currents of anticipation surging through her as his mouth and tongue brought her the first touches of ecstasy. She felt him slide his hands down across her bottom and pull her against him. She felt the extent of his own need, and she wrapped her arms around his waist, holding him as tightly as he was holding her. Aching to bring him the same pleasure and delight that he was bringing her. Eager to love and be loved in return. *Yes,* she cried out in the secret silence of her mind. *Yes.*

Suddenly he tore his mouth away from hers and threw back his head, closing his eyes and sucking in air in great choking gasps. His arms became rigid, and the heat spreading through his body burned through their clothes like a raging inferno. He swore softly. Harshly. Very unsteadily.

"Danaker?" she whispered, wondering how badly he was hurting, what she could do to make it easier. The ache in her own aroused body came through in her voice, in the way she said his name.

He opened his eyes, which were glittering with blatant sexual fire and the struggle to keep it under control, and looked down at her. "I'm here," he said, his voice strained as he managed a sliver of a smile.

She caressed his cheek, tenderness welling up in her heart. He was trying so hard to be noble about this, she realized. Even now, wanting her as desperately as she could see that he did, he was making a supreme effort to give her another opportunity to tell him she'd had enough, that she wanted him to stop. His face was flushed and tight, muscles clenching as he fought to control himself. And the expression on his face literally took her breath away. It was that of a man balancing on the knife edge of taking her down on the tiles and finishing it right here. Right now.

The idea that he could want her that intensely was incredibly exciting to her. If it had been any other man, she wouldn't have felt that way at all, but his desire for her was welcome.

Most definitely welcome. She'd passed the stage of wondering
why that was. She just wanted to rejoice in it. And enjoy it.

Joy. He gave her joy, she realized, rather stunned. *Oh, Danaker, I'm falling in love with you. Stranger you may be, but not
to me. Somehow, not to me....*

"Let's go upstairs," she murmured shyly. She couldn't help
blushing. Flushed with passion as she already was, she doubted
that it showed.

It showed. To him. And so did the shy catch in her voice. His
heart missed a beat. He bent to kiss her, only this time with all
the gentle encouragement he could put into it.

Shaking in response, Daphne stared at him wide-eyed as he
lifted his head. He wasn't smiling. He looked deadly serious.
And then he simply turned her to face the stairs and gently
urged her forward. He left his hands possessively on her hips
near her waist, though, and brushed a kiss across the nape of
her neck as she led the way up to her bedroom.

Daphne was amazed she made it. Her legs were as weak as a
newborn kitten's, and her hand trembled on the railing.

Her room was at the end of the hall. A corner room with
windows on two sides and a bathroom all its own. The navy-
blue linen curtains were open, and the apple trees that stood
just outside were in full view, their limbs embellished with dry-
ing leaves in the early colors of autumn...and two plump, gray
birds. They were staring round-eyed into the bedroom, only
mildly curious. Mourning doves settling down for the night.

Danaker hesitated in the doorway. He allowed Daphne to slip
away from him and he took a moment to absorb the surroundings. He would have recognized it as Daphne's room anywhere, he thought, just from the scent of it...sultry, intoxicating and definitely hers. The bed, a double, was neatly
made, with a hand-sewn quilt folded carefully at the foot and
pillows plumped at the head. There was a nightstand with a
banker's lamp and a half-dozen paperbacks under it, including one with a bookmark in it. The large oval rug in the middle of the room was hooked by hand, he thought. Maybe forty
years old. He smiled, which wasn't easy, since he was still fully
aroused and aching from his hips to his knees. The damn rug
looked like one his great-aunt had in her cabin in the moun-
tains.

He turned his attention back to Daphne then, and frowned
as he saw her scrabbling through things in her dresser. What in
the hell was she rummaging through her drawers for? He came

up behind her and put his arms around her, bending to murmur seductively against the back of her neck, "Look for it tomorrow, sweetheart. Whatever it is, it can wait. *We* can't." He nipped her delicate nape, making her curl back against him and murmur incoherently.

Daphne turned in his arms and buried her flaming face in his neck. Bracing herself, she muttered, "I was looking for my dia..." Her voice trailed off into a whisper so faint that it couldn't be heard. She felt like an idiot for being so embarrassed. What on earth would he think of her?

Perplexed, he asked her to repeat the word, holding her close so she wouldn't have to face him but could simply mumble whatever it was in his ear.

Daphne swallowed hard, tensed her shoulders and said the word again. This time he heard her. She could tell, because his body shook like a man trying not to laugh. She leaned back and saw he was grinning.

He reached into his pants pocket and removed the small package he'd picked up in the drugstore earlier in the evening. "Don't worry about it," he said, punctuating the comment with a kiss.

Daphne sighed and buried her face gratefully in the hollow of his shoulder. "I'm glad one of us is still thinking straight," she murmured. "To tell you the truth, it's been so long, I don't know where it is," she admitted sheepishly. "Or whether it's still any good." Maybe the same should be said about herself, she thought. But then, she'd never been a red-hot lover anyway. Maybe Danaker wouldn't mind, she thought wistfully.

Still grinning, he opened the package and tossed a couple of the small packets onto the night table next to her bed. Then he turned his attention back to the woman hiding her face against his body, cuddling against him like a frightened lamb.

"It's all right, Daffy," he murmured. "Everything's going to be all right."

He deftly tugged her blouse from the waist of her slacks and dropped it carelessly on the nearest chair. A downward pull of a zipper, a few distracting kisses, and she was stepping out of her slacks, her hands trembling on his shoulders for balance as he slid the slacks down her thighs, then straightened to toss them onto the chair with the blouse.

He let his gaze roam over her, enjoying her graceful curves, the shadowy triangle beneath her nylon panties, the delicate swell of her breasts beneath the unfastened bra still draped over her flesh. He removed the bra, their smiles fading. And she stood before him, her heart in her eyes.

He swallowed hard, took her hands and brought them to his shirt front. "Take it off," he suggested softly. He felt the tremor of her dainty fingers as she unbuttoned the shirt and slid it off. She watched him in fascination as he pulled off his T-shirt a moment later. The look in her eyes made him burn. He thought it might not be a good idea to let her undress him further. If her hands touched him any more intimately, he wasn't going to be able to make this last very long. And he wanted it to last a long, long time. For both of them, but especially for her. There was something pathetically wistful about her, he realized. She was looking at him as if he were a Christmas tree and she'd never been allowed to have one, he thought. Well, honey, your time has come, he promised her silently.

Daphne couldn't help herself. He was so handsome. So very male. She stared at his bare chest, dusted with dark gold hair gleaming in the light of the lamp hung from the ceiling. Sultry swirls of pale brown and silvery blond hair arrowed down until they disappeared into the waistband of his pants.

She blinked and looked away. Suddenly she felt very... exposed. And woefully inexperienced. Oh, Lord... She wished she could hide in the shadows, where her shortcomings would be easier for him to overlook. She hoped.

He leaned over and turned off the light at the wall switch.

Surprised by his unexpected understanding, she shyly looked at him. "Thank you."

"You're welcome," he told her softly.

He gently tilted her face up and brushed a soft kiss against her trembling lips. He could see that her nerves had returned. Perhaps because they were practically naked, nearly in her bed making love. Was she thinking it over? Wondering if this was going to turn out to be a mistake? He wasn't going to let her think about it anymore. He'd already decided for both of them. He never should have stopped touching her, he thought. As long as they were in physical contact, her body kept all the messages honest and clear and uncomplicated. Now her arms were wrapped around her middle, and she looked as if she felt overexposed. Well, he had a sure cure for that.

"Lie down, sweetheart," he suggested huskily. He moved with her to the bed. It only required a few steps. Then he put a hand on her shoulder and another on her hip and gently pressed her back onto the soft coverlet, bending over her long enough to press a reassuring kiss against her lips.

He sat down on the bed next to her and removed his remaining clothes in silence, standing to unfasten his belt and drop his slacks. Then he joined her on the bed, stretching out full-length beside her.

"Frightened again, Daffy?" he whispered, gathering her into his arms and sliding his leg possessively over hers. He thought she shivered, but when she burrowed into him like a soft little ground squirrel, he decided that at least her fears weren't going to keep them apart. "Daffy? Talk to me, baby. Don't be scared. I want to make this easy for you...and good for you."

Her violet eyes were the color of indigo at midnight, swimming with emotion, as she gazed into his very serious expression.

"I am a little nervous," she admitted. "But it isn't *just* that I'm afraid or frightened." She struggled to explain, trying to sort out the complex emotions coiling inside her. "You see, I've never felt so alive as I have with you," she began, humbled and grateful to him for that.

He smiled. "Thank you. So...what's worrying you, Daffy?" He ran his fingertip over her shoulder, enjoying the way she responded to him even now, while she struggled to tell him what was worrying her.

"Well, you see...I...I mean...it's just that..." She squeezed her eyes shut. Darn it all, she thought anxiously. *Just spit it out, Daphne. Just do it.* She took a breath, as if to fortify her courage, then finished, the words tumbling out, "I'm not very *good* at this. And I hope you won't be ... disappointed."

She felt his finger still, and the silence stretched between them until it hurt her. She opened her eyes tentatively and ventured to look at him to see how he'd taken her admission.

"Disappointed?" He was staring at her in amazement, hardly able to say the word. He was incredulous that she had suggested the possibility, actually. His only worry was whether he'd be able to survive the pleasure. He had no doubts about how he was going to feel about making love with her. Unlike her, he trusted his instincts implicitly. He would have laughed at her anxiously stated fear, except that he could see that she was very serious.

So that was what her nerves were about, he thought. Stage fright. He wondered if her husband had taught her that, too, along with all the other disappointments he'd handed her. Anger flashed through him with unexpected force, but he squelched it immediately. He didn't want it to show, didn't want Daphne to have to worry about that, too. Later, he promised himself. There would be time for that later.

He wanted to make sure, though. "Why would I be disappointed?" he asked softly, his eyes running over her, letting her see how much he enjoyed what he saw.

Daphne's whole body blushed with pleasure at his appreciative examination. His obvious interest gave her the courage to answer forthrightly. "Connor was. He must have been. To have lived with me for so many years, cheerfully willing to stay celibate. At least, celibate with me..."

"What about you, Daphne?" he asked softly, sliding his fingers along her waist, stroking the fine resilient flesh of her hip and thigh.

She sighed and half closed her eyes, enjoying his touch enormously. "Me? I..." She couldn't remember, really. In the beginning, it had been exciting...mysterious...pleasant. "It was...all right," she said, groping for the word that would best describe it. "It was not torture, or anything like that. I enjoyed it."

Danaker tried not to look flabbergasted. *All right? Not torture? I enjoyed it?* "Your description sounds less than satisfying," he pointed out, trying to make it sound like a purely academic observation. He didn't want her to think about the man, let alone remember any intimate experiences. He ran his hand lightly over her body from her shoulder to the top of her thigh, watching her indigo eyes slide half closed with pleasure. Beautiful eyes.

"I don't know what to say about my...sex life...back then." At the moment it seemed about two hundred thousand years ago to her. Besides, she much preferred her present experience, which, to her delight, seemed to have resumed. He was now caressing the other side of her body from shoulder to thigh, just as he had the first a few moments earlier. A sigh of pure pleasure slid effortlessly from Daphne's lips. "But I think I'll have to invent new adjectives to describe my sex life now," she added fervently.

He smiled and kissed the hollow of her shoulder, murmuring, "Tell me what you like, Daffy. And don't be shy. The bedroom is no place for shyness." He kissed her breasts, reverently, tenderly, sliding his tongue over the coral nipples standing proudly for his attention. "You're very beautiful,

Daphne.'' He stroked her again, wandering over the soft skin of her stomach, gliding downward over her hips to her thighs and inexorably upward again. He found the damp, female heat at the triangular juncture of her legs and cupped her intimately but lightly, sending a shiver of anticipation through her flesh. ''Do you like that?'' he asked thickly, tightening his thigh around her leg, then releasing her to slide his knee suggestively between hers.

The rich tenor-baritone of his question vibrated deliciously in her bones, mysteriously softening them. ''I like *everything* you do,'' she moaned fervently, closing her eyes and looping her arms around his neck in surrender. ''Everything...''

Her response sent heat racing through him, making his skin burn; his loins were urgently heavy, and his fully aroused male flesh pulsed with fierce need. He wanted to bury himself in her soft heat and feel the hot lava of satisfaction erupt inside them both. He clenched his teeth and tried to think of cold showers to keep from rolling on top of her and stroking himself into heavenly oblivion immediately. He wanted to be sure she was with him, and he was just getting to know her body, her needs. Somehow he had to deny himself the satisfaction he hungered for like a starving man. Just hold on a little longer, he told himself grimly. Just a little longer.

Daphne wanted to kiss his hands for what he was giving her. He was a persuasive lover. Tender and skillful and careful of her. He seemed to instinctively know where to touch her and how to touch her. When to press harder, when to ease up and move on to another eager point on her body. She loved it. All of it. And she told him so with every soft sigh, every startled smile, every twist of her astounded body, every shyly returned caress of her own.

When he found the velvety warmth of her inner thighs, her whole body felt a soft jolt of pleasure. And when he slid her panties off and explored the damp heat between her thighs, she buried her face in his naked shoulder, caressing his hot skin in instinctive response. She felt him twist and realized that he was now completely naked beside her. Before she could fall back into a renewed sense of shyness, he was touching her again, and all she wanted was to belong to him. Completely.

He trailed a path of liquid fire over her with his hands and his lips, with his hot murmurings and his lightly grazing teeth. Slowly. Surely. Gently. Bringing her to the edge with him. He could feel her response like the fine shimmering of heat on the horizon in summer. Her flesh was dimpled and rosy and trembling beneath his touch, and her head rolled from side to side. Her soft moans and sighs told him how deeply she was responding. That and the fierce tightening of her fingers in his hair, on his back, across his bare hip. Even the tentative caress she ventured across his thigh. He caught her hand just in time. How much more of this torture could he take? he wondered. Sweet, sweet torture.

"If your fingers had dropped another inch, I'd be gone," he growled, kissing her startled mouth and rolling half on top of her. "Your body feels so good," he told her on a sigh of profound pleasure at the feel of her silken body in full shoulder-to-thigh contact with his.

"Gone?" she whispered, smiling as he pulled her hands up over her head. Feeling emboldened by his obviously intense attraction to her, she teased, "Let me see...."

"You can put your hands on me later," he promised, his voice thick with the depth of his unsatisfied need. "You can put your hands anywhere you like later, honey, but not right now," he swore as she wiggled sinuously beneath him. "Oh, that feels good, but don't do it," he ordered. He looked into her eyes. "Later, honey. Next time..."

Next time. He wanted a next time, she thought, thrilled that this wouldn't be the only taste of bliss she would ever have in her life. Because that was what it was. Bliss. She held still, wanting to please him so that he would let her have a next time. So that she wouldn't ruin his "this time" by making him climax before he was ready. Although, Lord knew, she was ready. Not to climax. She'd never done that. At least, if she had, it certainly hadn't lived up to the descriptions. But the feelings she was having here in his arms were as hot and fiery and thrilling as anything she could have imagined in her wildest dreams. She groaned. Maybe better, she added silently, exhilarating in a new rush of sizzling pleasure as he lifted himself over her, kneed her thighs apart and settled himself intimately against her damp and swollen body.

His breath came out as a painful hiss, and his tight expression was one of pain.

Anxiously she asked, "Does it hurt?"

"Like hell. Like heaven," he said through clenched teeth.

His eyes were tightly shut, and he was holding completely still. He looked a hundred years away from her, as if he were mentally transporting himself to some other planet. Come back, my love, she thought unhappily. She missed his caresses, his closeness. Had she done something to disappoint him? Had she driven him away? Had she done something wrong?

Instinctively she yielded against him, pressing her breasts and belly against his rigid midsection. She felt him stiffen further, felt the throbbing pulse of his aroused body notched tightly against hers. When he didn't speak, but started breathing in long, measured breaths, still obviously struggling with some deep discomfort, she slid her thighs up around his and tilted her hips, welcoming him.

He moaned and tightened his hold on her wrists. Grimacing, he tried to hold himself back as much as he could. It was damned hard. Her body was sliding against him, and if he flexed his hips he would be entering her soft warmth. He tried to think of something, *anything,* to slow down the driving need to thrust into her. Then he felt her lips against his, pleading.

"Make the ache go away," she murmured encouragingly. She was thinking of his aching, although she was vividly aware of an ache of her own that she'd never had before. She tilted her hips and moved her thighs higher, bringing him partly into her body.

The warm, soft heat and her explicit invitation were more than he could handle. With a groan of total surrender, he thrust into her. When she moaned and writhed against him, he freed her hands and caught her hips. He tried to withdraw slowly, to hold on to the pleasure between them.

But she was on fire, and there was something she could almost reach, something deep inside that he had the key for, but she needed him moving to find it. She wrapped her arms around him and begged him with her body to help her.

His blood raced like wildfire through tinder, and he couldn't hold back anymore. He thrust into her, crushing her against his desperate hunger, feeling her shimmer in his arms, hearing her cry of surprise and satisfaction. Followed by his own. And then an endless kiss, entwining their hearts as deeply as their satiated bodies.

Chapter 11

The soft coo-cooing of a mourning dove stole quietly into Daphne's sleeping mind. Gently she floated back to reality on the bird's poignant lament. She had no sense of time or space at first, just an all-encompassing contentment that made her want to float in the mist between waking and sleeping a little longer. The dove cooed again. She stretched and struggled to find the energy to open her eyes. She didn't know how long she had dozed, but it was still dark outside. The dawn had not yet come.

And Danaker had not yet left. A little burst of joy illuminated her heart. Silly to take such pleasure in his lingering, she told herself. Ah, but she was so glad he was there. She hadn't realized how lonely she'd been until he'd shaken up her existence.

He was stretched out next to her, one arm still around her shoulders, one muscular leg fully pressed against hers.

She carefully rolled onto her side, trying not to disturb him, wanting to see him as he slept. He looked relaxed. And a little vulnerable, she thought, smiling tenderly. Even unconscious, he looked like a man you wouldn't want to take a swing at. Unless you wouldn't mind losing your front teeth and a couple of ribs. She studied his face, memorizing the weathered creases at the corners of his eyes, the strong clean lines of his jaw and his cheek.

Yes. He looked completely relaxed. As she thought about it, she realized that she was, too. She ventured a delicate kiss on his firm lips and softly whispered, "Thank you."

He stretched lazily, pulling her closer and opening his eyes, and fixed her with an amused and somewhat surprised stare. "Thank you?" he echoed dryly.

She blushed. "For...well...I never..." She nudged him in the ribs with her elbow and laughed. "You know what I'm trying to say."

"You never . . . ?" He whispered the indelicate word for her helpfully.

"Yes. I mean, no. I didn't. Until now. With you." She didn't know whether she was mostly thrilled or embarrassed or just plain astonished.

He saw all those emotions chasing each other across her face and caught her head with his hand, kissing her, gliding his tongue into her mouth for a deeply intimate show of his own feelings about their lovemaking. "I'm honored, Daffy," he whispered against her cheek as he cradled her in his arms. "And you're very welcome, baby. The feeling is mutual. Believe me."

She hugged his hard, warm body close, tangling her legs with his for good measure. She closed her eyes and sighed.

He twisted around to check the time on her clock. "I'd better get out of here," he said with a note of regret.

She rolled fully against his body and snuggled against his shoulder, as if, by doing so, she would absorb the feel of him being with her, imprint it in time and hold it there forever.

"How long have you slept alone?" he asked, sliding his fingers through her hair in a tender gesture of affection.

"Years."

"Feels strange having a man in your bed again?" he asked wryly.

She smiled against his shoulder and nodded.

"Feels a little strange to me, too," he admitted.

She opened her eyes and leaned on her elbow, looked down at him. "Does it really?"

"I've been sleeping alone for quite a few years myself, Daphne. Remember?"

She nodded thoughtfully. "I'm honored, too, then," she murmured shyly. "That you broke your fast with me...."

He laughed. "That's a hell of a good way to put it." He leaned over and devoured her with another thoroughly ravishing kiss. "And if I don't get out of your bed, we're going to have another big feast right now. I'd be more than happy to stay," he was quick to add, "but it might give your neighbors less to gossip about if I managed to leave before they get up for their Sunday-morning papers!"

He kissed her soundly, then jackknifed into a sitting position and swung his legs over the edge of the bed. He ran his hands through his hair a couple of times to wake himself up. It had been good lying there with her, he thought.

They put on their clothes and went downstairs holding hands.

She wanted to walk him to his car, but he firmly stopped her, standing in the foyer with his hands on her arms and a stern look on his face.

"I want you locked in here safe and sound," he explained, his brows forming a no-nonsense frown.

She gave a halfhearted laugh of mystification. "All right, but I think you're overdoing it a little. I haven't even seen the police patrolling much anymore." She had hoped that would reassure him, but it made him look less pleased than ever. His concern was very sweet, but she didn't want him to get needlessly carried away from it. She struggled for a persuasive argument that would lay to rest his lingering fears about her safety. "I really don't think there's anything to worry about, Danaker," she said seriously. "Whatever violence touched Connor's life obviously has nothing to do with me."

She thought something flickered in his eyes. But then it was gone.

"Yeah. You're probably right. But an extra dose of paranoia never hurts in a case like this."

With a sigh of defeat, she rested her head against his chest and looped her arms around his waist. She could hear the strong, steady beat of his heart, and it made her smile. "Okay. You can be paranoid for both of us," she conceded reluctantly.

"What do you usually do on Sundays, Daphne?"

"Sleep late. Read the paper. Go down to that doughnut shop for something sinfully sweet. Run along the Potomac, or one of the trails around here."

"Mind some company?"

She looked up at him, her eyes shining. "Today?"

He smiled. "Yeah."

"I wouldn't mind. I wouldn't mind at all."

He grinned and ruffled her hair affectionately. "Name the time, sweetheart. I'll be there."

She'd run along the Mt. Vernon trails for years and never noticed just how beautiful they were. Tall, stately trees bent over the light underbrush. Through the autumn-colored forest she could occasionally glimpse the deep blue color of the Potomac River, broad and smooth as it flowed nearer to the bay. Normally she'd see a few new faces on the trail and a whole lot of familiar ones. They rarely exchanged names, but they knew each other just the same.

Today they were all staring at her in surprise.

Because Quinn Danaker was running beside her.

"I feel like I'm being photographed for a police lineup," he teased her as they rounded a bend.

"Sorry," she said, laughing. A small valley rolled out in front of them, with an old mill race cutting through alongside the trail. "They're not used to seeing me with a man."

He grinned at her. "They'll get used to it."

She glanced at him, wondering how seriously he meant that. How personally. But he was scanning the small glen and the other runners and the trees ahead. Always keeping an eye out, she thought. Well, that was nice. Unnecessary, in her opinion, but very nice.

"We'll be back at the car in about five minutes," she announced, beginning to breathe a little harder. They'd run about five miles. She was wearing lightweight running pants and a zippered jacket, and in the warm morning sun the chilly weather had melted away, making her feel hot and thirsty. "Want to stop for something to eat on the way back?"

He caught her hand and kissed it suggestively.

She snatched it back, laughing. "That too," she teased, "but after I've had my coffee."

He rolled his eyes mournfully. "Where's your sense of romance?" he demanded, wounded.

They slowed to a walk, and he draped his arm around her shoulders as they finished the last half mile at a leisurely speed, cooling down.

"You make me feel like I'm a kid again, Danaker," she admitted with a sigh.

"How old are you?" He glanced over her curiously.

"Thirty-six."

He snorted a laugh. "You *are* a kid."

She eyed him speculatively. "Oh? And how old are you, Oh Ancient One?"

"Old enough to know better," he said half seriously.

She gave him an affectionate bump in the ribs. "How old?"

"Forty-five."

"Geez! You give me hope for the years that lie ahead, Danaker," she said with an awe that didn't quite ring true. And an irreverent gleam in her eyes.

He swatted her on the bottom. "Watch it, kid, or I'll give you a new appreciation for the next five minutes of your life," he warned, laughing.

She was rather sorry he didn't make good his threat. She wouldn't have minded being madly kissed and pulled down onto the grass, rolling around in his arms. She stared into space, thinking about it with a dreamy expression in her faraway eyes.

He kissed her, and she blinked.

He arched a brow. "Remember all those people running by us with such startled looks on their faces? Well, they're going to be waving at you again next Sunday. So if I take you down on the grass now, you'll be a long time living it down."

"Can you read my mind?" she demanded, dumbfounded at her transparency.

His lips twisted. "Sometimes. When you're thinking the same thing I am." He pushed her gently into the car. "Let's get outta here, Daffy. I'm getting hungry."

The look he gave her made it clear that he wasn't just hungry for doughnuts, either.

The doughnuts tasted good. So did the coffee. And so did Quinn Danaker when he led her down his hallway a half hour after they'd left the doughnut shop.

His mouth was decorating her collarbone with luscious sensations and his hands were sliding down across her hips. Weakly she murmured, "I'm all sweaty...."

"So am I," he pointed out, returning to her breasts and sliding his tongue erotically over the stiff little nipples.

She squirmed against him. "Don't you have a shower around here somewhere, Danaker?" she asked breathlessly, helping him out of his clothes as he helped her out of hers.

"This way...."

So he introduced her to his shower. And to himself. Again. Standing up against the pale yellow tiles, with warm water sluicing down over them, his mouth fastened hungrily on hers, his body sliding powerfully into hers. Until she was crying out. Shaking with need and the incandescent explosion of satisfaction that he brought her. As he groaned and stiffened and crushed her in his arms, she knew what it was to be made one with a man. Sweet heaven. One with him....

Quinn Danaker... I'm falling in love with you. Madly. Irrationally. Wonderfully.

She smiled as he bent his head against her neck, surrendering a little more of himself to her. He let her slide down until she was standing. She heard him mumble hoarsely against her throat, "A couple of old folks like you and me probably need their rest after this."

"Probably..." she agreed, but she had to laugh, because it was obvious that his body was not interested in resting at all. She slid her hand down over his aroused flesh, feeling a rush of pleasure as he groaned and shoved himself against her. "Why don't you show me your bedroom now?" she suggested huskily.

She didn't have to ask twice.

It was early afternoon when they woke up the second time. This time in his bed. Coffee-colored sheets tangled around their hips. The sunlight was filtering lazily through the nearly closed vertical blinds, laying a pattern of straight lines over their curved bodies.

"Quinn," she murmured, curling into his arms and pressing a kiss against his cheek.

"Mmm?" He didn't open his eyes, just slid his hand possessively over her soft breast, thumbing the velvety skin in slow and tender fashion.

"I've got to get back. Kyle will be home in a couple of hours...." It was hard to keep the regret out of her voice. She didn't quite succeed. And she didn't care, either. She trusted him with her feelings, she realized. She felt relieved and wondrous that he could inspire such trust in her. She had feared once that she would never trust again. *Thank you, Quinn....*

He pulled her closer, locking his legs around hers and pulling her on top of him. His eyes were still closed, his body still relaxed. "In a little bit . . ." he promised. "You can go . . . in a little bit."

He sounded as if he were talking in his sleep. She wiggled against him. That got an immediate rise from him, and she giggled.

He smiled. "If you keep wiggling your delectable little body like that, you're going to be here a lot longer, honey." He pulled her closer and fitted his partially aroused body intimately between her thighs. "Damn, that feels good," he said with a sigh.

She put her arms around his neck and buried her face against his throat. "I wish I could stay."

They lay there in a long, intimate moment of silence.

He wished she could stay, too. More than he'd expected. And he'd braced himself to expect a pretty strong desire in that area. It was more than having been alone for so long, more than needing the physical contact or the purely sexual release. It was more than enjoying her lovely body simply because it was hers and he liked her, was utterly fascinated by her. It was more complex than that, he thought. Deeper than that. If he'd been twenty years younger, he would think he'd fallen in love with her that night at the hospital. At first sight. Bang. A goner.

But, hell, he was in his forties. He knew better. Lust at first sight, sure. But love . . . love took more than a few days or weeks to grow, he felt obligated to tell himself. He might be falling for her, but he needed to keep some sort of rational perspective on all this. For her sake, at least. She'd already been through the wringer once with a man. He didn't want her to go through that kind of pain again. He didn't want to hurt her. Not even by accident. But hell and fire, he wanted her. His body's volatile response to her made that damned clear, he thought wryly.

"You know what?" he murmured, running his hand down across her bare back in a slow, possessive caress.

"Hmm?" she mumbled against the heavy pulse in his throat.

"That's the first time you've called me by my name."

"Danaker?" she asked in surprise, lifting her head to look at him. Then she remembered and smiled. "Quinn."

He liked the way she said it. And he showed her how much.

There was someone at the door, pounding on it with a cane, by the time they'd reluctantly gotten out of bed and started to dress.

"Who the hell is that?" he growled, zipping up his slacks and pulling a soft cotton shirt over his head. Barefoot, he stalked down the hall to find out.

Daphne finished putting on her socks and shoes, borrowed his brush to bring some semblance of order back to her tangled black hair and followed him. Cautiously.

"Help yourself to the coffee," Danaker was saying to someone. Catching sight of Daphne hanging uncertainly in the hall, he gestured for her to come out of hiding. Grinning, he introduced her to his guest. "Daphne, this is my uncle, Jerome Danaker. Jerome, this is Daphne Jamison."

Danaker pulled on a pair of boots that had been sitting neatly on a rubber mat near the door. Uncle Jerome stared at Daphne, his mouth open, his eyes shocked.

Daphne blushed and tried not to stammer like an adolescent caught in the act with her boyfriend, which was how Uncle Jerome was making her feel at the moment.

"Hello, Mr. Danaker." She inched forward and held out her hand politely.

"Call me Jerome," he ordered in a crusty voice. He shook her hand in a crushing grip. "Well, I'll be damned." He turned to look at his nephew. "I'm sorry. You should have called and told me not to drop by."

Danaker laughed. Daphne thought he actually looked a little embarrassed. She wilted inside. Oh, dear.

"To tell you the truth, Jerome, I've been a little preoccupied. Didn't even think of you, old man. Besides, you don't always drop in. Just when you've run out of wood for your fireplace."

"Which is most Sundays this time of year," Jerome reminded him dryly.

Danaker shrugged it off. "It doesn't matter." He was pleased that he had a chance to let Daphne begin meeting some of the people in his life. He wanted her to feel they had more connecting them than just his interest in solving her late husband's mysteries for her. He gave Daphne a parting grin. "Don't believe half of what he says."

And with that Danaker walked outside, leaving her with his uncle.

The man was still staring at her, and he began shaking his head, as well, scratching his ear as if he couldn't quite believe he had seen a woman walking out of his nephew's bedroom.

"Could I pour you a cup of coffee?" Daphne offered, desperately taking refuge in being a hostess. She hurried into the kitchen, found some mugs in the cabinet and turned anxiously to see what he would answer.

"Yes. And I'll take a shot of Irish whiskey in it," he added.

Daphne frowned doubtfully. "Uh...now?" she asked weakly.

He chuckled like a gnarled leprechaun. "Don't worry. Normally I'm not given to drinking at this hour. But this calls for a celebration. You see, I'd just about given up hope that Quinn would ever get involved with a woman again," he explained, as he stepped into the kitchen. He had a cane, she noticed, and he was leaning on it now. At least he wasn't waving it at her and expounding on her lapse of morals, she thought in relief.

"I don't know that you could say he's *involved* with me," she murmured unconvincingly. She felt an obligation to protect Quinn from any misunderstandings. She didn't want his family misconstruing their...intimacy...as anything serious. After all, they hadn't exchanged any long-term commitments. She doubted that Danaker would appreciate having to fend off a family bent on getting him tied down to a woman simply because he was sleeping with her.

Jerome Danaker took the mug of coffee from her and, without looking at it, reached over to pluck a bottle of whiskey from behind a cereal box on the counter. He poured in a healthy dollop and offered some to her.

"No, thank you," she hastened to decline.

He shrugged and returned the bottle to its hiding place. Then he clinked his mug with hers and raised his eyes appreciatively to heaven. "Thank you, Lord. Thank you."

She watched him take a drink. The man really looked pleased with the world.

"You're a very pretty lady," he said. "Why don't we go into the parlor and you can tell me where you met him and what you've been doing ever since that blessed day. Mehitabel is going to pump me for the details," he added with a sigh of defeat. "That woman can browbeat a stone into pleading for mercy."

She trailed after him in bewilderment. Danaker actually did have an aunt by that name, then. Correction. A great-aunt, he'd said. "Mehitabel?"

"She's his great-aunt. On the other side of the family from me. I'm his father's brother. She's his mother's father's sister. If you follow me..."

It wasn't easy, but Daphne tried.

"She's tough as nails. Tenderhearted, though. With a big soft spot for Quinn." He settled down in a comfortable black leather chair and gestured toward a settee near it, eyeing her quizzically. "I'll trade you fair and square. You answer my questions about you, and I'll tell you anything you want to know about him. I'll bet he's kept his mouth closed about himself, hasn't he?"

"Well...yes...but..."

Jerome laughed. "He's putting my wood in my truck. He keeps it in back of his garage for both of us. In about ten minutes, maybe less, he'll march back in here. And if I know him, he's going to want me to keep off the subject of you and him. So...how'd you come to meet?"

"Actually...it was in a hospital.... My husband had been shot, and Quinn was there when it happened...."

"I see. Go on...."

Uncle Jerome was a shrewd and kindly man, she discovered. He let her talk without interrupting, and he read between the lines very astutely.

"Maybe that's what broke the ice for him," he said after she'd finished.

Daphne took a sip of her own coffee and frowned. "What do you mean...'broke the ice'?"

"He's lived like a monk since his wife died. He's wrapped himself up in this new business of his and ignored all the offers people have shoved at him to start seeing women again. Maybe it was the violence that got through to him. Maybe he needed something that awful to get him out of his shell, bring him back into the sunshine, if you know what I mean."

Daphne blinked. "I guess I do."

She hadn't looked at it that way until now. The trauma of that night had shaken her out of her world, but perhaps Jerome was right. It could also have shaken Danaker out of his. Did that make her the first woman he'd actually been able to see clearly, then, once the shackles of his past had been removed? Had he been drawn to her simply because she was the first reasonably attractive female he'd let himself be aware of since his wife had died? It was a surprisingly depressing thought, and it made her heart ache. She wanted him to be attracted to her because ... well, because they would have wanted each other no matter what. No matter where or when they'd met. Was that so unreasonable?

"Sorry about your loss," Jerome said sympathetically. He sighed. "It takes a while to get over grieving," he stated slowly, as if thinking back over losses he, too, had suffered.

Then his eyes narrowed, and he stared at her again. He obviously didn't think she looked very grief-stricken.

Embarrassed at the accuracy of his assessment, Daphne attempted to defend herself and laid the story straight for him. She didn't want Jerome to think badly of her. He was, after all, Quinn's uncle. And she wanted Quinn's family to have some respect for her, to like her.

"My husband and I had been ... estranged ... for a number of years."

He nodded sagely. "I understand."

And she thought he probably did.

Danaker stomped into the living room, deposited his boots on the mat and looked at the two of them curiously. "Your wood is in the truck, Jerome." He glanced at a small clock on one of the living room tables. "I'm sorry to have to bring this little visit to an end, but we've got to leave. Daphne needs to go home. Her son's going to be showing up pretty soon, and he'll wonder where she is."

Jerome's eyebrows lifted. "Her son?"

"Yeah. Nice kid. Named Kyle." Danaker walked back to his bedroom to put his shoes and socks on, and to pick up his wallet and keys.

Daphne rinsed out the mugs, feeling like a dutiful wife. How intimate this must look to his uncle, she thought uneasily. She shuddered to think what kind of image Jerome might convey to Quinn's great-aunt Mehitabel. With a name like that, she must be a formidable woman, Daphne thought faintly. And she was a stickler for good manners. Danaker had pointed that out the first night she'd come to see him.

"Come on, Daffy," Danaker said, draping an arm easily over her shoulders. He held the door for his uncle, who limped out ahead of them, his blackthorn cane sternly tapping the way.

"Delightful to make your acquaintance, Mrs. Jamison," Jerome said briskly.

Danaker frowned slightly. "Her name's Daphne."

Jerome looked very amused. "Ah, yes. *Daphne*. The beautiful nymph who drove the handsome Greek god, Apollo, wild with unrequited love. Beautiful name. Daphne." He glanced at Daphne, and his smile became warmly avuncular. "You do justice to your namesake, my dear. I hope I'll be seeing you again."

Danaker laughed. Daphne blushed. And Uncle Jerome spryly climbed into his truck, looking very pleased indeed.

They beat Kyle home. But just barely.

"Hi, Mom!" Kyle shouted as he tumbled through the front door, his sleeping bag, pajamas and assorted favorite possessions spilling all over the living room floor. Crestfallen, he stared at the mess.

"Have a nice time, honey?" Daphne asked with a smile as she stood between the living room and dining room. Watching Kyle was like trying to track an unguided missile. He was always going off in all directions at once, full of life and all its exciting possibilities.

"Yeah. Crabby traded me his ant house for my worm hill. and I got the last card I needed for this year's Rookies and All-Stars."

Daphne's smile slipped a little. She hated the worm hill and wouldn't be sorry for a minute to see it leave the house forever. But Crabby's ant house? Yuck. She shivered in disgust. She shot a glance in Danaker's direction. He had been lounging against the dining room window that overlooked her backyard, casually looking things over, when Kyle had blasted into the foyer. Now he'd straightened and was walking closer to her, trying not to grin too broadly at the disaster area covering a sizable corner of the living room floor.

Kyle was mournfully gathering up his treasures on his hands and knees, muttering youthful curses for the Fates that forever flung his possessions to the floor. As he balanced the precarious load in his youthful arms, he noticed the man standing beside his mother. He looked at her in surprise.

"Say, Mr. Danaker's here," he blurted out.

"Yes," Daphne said soothingly. She had no intention of pushing Quinn into Kyle's life or Kyle into Quinn's, but she sensed a pair of males measuring each other, and that alarmed her a little. Kyle looked confused, she thought worriedly. "Mr. Danaker and I went running together this morning," she said lightly.

Better she should tell him as much as she could, she thought, rather than have him hear people talk and begin to wonder. After all, he'd barely had a father, but he'd lost even the little scrap that he'd had. And so recently. Her heart ached for her baby. And at the moment her "baby" was looking very uncertain as to whether he liked having this new man around for two days in a row.

Kyle frowned and staggered up the stairs and down the hall to his room.

Daphne looked apologetically at Danaker.

"I'm sorry," she murmured, lifting her hand in a helpless little gesture. "He's not going to like another man being around, I'm afraid."

He didn't seem surprised to hear it.

"Um...now that I'm home, and Kyle's home..." She caught her lower lip between her teeth and pulled on it a little.

"Do you want me to leave?" he asked softly.

She looked away. "Not really." She smiled weakly. "I don't have anything for entertainment...." Now that really sounded dumb, she thought. But what should she suggest?

He pulled her back into the dining room, where no one could see them through the windows and Kyle wouldn't catch them, because they would hear his thundering feet charging down the stairs first.

He put his hands on her shoulders and made her look straight into his eyes. He had that faint, heart-stopping smile. She couldn't help melting a little.

"Do you have any work to do? That I can help you with?" he asked softly.

"I guess..."

"Want to watch a little television later on and have some popcorn?"

She could hardly believe her good fortune, and her smile was like the sunrise. "You do things like that?" she asked faintly.

He grinned. "What did you think?"

She leaned against his chest and closed her eyes in pleasure as his arms closed protectively around her. "Oh, I don't know. Chase down evil geniuses...rescue fainting maidens...jump over buildings in a single bound..." She felt him laughing, heard the warm rumble in his chest. It went straight through her. As dearly appreciated as his kisses, she thought.

He tilted her chin upward and kissed her warmly on the mouth. "We can't do any more of this while your chaperon's around," he whispered huskily. "But this isn't the last kiss, my little nymph," he teased.

She fervently hoped not.

She was surprised how well it worked out. Danaker dutifully allowed himself to be supervised doing some of the heavier yardwork. And when Kyle meandered downstairs, he couldn't resist coming out to help, too. That slowed down progress considerably, because he kept finding one question after another to put to Quinn. And Pooch and Cleo being underfoot didn't help much, either.

All the neighbors seemed to poke their heads over their fences to say hello, too, Daphne noticed suspiciously. And each one made a point of ogling the tall man shoveling mulch and straightening lattices for her, while they brought her up-to-date on the latest worries of the homeowners' association.

No one seemed upset about Quinn's presence, though, she realized, and that puzzled her. She'd been expecting at least a few nasty innuendos about a new man coming around, since she'd been so recently widowed. Stoically, she sighed and pulled the last of the weeds from her small flower garden. *Just be grateful that they're being nice about it,* she told herself sternly. "Don't borrow trouble," her mother had always said. She concentrated on that.

"What next?" asked a familiar male voice.

Daphne was squatting on the ground and had to look up and over her shoulder to see him. She nearly lost her balance, but he steadied her by gently grabbing her shoulder. Even that light touch made her feel light-headed again. The blood raced to her cheeks, and she struggled to her feet. They were both getting a little sunburned in the face. Not to mention hot and sweaty. Which reminded her of earlier in the day. And the yellow-tiled shower...

He grinned. "If *that's* next, I'm a happy man," he teased.

Daphne tried not to look as happy as she felt. "If you're reading my mind, that means you're thinking the same thing."

He nodded and looked around. "Think your neighbors are going to give you a hard time?"

"About you being here?"

He nodded again, more soberly.

She shook her head. "I don't think they're going to give it any thought at all. I wish I knew why...."

Danaker recalled his conversation with Sammy Wong, and Sammy's awareness that Daphne and Connor hadn't been happily wed. He was about to suggest that her neighbors might also have sensed a certain amount of that, but before he could, Kyle let out a war whoop worthy of a drunken scouting party.

"The ice-cream man!" he shouted, rushing over to them eagerly. "Can I get something, Mom? Please?" Kyle turned his most charming, boyish smile on her. Pooch and Cleo, puddled at his feet, stared up at her yearningly.

"I guess so." She wiped her hands on the cloth tied around her waist. "Let me go get some money...."

"There isn't time! He drives so fast!" Kyle wailed.

Quinn lifted his wallet out of his pocket and pulled out some bills. "My treat," he declared. "Want something, Daffy?"

She shook her head and watched as Kyle leaped up and down and galloped alongside Quinn as he strode toward the jingling ice-cream truck approaching the front of their house.

"The way to a *boy's* heart may be through *his* stomach, too," she said in amusement.

While the two bought their ice cream and sat on the lawn furniture trading tales about their favorite sports, Daphne threw out the weeds, washed up, then proceeded to do some laundry.

"Guess what, Mom!" Kyle yelled, bursting into the laundry room as she sorted clothes and put the first load in the washer.

"What?" she said automatically, paying only absent-minded attention as she plucked her delicate underwear out of a pile of scrungy-looking blue jeans.

"Mr. Danaker collects baseball cards, too."

She turned, a pair of blue lace panties dangling from her hand, and watched her excited son expound on the thrill of seeing truly old collector's items.

"Why, he's even got some from way back in the fifties and sixties," he said in an awestruck tone.

"That old, huh?" she said. She lifted her eyes and tried not to laugh. Quinn was standing a little behind Kyle, obviously enjoying the boy's enthusiasm.

"You'll have to come over to my house sometime and look through them," Danaker suggested. "If it's all right with your mother."

"Oh, she won't mind," Kyle assured him with an easy grin. "Will you, Mom?"

"Of course not." Then she noticed that Quinn's gaze had shifted to her hand, and she remembered what she was holding. She quickly stuffed the delicate item down into a pile of laundry, well out of sight. "Why don't we see about dinner?"

Kyle shrugged. "Okay. But I'm still full of ice cream." He grimaced. "You know, this new guy's no good."

"New guy?" Daphne asked vaguely. She wasn't paying very close attention because she was trying to remember what was in her refrigerator that could be thrown together into some semblance of a meal.

"Yeah," Kyle complained. "The new ice-cream man. Well, it's a whole new truck, actually. A different company from the one that usually comes. This guy doesn't have the best stuff. And he never knows how much anything is. And he's kinda nasty. Wouldn't even give Crabby a second choice one day because he was in a big hurry...."

"Maybe he's having personal problems," Daphne suggested, frowning. Like figuring out how to make dinner out of the strange things she just knew were going to be staring at her when she opened the refrigerator door.

Danaker frowned, though, as he followed Daphne and Kyle into the kitchen.

"When did this truck first start coming around, Kyle?" he asked curiously.

"Oh...not too long ago..." Kyle wrinkled his nose, trying to recall. Then his face fell. "It was after Daddy got killed," he said stoically. His chin jutted out.

The three of them stood in the kitchen in silence for a moment. Kyle's chin quivered, and he buried his face in Daphne's stomach, throwing his arms around her and strangling a sob. She hugged him tight and pressed a kiss to his head.

Her eyes met Quinn's. She didn't feel alone anymore, she thought. Even though he wasn't touching her, he communicated an intangible message of strength and support to her. She smiled at him tremulously.

"Anybody in the mood for Sammy Wong's?" Danaker asked.

Kyle straightened and blinked away the tears from his dark lashes, then murmured, "I am."

"How about eating at the restaurant this time?" Danaker suggested.

Daphne looked at him strangely. It would be sort of like a family outing, she thought.

"Daphne?" he asked softly.

She looked at Kyle's face, tear-streaked yet undefeated. And then at Quinn Danaker's features, strong and toughened. They made an interesting pair, she thought.

"I'd love to go," she said finally. "But it's Dutch treat," she insisted primly. She didn't want him thinking she couldn't manage. Or that she was a leech.

"We'll see," Danaker replied, amused by her determination to keep him from spending money on her.

He wasn't so amused by the story Kyle had told about the ice-cream truck, though. Maybe Daphne was right, of course. Maybe he *was* becoming paranoid. But he tended to think kids were pretty astute observers of their neighborhood environments. And if Kyle thought there was something strange about the ice-cream man, Danaker was inclined to take a closer look.

He'd start with Yarbro and Foley. First thing Monday morning.

Chapter 12

"The *ice-cream man!*" Sergeant Foley exclaimed in sheer disbelief. "Come on, Danaker. Give me a break!"

The stark white light of the office made the balding spot on his head shine, and it cast stark shadows against the plain-colored walls, as the sergeant heatedly waved a thick manila folder in the air.

"Yarbro and I are up to our necks in three new felony assault cases! All committed in the last seventy-two hours—and the last victim was the grandson of a city councilman! Boy, does that ever get a lot of press. Poor guy's in the hospital with a fractured jaw, two broken ribs and a dislocated knee." He grimaced. "So we're a little busy here."

Danaker stood in front of Foley's nondescript desk, which was overflowing with paperwork, and crossed his arms in front of his chest. "I'm not asking you to research his ancestry," he pointed out evenly. "I'm just asking you to phone the Fairfax County police and request a check on the driver. Maybe get them to resume drive-bys again when the truck might be around."

Foley rolled his eyes, and then he looked at Danaker, obviously hoping that he could make himself clearly understood this time.

"Look, Danaker, the Fairfax police *also* have a few other cases to handle." He ticked a few of them off on his fingers. "They've got missing children and domestic violence. *Lots* of domestic violence," he repeated heavily, shaking his head sadly. "And they've got the usual range of gunshots, assault-and-batteries, burglaries, grand-theft auto...."

Danaker put up his hand. "I get the picture." It was difficult not to lose his temper, but he held on to it anyway. Anger wouldn't move Yarbro or Foley any faster. They were professionals. They needed rational arguments. Something that would justify their putting time in on *this* case instead of another one. "It wouldn't take very long to call the police who checked her house after the shooting. They might be willing to look into it. The case isn't closed, and they want to close it. Right?"

Foley sighed. "Probably. We never got any more on that," he added, peeling through a stack of folders and pulling the one labeled with Connor Jamison's name. He checked its contents and shook his head. "No. The ballistics didn't match. The bullet that killed Jamison and the one that was dug out of the wall at Mrs. Jamison's house were different calibers. Fired from different weapons." He shrugged apologetically. "I'd like to help you, Danaker. We don't like open cases, and Connor Jamison's murder is still an open case here."

"Working any good leads?" Danaker asked.

Foley's expression went inscrutable. "Nothing I could discuss."

"Not a damn thing," Danaker interpreted correctly. He saw the color rise in Foley's cheeks and decided he was right. "Whoever shot Connor Jamison was professional enough to elude you," he pointed out, not above rubbing it in a little. "Maybe he's done it before. Maybe he's got a long list of hits and you'd be doing the world a major public service to get the SOB off the street."

Foley's brows wrinkled in irritation. "Yeah. Yeah. We'd like to get him, okay? But he's not the only bad guy around. There's more than one out there, Danaker. Believe me."

Not as far as Danaker was concerned. Because there was only one Daphne Jamison. That made this case special for him. He stalked around the office, trying to come up with a more effective argument. He wanted that driver checked. Fast. Kyle's comment dug into him like a burr. Maybe he was being foolish; maybe he was grasping at straws. Certainly he hadn't come up with much to work with, either. His contacts in Europe had provided him with an interesting portrait of Connor Jamison's activities, but the names of Jamison's associates didn't ring any bells with Interpol. Or with anybody else he knew. Jamison's cronies were greedy and skirted the edge of the legal arms trade, but as far as he knew, none of them hired killers. Or, if they had, he couldn't find any evidence of it. Yet.

Lt. Yarbro, immersed in private conversation at his desk a few feet away, murmured into the telephone receiver, "Okay, Darlene. The mower should be fixed by this weekend. So if your mother doesn't mind waiting 'til Sunday, I'll do her grass after church. Will that make you happy?" He rolled his eyes. Then his craggy face relaxed as he heard her reply. "Great. That's what we'll do, then. Agreed?" He grinned into the space in front of him, but his lazily drooping eyes were obviously seeing his wife. His mind had apparently left the thorny subject of mowing his mother-in-law's grass and moved on to greener...and softer...pastures. "After that, maybe we could go down to Charlie's for steamed crabs and beer," he drawled hopefully. He began smiling like a sailor contemplating enjoying something a lot more satisfying than eating a dockside meal after months at sea. "We haven't been there for quite a while. . . ." he reminded her softly.

There was a distinctly suggestive note in his voice, obviously intended for his wife alone. Embarrassed, he glanced around to see if other ears had picked it up. His own ears turned red as he intercepted Danaker's amused but impatient expression.

Yarbro quickly cleared his throat, concluding on a much more businesslike note, "See you tonight." He choked at his wife's reply and briskly hung up the phone, staring at it a moment in surprise before he shook himself out of his personal life and back into his job.

He swiveled his chair and turned a military stare on Danaker. "Have you heard from that friend of yours yet? What was his name?" He reached for the folder on Jamison's case, but before he could search through it, Danaker supplied the information for him.

"Janisch?"

Yarbro nodded.

"No. His secretary hasn't heard from him since the day Jamison was killed. His answering machine's so full of messages, it's closed down. Our mutual friends in Europe haven't seen him or talked to anyone who has. The only lead I've got on Janisch came in on a scrambled message over the phone late last night.''

Yarbro and Foley said in unison, ''What?''

''Someone in Hamburg thought they spotted Janisch trying to get through the docks onto a freighter the day after Jamison was killed.''

The detectives both sat a little straighter. ''Got any names or facts to go along with that?'' Yarbro demanded crisply.

Danaker pulled a piece of paper out of his shirt pocket and handed it to the detective. ''I can't give you the name of the man who passed me the information, but there are the times and dates, the name of the freighter, its registry and its dock location.''

Both policemen looked decidedly suspicious. ''Give,'' Foley said.

''Come on, Danaker,'' Yarbro muttered irritably. ''We need the name of the man who gave you this.''

Danaker stood his ground. ''The man's an informant for a half-dozen intelligence agencies. He doesn't want them knowing what he's doing unless they're paying him for it. He would only give me what he knew when I promised to keep his name out of it.''

Yarbro looked both curious and highly skeptical. ''And why would he work for you? You paying for it, too?''

''No. He owes me.'' One hell of a lot, Danaker thought. And he'd be dead in a matter of days if some of what Danaker knew about him ever came to light.

Yarbro and Foley stared at Danaker. Then they exchanged glances. And looked back at him again. What the hell, they had nothing to lose.

Yarbro spoke for both of them. ''We'll call the Fairfax investigator and ask him to do us a favor.'' He grimaced, wondering what Fairfax would want as a favor in return. He didn't have time to go to the john, let alone squeeze in any favors, this week, damn it. He scowled threateningly directly at Danaker.

''Ask them to run an ID check on the ice-cream man and start some drive-bys again,'' Danaker said, wanting to push both items hard.

''Yeah. Both of them,'' Yarbro agreed irritably. ''But I want *everything* you get on Jamison. You hear me? *Everything!*''

Danaker laughed without a trace of humor. ''Believe me, I wish I had more to give you.'' He frowned thoughtfully. ''I've got one more fish on my string, and she should be calling in soon with whatever she's got. I'll tell you if she's got anything worth repeating."

"She?" Foley piped up, surprised and clearly interested. "A lady spy? Hey, maybe this will be just like the movies." He sighed, thinking of the pretty girls that always fell over James Bond. Life just wasn't like that here in Alexandria.

Danaker made no reply one way or the other regarding her status as a lady or as a spy.

"What are you hoping she'll find out for you?" Yarbro asked.

"Who Christina is."

Neither Yarbro nor Foley looked as if they thought Christina would be the answer to this case. "She's probably just his girlfriend," Foley said, trying not to sound too insensitive.

Danaker grunted. "Maybe." He turned a speculative stare in Yarbro's direction. "And speaking of people sharing everything . . . why didn't you mention that John Sarmien attended Jamison's funeral? He isn't family."

"How'd you find that out?" Yarbro demanded.

"Daphne told me."

"Daphne, huh?" Yarbro's eyes narrowed. "Have you been seeing her, Danaker?"

"Yes." He didn't apologize for it, either. As a matter of fact, the automatic suspicion he sensed in Yarbro irritated him. "She's a very nice lady," he added softly. "I'd like to make sure she doesn't get hurt."

"Hmm." Yarbro wasn't certain what to think about Danaker's explanation, and he didn't bother to hide it. "How's she doing?"

"Well enough," Danaker said, making it clear from his clipped tone that he wasn't going into any detail. The rest was strictly private. Not police business. Period.

The phone rang on Yarbro's desk and he grabbed it. "Lt. Yarbro . . ."

Danaker glanced at his watch and swore silently. He didn't have time to press Yarbro for the details about John Sarmien. He had an appointment with a client, and he would barely get back in time for it if he left now. Reluctantly, he turned to leave.

"Keep in touch," Foley suggested. There was a faint hint of warning in the way he said it.

"You can count on it," Danaker guaranteed, smiling sardonically at the thought that the police still didn't quite trust him.

He hoped they were equally skeptical about John Sarmien.

"You look different, Daphne." The woman who was speaking peered at Daphne thoughtfully. "You look...younger. Not that you ever looked old, of course," she hastened to add. She grinned nervously, embarrassed by her choice of words.

Daphne was perched on the desk that she shared with two other part-time employees of the small local newspaper for which she worked. She got it Tuesdays and Thursdays. It was lunchtime, and she was in the middle of scooping a spoonful of yogurt from its small carton, half thinking about her proof-reading and half thinking about Quinn Danaker as the woman announced her assessment.

As Daphne listened to her coworker's hesitant praise, she gulped. So the glow she felt inside showed on the outside, too, she thought uncomfortably. She smiled weakly and murmured, "Thanks."

The mousy-haired woman looked at her nails and sighed. "I think I'm going to try some of those fake nails. You know...the ones they sell in the drugstore near the nail polish? I've got a date this weekend, and I'm sick and tired of looking like small animals have been gnawing on these." She fanned her fingers out. They were smudged with printer's ink. She glanced at Daphne's nails enviously. "Yours always look nice. They're short, but never raggedy. You must eat a lot of gelatin or something."

Daphne had not been paying much attention to her nails, but she was grateful for anything that would divert Marlise from the glow that she'd detected. Just as Daphne was thinking that the danger was past, Marlise's bubble-weight mind bounced back to it.

"If it were anyone else," Marlise confided, a little slyly, "I'd say that glow you've got came from a man."

Daphne choked on her last swallow. Marlise pounded her on the back, making it worse.

Daphne slipped off the desk, managing to get out of Marlise's anxious but unhelpful reach.

"Are you all right?" the woman asked worriedly.

"Y—yes," Daphne croaked. She took a sip of her diet cola.

By now her boss and a couple of other people had looked up in concern. Most people were eating or reading mail or joking. A few were actually doing a little work during the lunch break.

The reporter was on the phone, as usual. Daphne struggled to put a reassuring smile onto her face. Most of the others turned back to their original activities, appearing relieved that they didn't have to remember the Heimlich maneuver. Her boss, however, came over for a closer check. Her heart sank. More sympathy. She really wished he wouldn't.

"Are you okay?" he asked, his face a portait of male solicitude.

"Yes," Marlise answered for Daphne blithely. "I was just telling her I thought she got that glow she's been wearing all week from a mysterious man we haven't heard about yet. Maybe she finally got her love life jump-started again. Or at least got a date or something."

He blanched, then sent a silencing look at Marlise. The whole office liked her, but she was always the person who said what everyone else was too polite to say.

"That's hardly the kind of thing to say to Daphne, Marlise," he pointed out reprovingly. "After all, she's still newly widowed." He turned a somber smile on Daphne. He'd pulled it out with regularity ever since Connor's murder.

Daphne told herself that she should appreciate their solicitude, their affection and support. But she felt like they were chaining her up, expecting her to live a charade and act like a grieving widow, even when she wasn't prostrate with grief. She couldn't help feeling guilty about her lack of deep sorrow, though. People so obviously expected it of her. And Kyle expected it. She thought he did, anyway. So she kept telling herself that she only needed to endure this for a few months. Surely she could persevere in being a mourning widow that long, for Kyle's sake, at least. He *was* mourning, although not as much as she had expected, she had to admit.

But Marlise cut through the charade like a dustmop going through cobwebs. "She's not newly widowed, Bob! I don't know why you all keep trying to make her feel she has to go wear black and all."

Bob was aghast. Daphne was newly widowed, no doubt about it, as far as he was concerned. His expression became wrathful as he narrowed in on poor Marlise. "That's an awful thing to say!" he said righteously.

Marlised looked annoyed, and her pale brows beetled stubbornly. "You know very well that Daphne has lived like a widow as long as any of us has known her. Why, you even said that her husband was gone so much that Daphne made 'golf widows' look like new brides!''

Bob turned a pretty shade of crimson all across his cheeks. He choked and tried to babble an apology at Daphne.

Daphne was frozen, at first in horror at the revelation that her office mates had gossiped about her behind her back, apparently with candor and on more than one occasion. Then she began to feel a certain thawing. Marlise's honesty, while a little overly blunt, was well meant, and it might free her of the need to accept condolences she really didn't want.

Daphne stared at Bob and Marlise as the scales fell from her eyes. *They knew she'd been unhappily married.*

Marlise prattled on. ''Why, if I'd been married to a man who was gone that much, I'd have divorced him long ago.'' She frowned thoughtfully. ''Well, actually, I guess that's what I did with Edgar, my first husband. He was a train engineer . . . liked to be gone all the time. . . .'' Her face acquired a definite scowl. ''He also liked to play with a new girl in every town. . . .''

Bob was nearly beside himself, and he tried to draw Daphne away. ''I'm sorry, Daphne. . . .''

She patted him on the arm. ''It's all right. Actually. . .'' She took a deep breath. ''Actually, she's not completely wrong, you know.''

His eyes flickered. He was surprised she'd admitted it. But he clearly wasn't shocked by what she was saying. That made Daphne bold enough to admit a little more.

''Connor and I had been having problems for quite some time.''

He smiled gently and nodded. ''I rather thought so.'' He blushed. ''But, uh, it didn't seem like a very polite thing to bring up, uh, after what happened to him. . . . Besides, a violent death can make you mourn out of shock alone.''

Daphne glanced around the room. Everyone was busy with their own responsibilities. No one was paying them particular attention. ''Do they all know that?'' she asked curiously.

He lowered his gaze and cleared his throat. ''I think so.''

Daphne breathed a long sigh of relief. ''I'm glad. They won't be disappointed, then, if I don't wear widow's weeds, will they?''

He caught her drift and smiled reassuringly. ''Nobody will be disappointed, Daphne. I think I can promise you that.'' He looked at her differently then, as if really seeing her for the first

time during the conversation. "You know, you look...
younger...."

She smiled. "Funny, I think I feel that way, too."

When she walked to her car later, she realized that there was
a spring in her step and an anticipation in her heart that hadn't
been there for years. She knew why they had returned.

She was free. And Danaker was going to call her later that
evening. She'd hear his voice again. She smiled in anticipation. Then the smile turned into a lighthearted laugh.

He made her feel wonderful. He made her heart glow.

Danaker sat in his study, in his underground business cham-
bers, staring at an old picture.

It was a photograph of his dead wife, Cherie, taken the day
before she was kidnapped. She was sitting on a lounge chair on
the veranda of a hotel outside Vienna. The smile on her face
was warm and open and very happy.

He'd loved her. Very much.

But she was gone. What they'd had together was gone. Like
sand running through a man's splayed fingers, their happiness
had returned to the eternal well from which such things came.

He was surprised to find that he could think about it dispas-
sionately. That was a good sign, he decided. Evidence that he
was fully ready to move on with his life. He wouldn't look back
in regret.

Ironically, he thought that if Cherie and Daphne had met,
they would have liked one another. They shared some of the
same openheartedness. The same basic sense of integrity and
honor.

He felt honored to have had the fortune of knowing both of
them.

He put Cherie's picture back into the small album from
which he'd taken it. Then he slid the album back into its place
on the bookshelf not far from his desk.

He lifted the phone to call Daphne. There was a smile on his
face as he leaned back, propping his feet on his desk, as he
waited to hear the sweet cadence of her voice saying hello.

Later, when he was lying in his bed, he forgot about the picture altogether. His thoughts focused exclusively on one
woman. She had silky black hair and eyes the color of violets
dampened by a sudden spring shower. He turned onto his
stomach and rubbed his face against his pillow, smiling as he

found what he sought. He could still smell her scent there. It made him recall in vivid detail having her there in his bed, and it made him grow hard with renewed desire. The frustration was something he was getting used to. It was a price he was willing to pay for the pleasure of her company, real and imagined.

Daphne was the name he murmured as he fell asleep. Daphne's was the face he saw. And it was Daphne who filled his restless dreams. She, and she alone.

Daphne saw the big yellow school bus pull up at the end of the block and belch out its load of kids. One of which was hers, she thought wryly, watching for his dear face among the squealing schoolchildren.

She was standing in her front yard, a pair of garden shears in her hand and her back toward her driveway. She didn't hear the car pulling in until the driver killed the engine. At that moment she caught sight of Kyle, laughing at something Crabby had just said. The two boys poked and taunted each other with the insulting abandon that eleven-year-old males considered perfectly normal. She sighed, despairing that they'd ever discover a more civilized form of communication. One not based on who could more deeply insult the other.

"Daphne?"

She turned to face the visitor who'd gotten out of his car and was walking across her lawn, smiling diffidently at her. When she saw him, she nearly dropped her shears on her foot. "John...what a surprise! I wasn't expecting to see you again," she said.

Habit pushed her hand forward and draped a smile on her startled face. John Sarmien reciprocated, clasping her hand in his as soon as he was close enough to do so.

John Sarmien, she thought. A few weeks ago she would have been happy to see him. He'd always been very nice to her. Polite. Attentive. Concerned for her and for Kyle. He'd gone out of his way to facilitate the paperwork at Corday after Connor had died, greasing the way for the benefits to flow to her. That had made the first month much easier to bear.

But she couldn't forget what Quinn had told her about Corday and Connor and John Sarmien. The man holding her hand and smiling so solicitously into her eyes was a weapons salesman. He was also a man who tried to hide that fact. And he worked on the ragged edge of this side of the law.

Her handshake was a little less firm than usual. And her eyes betrayed her uncertainty about him.

Something flattened in the cordial depths of his eyes, and the smile that neatly curved his thin lips dried ever so slightly.

Daphne swallowed and searched for a way through this precarious new mine field. "Would you like to come inside, John?" she asked, trying to be as gracious as he would expect. "I just made a fresh pitcher of iced tea with lemon. Would you care for a glass?"

"Yes. Thank you, Daphne." He followed her up to the house, watching her body curve as she put the shears and her garden gloves on the steps. As he passed through the front door, he said, "I hope you don't mind my dropping by unexpectedly like this."

"No. Not at all." She'd never felt like such a liar! She regretted that people were supposed to say such things. But it seemed safer to take refuge in the customary pleasantry rather than tell him that she was both disconcerted and surprised.

She could hear Kyle laughing outside. It sounded as if he and Crabby were dumping their schoolbags on the front lawn and getting Kyle's skateboard out of the garage. At least he'd be out of earshot, she thought, as she got the pitcher of tea from the refrigerator and two tall glasses from the cupboard. She'd never felt totally at ease with John Sarmien, but she'd always put it down to not knowing him very well and to the fact that he had been Connor's boss. Now she wasn't so sure.

Sarmien received the glass of tea from her with a smooth smile. "Thank you." He drank some of it and complimented her. "Delicious. Just delicious!"

Daphne smiled. It was only iced tea, she thought. He was making more of it than was necessary. She wondered why he was trying to ingratiate himself and what he was doing here. The hair on the back of her neck tickled as she waited for him to explain. Something about his visit worried her at a very elemental level. She supposed she had Danaker to thank for that, too. *Trust your instincts,* he kept telling her.

Sarmien's gaze floated away from her to roam the room in a slow, desultory survey. "I suppose you wonder why I'm here...." he said conversationally.

"Yes. You haven't been a frequent visitor," she pointed out dryly.

His smile was as clear as varnish. It made her skin crawl.

"True. I often wanted to get better acquainted with you, Daphne. But when we moved our section of Corday overseas—" he shrugged "—it was difficult. I'm sure you understand." He smiled in a way that encouraged her to agree.

"Of course." She obliged him out of habit. She wished Quinn were here listening to this. She wondered what he would think.

"But since Connor's tragic death," Sarmien went on to say, "I thought that it would be helpful if I kept in touch with you. We don't want you to feel abandoned, Daphne."

He leaned toward her and caressed her hand in a gesture of concern. Daphne experienced a strong desire to recoil from his touch. It was about as pleasant as being licked by a lizard.

"We want to make sure that you're managing all right, that you don't need anything." His brows lifted in unmistakable question. "*Do* you need anything? Are the bills under control? The benefits arriving as we'd expected?"

"Yes. In fact, the benefits are being paid even more quickly than I had expected." Surely he would know that, she thought. She wondered why he'd asked. "We're doing well," she said evasively. She didn't want to share the details of her financial life with this man. "The bills are as 'under control' as they ever were," she admitted on a lighter note, hoping he would take the hint and not pursue it further.

"Good. Good." He put down his glass of tea. "I'm very pleased to hear that."

Daphne had the impression that he was leading up to something, and she waited, wondering what it could possibly be.

"I had another purpose in coming to see you today." He smiled like a man embarrassed by a soon-to-be-admitting failing. "We have discovered a small problem at work...."

"Oh?" Daphne felt a chill on the back of her neck.

"It isn't anything cataclysmic...." he assured her smoothly.

"It must be fairly serious," she pointed out reasonably. "Otherwise you wouldn't be here, would you, John?" She tried not to sound overly suspicious. After all, he wouldn't be aware that Quinn had told her about Corday's semisecret arms dealings. Instinctively, she tried to draw him out without giving that away.

He smiled thinly and nodded. "You're very perceptive, my dear. If it were minor, a secretary would have called, or an accountant might have drafted you a letter." He paused, considering exactly what approach to use with her. "I thought it would be wise if I came in person for two reasons. First, because I wanted to make sure you were not still so deep in your grief that this conversation would upset you more than necessary."

"That was very considerate of you," she said, acknowledging his profession of concern with only a faint smile. She didn't believe him for a minute. Whatever else had held him back, it wasn't worry about her emotional state, she thought. There was something about the way he looked at her that just didn't let that sentiment ring true.

"The second reason is a bit more ... delicate."

She waited for him to explain, her fingers tightening.

"We seem to be missing some items that Connor should have had with him at the time of his death."

"What sort of items?" she asked, frowning in surprise. Sarmien's eyes flickered strangely. Daphne felt her sense of distrust for the man deepen.

"Some information," he explained, watching her closely. "It might appear to be a report, or a file of loose papers. And, uh, a key."

"A key?" Daphne wondered if she were becoming needlessly paranoid, or if Sarmien were really as intent as he seemed beneath the smooth exterior he was presenting. Was it her imagination? Or was it real? "What kind of key?" she asked, searching for more information.

"Small. One that would fit a lock box or a locker in an airport, for example...."

She looked at him as if he were crazy. "A locker in an airport? Connor?" Her brows formed a mystified vee. "What's going on, John? What's missing?"

He waved his hands as if to smooth over any upset he was causing and rose from the table, apparently wishing to bring the discussion to an early end. "It's nothing for you to worry about, my dear. Just business." Seeing the doubt in her eyes at that vague excuse, he expanded a bit. "He had some contracts for the deals he'd been working on in Europe just before he died. We haven't found all of the documentation in his files at work." He shrugged and gave her the fatalistic smile of a merchant who'd just sold something very valuable at a steep loss. "It occurred to me that he might have been in a hurry the night he came home, and that he might have put something in a safe location until he came to work."

"I see." Daphne followed him to her front door. It required an effort for her not to shrink from his touch when he patted her on the arm.

"It was just an outside chance that you might have come across something," he assured her. His eyes bore into hers searchingly, though. "If you find anything...papers, notes, a computer diskette, a key...anything that might be work-related...call me, Daphne."

"Of course." She held the door for him. He lifted his head to look out to the street in front of her house, and he stiffened at what he saw there. "It appears you have another visitor."

Daphne looked to see what had affected him and saw Quinn Danaker pulling his car up behind Sarmien's. Quinn looked as unpleasantly startled to see Sarmien as Sarmien was to see him. For a moment she wondered if the two men knew each other. That was ridiculous, she scoffed. Quinn would have mentioned it. So why did they look with such distaste at one another?

The two men passed each other at the midpoint between the street and the house.

"Sarmien," Danaker acknowledged curtly.

"Danaker," Sarmien replied coolly. "I'm surprised to see you here." He failed to sound like it, however.

"I doubt that," Danaker said coldly.

Sarmien's smiling eyes iced over. "For a man known for his cool self-control, you sound warm, Danaker." He glanced significantly at Daphne, who was standing in her front doorway, watching them. "Perhaps *hot* is a better description."

Danaker's jaw tightened, and he felt more furious than he had in a very long time. His eyes narrowed predatorially. "I'll take it very personally if anything upsets Daphne," he said in a deadly soft tone. "Or if any more violence comes into her life."

"That's very interesting, Danaker. Very interesting indeed." Sarmien stared at him, and a chilling smile spread over his face. "But why tell me?"

"I think it's something you should know."

"You know, Danaker, it's amazing we've never met before," Sarmien said reflectively, choosing to ignore the quiet threat that had just been made.

"Just my good fortune," Danaker growled.

Sarmien flushed at the insult. "You'll have to excuse me," he said with saccharine sarcasm. "I was just leaving. We'll have to postpone our further acquaintance until some other time."

"And some other place," Danaker added warningly. From Sarmien's stony gaze, he was sure that he'd gotten the point: Steer clear of Daphne Jamison.

Danaker's face was granite hard as he watched Sarmien depart. When he joined Daphne, he was still feeling grim, and his opening comment was curt. "What did Sarmien want?"

As she drew him inside to explain, Kyle rocketed down the sidewalk on his skateboard and careened up the drive to the front steps. "Hi, Mr. Danaker."

"I'll tell you later," Daphne promised Danaker softly before Kyle got any closer. When he frowned, she pulled him behind the door and gave him a quick hug and kiss.

He couldn't help it. He responded to her instantly. His body heated at the touch of hers, and his mouth quickly sought a deeper intimacy. When she pulled away laughing a few moments later, he realized that the edge of his anger at finding John Sarmien sniffing around her had been blunted.

"I'll tell you after dinner," she promised, smiling into his half-worried eyes. "Kyle won't get in the middle of it then."

"All right," he agreed with some reluctance. She had a point, but he didn't like being kept in the dark. The more he'd heard about Sarmien's most recent deals, the more convinced he'd become that Connor's death had something to do with them. "But I want a full, detailed report on everything he said."

Daphne was a little surprised by the anger she sensed in him, and the determination. It was as if Danaker had already guessed what Sarmien had told her. But that wasn't possible, she told herself.

She must be getting overly imaginative, she thought. She'd feel better later on, after Kyle was asleep, when she and Danaker could be alone. Anticipation made her skin tingle. Quinn would soothe her ragged feelings, make her feel safe again. And wanted. Fiercely wanted.

Chapter 13

Much later, after the dishes were done and Kyle had fallen asleep, Daphne closed Pooch and Cleo in the laundry room for the night and went into the family room to join Quinn.

He was sitting on the old couch, watching the late-night news on television. As she came over to him, he loosened his tie and unbuttoned the top couple of buttons beneath it in a gesture of intimate relaxation, which made Daphne feel suddenly very tender toward him. When she reached the sofa, she stroked the fine wool fabric of his suit jacket, which he had casually draped across the back of the couch. She liked having him here. Felt comforted by it. Enjoyed it.

Danaker reached around, circled her wrist and pulled her hand down over his shoulder. He placed a soft, teasing kiss against the back of her hand. Then he pulled her down lower and found her mouth with his in a lingering kiss of such delicacy that tears began to press against her closed eyes.

"Mmm," she murmured appreciatively against his mouth. "Is this dessert?"

He grinned suggestively and pulled her around the edge of the sofa, flicking off the television using the remote control in his free hand.

"Yes, my sweet. This is dessert for the adults. But there are several courses, and this is just a tiny bite of the first one," he teased. He pulled her yielding body down onto his lap. As his arms went around her, his eyes darkened and his smile began to fade. "I've been waiting for dessert for hours. Come here, you sweet little tart, you."

He brought her head close with one sure hand and kissed her hungrily. He felt her arms slip around his neck, and he heard her moan softly. The husky sound vibrated in his mouth, since they were still kissing. It ran right down through him like a current of electricity, shocking every nerve it hit along the way.

He lifted his head and looked into her eyes, half-closed with desire. Before he could tell her how much he had missed her all day, she drew him back and found his mouth with her own, eagerly teasing his lips and the warm interior of his mouth with her own spritely tongue.

Her eager responsiveness to his caresses was like gasoline sprinkled on a flickering flame. Fire licked across his skin, seethed hotly inside his loins, burned deeply in his belly. He lightly caressed the yielding flesh of her tongue with his, parrying her gentle thrusts, sliding deeply and intimately into her mouth, just as he ached to do to her body.

Daphne melted against him as a heat wave of desire seared her. She, too, had thought about this moment all day, ached for it ever since they had parted. Her hands slid shyly over his clothed body, relearning the contours of his muscled ribs beneath the long-sleeved dress shirt he was wearing. From there they timidly slipped down to his firm waist and belly and his lean, solid hips.

Molten fire intensified inside her mouth. She was utterly lost in the rhythmic stroking of his seductive tongue, the skillfully applied suction, the delightfully sensitive changes he somehow made in pressure. Like hot lava, delectable sensations poured through her body in slow-moving rivers of steamy pleasure.

Unwilling to lift her mouth long enough to speak, she told him with her body just how wonderful he made her feel. She told him with every shaking caress of her fingertips, in the eager way she pulled loose his shirt and lifted his undershirt, and in the small sound of pleasure she made as her hands found his warm, muscled flesh.

He wrapped his arms around her more tightly, and his velvety tongue explored her with even greater urgency. Breathing became harsher. The textures, the sensations and the sounds of their passion turned Daphne's body to flame. With trembling fingers she began fumbling with the belt at his waist, moaning against his mouth as he finally broke the kiss to catch his own now-ragged breath. As he buried his face in her hair, his fingers slid up and over her breasts.

With a couple of quick twists of his hands, he pushed up her blouse and her bra and found the tender flesh beneath. As he ran his hands gently over her, cupping her, then feathering each bare nipple lightly with his fingertips, he felt her back arch against his arm in pleasure. Her movement sent an answering surge of desire straight through him, tightening his gut and igniting his blood.

"I can feel the fire race through you when I caress your breasts," he murmured hoarsely against her throat. "It burns me, Daffy. God, how you burn me up, baby." He caressed her down the midline of her body in a slow, intimate stroke that spoke of tender endearment as well as physical excitement.

She arched against him helplessly, letting her body rub against his attentive, magical hands. She wanted them all over her, wanted his mouth all over her, wanted his hard body filling her, thrusting into her. He was a demanding lover and yet very giving. So incredibly giving.

"Now for the next bite of dessert," he teased her in a voice a little more strained than normal. He eased her clothes loose, although he didn't take them completely off.

"Isn't this a little cumbersome?" she asked, laughing and looking a little dubious.

"We'll see," he muttered philosophically. Then, with a rakish grin, he took a leisurely moment to enjoy looking at the parts of her that he had bared. He ran his fingertips over her lightly, making her shiver in delight. When his eyes met hers, they were serious. "I'm trying to remember we're hiding out in the basement, Daffy," he explained softly, the huskiness in his voice betraying the strain he was under. "We aren't in your bedroom or mine with the door locked."

His attention shifted to her breasts, and he lowered his head to let his lips follow where his hands had been a short time before. He kissed the slopes and curves, nuzzled her gently, breathed on her skin and grazed it lovingly and oh-so-lightly with his teeth. He ran his tongue over her, swirling around the puckered nipples, lightly caressing the tight little beads with his warm wet touch. Whenever he heard her sigh, felt her arch toward him or clutch him harder, he repeated the slow motion of his tongue on the sensitive spot.

Daphne whimpered in pleasure as each nipple was carefully attended to, delicately aroused and teased and loved. She felt

his hands slide down across the bare skin of her hips, and she
wiggled to ease his way.

"Let's try a little dish of this, sweetheart," he murmured,
easing his knowing fingers down across the sensitive skin of her
thighs, then slowly between them, and finally up across the
delta of fine curls, where he luxuriated in exploring her in light,
circular caresses. He palmed her hidden secrets, feathered the
darkened triangle with his fingertips.

Daphne was torn. She could easily have lain in his arms and
shamelessly writhed in pleasure and enjoyed his inventive attention. However, she also wanted to caress him, both for the
pleasure that gave her and to give back to him a small part of
the extraordinary gift that he was so willingly giving to her.

She reached out, and she could tell by the increasing heat of
his body, by the rougher way he touched her, by the way he
tilted his body to make it easier for her to caress him, that he
was thoroughly enjoying the attention she was paying him. It
made her nearly tearful with happiness that he reacted with
such alacrity to her gentle hands as she sought to discover what
pleased him. She felt a deeply personal pride that he responded so quickly and so easily to her. It strengthened her
confidence, and it made her feel loved. So when she felt his
aroused male flesh press against her thigh, she caressed him,
closing her hand over him in a slow, tender motion, sliding her
palm over the lambskin-soft sheath of hot male skin covering
his hardened manhood.

He moaned and thrust himself against her. Then he hissed
and grabbed her hand, holding it still over himself for a long,
painful moment.

"That feels so good I may not make it to the last item on the
dessert list, Daffy," he muttered through his teeth. He put her
hand back up on his bare ribs.

Then he pulled her over him and let her slide across him, so
that she was half sprawled on his left side and half open for him
to touch. Their eyes met, and he slid his left arm up behind her,
pulling her head down for a deep and tender kiss. As their
mouths mated, his fingertips slid down her body, rediscover-
ing the humid warmth between her thighs. Her legs parted
willingly, and he caressed the sleek and silky lips that were shyly
hidden beneath her delta of downy curls.

With each slow stroke of his long fingers, she was inundated
by a new wave of deep, deep pleasure. Each wave was stronger
than the last. Each dragged her deeper into a dark vortex of

excitement. She moaned and moved against him, unable not to. She buried her face in his hot neck and kissed him, rolling her hips in counterpoint to his thrusting fingers. The undertow dragged harder against her. Pulling. Pulling. Deeper. Smoother. Harder. Sweeter.

His arms tightened around her as he felt her grow taut, heard her breath turn into a soft, staggered pant.

"Quinn," she whispered, barely able to talk. "Please . . . I need you inside me . . . don't make me . . ." She still couldn't quite bring herself to say the word. "You know, don't make me do it alone. I want you with me. Please." She caught a sob of frustration. "Stop! Oh, please . . ."

His fingers slowed, but never quite left her. His voice vibrated with wanting and regret. He didn't have much choice. "I came straight here after a meeting in Washington, honey. I didn't bring anything with me," he confessed ruefully. "Believe me, I've been cursing that meeting ever since I left it." He could still visualize the box where he'd left it next to his bed.

She put her forearms on his chest and propped herself on them. Her eyes were glazed with passion but softened by a mischievous glint. "This time, *I'm* prepared," she announced rather breathlessly. She blushed in spite of her best intention not to.

He became completely still. "You found your, uh, equipment?" he guessed in amusement.

She grabbed his ears affectionately and kissed him soundly. "No! But I drove halfway across the county to a drugstore and picked up something suitable. Something they didn't have back in the 'old days,'" she added, lowering her voice suggestively.

He was beginning to smile. "Do you need to get up and do anything at this point?"

She laughed and draped herself over him wantonly. "No. I've already done everything I need to."

He quickly removed the necessary clothing from both of them and pulled her over on her side, so that they were lying facing one another. He looked into her eyes and felt robbed of his breath, as he so often did when he gazed into those rich violet depths. They were dark with wanting, transformed into the mysterious color of indigo.

He felt the most irrational urge to tell her that he loved her, and he captured her face in his hands and kissed her quickly to prevent the words from tumbling out of his mouth. He slid his knee between her thighs and pulled her leg up over his hip, easing himself deliciously close to her and settling his fully aroused flesh boldly against her soft, damp warmth.

As he wrapped his arms around her and kissed her throat, he murmured how beautiful she was, how hot he was for her, how much he wanted her, how sweet it was to hold her in his arms.

Something in the way he touched her, in the hoarse sound of his voice, made Daphne feel loved. She knew he wasn't saying that, but she glowed at the possibility that he was going through the same incredible experience that she was, falling in love with a virtual stranger.

He thrust his manhood teasingly against her dewy flesh, letting the slippery caress drive them both a little crazy.

That teasing intimacy, his passionate kisses and the hotly whispered love words combined to drive her wild with wanting. And it weakened her resolve to keep her love for him in the closet, where it couldn't alarm him. Or her.

When she looked at him, her heart and her surrender were there for him to see. She saw his eyes darken in response.

"Sweet Daphne. I never thought . . ." He caught his words, biting them back with an effort. He closed his eyes for a moment, struggling with himself.

He looked as if he were seeking absolution for some sin, she thought. Like a man wrestling with a demon. Aching to comfort him, to reassure him that whatever he was worried about could be worked out, Daphne pressed her lips gently against his and kissed him with all the tender love in her heart.

When she lifted her lips from his, she thought he looked even more shaken. But then he took a deep breath, and whatever it was disappeared.

"You're *mine*, Daphne," he whispered fiercely against her throat. "No matter what happens, you're mine. And I intend to keep you."

"Yes," she whispered back, thrilled down to the marrow of her bones that he wanted her so desperately. "Yes."

"Look at me, Daphne," he ordered hoarsely.

As she gazed into his fierce, golden brown eyes, he grasped her hips and thrust slowly into her. Their eyes were locked as he pushed deeply into her flesh. She felt possessed in body and soul in that instant, as bound to him as she could ever be to a man. And she thought that he felt that way, too. It was like a sacred vow, watching each other as they took one another in the most intimate form of possession possible.

She wrapped her arms around him and unerringly found his lips, even as her eyes closed in ecstasy. He thrust into her in long, slow, possessive strokes. Each hard thrust fueled the fire of need raging deep inside her. Every time her body lifted to meet his, she felt him tighten and clench, and that thrilled her to the core, too.

He twisted a little and changed the sensitive point of contact between their bodies just enough so that the next time he thrust into her a brilliant burst of joy began deep within her.

She gasped his name and tightened her arms around his shoulders, desperate to get so close to him that they could never be parted again. He growled in satisfaction and murmured encouragement, then twisted again. The brilliant burst erupted again, only this time it was like the beginning of the sunrise. Suddenly it expanded and grew, becoming brighter and hotter and filling her with a blinding radiance greater than anything she had ever imagined. She tumbled into a supernova and heard a soft, wild cry. She knew it as hers just as he urgently covered her mouth with his and convulsed violently against her in his own brilliant, scalding rebirth.

As he shuddered against her in a series of strong aftershocks, he was groaning a name. When he tore his mouth free of hers and buried his face against her damp neck, she heard at last the name he'd been crying out. The name was hers.

Daphne was grateful that he didn't want to move for a while. It was so good holding him, feeling his arm around her, listening to his slow breathing by her ear. She slid her fingers through his soft dark blond hair, watching it fall through her hands. She noticed a few silvery glints. He was beginning to gray, she thought affectionately.

"I think I'll call you 'The Silver Fox,'" she murmured.

"Hmm?" he mumbled into her shoulder. He turned and lifted an eyebrow.

"You're getting a few gray hairs," she pointed out with a smile. She affectionately ruffled his hair. "It'll make you look distinguished." Her eyes twinkled. "And not so dangerous," she added, remembering how he'd looked to her in the strange lighting at The Farmer's Mouse.

"Dangerous?" he repeated softly. He'd been watching her with a lazy smile, too thoroughly saturated with contentment to want to do anything but wrap his arms around her and hold her tight. But that word—*dangerous*—brought a lot of things back to him that he'd been ignoring for far too long. He sighed, and his smile gradually turned bittersweet. "I'm surprised you haven't found more than a few of them," he conceded dryly. Considering some of the hair-raising experiences he'd had, it was a miracle he hadn't grayed out years ago. "Come on, Daffy," he said firmly, pushing himself up and bringing her along with him. "Dessert's over. You and I have to talk." He pulled on his pants and absentmindedly handed Daphne hers. "There are some things that we need to discuss," he added, frowning as he began to think about the conversation that lay ahead of them.

"Hmm," she said, kissing his bare shoulder before it could disappear beneath the shirt he was pulling on. "We're back to being serious, I see," she observed regretfully.

"Very serious." He tucked his shirt into his trousers, zipped them up and fastened his belt. Then he helped Daphne along by handing her the rest of her clothes and frowning at her as she stepped into them very slowly and with a couple of shakes of her bare bottom that made Danaker wonder if he weren't making a big mistake after all.

"You certainly are in a hurry to get me covered up," she noted humorously.

Beneath her effort at lightheartedness, however, she was beginning to feel a little hurt. He was obviously in a big hurry to wrap things up and get down to business, but that wasn't what Daphne needed now. She was still basking in the warm afterglow of lovemaking and longed to be cuddled and held, yearned to sleep next to him and enjoy the deep relaxation that followed such profound release, such an intensely intimate emotional union.

He saw the hurt in her eyes and debated whether to yield to her desire to play awhile longer. He had noticed her reluctance to break up their intimacy. Her hands had lingered on him when he rose. She was slow to take the clothing he handed her. And she was taking her sweet time pulling her damned bra closed at the moment. He dragged his eyes away from the bare breasts enticing him and stepped forward to briskly fasten the closure. With stiff-fingered efficiency he helped her into her blouse without saying a word. He was old enough to know that saying the wrong thing could cause more trouble than keeping one's mouth shut before you'd given the situation enough thought. Grimly, he contemplated his options.

She stared at him as if he'd become a different man. He'd withdrawn from her emotionally, something he hadn't done the other times they'd made love, she realized in retrospect. What was bothering him? *Quinn? Talk to me,* she wanted to say. Her old shyness came back to plague her anew. Maybe she shouldn't press him. Not yet, anyway.

Hell, he thought angrily. He couldn't let her feel he was simply abandoning their intimacy, even though that might be the best thing to do at this point. But he remembered the piercing sweetness that had bolted through him a little earlier when he'd seen the love that bordered on adoration in her eyes. His guilt at not having told her everything had been back-breakingly hard to bear then. He had never wanted to deceive her. Not in the way it had turned out, anyway. And now she was falling in love with him before he'd explained the facts of his connection with Connor Jamison.

He grimly wished that he could roll back time to that night in the hospital. Knowing what he did now, he should have told her then that he was to have met Jamison. He could have been a little vague at first, then gradually filled her in as they became better acquainted. Now . . . now he was faced with telling a woman he wanted with every breath in his body that he wasn't exactly who she thought she was. She would have every right to feel betrayed. What he now feared, though, was that the damage might go deeper than just anger and a shouting match.

He was well aware that Daphne had built a protective wall around her heart and her body long ago. She had lived with betrayal for a very long time, and she knew it for a cold, unsatisfactory partner. Then she'd discovered ecstasy when he'd breached those walls and won her trust. On faith. On instinct. Trust your instincts, he'd told her, and she had.

Now she was much more vulnerable to serious wounding, he thought. Partly because it would appear to be a second dose of the same poison she'd been handed once before by a man. And partly because she was physically attracted to him in a way she hadn't been to her husband. She had surrendered to him in the most personal form of vulnerability and trust that a woman could yield to a man. How would she react if she believed that he, too, had betrayed her? Would she let him explain? Would she give him an opportunity to make some sort of amends for his blunder? Would she listen to him at all?

He recognized the cold sick feeling sliding through his gut now. It was fear. It tasted sick and sour in the pit of his stomach. Damn it, how could he have known they would be like flint and steel to one another? They only had to look at each other and... He swore aloud.

Well, he had no choice but to try to begin some sort of explanation, he thought. Perhaps if he eased into it gradually, over a couple of days or so, she might accept the truth more easily. If he were incredibly lucky. Or if Daphne really had learned to trust her instincts. Two chances were better than none, he told himself grimly.

Daphne finished fastening the waistband of her slacks and wondered what he was planning on saying at this serious discussion. If he had behaved differently, she might have entertained the enchanting possibility that he would tell her he was falling in love with her, or something satisfyingly close to that.

But there was a grimness about his eyes that made her think the conversation he was planning would have very little to do with their relationship. It was more likely he wanted to discuss the mystery of Connor's death.

A small dart of guilt pricked her conscience when she realized she was no longer as deeply interested in solving that mystery as she had been immediately after Connor's murder. But then, a great deal had changed in her life since that night. A lot of old shackles had rusted through and fallen away, freeing her.

And all her most exhilarating discoveries involved Quinn. She flushed from her shoulders to her hips thinking about the dramatic change he had made in her tidy little existence. He had opened doors for her that would never be closed again.

"Stop looking at me like that, Daphne."

"What's the matter, Quinn?" she asked him softly, searching his face for some glimpse of a clue. He was frowning, but it was frustration rather than irritation that she saw in his eyes. "We were so close just minutes ago, and now..." She made a helpless gesture. "What happened?"

He ran his hands through his hair and paced across the room. *Don't blow it already.* "I'm sorry, Daphne. This is going to take a little time...." He sighed. "And I'm not at my best. It's been a long day." And a long several weeks.

She watched him struggle with himself and wondered if perhaps this was more serious than she had thought. Had she misjudged his interest in her? Just as that awful thought began to ice her down, he crossed back to her and took her shoulders in his hands. She was immediately reassured by his touch, and the warmth and sincerity in his eyes quickly cast off the dreadful fear that had gripped her. No, she thought, taking heart. He does care. I couldn't be that wrong....

"Do you remember when I told you that I was sorry we met when we did?" he asked.

"Yes. At my dining room table..."

"Yes. I want you to know that I still feel that way, Daphne." He drew her close and wrapped her in his arms for a long moment. Then he firmly held her away and looked straight into her eyes. "After the mysteries are cleared up, promise that you'll let me start all over again."

She laughed a little uncertainly and gazed up at him in surprise. "I'd much rather we just kept on going from where we are now." She felt her cheeks grow hot with embarrassment. She'd never thrown herself at a man, and that was pretty much what she'd just done. But Quinn didn't look particularly concerned about that one way or the other. He seemed preoccupied and not at all relieved by her reassurance. Her smile faded into oblivion and she touched his cheek. "What's the matter, Quinn?"

He sat down in the chair and motioned for her to sit in the old wingback across from him. She did, wishing that he'd pulled her onto his lap, or at least let them sit on the couch, where they could touch. She missed the simple pleasure of being in physical contact with him. Not wanting to seem like a clinging female, she tried to keep a stiff upper lip and bear the disappointment without complaint.

He thought the easiest way to begin would be with Sarmien's visit. From there, he could start giving her a few pieces of his past. That would be a beginning, at least.

"Why was Sarmien here?"

The question was unexpectedly to the point, and Daphne blinked in surprise. Aside from the unvarnished bluntness of it, she had the strangest impression that Quinn already knew Sarmien. But that was impossible, surely. She distinctly recalled mentioning that John Sarmien had attended the funeral and that he had been Connor's boss. Danaker had remained silent then. If he'd known Sarmien, he would have acknowledged it, she was sure.

"I was very surprised to see him," she admitted, curling her legs under her.

"You weren't expecting him?"

"No." She wrinkled her nose thoughtfully. "He began by expressing his concern for me, hoping everything was going well, wondering if the company benefits were being paid promptly, that kind of thing."

"And after he finished all the standard platitudes, then what?"

She was amused by his confident and absolutely accurate description of Sarmien's opening ploy. Danaker certainly knew how to size a man up in a hurry, she thought admiringly. "After the, er, 'platitudes,' he told me some items were missing that should have been among Connor's things at the office. He was wondering if I'd seen any of them."

"What kind of items?" he asked.

"Let's see." She frowned in concentration. "Papers or files with papers in them, possibly a report or several reports . . . He was a little vague. Oh, yes, and a key."

"A key?" Danaker leaned forward intently.

"He thought the missing papers might have been temporarily placed in a locker in the airport or a lockbox or something similar." Daphne shrugged and shook her head. "I thought the whole thing sounded pretty strange, to tell you the truth." She looked at Quinn with curiosity. "I was wishing you could have listened to him when he was telling me all that," she confessed softly.

He smiled slightly. "Yeah?"

"Yeah," she echoed, inflecting the word as he did. "I thought you'd be better at figuring out what he was up to than I was."

"Is that so?" he said, amused.

"Yes."

"Why do you think that, Daffy?" he asked softly.

"I think you've got a lot of experience dealing with men like him," she explained.

"Really? What kind of experiences were you envisioning?" He trod carefully, but he tried to lead her gently toward some of the other topics he wanted to air.

Daphne clasped her hands around her knees and cocked her head to one side, studying him. "I really don't know much about you, do I, Quinn? I mean, I really can't answer that question, because I don't know what experiences you've had."

"That's right." His gaze did not waver, and the warmth never flickered. "Would you like to take this opportunity to ask me some questions?" He smiled at her, but it couldn't quite soften the seriousness in his eyes. "I'll answer them. As truthfully as I can."

"I know you will," she assured him with great warmth. "You're an honest man, Quinn Danaker. All my instincts tell me so."

She had hoped her passionate avowal of support would soothe him, bring them closer together again. To her surprise, the moment she said the word *honest*, he seemed to stiffen, as if she had slapped him instead of complimented him.

"If you ever doubt that, tell me. Let me give you whatever proof you want, Daffy," he said huskily, a strange light in his eyes as he gazed at her.

She was puzzled. "All right, but I can't imagine . . ."

He shrugged. "Life can be strange."

"I suppose." He'd urged her to ask questions, she realized, and the one that had most recently occurred to her forced its way out. "Did you ever meet John Sarmien before?" she asked curiously.

"No. Why?"

"Well . . . it just seemed to me that you greeted each other as if you were acquainted," she admitted sheepishly.

He nodded. "You're very perceptive."

Daphne blinked in surprise. "Does that mean you do know him, then?" she asked in confusion.

"I know him by reputation," he explained.

"And does he know you?"

"Yes."

"By reputation?" she surmised.

"Yes."

She leaned forward and gave him a somewhat perplexed look. "What reputation?" she asked naively.

Answering that candidly would certainly fill in a lot of blanks in his life for her, he thought grimly. How could he supply some of the truth and not be accused of deceit? He needed to feed her the truth gently. Very gently.

"I worked for a European-based company before I retired to my current business," he reminded her.

Her eyes lightened. "Of course." A shadow passed over the lightness. "But Europe is a very big place," she quickly pointed out. Then, curiously, "What kind of business were you in? Surely not the same kind of consulting that Corday does." She smiled. She just couldn't see Quinn pushing papers and endlessly consulting on educational- and management-training issues.

He could see she'd forgotten about the under-the-table business Corday was involved in. "I was in exactly the same business."

Daphne had been smiling, but something in the steady way he was regarding her sent a slow curl of apprehension through her. For one silly moment, she even remembered the borderline legal arms trading he'd claimed Corday was involved with, and she wondered if that was the business he was talking about.

It wasn't the looniest thing she'd ever thought. After all, he was involved in small-arms trading now, of an antique variety, of course. It would be easy enough to progress from one to the other, she supposed. But that was ridiculous. He would have said something.

"Quinn . . ."

They were interrupted by a loud yell from upstairs.

Kyle.

They dashed up the stairs and found him thrashing around wildly in his bed. His head rolled from side to side, and he was muttering unintelligibly.

"It's just a nightmare," Daphne exclaimed in a whisper, sagging with relief. It was dark in Kyle's bedroom, and she went inside to make sure he was still asleep. He was, but when she bent over him to see, she noticed the balled-up jacket he was clutching. It was half-buried under his pillow, half cushioning his cheek.

"I think I've just found what we've been looking for," she murmured.

She gently removed the jacket from Kyle's loosening grip.

Triumphantly, she removed a crumpled envelope from the inside pocket. To her surprise, something fell to the floor with a metallic clink.

A key.

Chapter 14

Danaker picked up the key and examined it. A serial number and USPS-DO NOT DUPLICATE had been engraved on it.

"This is a key to a post office box. Do you recognize it?" he asked, turning his steady, amber eyes on her.

Daphne, who had closed Kyle's door and joined Danaker in the hallway, peered at it in the subdued illumination provided by the night-light. Her brows gathered into a pensive frown, and she slowly shook her head.

"No. I've never seen it before. Connor never mentioned having a mailbox...."

He heard the note of faint surprise, followed by resignation, in her voice. At least she no longer experienced major shock or hurt when they uncovered a new deception by her late husband. That pleased him.

When he dragged his mind back to the substance of her reply, however, he frowned. If she didn't know which post office Jamison had used, it would be difficult to locate the box, unless they notified the postal authorities or the police. He preferred seeing the box's contents first, if possible, just to avoid any unwanted complications.

He turned his attention to the jacket that Daphne was clutching in her arms and the white envelope crushed in one delicate fist.

"What else did you find?" he asked smoothly.

She led him back down to the living room, where the light was much better and they could speak without fear of waking Kyle. She stopped close to a floor lamp and placed the envelope on a small coffee table. Then she carefully felt through each of the pockets, withdrawing loose change from one and two printed bus schedules from another. She looked up at Danaker.

"That's all," she said. She felt like she should be apologizing. She didn't think these were much to go on.

He picked up the envelope and looked at it. It was addressed to Jamison at a post-office box in Merrifield, Virginia. He turned it for Daphne to see, and when their eyes met, they were both beginning to smile.

"That answers the question of where the box is," he pointed out dryly.

Daphne hurried to flip open the bus schedules.

"One is for the route from Springfield to Pentagon City," she told him. "The other is from Pentagon City to Fairfax." She frowned and ran her finger down the stops for the second route. Her expression cleared and she added excitedly. "And one of the stops is at Merrifield!" She looked at Danaker, relieved that one mystery had just been solved. "He must have taken the bus to the Merrifield post office that day."

There was a sense of triumph in solving that particular mystery. She wondered if perhaps she hadn't missed her calling in life. Maybe she should have been an investigator of some sort.

Quinn nodded. "You're probably right."

Daphne's brow knitted into another small frown. "Why would he go way out there to get a postal box?"

Danaker shrugged. "Hard to say. It isn't the post office closest to your house, obviously. On the other hand, since it's the regional mail-handling facility, they're open seven days a week and have tellers available until midnight on weeknights and into the evenings on weekends. It's the first stop for letters and packages when they arrive in Northern Virginia, so it may speed up delivery by a day or so." He knew because he used that facility himself when the occasion warranted it.

He flipped the key lightly in his palm. He wanted to examine the contents of Jamison's postal box as soon as possible. If it contained some clue about Janisch's whereabouts or the message that he had been trying to send to Danaker, the more quickly they discovered it, the better.

"I don't suppose you would care to see what's inside the box?" he teased.

"Oh, yes, I would! I don't like unsolved mysteries!" She saw his mouth twitch into a grin and realized she had shamelessly risen to the bait.

"It isn't just a matter of facing the truth about Jamison's life anymore, is it?" he asked softly.

"No." She smiled at him sheepishly. "That was my reason in the beginning. But now I feel like I'm on a scavenger hunt. I'd like the thrill of discovery."

He laughed. "The thrill of discovery, huh? I think I've encouraged a genie to pop out of her bottle."

She thought perhaps he was right. She *did* want to find out what was in the box, not so much from a desire to unearth the extent of the mockery that Connor had made of their marriage, but simply to know the truth. She must have caught some of Quinn's unflagging curiosity.

He tossed the key again.

"It's too late to drive over there now," he said pensively, as he considered the possibilities. "They lock up at midnight on Fridays."

She was not surprised that he knew such operational details. She had seen some of his correspondence, stacked and ready to be mailed, when she had been at his home, and she knew that he was an astute businessman. She simply assumed that he had discovered the efficiency of the Merrifield facility in the course of conducting his own business. Besides, she wouldn't have been surprised by anything he knew. She was beginning to believe that Quinn knew something about almost everything.

"We could go tomorrow," she suggested hopefully.

It was a delightful excuse for her to invite him to spend some time with her, she thought happily. She hoped that he didn't have anything else planned, and that he didn't think she was involving him in her life more deeply than he wanted. She was sure that he had enjoyed the time they spent together, but still had his own life, separate from hers. She was having a hard time remembering that lately.

He relaxed. She'd taken the words right out of his mouth.

"What time?" he asked, pulling her into his arms. He kissed her cheek and leaned his jaw against her temple.

It was all she could do not to purr. Whatever had caused him to be distant earlier had faded. He was warm and intimate again, just as she wanted him to be.

"Kyle has a soccer practice tomorrow morning. They don't have a game, so the coach told them to get in some extra drill time. He was going to go with Crabby and his father. They'll be gone from nine until about noon, I think. We could run over to Merrifield while he's gone." She leaned back in his arms and looked at him questioningly. "Would that be all right?"

He smiled slightly and kissed her lightly on the mouth. "It's fine with me," he agreed. "Although I wouldn't mind kidnapping you after we've been by the post office." He lowered his mouth to kiss her neck in tender persuasion on behalf of his thinly veiled proposition.

The sensation of his lips and tongue caressing her skin made her bones soften and her stomach melt.

"Kidnap?" she murmured doubtfully as her eyes closed in pleasure. Her arms tightened around him, and she pressed herself against him like a cat curling around its favorite catnip. "Where were you thinking of taking me?" she finally managed to ask.

"To my bed," he whispered in her ear.

"In that case, I won't press any charges," she assured him. Her voice was as unsteady as her knees.

He found her mouth with his and kissed her intimately, deepening the kiss as he felt her tighten her arms around his neck and moan softly in her throat. Blood heated and pulsed through his body, forcing him to break away before it became awkward for him to walk out her front door. Considering their love play earlier, he shouldn't have been so easily aroused. Obviously his body wasn't aware of that.

Their eyes met. Hers were soft and adoring. His were hot and becoming clouded with concern.

"I want to talk to you tomorrow, Daphne," he said seriously.

"Talk?" She slid her hand through his hair playfully. When she let her other hand glide provocatively down his chest and waist, he caught it and pressed a kiss on her mischievous palm.

"Yes, talk, you lusty wench," he growled, smiling. The smile did not banish the serious light from his eyes, however. "I want to tell you the story of my life. I believe you asked for it once, and I put you off. I think the time has come for you to hear it."

She laid her head against his chest and wrapped her arms around his waist. He wouldn't make an offer like that if he wanted to keep his distance from her, she thought, reassured.

Whatever had made him withdraw from her earlier obviously wasn't anything serious. She smiled contentedly.

"Lusty wench, huh?" she teased him back. "I'll be looking forward to hearing all about your checkered past!"

I hope you feel the same way about me after you hear it, he thought, unconsciously tightening his arms around her and drawing her closer. She was warm and loving now, but how would she feel about him when she knew the truth? Unfortunately, there was only one way for him to find out. By telling her.

The key fit easily into the jagged slot in the mailbox.

Daphne turned her hand, and the metal door sprang open. She grinned at Quinn, who was standing beside her, waiting.

"Here we go," she said dramatically, and she reached inside to remove the contents.

It was a large box, and it contained a fair number of things. There were several large envelopes, which from the feel of them were filled with what could have been reports. There were also three legal-size envelopes thick with what felt like letters of several pages in length.

Daphne handed them to Quinn and pulled out a padded envelope with a flat cardboard box in it. Whatever was inside the box was heavy. She passed it to him, shut the postal box door and locked it. When she turned to take a closer look at everything, he was pensively hefting the padded envelope, trying to gauge the contents.

"Shall we go over there to open everything?" she asked. She pointed toward one of the broad tables available for postal patrons to use in addressing forms and stamping envelopes.

"That might be a little public," he said gently. He wasn't sure what the mail would reveal, but he didn't want Daphne to take any additional insults from her late husband in front of an audience. And he didn't want her to discover his identity that way, either. "Why don't we go back to my place? No one will interrupt us there."

"All right."

She remembered his threat to kidnap her afterward and tried not to look as excited as she felt. It wasn't easy, though. Even thinking about Quinn made her grow very warm. And being with him was worse.

He saw the telltale blush of color that stole across her cheeks and he grinned wickedly, guessing the direction of her naughty thoughts. "We don't need interruptions for *that*, either," he told her in a low, intimate voice.

She turned startled eyes on him.

"Yes. I'm reading your mind again." And he didn't look apologetic about it, either.

She couldn't help laughing. "That means you're thinking the same thing," she reminded him rather primly.

His white teeth flashed in an unsettling, wolfish grin.

When they got to Quinn's they spread the mail out over a large, rectangular table in one of his gunrooms.

They opened the big padded package first. It was addressed to Jamison, but there was no return address on the outside. It had Austrian postage on it, but the stamps had never been canceled. Apparently it had been placed in the box for safe-keeping. Connor must have brought it with him in his luggage on the airplane, she thought.

Daphne opened the box inside the padded envelope and removed the item inside. The minute she saw it, she had a strange feeling again. It was the same sense of unease she had experienced the night before, when Quinn had seemed distant and unknown for a moment. Her instincts all clamored: something is wrong here.

"It's a gun!" she exclaimed. She handed it to Quinn. "I don't think Connor even knew how to shoot. Why on earth would he have this? It doesn't look like an ordinary gun. It looks more like something a collector would have. Like something *you* would have."

"You're right." He stared at the small weapon. He recognized it as soon as he saw the two initials engraved on the silver under the barrel. JK. It belonged to Janisch Kopek. Or, at least, it had the last time he had seen it. Was this what Janisch had been sending him? If so, why hadn't Jamison brought it with him? And if not, why was there no note or bill of sale accompanying it?

He couldn't believe that Janisch would have sold this particular gun to anyone. It was his personal favorite, the first gun he had ever bought with the intention of keeping. Before, he had always bought to resell for a profit. But this one had intrigued him, and he had kept it in a glass case behind his desk. Gradually he had bought a few other collector's items. But this small gun had been special. The queen of his harem.

It was a small pistol, the size and shape of a derringer, exquisitely formed of polished wood and fine metal. To Daphne's untrained eye, it looked quite valuable.

She watched him handle the little gun, turning it over in his hand, examining the various parts with knowledgeable eyes. His palm molded the finely finished maple stock as if it had been made for him. His lean fingertips glided along the plate of etched silver that flowed down from the stock and covered the petite barrel. She was reminded of the effortless skill those same fingers displayed when caressing her.

He lifted the gun, pulled back the hammer, looked down the sight and ever so gently released the hammer again. He held the little gun like a man who could hit a dime at forty paces in a driving rainstorm, she thought.

"What kind of gun is it?" she asked curiously.

"A .41 Williamson metallic cartridge derringer with brass and silver mountings."

"Is it as expensive as it looks?"

"Yes."

"Why do you suppose Connor had it?"

"It might have represented some sort of payment," he suggested slowly.

"Payment for what?"

"For rendering a service to someone."

"Why wouldn't they just pay money?"

"Maybe Jamison didn't want money. Maybe he preferred the Williamson. Or maybe this was the only thing that the person had to pay him with."

Daphne stared at him. She had the eerie feeling that Danaker had a whole scenario in his mind, but that he was only sharing a small piece of it with her. He was speaking as if he had been standing in a room somewhere watching the deal being cut between Connor and this unnamed person who had owned the gun.

She shook her head, trying to rid herself of the bizarre image. She was letting her imagination run away with her, she thought. This was crazy.

She tried to imagine who could have given Connor the pistol. Sarmien? One of Connor's mysterious acquaintances in Europe? The elusive Christina?

"You look like your head's about to crack," he told her, joking with her to try to keep her in a reasonably good mood.

"It is. From thinking too hard," she muttered darkly.

He picked up the envelopes and quickly checked the postmarks and return addresses. None of them looked like anyone he knew.

"Here...you start on these, and I'll work on the others. We'll trade when we're done until we've both read everything."

She agreed, opened an envelope and began to read.

Daphne didn't have to know a thing about the international weapons business to recognize that the reports summarized three secret deals that Connor had been working on for Corday International. Arms deals. Big ones. And quite illegal.

Corday was quietly purchasing both highly sophisticated equipment and large quantities of traditional armaments from a dozen different legitimate sources scattered throughout Europe, Asia and North America. They were giving the sellers a guarantee that they would not sell the equipment to any person, group or government who was prohibited from purchasing it by the country in which the weapons were manufactured. This was the typical "end-use" restriction applied worldwide and almost impossible to enforce.

At the warehouses, the weaponry was then dismantled, making it appear less technologically advanced than it was. The pieces were relabeled, to get around the end-use restrictions. Then the repackaged, disassembled parts were identified on shipping manifests as agricultural equipment or arms replacements and spare parts for rural police and army units in half a dozen countries around the world.

"Good heavens!" Daphne exclaimed, appalled. "Who do you suppose is getting all this?"

Quinn looked up from the report he had just finished. He had put on his reading glasses and was staring at her over top of them.

"The companies paying for that equipment are all probably fronts for a dozen loosely connected and very ambitious terrorist groups."

It was an educated guess, but he knew that two of them were fronts, and he would be very surprised if the rest weren't also. He had also recognized the delivery route being used on one of the operational plans. It had been used seven years ago by the terrorist group that had killed his wife. Seeing the route's resurrection ignited a great deal of anger in him.

It also aroused a very bad feeling about this whole situation. He didn't believe in coincidence. Janisch must have discovered the connection, too. Perhaps that was what he had been trying to tell Quinn. Secretly, so that they wouldn't be aware their plan had been discovered. But Janisch surely would have notified the authorities who kept track of such breaches in arms trading. So why was there no record of any of this? His friends should have stumbled onto something if there were any kind of surveillance going on. Any open case on file.

Daphne was unaware of Quinn's pensiveness. She was horrified at this latest revelation. Just when she thought Connor could do nothing more to surprise her, he had.

"Connor was the go-between in arranging sales of military equipment to terrorists?" she exclaimed, aghast.

"I'm afraid so."

She felt sick. She knew she wasn't responsible for what Connor had been doing, but she felt as if she had been connected to it anyway. After all, he *had* been her husband. His sins were not as distant from her as a stranger's would have been.

"Are you all right, Daphne?" he asked quietly. He saw her pale, watched the dawn of revulsion in her eyes. "If you'd rather not read any more of this, I can do it for you," he offered. "You can look around my business...."

They were beneath the earth, surrounded by rooms filled with antique weapons, with his office down the hall.

Daphne shook her head. "I'd like to see your antiques later," she admitted with a shy smile. More seriously, she added, "But I want to read everything. I want to get it all out in the open and then get it behind me. I just...wasn't expecting this." She sighed. "I know Connor stretched the boundaries of ethics until you could hardly see them anymore, but I never thought he'd be so eager to make money that he would actually break laws and provide weapons to dangerous people." She lifted her chin in determination. The shock was behind her now. What other damaging news could she possibly hear?

Danaker got out of his chair and gathered the reports. "I'd like to fax some of the names, dates and figures in these files to my contacts in Europe." He raised his eyebrows questioningly, waiting for any objection she might have.

"All right." She followed him, carrying the letters with her. "This place is really amazing," she told him sincerely as they walked down the hall.

"Thanks. Look around if you like. This may take some time," he said, frowning.

He unlocked his office and walked inside, leaving the door open so that she could enter whenever she wished. Lights automatically turned on as he passed through the electronic sensor over the entrance. He went straight to his computer and turned it on.

Daphne read the letters and left them on a table within easy reach for him. The letters were all from a woman named Lilli Marlene. They had been mailed from Austria, Switzerland and Italy. They also contained details of arms deals. They seemed to discuss deals similar to those described in the reports, but there were subtle changes. The types of weapons the buyers wanted were clearly stated and very similar to what was in the inventory in the other reports. But the dates of shipping, the destinations and the people engaged to transport the arms were different.

There was something else in the letters, too. These were not just impersonal business correspondence. They were love letters. Well, "lust letters" might be a better description. The woman had obviously been sleeping with Connor and enjoying it. She was looking forward to their next tryst. Daphne had felt a slight flare of anger at that. Not that she cared if Connor were physically intimate with this woman. It was just such an insult to her. She would have given him a divorce if he had wanted to marry this Lilli Marlene. But instead he had cheated. Daphne had been bound by their marriage contract. Out of a sense of honor and decency, she had remained celibate. He had not. And quite flagrantly, too, she thought, at a resort outside of Salzburg in one of the letters. Daphne remembered seeing the bill for that come in. And she had *paid* it! She was so disgusted, she tossed the letter on the table and jumped to her feet.

Quinn looked up in surprise.

"I'm going to take the grand tour," she announced briskly.

He was a little perplexed by her strange attitude. "Something bother you in the letters?" he asked, following her malevolent glance at the pile near his elbow.

"I just wish I'd read *that* one before I paid a certain bill," she said through gritted teeth.

He had read the letters and took a wild guess. "The hotel tab from Salzburg?"

"That's it."

He frowned. "I thought you didn't care."

"I don't!" She stalked out.

He felt a searing irritation. Jealousy. He didn't want her caring one way or the other what Connor Jamison had done. He thought she was probably just angry at having to pay for Jamison's adulterous entertainment with another woman. He could understand that. He would have preferred that she didn't give a plugged nickle one way or the other, but he did understand. He turned back to the computer and fed some more data to his network of friends.

"Come on, Peter," he muttered. "Get the hell out of bed. It's only four or five in the morning. Early riser gets the worm. Or, in this case, the answer to the riddle."

Daphne didn't hear his comment. She hadn't even seen the perplexed expression on his face as he watched her leave his office. She was fully absorbed in exploring his hidden caverns.

This was the first time she had been able to take a leisurely tour of his business. He had brought her down here with him on a couple of occasions when she had visited, but they had only lingered long enough to retrieve something and return to the house. He had shown her one of the cases of guns, patiently answering her questions and explaining what she was too naive to ask about.

Quinn had always been with her before. Now she was on her own.

In his office, Quinn leaned over to push some buttons on a console hidden beneath the computer table. "I've released the locks on all the doors," he told her over the intercom system. He grinned slightly. "If you see anything you'd like, let me know. I warn you, though, I drive a hard bargain. You won't find me as easy in a business negotiation as I am between the sheets."

"Easy?" She laughed at his teasing comment floating warmly through the air, making her feel his welcome presence was magically all around her.

A central tunnel ran from his home down underground. Rooms had been built off the tunnel. One was his office. One was a warehouse for items that had just arrived or were being packed for shipping. Other rooms were used for display.

It reminded her of a private museum. Each piece was carefully placed on a glass shelf in a thick glass case. Soft white spotlights in the ceilings automatically illuminated the room and its contents when she passed through the door. Everything was pristine and inviting.

Unlike in most museums, however, her tread was silent. Quinn had soundproofed the walls and ceilings and installed wall-to-wall carpeting in the rooms and hallways.

The display cases were filled with weapons as beautiful as they were deadly. These were not crudely manufactured things. They were works of art. The craftsmen who had made them had poured all their skill and talent into each one. A label had been placed beneath each weapon giving its name, maker, date of manufacture and any interesting details about its history.

One pearl-and-silver derringer had been owned by Bat Masterson. And a rifle with fancy carving on its fine walnut stock had once been used by the great Annie Oakley. Daphne couldn't resist a smile. She could understand the temptation to want to own something that a famous marksman had once used. Perhaps all collectors enjoyed the illusion that they were somehow touching genius when they handled something a genius once used.

She wandered into another room, one filled with pistols, revolvers and their elegantly crafted cases and carefully preserved cleaning equipment. One set was said to have been carried from St. Louis to Cheyenne by Buffalo Bill Cody. And there was a pair of early eighteenth-century dueling pistols alleged to have been used by one of the Lees of Virginia.

There was a room full of infantry carbines and military pistols, all over one hundred and fifty years old, and knives used in warfare for hundred of years. The blades were as sharp and gleaming as the day they were made. Only a few pits and dents whispered that they had once been used against a person in desperate hand-to-hand combat. To the death.

The last room had a bookcase of reference books with photographs and details used by experts in identifying various weapons. The room contained some of the oldest pieces displayed in Quinn's collection. Daphne was fascinated by a pair of eighteenth-century Scottish flintlock pistols with a ram's horn grip and a trigger shaped like an acorn. And a graceful sixteenth-century long-barreled matchlock arquebus from Japan, painted with a delicate design in a gold leaf and displaying the symbol of the ruling Tokugawa family, nearly took her breath away.

In a neighboring glass case, she found a seventeenth-century Italian flintlock with a walnut stock and gold damascening on the smooth, long barrel. The lock was whimsically carved in the shape of a nymph rising naked from her bath. Daphne couldn't

help wondering if the shootist had smiled every time his thumb
caressed it. She wondered what the figure might have been if the
gunsmith had been a woman. An image of Quinn's magnificent body modeled in silver and fashioned as a lock flashed
unexpectedly through her mind. A lighthearted, happy smile
brightened her face as she thought of him.

There were many other firearms, each with a unique combination of engravings, fine woods and precious metals. Some
were accompanied by animal horns or silver flasks for gun-
powder. Others had matching knives.

Finally she came upon a pair of very old wheel-lock pistols
from Germany that had been made for a duke. They were in-
laid with bone, silver and gold in a complicated baroque design. Daphne wouldn't have been surprised to learn that they
had never been fired. They gleamed as if they had been fashioned yesterday. Maybe the duke had tucked them in his pan-
taloons, or wherever such pitsols were worn, just to look
impressive. He would have succeeded with that pair, she decided.

What stories these weapons could tell, she thought as she
drifted back to Danaker's office.

She found him frowning at his computer monitor. Feeling a
surge of tenderness and love, she went to him, looping her arms
around his broad shoulders and standing behind him with her
chin resting affectionately on his head.

"How are we doing?" she asked. She couldn't stop smiling.
And it was all because of him. He made her darkest hours
lighten with happiness. She kissed his temple and rubbed her
cheek against his hair, inhaling its familiar fragrance.

"I think we're beginning to see a pattern," he murmured. He
was glad she was back. He had been wondering where she was
and wishing that she were close enough for him to glance over
and see her once in a while. But now that she was here, he could
feel his train of thought begin to slip.

He tried to concentrate. Then he felt her hands wandering
curiously down across his chest, and his mind began to fray.
Her shy exploration of his pectorals sent a wave of damp heat
across his skin and curling down deep into his belly.

"You aren't making this any easier," he complained with a
husky laugh.

He found he had to clear his throat as her fingers played over
his pebble-hard nipples. Suddenly electricity arced from the
point where her soft fingertips touched his chest and raced

down into the depths of his loins. There it swirled and coiled and slowly set him afire.

He was clenching his jaw, determined to wrap up his last damn sentence, when she found his ribs and waist, adding to his sweet misery. He was mangaging to handle that when a soft, sultry moan of pleasure caught in her throat and somehow lit every nerve in his entire body.

"Daphne..." he objected, simultaneously laughing in pleasure and groaning in frustration. He closed his eyes. The last two lines on the monitor made no sense. At least, he didn't think they did. He lost his train of thought completely as her clever hands glided shyly down to his muscled thighs. Again and again. Brushing dangerously near the part of him that was achingly hard.

He swore softly and tried to remember what in the hell he was supposed to be writing on the screen.

Daphne nuzzled his throat and began kissing his ear. Encouraged by his groan of pleasure and the way he tilted his head to give her easier access, she traced its lines with the tip of her tongue.

He hit two keys in succession, turned off the computer and swung around in the chair. Before she could do anything but gasp in surprise, he'd swung one arm around her and dragged her down across his lap. His eyes burned and his body ached. He was hard and ready, and it was all he could do not to strip her pants off and free himself enough to slide into her satiny warmth to ease this wonderful suffering.

Her eyes were laughing down at him, and the love and tenderness he saw in her face made his heart ache. Somewhere along the way, he had fallen in love with her. And he had fallen hard.

"Damn it, you've bewitched me," he whispered hoarsely. "You're as necessary as air is to breathe." He found her lips and kissed her, gliding his quicksilver tongue into the sweet welcome of her mouth. He circled her breasts with his hand and sucked his cheeks in, drawing her tongue into his mouth to play.

The intimate caress of his tongue sent fire coursing through her veins. His hand gently traced the shape of her breast, then swiftly burrowed beneath her clothes to find the turgid nipple. The dull ache of pleasure that had been slowly building between her legs as she had touched him suddenly became very uncomfortable to endure. Desire swept through her, and she fastened her mouth on his, moaning his name in surrender. It was a very clear plea, and he was already attuned to hear it.

To her very great surprise, he lifted her into his arms and surged straight out of the chair. She was so startled at that feat of strength that she leaned against his shoulder and looked into his eyes.

"Good Lord but you're strong," she whispered.

Her open admiration of him was almost more than he could bear. He laughed, but it took quite an effort, because he desperately wanted to take her right where they were. The primitive urge to thrust into her silken body and bury himself in her loving warmth was nearly overpowering.

"Daphne, put your face against my shoulder," he told her, using what he would gather of his stern and no-nonsense voice.

She did, but she couldn't help mumbling against his shoulder, "Why?"

"Because I want to make it to the bed, damn it! If you do one more provocative thing, it's gonna be right here on the floor." He felt her begin to smile and knew she was taking it as a dare. "Daphne!" he warned her, striding down the hall a little more briskly.

She giggled softly, which wasn't much help, but he made it to the bedroom. He had no idea how he managed to get there. His mind was in a red haze. He went through the door and let her slide to her feet while he rapidly stripped clothes off her as fast as he could lay his hands on them. The fact that she was doing the same with his clothing should have helped, but it only made him more desperate to have her. The touch of her hands and her open, eager desire drove him wild. They staggered to his bed, mouths fused in a hot, deep kiss. As he eased her down, he slid his hand between her thighs. They fell open to him, as if he had every right to her. She was wet and squirming and moaning for him to enter her. He rolled between her thighs and entered her in one smooth, long thrust that buried him fully in her satiny warmth.

"Daffy, Daffy," he murmured between kisses. "I'm so hot for you I can't think."

"Me too," she gasped as his mouth went quickly over her shoulders and down to suckle each breast. His wet tongue slid across her nipples in rhythm with the slow, deep thrusts of his body into hers.

They were a quick tangle of loving hands and eager mouths and hoarsely whispered words of love. He found her mouth again with his and felt as if his body and soul had fused with hers. He was too deeply aroused. The quick, hot flash of desire she had ignited in him could not be prolonged. He was losing control, and he couldn't get it back. The feel of her soft body yielding and moving hungrily against his made him begin the deep, rolling ride to his climax.

He cried out her name—mournfully, because it was too soon, and triumphantly, because he loved her—and she was his.

The convulsions of his body triggered her own deep release, and they clung to each other as wave after wave of satisfaction washed through them.

She hugged him as hard as she could. Her thighs wrapped around his, her body pressed so tightly against his that they could not be identified as two separate beings. She wanted to tell him that she loved him. That had been pushing against her heart for a long time, and she could not hold the words back any longer.

"I love you," she whispered on a deeply ragged sigh.

He was still for a long moment. Then he lifted his head and looked down at her. "Daphne . . ."

It sounded like a benediction. Like the dearest words of love. His eyes were dark with emotion. She was sure that he loved her. She was so happy she thought she might burst. And yet, in the depths of his eyes, she glimpsed a shadow. What was the matter? She ran her hand over his shoulders, yearning to comfort and soothe him, to chase away the shadow that dared to haunt their happiness.

He closed his eyes and rested his forehead against her shoulder. He *had* to tell her, he told himself. He *had* to.

She enjoyed the sensation of his body draped, relaxed and heavy, on top of her. He seemed vulnerable this way, she realized. She liked him vulnerable. And intimate. And close. And hers. She was smiling again. And she knew that if she looked in a mirror, her eyes would be sparkling. Her heart was racing, and her body was deeply contented.

All because of him. She kissed his cheek tenderly.

He rolled off her onto his back and stared at the ceiling. Blindly, he found her hand with his and brought it close to his body.

"Daphne," he began, "there are some things you need to know."

Chapter 15

"About you?" she asked sleepily.

"Yes."

Daphne laced her fingers securely through his firm clasp and smiled. She felt like chocolate melting in the bright summer sun, warm and sweet, and much too satisfied for anything to upset her. Besides, Quinn was holding her hand and lying close to her, their bare bodies touching lightly. She always felt confident and relaxed and happy when he was in physical contact with her. She sighed and stretched like a well-fed cat.

"Am I finally going to hear the story of your life, then?" she teased.

"Part of it."

She was oblivious to the faintly grim undertone in his voice. Even if she had heard it, however, her first reaction would have been to deny it, to push it away as an unwelcome disruption. She wanted nothing to disturb the delicious feeling of contentment in which she was floating. After so many years of emptiness, she wanted to enjoy this magical happiness.

He frowned and tried to decide where to begin, how much to tell her this time, and what bombshells to leave for tomorrow.

"We were talking about my past last night, but then we heard Kyle and found Connor's jacket and afterward we never returned to our conversation," he began, attempting to pick up the slender threads of explanation at the point they had been dropped.

She drowsily allowed her eyes to close. Listening to his low, masculine voice was a pleasure. It didn't really matter what he talked about, just so long as his rich tenor-baritone continued to caress her. She found it as soothing as a massage.

"Mmm," she mumbled, encouraging him to go on with whatever he intended to say. She wanted him to know that she was listening, even though she was giving every appearance of falling asleep.

"I told you that I used to be in the same line of business that Corday is in."

Her mouth lifted in amusement, but her eyes remained blissfully closed. "I still can't imagine you as an educational or business consultant," she admitted sleepily.

"You can stop trying. That wasn't the line of work I was in."

She realized he had ceased talking, as if to emphasize his point. The languid feeling that she had been enjoying began to recede. She frowned slightly, then slowly opened her eyes.

"Are you trying to tell me that you were in Corday's *other* line of work?" she asked incredulously.

"Yes."

She felt reality intrude like a cold shower, clearing her mind and banishing her relaxation. She turned her head to look at him and found his gaze already on her. He looked watchful, but otherwise his expression was difficult to read. A chilly curl of anxiety formed in the pit of her stomach.

"Go on," she said, amazed at how reality firmed her voice and gave it a calmness she didn't feel.

"I worked for a man named Janisch Kopek. He's an arms trader."

She stared at him. "An arms trader." She repeated it as if making certain she had heard him correctly.

He saw the disbelief in her eyes, felt the stiffening in her limbs. "It can be an honorable business," he pointed out grimly.

Her delicate brows drew down into a graceful frown. "Can it?" she challenged.

He felt a twinge of anger that she could so quickly back off from the complete trust she had been giving him. He told himself that he would react the same way if their positions were reversed. It didn't help. He wanted her to have faith in him. Blind trust. Complete confidence. The kind that a woman in love would offer to her mate.

He pulled her hand across his chest and stared at the ceiling again. It was easier to keep calm and rational that way. He wouldn't have to see the emotions in her eyes as she heard the truth.

"I met Janisch when he was buying a warehouse full of M-1 rifles and British hand grenades in Singapore. He was looking over the goods, and I walked in. I knew the warehouse owner. He and I had served in the same army unit stationed in the Philippines. I was in town for his wedding. He was selling the rifles and grenades to pay for a honeymoon for his new bride." He had to smile at the irony of that.

Daphne struggled to take in what he was saying. She had the strangest feeling that her world was dissolving. Something was slowly going wrong. She frowned, recalling that he had mentioned those places once before to her, on one of the nights when they had ordered Chinese food.

"You told me that you did some business with Sammy Wong's relatives in Singapore and the Philippines."

"Yeah. They don't know my old army buddy. But I met them because they wanted to buy what I had to sell. Modern rifles, retooled tanks, a few small naval vessels destined for mothballs. I traveled there a lot when I was working with Janisch. They told me to look up their cousin Sammy's restaurant when I was in Washington. That's how I got to know him." He grinned slightly. "That's why they drop off food after hours at my house and let me eat in the kitchen. I'm sort of an honorary cousin."

Daphne felt an awful coldness begin to slink across her body. He had a secret life. That was what it sounded like, anyway.

"Why didn't you tell me this before?" she asked in a soft, thin voice.

"It didn't really matter in the beginning. I was trying to help you solve your husband's murder, and my employment history certainly didn't come up naturally in any of our conversations, if you'll recall. I told you that I would contact a few people I used to work with and ask them if they knew anything."

"Yes. But I had no idea . . ." Her mind began rolling out the memories then. She recalled him saying something about having worked with security arrangements. "These former business associates . . . are they the kind of people who have their names on the company letterhead? Appear in the annual report? Or do they hide their identities, too?''

"I never hid my identity," he said bluntly. "I admit I didn't go into what I'd done in the past, but that's not the same thing. As for my contacts . . . yes, they keep a low profile." He sensed her withdrawing from him further. Her hand was cool, and she kept trying to slide it away from him. He tightened his grasp, refusing to let her go.

"They're *spies?*" She stared at him so hard that he swore it felt like a laser boring through his cheek. He abandoned his view of the ceiling and returned her gaze with as much firmness and calm as he could still muster.

"Some people might call them spies, I suppose. They aren't government agents. At least, most of them aren't. But they make a fair income by knowing what's going on and who is doing it. They gather and sell information. The highest bidder gets it first."

"And what was your connection with them?" She wasn't sure she would like the answer, but she had to ask.

"I asked them questions that couldn't be answered by reading the newspapers or through other conventional forms of information gathering. When they located what I wanted, Janisch and I paid them. I guess you could say we kept them on retainer."

She simply stared at him, searching for the man she had known up until a few moments ago, wondering who this new man was.

"It was a job that I liked," he said matter-of-factly. "I had been a good shot in the army, and working for Janisch gave me a chance to keep my hand in. Janisch asked me to test fire some of the rifles for him that day in Singapore. We got into a rather lengthy conversation about military firearms afterward and ended up having dinner together later. He impressed me as a decent, honest man with exceptionally shrewd business sense and a great network of connections worldwide. Janisch's business had grown so extensive, he needed a second-in-command. I didn't know it then, but he had decided I might serve him well in that role. He offered me a job, and, since I didn't have any more interesting prospects at the time, I accepted."

"I see," she said quietly. She swallowed hard. "Who did you sell your weapons to? The same people that Corday does?''

His jaw tightened in anger. "Come on, Daphne. I'm the same man I've been since we met. Do you think I'd sell guns to terrorists?"

She closed her eyes against the pain. "I don't know you, remember?" Could she have been such a fool as to be tricked again? The thought was too horrible to be true. She refused to let herself think it.

He rolled onto his side and released his hold on her hand in order to grip her soft shoulder. "You're wrong. You know me. You just haven't heard all the trivial details of my life," he argued in a low, tense voice. "I told you once before . . . you already know all the really important things."

Her eyes fluttered open, and she looked at him wistfully. "You don't know how much I wish I could believe that." She bit her lip. "But I feel like I'm in a revolving door and my life is starting to repeat itself. You're telling me this because you feel guilty, aren't you? You know you should have said something earlier, but you didn't, and now it's coming out like some sort of confession."

He sighed. "Yes. But, hell, don't I get any credit for trying to clear the decks with you? Would you rather I didn't say anything?"

"Of course not."

She looked so miserable that he pulled her into his arms without thinking.

"Daphne, I'm falling in love with you," he whispered. "I'm trying to get things straight between us because I don't want you to have any doubts about me."

His words of love penetrated all her fears, and she wrapped her arms around him, clinging tightly. He kissed her and petted her and caressed her, giving her the reassurance she so dearly craved. She badly wanted to believe him, so she temporarily banished all her remaining questions. She framed his face with her hands and kissed him with all the tender passion that filled her heart.

"I love you, too, Quinn Danaker. You have made my life so very beautiful."

Her lips moved softly against his as she spoke. When he kissed her back and slid his tongue provocatively over the soft contours of her lips, she relaxed a little more against him.

"Honesty is very, very important to me," she admitted huskily. "It would be so hard to be lied to again. . . ."

"I know." He drew another breath, intending to explain his remaining lie of omission—the rendezvous with Jamison on the night that he was shot—when the telephone rang harshly. "Damnation!" he cursed. He reached back and got the phone. Angrily, he said, "Hello?"

Daphne saw the frustration in his face turn to a mild form of embarrassment.

"I'm sorry to hear that. Yes, Daphne's here," he said, in a much friendlier tone. "I'll let you speak with her." He handed the phone to Daphne with a rueful grin. She had told the baby-sitter where to reach her in an emergency. Now they were reaping the results.

"It's Mrs. Corrigan. She wondered if you could come back a little early. She broke a tooth biting down on a walnut, and the dentist said he can take her as an emergency patient in half an hour if she can get there."

Daphne jacknifed into a sitting position and lifted the receiver to her ear. Painfully aware of her nakedness, her cheeks were suffused with the rosy color of shame. She knew Mrs. Corrigan couldn't see her, but...

"Millicent? I'm so sorry about your tooth! I'll be there in half an hour," she quickly assured her. "Don't wait for us, though. You go straight to the dentist! Kyle can manage on his own until I get there. He's a big boy now." She smiled and batted away Quinn's playful hand, which had found its way to her breast.

As soon as she hung up, she began to dress.

Quinn considered explaining the truth about having to meet Connor on the night he was murdered. But he hated to do it while he was pulling on his pants or driving the car. If Daphne were upset by it, they would have no time to thrash things out. They would soon be at her house, and Kyle would be there. This wasn't the kind of discussion to have in front of an eleven-year-old boy, in his opinion.

She saw his frown as he dressed, but she put it down to their being interrupted just as they were starting to make up. She had to admit, she didn't feel quite happy about what he had said.

As they drove to Springfield, she looked out the window beside her and muttered fretfully, "I still have some questions to ask you."

"I thought you would."

From the humor in his voice, she thought he intended to patiently answer until her every suspicious worry had been thoroughly laid to rest. That made her smile. Also, she remembered the hoarseness in his voice when he had told her that he loved her.

She was sure he could explain everything. She was uneasy, but he would be able to dispel her fears. She stubbornly told herself to believe that.

Kyle was feeling quite proud of himself. He was home alone. No mother. No baby-sitter. Nobody at all. He was all by himself.

At his age, he thought that he should be able to do many more things than his stodgy old mother permitted. He wanted to roam far, stay up late and skateboard fast. Every time he pushed the limits, she turned into a wall of maternal resistance. His mother was such a worrier. No fun at all.

He was pondering the experience of being his own man when he heard the friendly jingle of the ice-cream truck's bell down the street. From the sound, he estimated it was around the bend and moving very slowly. It should reach his house in about four minutes. More if one of the kids up there had a hard time making up his mind.

He dashed up the stairs and tore into his room, tossing clothes and toys out of their scattered heaps in a desperate search for his weekly allowance. He knew he'd dropped it here somewhere.

Finally the five-dollar-bill appeared, poking out from beneath his worn and dusty backpack. With a boyish grin of triumph, he snatched it up and raced back down the stairs.

He knew just what he wanted: the big tin roof ice cream on a stick coated in white chocolate and sprinkled with brown chocolate jimmies and tiny bits of peanut-butter brickle. It came with a little plastic toy shaped like a cartoon character. Every week a different "toon." Kyle *loved* cartoons.

He arrived at the curb thirty seconds before the truck did. Perfect timing, he thought, as proud as a little peacock. It wasn't until the truck was a mere four feet away that he realized instead of stopping, it might hit him. Astonishment froze him in place. Then fear hosed him down with high-pressure adrenaline.

The brakes on the truck squealed, and he heard himself shriek in terror as he tried to jump clear of the fender. His last mournful thought before he hit the lawn was that his mother would probably never let him get anything from the ice-cream man again.

Not to mention stay home alone.

Daphne saw the small crowd of neighborhood children as soon as Danaker turned down her street. They had formed a raggedy circle around something on her front lawn. The ice-cream truck was parked at a peculiar angle near her drive. One of her neighbors was craning her head out the front door, looking anxiously in several directions, as if waiting for someone else to take the initiative and do something.

By the time they'd stopped and gotten out of the car, Daphne could see a body lying on the ground in the middle of the circle. She recognized the clothes immediately. Her blood ran cold with fear.

"Kyle!" she cried, running to him.

The children moved away, and she fell onto her knees beside him, her heart contracting painfully with relief when she saw him. He was sitting up and yelling at one of the kids.

"Well, you didn't have to push me *that* hard with your toe!" he complained with venomous indignation.

"I just wanted to see if you were dead," the kid explained reasonably. He obviously thought that Kyle must have suffered a permanent brain injury if he couldn't understand *that*. "I wouldn't want to touch you if you were dead!"

Kyle glared at him. "I wouldn't want you to touch me if I were *alive!*" he declared loudly, oblivious to how nonsensical that sounded. Then he felt Daphne's gentle hand on his shoulder, and he turned. As soon as he saw her, his ferocious bravado began to crack. He blinked his eyes and leaned his face against her blouse. "I was just gettin' some ice cream, Mom," he wailed in a voice that trembled. "I didn't mean to get run over." He tried not to sob.

Daphne looked at him, horrified. "Run over!" she exclaimed. She ran her hands over his arms and legs. "Are you all right? Does anything hurt?"

Kyle had to think about that. He wasn't sure whether he hurt or not, but it occurred to him that his mother might not punish him so severely if she were terrified that he might die. He lay back and moaned, letting his eyes flutter half-closed. Watching her through the slits, he murmured weakly, "I don't know. Everything went black when I went through the air...."

Danaker, who had been standing behind her, watching the drama, had seen the calculation in the boy's eyes. He almost laughed. Smart kid, he thought. Daphne was so worried, she'd skin him alive for scaring her to death. He understood her feelings perfectly. Seeing the child on the ground had scared him, too. He had been tremendously relieved to hear the feisty way Kyle had argued with his friends, a sure sign he was all right.

Daphne looked anxiously at Quinn. "Should we take him to the hospital or call an ambulance?" she asked worriedly.

He knelt beside her and gave her shoulder a reassuring squeeze.

"I had some emergency medical training years back," he told her. "Let me take a look at him first."

As he felt the boy's arms and legs, gently palpating his abdomen and asking questions, he decided it was very unlikely anything serious was wrong. He straightened up and looked around, wondering what had happened to the ice-cream man.

"Where the hell did that driver go?" he asked. His stern glance swept the awed crowd of children and the lone mother who had finally ventured out of her front door across the street to join them.

The children all pointed toward Daphne's house.

"He went in there to make a phone call," one of them piped up helpfully.

Daphne was tenderly stroking Kyle's head and crooning reassurances. The boy began to moan a little and clutched her blouse tightly. "I'm sorry, Mommy," he cried. "I didn't mean to—"

"It isn't your fault," she assured him, her heart breaking at his suffering. She looked up at Danaker, not hesitating to trust him to advise her. "What do you think?"

He tore his frowning gaze away from the house. His expression softened as he looked at her. His voice was firm but gentle as he gave his assessment.

"Kyle says he feels bruised, which makes sense, since he jumped like a deer and fell pretty hard. He doesn't remember the truck doing anything but breezing very close to him, so he probably wasn't struck. He doesn't appear to have any broken bones. He didn't pass out, so he probably didn't hurt his head. Everything else seems to be functioning normally. Why don't you just keep an eye on him for the next fifteen minutes? Watch for any symptoms. If nothing crops up, I think you can figure you're in the clear."

She was tremendously relieved to hear it. She thought Kyle was mostly shaken by the close call, but it was reassuring to have another adult come to the same conclusion. That kind of backup had been absent for years. She'd had all the responsibility herself. It was she who decided whether Kyle was sick enough to call the doctor or not. She who did all the disciplining. Alone.

The expression of gratitude and love in her eyes was eloquent. He found he couldn't smile, because the look in her face made him ache for her, made him want to fold her in his arms and tell her again that he loved her.

He couldn't do that, unfortunately, since they were surrounded by a lilliputian crowd that was riveted to their every word and gesture.

He gave Kyle a very direct look. "Don't overdo it," he advised sternly.

Kyle's eyes flew open in surprise, and his mouth dropped. He'd been caught! His eyes went anxiously to his mother. She looked a little uncertain. He relaxed. She hadn't caught on yet. It was only Mr. Danaker who realized he was making the best of a bad situation. Okay. He wasn't dumb. He'd sit up and start limping around and act all right in a few minutes. Then maybe Mr. Danaker wouldn't tell his mom. He hoped.

Daphne watched Danaker leave them, heading for her front door.

"Where are you going?" she asked, dismayed that he would leave them so quickly.

"To see what in the hell the driver's doing in your house," he growled.

She stared as Danaker disappeared inside. It was very strange that the driver had been in there so long, she realized, now that she was no longer worried that Kyle was in imminent need of medical help.

A few moments after Quinn went through the front door, the driver exited. He made a straight line to her.

"Sorry," he mumbled, nervously looking back.

Danaker had been upstairs making a quick check of the premises when he heard the man leaving through the front door. He couldn't linger, however, if he wanted a word with the man, so he came outside again and caught up with him.

"What were you doing in her house?" he demanded. His voice was as hard as iron. So were his eyes.

"Just calling my company, mister," the man said. "But the line was busy, and I had to try a coupl'a times before I could get through."

"Why in the hell were you calling your company?" Danaker demanded angrily. "You could have called an ambulance, or stayed with the boy to see if he needed help."

"I don't know nothin' about hurts like that. Besides, I never touched him! He jumped like a rabbit and banged himself up on the hard ground. The company rule says call right away if there's any problem. They don't want to be sued. Not that I did anything wrong! I never touched the kid!"

The driver backed away fearfully.

Danaker didn't believe him, and he followed the man to his truck, intending to get a more truthful answer out of the bastard.

"I think I'll go now," the man said fearfully as he saw the deadly light in Danaker's eyes. "The boy's all right, isn't he?" he challenged, as if that should keep Danaker from exacting any revenge.

"Yes. No thanks to you," Danaker said in a voice so soft it sent a shiver of alarm down the driver's spine.

Danaker grasped the man's shirt front just as he began to get into the truck. He twisted his fist until the man began to choke.

"What were you looking for inside her house?" he demanded.

"Nothing." As Danaker's fist tightened, the man squeaked, "The phone . . . nothing more, I swear. . . ."

Danaker's lip curled back. "I've listened to much better liars than you. Try again." He pressed two fingers straight into the driver's stomach.

The man's eyes widened in severe pain, but he could only make a strangled yelp, because Danaker's fist was still knotted at his Adam's apple. His back was flat against the truck, so he couldn't get enough room to kick with any effect or swing a solid punch. From the solid muscle he had seen in Danaker, he knew anything less than a very hard blow would be worse than useless. It would only enrage the man further. The current state of Danaker's rage was bad enough.

"They'll kill me if I tell," he rasped, gasping for breath.

"I'll kill you if you don't," Danaker whispered, smiling coldly.

For a moment they hung together in a battle of wills. Danaker's will, however, was by far the more persuasive. He didn't care if he were wrong about the driver's guilt. And the driver could see that.

"Stop choking me to death and I'll tell you," the man gasped. His face was beginning to turn blue from lack of oxygen.

Danaker loosened his grip. But just a little.

"They told me they'd pay me a thousand dollars if I could get the kid to tell me what was going on at home. Especially anything about his old man's business."

"Keep talking," Danaker ordered coldly.

"I heard him last week talking to one of the kids about having his father's jacket and finding a key and stuff, and I thought if I could get them, maybe I could get more than a thousand dollars. So when I saw the kid today, and no one around, I thought I'd take a chance."

"You went in to search the house?"

"Yeah."

Danaker's eyes narrowed. "Do you ever have anyone with you in the truck?" he asked softly, thinking of the day he and Daphne were shot at and he had heard the jingle of the ice-cream truck.

The driver paled, and his eyes wavered nervously. He licked his lips. "Naw. I don't need the help."

Danaker knew the man was lying, and his smile was enough to freeze the blood of a fever victim. "You're wrong. You need help. Lots of it. And you're gonna get nailed, pal. It's just a matter of time."

The man saw the children and neighbor gathering behind Danaker in a semicircle, their faces filled with curiosity.

"You wouldn't do anything to me in front of witnesses," the driver said, emboldened in spite of his fear of Danaker.

"Don't count on it," Danaker said in that same chilling voice. "Who was paying you?"

"I don't know their names," he said quickly.

Too quickly, Danaker thought. But if he pressed, the man could make up names, and he would have no way of knowing whether they were false or not. If the Fairfax investigators had checked him out, maybe they had stumbled across his contacts. Danaker hoped so. Unless he wanted to ride around in the truck with the man, he couldn't do much more. Just let him run to ground and see if the police could track him to his bosses.

Reluctantly, Danaker released his hold. He didn't want to be on the receiving end of an assault charge, and he was sure the man wouldn't repeat his confession unless someone were threatening physical violence. He wondered how he could come up with some nice, solid evidence for the police. Maybe the idiot had left fingerprints, he thought. As dumb as the guy was, it was possible.

The driver scrambled into his truck, turned it on, slammed it into gear and stepped on the accelerator with gusto.

Danaker went back into the house to call the Fairfax County police. And Yarbro and Foley, just for good measure.

By the time the police had left, it was dinnertime. Daphne just took it for granted that Quinn would stay, and so did he. Kyle pleaded for Chinese take-out from Sammy Wong's, but Daphne ruled that out, saying she had to feed them the hamburger she'd thawed. It would be burgers and mashed potatoes and whatever she had in the refrigerator that could be tossed into a salad. Period. Well, maybe a little cherry pie for dessert, if she defrosted the one in the freezer.

Two male faces smiled at her beatifically. It made her feel like she'd just won the Kentucky Derby.

After dinner, Danaker lay on his back on the living room couch, tossing a baseball through the air toward Kyle, who was sprawled on the floor across the room. They were challenging each other with baseball trivia questions while Daphne paid a few bills at her desk upstairs.

When she finished and came to rejoin them, she couldn't help standing in the stairwell for a moment and watching them. They got along well, she thought. A warm feeling spread in the region of her heart. She could easily imagine Quinn doing all the things with Kyle that Connor had always been too busy to do. And she thought that Kyle could grow up loving and respecting Quinn as much as he ever had his natural father—or more. She couldn't help feeling a little maternal pride in her son's good sense. He could already see what a fine man Quinn Danaker was. He was a man's man, and yet he was a woman's man, too.

Danaker, sensing her presence, twisted his head to see her. Since he had the baseball, the game with Kyle came to a halt.

She smiled at him. He smiled back. And something else invisible passed between them. An understanding. A kind of comfort that was like a tender kiss.

"Time for bed, Kyle," she announced in her most authoritative voice.

"Aw, Mom!" he whined automatically.

Danaker turned to look at the boy. He didn't say a word.

Kyle shut his mouth and scampered up the stairs, heading for the shower without another sound.

Daphne stared in amazement in the direction of the suddenly noisy bathroom. "How did you do that?" she demanded incredulously.

He grinned and pulled her down on top of him. "What'll you give me to tell you?"

She captured his face in her hands, and she was laughing. "Nothing! You're not so tough! I'll torture the truth from you!" she threatened.

He pulled her head down, and their mouths met in a warmly intimate kiss, tongues tangling as the hot sensations traveled down their bodies like wildfire. He broke it off with a groan of frustration and held her close.

The sound of the shower upstairs reminded them that they wouldn't have this moment of privacy forever. Daphne whispered in his ear, "Really...how did you do it? I've got to learn the technique or I'll sound like a shrew. Sometimes I scream at him to do the simplest things. It's so exasperating. If I could just look at him like you did, I could sound grown-up and dignified, and I could get some cooperation at the same time."

She felt him smile, then begin to laugh. She lifted herself on her elbows and fixed him with a deadly stare. "Tell!"

"You'll have to put in a few years in an infantry division," he explained, grinning. "That commanding, don't-mess-with-me look is the product of years of learning how to order men in a rifle company to do things no one in their right mind would willingly do."

She softened and caressed his hard cheek. "Is that where you got your emergency medical training?" she asked quietly.

"Yeah."

The shower turned off. Daphne gave him a last, quick kiss, and he reluctantly let her go.

She was standing beside the couch, holding his hand lightly in hers, when he gruffly announced, "I'm staying here tonight."

She blinked and looked down at him in surprise.

"After what happened this afternoon, I'd feel better if I were in the house, Daphne. I'd worry about you otherwise," he explained.

She looked at their hands and nodded. "Actually, I'd feel safer, too. I don't agree with your worries all the time, and this may be another exaggeration...worrying about something that's really nothing at all to fret about...but..." Their eyes met. Their fingers tightened. "I would like you to stay," she told him softly.

He kissed her knuckles. "Not worried about what the neighbors will say?" he asked huskily. He was relieved she hadn't argued about it, but he didn't want her to be in an awkward position, either.

She shook her head. "I used to be." She smiled ruefully. "When there was nothing for them to worry about, I was always careful to live a very upright life," she said, making a little fun of herself, but meaning it. "I don't care what anyone says now." Her eyes were as soft as spring, as warm as the summer sun. "I'm totally without shame where you and I are concerned."

He would have argued about her choice of words, but her tender, heartfelt sentiment made it difficult for him to say a thing. Then Kyle was hopping down the stairs, demanding a last glass of something to drink, and Daphne regretfully pulled free of Danaker.

Later, after Kyle went to bed, they stretched out on the couch together. Daphne was exhausted, and Quinn held her in his arms, caressing her until she fell asleep.

He wouldn't mind doing this every night, he thought, half-asleep himself. That meant getting married, he realized. It was the first time he had admitted it to himself in so many words. He wondered if she would be willing. Whether Kyle would make it difficult for her. Whether he could convince her.

And how long he would have to wait.

He'd waited seven years for her to fall into his life. He would wait as long as necessary.

He kissed her on the mouth. Even in her sleep, she responded, curling closer to him, smiling.

He remembered then that he had never gotten around to explaining about the rendezvous with Connor. In all the excitement, the time had never been right, and he had forgotten about it until now.

Before he started talking to her about marriage, he needed to explain about that.

He sighed and stared at her pretty face, relaxed in sleep.

He hoped to hell she took it the right way, but he had a feeling it was not going to be easy. Why in hell hadn't he told her when they first met? Silently he cursed his lack of foresight.

Quinn tried to show her by his tenderness as he held her in his arms that he loved her, that he would never do anything to harm her, that he would protect her with his life.

"Trust me, Daphne," he murmured against her lips. "Trust me."

Chapter 16

Monday turned out to be a very busy day.

When Danaker finally got back to his house, he found that a pile of messages had come in, only half of them related to business. The rest were the fruits of his labors on behalf of Daphne Jamison and Janisch Kopek.

Some of them had come in on his facsimile machine. One was a picture of a woman. Her name was Christina Douros.

When he called Yarbro and Foley, he found them at their desks for once.

"Yarbro? This is Danaker. I've got more information for you," he said, skipping the conversational preliminaries without a hint of apology.

"Great," Yarbro drawled. "You know, every case should have someone like you working on it, Danaker. We could get a lot more done."

Danaker laughed. "What? And prevent you from earning your pay? I wouldn't think of it."

An hour later he was in the detectives' office, explaining what he had learned. For once they returned the favor and shared their most recent findings with him. When they put everything together, they almost had the puzzle figured out.

Then the telephone rang.

Yarbro answered. His face went smooth in amazement.

"Yeah. We'll be right over." He hung up and turned to Danaker. "That was Fairfax Hospital. They've got a John Doe in their intensive care unit. He's been there for about a week. He was comatose on arrival. Somebody found him in a phone booth at Dulles, slumped over the phone, unconscious. He had been given a toxic injection. It should have been lethal, but not all the poison got into him. He must have struggled or twisted when his assailant tried to shove the hypodermic in. That, the thickness of his clothes and his extra weight all helped enough to keep him alive. Barely."

Danaker listened grimly. "Who is he?"

Yarbro hesitated. "They think he's your missing friend, Janisch Kopek."

Danaker clenched his teeth, then muttered a curse. At least Janisch was alive. If it was Janisch.

Yarbro and Foley got up and started toward the door. Danaker fell in with them.

"They couldn't match him with any of the local missing persons," Yarbro explained as they went to the parking lot. "Since we've got an international community here in Washington and he was found at an international airport, they checked with Interpol. Once they had some passports to match him against, they compared his prints with the information on file. We'd left word with just about everybody's computer that we were to be contacted if he was found, so they're calling us to come check on him."

"He didn't have any identification on him?" Danaker asked, frowning.

"Nope. It looks like whoever stuck him did a professional job of stripping his ID. And the airport security carmeras didn't show the booth clearly enough to see who'd gone in after him. The guards were busy with people checking in for flights, what with all the extra precautions they're taking these days. They didn't notice anything until they found him."

"You want me to ID him for you." Danaker assumed that was why he was being invited along.

"Yeah." Yarbro patted Danaker on the shoulder sympathetically. "I don't know whether to hope it's him or not. At least he's alive, if it is your friend."

It was.

* * *

Daphne was sure no thief ever felt a greater thrill of danger than she did as she slipped into Danaker's home that Monday afternoon. She intended to surprise him by showing up a little earlier than expected. She could hardly wait to see his face.

He had given her the keys that morning, along with detailed instructions on the security codes for getting into the business wing. She had been shocked when he had pressed the keys on her, folding her fingers around them and taking no arguments from her.

"I'd like to see you tonight, if you can get away for a few hours. Do you think you can?"

"Sure. Kyle's class is going on a field trip and they won't be back until about ten this evening." She had looked at the keys. Then back at him, rather humbly. She took his gesture as quite an honor.

He kissed her, and she felt so much a part of him that it physically hurt her when at last he pulled away. In an attempt to lighten the atmosphere between them, she tried to tease him.

"Aren't you afraid I'll run off with your valuables?" she joked.

He didn't even crack a smile.

"No. But you're welcome to them. You already have the most important things that belong to me," he told her softly.

He wrapped his arms around her, and she clung to him, thinking, *This is what I wanted to have in a marriage. Exactly this.*

"Will you come see me tonight?" he asked, nuzzling her.

"Of course. Whenever you want me."

"I want you all the time," he said with a sigh. Then, cupping her face, he suggested, "Could you come around dinnertime? I may be out this morning, but I'm sure I'll be back by then."

"All right."

And when he left, she had the keys and an open invitation from him to use them whenever she wanted, to make herself at home in his house, in his museum-quality collection of firearms, in his office. In his bed.

Anytime. That was what he had said.

So here she was. Tiptoeing into his unguarded domain, like a timid mouse slipping cautiously into a lion's empty den. She had parked in the paved space on the far side of his garage, where he was unlikely to see her car. She carefully relocked the doors after her, except for the electronic lock that was automatically reset when she passed through the tunnel into the business wing. She unlocked the door to his office and went inside, feeling exceedingly pleased with her success.

She perched on his desk and smiled. Now what should she do? He might not be back for a while. Her eyes fell on the pile of papers neatly stacked by his small photocopier. A woman's face was on the sheet on top. Curiously, she looked at it, and then began to read the paragraph beneath the picture. The name stopped her cold.

"So you're Christina," she breathed in surprise.

It came as a shock, because she hadn't expected to stumble on it. Quinn had absorbed her thoughts to the exclusion of all else today. She had nearly forgotten her desire to know who Connor's "Christina" had been. She had been sitting next to Danaker when he requested this information, however, and she was confident that he intended to tell her all about it. He simply hadn't had the opportunity yet. She was certain that he wouldn't mind her going ahead on her own.

It was rather pitiful, she thought, and it still left a number of questions unanswered, but she did begin to get the picture.

Connor had originally met Christina Douros in Cyprus two years ago at the auction of some military vehicles. She was the widow of a man who had died as a rebel fighting for one of the endless political causes that plagued the Middle East. She had lived in Europe most of her adult life—in Switzerland, to be precise.

Apparently she had seduced Connor quite skillfully. She might or might not have fallen in love with him. The informant wasn't too sure about that. But there was apparently no doubt that Connor had fallen hard for her. He'd stopped seeing the other women he'd been squiring around the major capitals of several countries. Daphne felt a certain amount of disgust reading that statement.

For the past year and a half he had pursued Christina through half a dozen contries. Fortunately, their businesses took them to the same locations. She was quietly arranging for the purchase of military equipment to rearm her late husband's political group, and Connor was buying hardware for Corday International, to resell to buyers worldwide.

Apparently Christina's group became affiliated with a known terrorist organization. Their need for weapons, ammunition and related items suddenly increased dramatically, but some of their old sources were reluctant to sell to someone so closely connected to a terrorist group. Christina used Connor to help arrange some extra sales. She even persuaded him to skim off some of the weapons he obtained for Corday. They were then diverted to her friends and relatives and their paramilitary group.

Daphne sat and stared into space. Connor had been betraying Corday, too, she realized, amazed again at his unreliability. She looked at Christina's picture. The woman was very beautiful. Young. Perhaps twenty-eight or so. With the straight nose and beautifully arched brows of the Greek beauties immortalized by ancient urns and marble statues. Her hair was stylishly cut and most likely black, although Daphne could only guess. The fax wasn't in color.

She glanced through some of the other papers. It appeared to the people communicating with Danaker that Christina and Connor had carefully arranged a very large diversion of military supplies for the near future. They had piggybacked Christina's purchase on Corday's, using the terms, shipping routes and contracts with Corday to help conceal her consignment. The arms intended for her group were to be separated at three different points and sent to Nicosia. From there they were to go to warehouses held by two religious groups who secretly fronted for Christina's political cronies. Lilli Marlene had been her code name.

Daphne sighed and shook her head. How could Connor have gotten mixed up in something so illegal, so dangerous? Surely no woman was worth the risk. It had cost him his life. And the fallout had endangered Kyle and her. That made her very angry.

The document from Peter Trevor speculated that someone at Corday had gotten wind of Connor's activities, discovering that he was double-crossing them, stealing from them. Since they had so little fear of the law, he argued they might have shot Connor simply to put a stop to his shenanigans. It might have been difficult to fire him, after all, because he could have threatened to expose Corday's illegal-arms activities. Murder would have been a nice, clean solution from their cold-blooded point of view.

Daphne put the papers back and curled up on the small
couch, thinking about Connor and Christina and Corday's illegal activities. Her eyes widened in horror. *Sarmien!* He had
been sniffing around her house, making oblique references to
missing business files. He must have been involved. She was
willing to bet that he had been the one to uncover Connor's
plan. Sarmien had never shared power with anyone, as far as
she knew. He jealously guarded it, and he would have resented
Connor's independence. He would have been infuriated by the
lack of loyalty. She had heard enough about the man to be
fairly confident of that.

She leaned back and watched the closed-circuit television
monitors banked along the ceiling. She could see into each
gunroom with them and could enjoy looking at Danaker's
handsome antiques, faintly visible in the subdued lighting that
he kept on twenty-four hours a day for security reasons.

"I think I prefer old guns to new ones," she murmured
wryly. She closed her eyes, waiting for Quinn to come home.

He was going to be so surprised.

The minute that he walked through his front door, Danaker
thought Daphne was there. He looked around, but she was
nowhere in sight, and he didn't hear any sounds that would in-
dicate she was present. Her scent must still be in the air from
her visit yesterday, he thought wryly. Or he was going crazy.
Always a possibility.

Yarbro and Foley followed him into the tunnel, down to the
gunroom where he had left the Williamson pistol. They were
fairly sure they had figured out what Jamison was up to and
why Sarmien or his hirelings might have killed him. But they
hadn't come up with a plausible reason for Janisch to be involved. And they'd come up equally empty trying to guess why
Janisch would have sent Connor to Danaker.

Perhaps it had something to do with the pistol. Maybe Janisch had been sending that to Danaker. Maybe Jamison had
been trying to lose his pursuers and hadn't been able to get back
to the mailbox to retrieve the pistol and bring it with him.

They were all convinced that Jamison had tried hard to keep
the existence of the mailbox a secret known only to himself,
Christina and the postal service. He'd used it to stash some
items, but only letters and packages addressed in Christina's
hand had actually been mailed to him there.

So, what had Janisch been trying to tell him? Or send him? And why?

"Here it is," Danaker said, removing the pistol from the locked drawer in which he had placed it earlier in the day. He retrieved some tools from a nearby cabinet and gestured for the detectives to take a closer look at the little gun. "We can take it apart here, or have it X-rayed first and taken apart at a police lab. You're welcome to send it to the FBI lab, for that matter. Peter could probably expedite a request for us, if you want to hurry it up."

The men stood around the table, each in turn looking the weapon over carefully. Daphne, who had fallen asleep in Danaker's office, awakened to see them there, displayed on one of the monitors. She slipped off the couch and quietly made her way out of the office and down the hallway. It was easy to be as silent as a cat burglar with so much soundproofing and carpeting, she thought with a grin.

"If the doctors at Fairfax Hospital are right, he may be coming around. If he regains consciousness, Kopek could simply tell us why he was trying to contact you, why he didn't call or write and explain, and whether the pistol had anything to do with it."

Daphne could hear their voices as she reached the door, but it wasn't making much sense to her. She recalled that Danaker had worked for a man named Kopek, but it seemed strange to hear Yarbro talking about the man being in a local medical facility, or trying to contact Quinn. Maybe she was groggier than she realized.

She was just outside the open door when Foley began to talk.

"Can't you come up with *some* reason why you were supposed to meet Jamison that night down in Old Town, Danaker?" he demanded in exasperation. "*Any* reason at all? No matter *how* farfetched?"

Danaker saw a movement out of the corner of his eye and whirled to see Daphne. She was frozen in the entryway, an expression of absolute horror dawning on her face. He took a step toward her, realizing what she had just heard.

"Daphne," he said softly, extending his hand toward her.

She stepped back, shaking her head, as all the color drained from her face. Disbelief, hurt, dreadful pain, all crossed her pretty features.

"You were *meeting* Connor that night?" she asked, dumbfounded. Each word was carefully pronounced, as if she were making absolutely sure that there was no mistake.

Danaker slowly let his hand drop to his side. Grimly, he answered, "Yes."

She flinched as if he had struck her. It hurt him to see it.

"Daphne, let me explain...."

"No!" she cried out. "I won't hear any more lies! Not from any man." Her violet eyes were awash with tears, and her voice caught painfully. "Especially not from you!"

She whirled and ran down the tunnel, desperate to escape. She wanted to run away from all the pain he had caused. All the joy he had brought her under a veil of deceit. He had lied to her! Lied! She couldn't bear the thought of it.

His front door slammed against the frame as she stumbled outside, finding her car through intsinct. She was blinded by her tears. She fumbled with her keys. Thank God she'd had her purse slung over her shoulder out of habit, she thought bitterly. Mother had said, Always keep your purse with you. *Thank you, Mother.*

Finally the key fit, and she swung the car door open, but before she could get inside she felt a pair of very strong hands clamp down hard on her shoulders.

"Let me go!" she screamed, not caring what anybody thought. She'd never made a scene in her life, but she whirled, scratching at him, trying to push him away.

He caught her hands behind her back and held her tightly against his chest.

"You can't drive in this state," he growled. "You'll kill yourself."

She glared at him through the blurriness of tears. "No, I won't!"

He pulled the keys from her hand behind her back and let her go. "I'll drive you," he said tightly.

"Absolutely not! Give me back my keys, you...you..." Words bad enough to describe him simply would not come to her, and she stamped her foot in frustration.

He saw Yarbro and Foley coming out his front door. "Lock that, would you? Daphne and I are leaving."

"We are not!" she delcared, horrified. The detectives smiled at her weakly and did as Danaker had asked. "A fine pair of Dutch uncles you've turned out to be!" she shouted at them angrily.

She made a heroic effort to get herself under control. Where was the icy disdain she needed at a moment like this? Where were the measured voice and the unmoved emotions that she had cultivated as a form of self-defense those many years with Connor? She couldn't find them anywhere. There was only this awful suffering, the hurt so deep she feared it would never heal.

Danaker pressed his lips together thoughtfully. "Would you be willing to go someplace neutral? Public?" He smiled without the slightest happiness as she latched onto that last word.

"Where you can't try to manipulate me again, you—" she sputtered furiously "—you aging Don Juan!"

He almost laughed and shook his head. "You *are* mad." He sighed. "Aging Don Juan, huh?" He opened the door for her. "I've got your keys, so you might as well humor me. I just want to add a little to what you've already heard. Then I'll take you home."

"I've heard enough already!" She glared at him. "Besides, if you drive me home, how will you get back here?" She expected him to try to stay at *her* house, as he had last night. The tears welled up again. Furiously, she brushed them away.

"I'll take a cab home," he said with a shrug.

She stared at him defiantly. She really didn't think he would hurt her physically. She wasn't afraid of that. Furious that he wouldn't simply let her leave, she plopped down in her car and fastened her seat belt. He did the same.

He started the engine, but before he reversed, he took a good look at her. She was wearing a pastel green shirt and dark purple running shorts. Each was trimmed with the color of the other. She had on new running shoes with hot pink laces and white cotton socks, and a purple-and-pink headband.

"You look very pretty in that. Were we going to go running when I got home?" he asked softly. "Or were you showing me a new outfit?" One he would have enjoyed taking off her, he added silently. He knew better than to voice the thought, however. She was already upset enough.

She refused to look at him or reply.

He hadn't dressed for a run in the park, but he hadn't dressed for business, either. He thought some exercise might not be a bad idea. They could run and be on public turf, as he had promised.

"Where are you going?" she demanded suspiciously, as he backed out of his drive.

"To the Potomac running trails, near Mt. Vernon."

"That isn't neutral," she objected darkly.

He glanced at her in surprise. Maybe he hadn't lost her yet. "I'm glad to hear you say that."

She could have bitten her tongue.

When they got there, neither of them was really in the mood to run, and they began by walking the trail, instead.

They had gone less than a quarter mile when Daphne halted and faced him. The walking had worked the edge off some of her initial hysteria, and she was able to speak with much more emotional control this time. "You said you had a few things to add to what I heard," she reminded him coolly. "Tell me. Then please take me home."

They were alone except for the natural fauna and flora. On weekday afternoons most people were at work or at school. However, Danaker preferred more privacy, for Daphne's sake. She would be embarrassed later if some stray person happened by while they were in the midst of a heated exchange. He was unconvinced that they could have a cool, detached conversation about this, although he was willing to give it a try.

He took her by the arm, but she immediately stiffened defensively and yanked herself free. "Don't touch me!"

"Let's go down by the old mill ruins," he suggested grimly.

Her cheeks were suffused with color. That place brought back very intimate memories. "No."

He lifted a brow. In a soft voice he challenged, "If you hate me now, what difference could it make?"

"None," she lied, as her pride smothered a more honest reply. She angrily turned on her heel and jogged toward the trail spur that led to the old ruins. "Let's get this over with. At least I can sit in the shade while you lie to me," she muttered scathingly.

His hands tightened at his sides as he loped alongside her. He would *not* lose his temper, he vowed silently. And he would keep his hands off her. *Off her.*

When they reached the crumbling mill, Daphne paced around the small meadow to cool down. Then she found a shady spot near one stone wall. It was as good a spot as any to stand her ground. "Well?" she demanded crossly.

But her voice shook, and she was dangerously close to tears again. She could have killed him for bringing her to this. Too proud to admit it, she glared at him and stuck her chin out defiantly.

He sighed and ran a hand through his hair.

"I didn't lie to you . . ." he began.

She rolled her eyes.

"But I didn't tell you the entire truth, either."

The look she gave him was insulting.

"The night Jamison was killed, I thought his death might have had something to do with whatever he was bringing to me . . ."

Suspicion joined the anger and insult in her face.

"And I needed to find out what that was."

Shock registered in her eyes. "That was why we searched his room so thoroughly," she whispered, seeing that event again.

"Yes."

She looked away. It hurt too much to bear. "I really fell into your plan like a baby, didn't I?" Her voice became embittered. "You must have thanked your lucky stars that night at the hospital when I took your business card. And then again when I actually showed up at your house!" She laughed, but the sound became choked. "What an incredible piece of luck for you. You could comfort the grieving widow, and while you were keeping her busy with your amorous attention, you could search her house for your missing delivery!"

"It wasn't quite like that."

"It was exactly like that!"

The expression in her eyes was worse than any blow she could have landed on him. It sliced through him like a sword, straight into his heart. He moved in front of her, trapping her between his body and the stone wall of the mill, but he didn't touch her.

"I had planned to quietly search the house," he conceded tightly. "But I hadn't planned on falling in love with you."

She laughed angrily. "You don't have to bother with that line anymore, Danaker! It isn't necessary. You've thoroughly searched the house—and me . . . ." She blushed and stumbled over the words. Her self-respect forced her on. "I know the truth now. Please take me home."

To hell with his vow. He grabbed her by the shoulders and pulled her against his body. Her lips were his, and as his arms closed around her, the rest of her was made his, as well. He wasn't gentle. He wasn't kind. It was the possessive act of a man bent on demonstrating that she was his and he had no intention of letting her go. Ever.

She struggled at first, but the scent of his skin, the feel of his body, the taste of his mouth, were too deeply associated with pleasure and love for her to remain unmoved. Tears of humiliation and defeat filled her eyes, but she knew she enjoyed his touch. Even now. Knowing what she did. When he lifted his head, his eyes opening slowly, she cried out, "Damn you! Why did you have to make me love you? Why did you have to show me what it was like to feel this way? Why couldn't you just have searched the house and left me alone? Why, Danaker? Why?" She went rigid in his arms, tears streaming down her face. Why, oh why, had he hurt her like this?

He pulled her head against him and nuzzled his cheek against it. "Because I fell in love with you," he whispered huskily. "That was not a lie, Daphne. It's the truth. Everything I told you was the truth. I swear it."

She swallowed and clenched her hands. She pushed her arms up between them and rested her fists on his chest, like a wedge between their bodies. "How can I believe that?" she whispered, desperate to be free of the enchantment before she was again lost to the strange witchcraft he exercised over her. "How can I ever believe that?"

He closed his eyes and rested his chin on her head for a moment, thinking. Reluctantly, he opened them again and lifted her face so that she had to look at him as he replied. He would have preferred saying this under other circumstances, but he had little choice now.

"If all I wanted was to search Jamison's things, I've done that. The police, my friends in Europe and I have enough of the puzzle figured out for me to say goodbye to you," he pointed out with deliberation.

She blinked. The words fell like arrows into her emotions.

He kissed her cool, unresponsive lips with all the tenderness in his heart. "I don't want to say goodbye, Daffy. . . ."

"Don't call me that!" she pleaded mournfully.

He smiled a little. "Sweetheart, then."

"No!"

"Darling?"

Her fists fell threateningly on his chest.

"My love?"

"I am not your love!" She tried to pull away, but he held her fast.

"When I gave you the keys to my house, I told you that you already had the most important things that belonged to me," he reminded her.

"Pretty words," she said, stubbornly refusing to believe him.

"*The truth.* You have my heart. And, if you want it, my life."

She looked away. It hurt too much to hear him speak with such sincerity, such intensity. She dared not believe him. As horrible as it felt now, how much worse would it be if she let him persuade her and then discovered later that he had still been leading her on?

"I want to marry you, Daphne," he told her softly, his lips brushing her cheek as he declared his intentions. "And I damn well don't have to propose to you. Even though you're hurt, outraged and angry, you know that's true. I could walk away if I didn't care. But I do care. I love you." His arms tightened around her as she flinched and cried out, trying to draw away. "I won't let you go!" he said fiercely. "You can have some time to cool off, to think it over, but that's it. Then I'm going to do everything I can to convince you to say yes."

She had thought the world had fallen on her head earlier, but his proposal of marriage tore her heart in two. She looked at him, her violet eyes filled with tears. Doubt and love warred within her.

"How can you be so cruel to me?" she whispered, the tears streaming down her cheeks.

He kissed the silvery paths, licking the moisture and caressing her eyes with his mouth. "I'm trying *not* to hurt you, damn it," he growled, his voice shaken now, too. "And if anyone's being hurt, it's *me.* Your pain is mine. Your tears slice into me. I'd do anything to undo the events of the past weeks, but I can't. If I had known that I was going to fall in love with you, I would have told you that day in your dining room, when we were going through the bills, that I had been in Old Town to meet Jamison. But I didn't know, Daffy. I was attracted to you the first time we met, but I put it down to lust. I kept telling myself no one falls in love that fast. But I did. I've been trying to explain to you for days, but I kept telling myself to go slowly. To give you a few facts at a time. I didn't want you to go into shock, to lose faith in me." He sighed. "I didn't want this to happen. But I dragged it out too long, and my worst nightmare has come true. Hell. You'd think a grown man would be able to avoid this kind of disaster. But you..." He swore. "I can barely think when I'm around you, Daffy. I love you so...."

His voice was strained, and he had to stop and clear his throat.

Surely he couldn't be pretending to hurt like this, she thought, staring at him, hearing the agony in his voice and the self-recrimination in his words. She saw an expression akin to fear shadow his eyes, but he brutally submerged it before she could be sure.

He held her close, rocking her gently in his arms, breathing in the sweet scent of her hair and soaking up the sensation of having her near.

"Did you know Connor?" she asked quietly.

"No. I never met him."

She frowned. "How can I know what to believe?" she wondered aloud.

He framed her face with his hands and kissed her. "Trust yourself," he suggested huskily. "I'll give you as much time as you want." He grimaced, immediately regretting his words. "Well, if you take longer than I can stand, I'll start sending in some troops to support my cause," he admitted.

She couldn't help but smile a little. "Such as?"

"Character witnesses." His expression lightened. Her smile was encouraging, he thought. "I may even introduce you to my great-aunt, if everything else fails. Mehitabel lives up to her formidable name. After she's worked on you, you'll be ready to have me recommended for sainthood."

Daphne couldn't help it. She laughed. Tremulously, perhaps, but it was laughter.

"Come on," he said, draping an arm around her. He couldn't bear to completely let her go. "I'll drive you home."

As they drove to her house, Daphne posed another question. "What do you think Connor was supposed to be delivering to you?"

"Damned if I can figure it out. It could have been a message or an object."

"Could the message or the item—whatever it was—have been connected with Connor's illegal arms deals?" she ventured, voicing her worst fear.

"I don't know. I can't see how, though. Kopek would have notified the authorities about that, and as far as we can tell, he didn't. I don't recognize any of the people he was dealing with, although they were using some of the routes the terrorists who killed Cherie used."

His wife, she thought. His voice still hardened when he spoke of that, she realized.

"Do you believe me?" he asked, glancing at her.

"I guess. After all, you're working with the police on this."

When they arrived at her house, he did as he had said he
would. He called a cab to take him back to his house.

They were waiting for it to arrive when she murmured,
"Maybe Kopek was just sending you a present."

Danaker frowned. "Why not just mail it? And tell me?"

"Maybe it was a surprise." She was thinking of the Williamson. It would have been a natural gift for Danaker.
"Maybe it was a birthday present," she joked, in a lame attempt at humor. She really had no idea what Kopek might have
been thinking, and she had so many worries of her own now,
it was hard to think at all.

Danaker stared at her as if he'd been poleaxed. "A birthday
present." Of course! Why hadn't he thought of it himself?
Damnation.

She shrugged. "I just said the first thing that came into my
mind."

He slowly began to grin. "If I thought you'd let me, I'd pick
you up and swing you around and kiss you until you fainted."

She looked at him blankly, although his words made her feel
warm and excited, in spite of all that had passed between them.

The cab pulled up in front of the house. He looked at her lips
regretfully. "I'll explain later," he promised. His eyes looked
clearer now. More certain. "I'll call you. I want your promise
you'll pick up the phone. Please?"

She nodded. The shock had worn off. She didn't need to hide
like a rabbit from him. "I promise."

Daphne watched as he left. She stood in front of her living
room window for a long time afterward, thinking. She wanted
to believe him. Her heart cried out that she should. She remembered his uncle Jerome's comments that day at Danaker's
house. She knew some things he had told her had to be true.
Jerome had confirmed that Danaker had loved his first wife.
He had mourned her deeply, and he had been alone for seven
long years after her death. He wasn't a playboy, and he didn't
think of her as a toy. She couldn't believe his passionate response to her was entirely feigned. And hers certainly wasn't.

But did she have the courage to trust him with her life? For
that was what he had asked her, when he had proposed marriage. He hadn't had to say a word about marriage to her. He
could have walked away. But he hadn't. He'd asked her to

marry him. She was sure he meant it as proof of his honesty and of his intentions toward her. Why else would he do it?

That really turned her fears upside down. Surely the only thing he could gain by marrying her would be herself. Wasn't it? She gnawed on her lip and wracked her brain. Had she missed something again? Did she dare trust him? Believe him?

Love him?

Chapter 17

A birthday present. Could it have been so simple? Such a ridiculous crossroads of events? Danaker thought about it for close to an hour. It was the first theory that made any sense and fit with everything else.

Janisch had told him years ago that, before he retired, he wanted to give Danaker a memento of their years of partnership. Janisch had given broad hints recently that he intended to wind down his business. That pistol represented the years of work he had put in. And Danaker would have inherited the business, had he been willing to take it. Janisch thought of him as the closest thing to a son he'd ever had.

The night Jamison was to have delivered Kopek's message was the eve of Danaker's birthday. He hadn't celebrated his birthday in years, and hadn't connected it with Janisch Kopek. His family sent him cards, of course, but Janisch and he hadn't bothered. When they had worked together, they'd gone to a bar and had a couple of drinks, using the event mostly as an excuse to relax and amuse themselves. But perhaps this time Janisch had used it as an excuse to give him the gift he had once promised. The token of their friendship and successful partnership.

Janisch could easily have known that Jamison returned to Alexandria regularly. Being in the same business, Kopek would have had opportunities to ask Jamison to carry something into the country for him. Janisch had always had a cloak-and-dagger sense of humor. He would have enjoyed the stealthy delivery.

And the message that Jamison would have given him? Happy Birthday. And the Williamson. Danaker swore. It all fit. Incredible.

Jamison must have gone to retrieve the Williamson at the post office, but Sarmien had had him followed, because of the other things which had nothing to do with Janisch's innocent gift giving. Jamison had been trapped, Danaker reasoned. He couldn't get the pistol without giving away the location of his postal box. He wanted to keep it secret, because he stashed his papers there and they outlined his plans to betray Corday and moonlight as an arms trader with Christina.

So Jamison had run. He'd tried to lose his followers. That had made him late for the rendezvous. But he hadn't been able to shake them. Perhaps he thought he had finally lost them when he'd come running toward Danaker that fateful night, but they'd hung on to him like death. And killed him.

Jamison had died because of his betrayal of Sarmien. His death had had nothing to do with Janisch's attempt to deliver an unexpected birthday present, a fond farewell to a warm partnership.

It made sense. And everything fit. But how could he prove it?

There's the rub, Danaker thought, frowning. Somehow he needed to trap Sarmien, tempt him into confessing to a piece of the crime. Draw him out in some way.

Quinn doubted that Daphne would be safe until Sarmien was convinced that she would not stumble across the evidence of Jamison's moonlighting. Such evidence would reveal a motive for Sarmien to have killed Jamison. He would become a suspect, the possible subject of a police investigation. He wouldn't welcome that.

As long as that threat hung over Daphne, Danaker knew he would live in fear that someone else would break into her house. They might fabricate some feeble excuse, or just plain break-and-enter. If there was a next time, they might find Daphne inside. They might hurt her. Or kill her. Or Kyle.

His stomach clenched, and the old sensation of being sick washed through him, sending a cold sweat over his skin. He wasn't going to permit that to happen. He had already lost one person he loved to violence. He would *not* go through that again. He *had* to find a way to remove the threat. Fast.

He smiled dangerously as he considered the possibilities. Why not simply tell Sarmien the truth: that he had the evidence? That would make Sarmien shift his sights to him. Daphne would be out of it. Then he would offer the man a trade: the incriminating papers in exchange for a finder's fee. Bait and trap. He had lived close enough to the world of illegality for Sarmien to believe him capable of blackmail. And it helped that dishonest people usually found it easy to believe that everyone else was as amoral as they were. He lifted the phone and dialed Yarbro's number.

After a brief explanation, he said, "I have a suggestion, Lieutenant."

"I thought you might." The detective chuckled. "Go on."

Daphne hadn't heard from Danaker in over twenty-four hours. At first she told herself she should be happy. She was free. Then she told herself he was giving her time to calm down. He had said he would do that. But finally she admitted that she missed the sound of his voice, the touch of his hand, the smile that lit his eyes. He had called to say good-night whenever they didn't see each other. She missed it. She'd been lonely last night, without his call.

She had considered what he had said at the mill and run the past few weeks through her mind. She remembered the times he had seemed preoccupied, had tried to guide their conversation toward his past. She recalled him telling her that he wanted to start all over again with her when the mess with Connor was resolved. The more she examined things calmly, the more she was inclined to believe his claim that he had been trying to break the news gently to her.

She might be making a tragic mistake, but her heart was being very stubborn. She wanted to listen to his explanations, to give him another chance. Give *them* a chance.

She still had the keys to his house. Night was falling, but she didn't want to wait, now that she'd decided. There was a school holiday tomorrow, and Kyle was spending the night with Crabby, so she didn't have to worry about a baby-sitter, or leaving in the middle of a complicated or strained discussion because she was needed at home.

She called to ask if she could come over, but his phone was busy. And busy. Busy. Busy. At least he was home, she thought wryly. She wrestled with her reticence. She really should call first. But her yearning for him gave her the courage to go ahead. The first time she had gone to his house, she had not been expected, she reminded herself. He had welcomed her then. He would do no less now. He said he loved her. She wanted to believe him.

She stood on his front porch, knocking on the door, when something swooped over her head. She ducked. The bat again. She shivered in revulsion. The door opened, and she turned to smile tentatively.

Quinn took one look at her and cursed under his breath. Aiming a worried look at the area behind her, he grabbed her by the arm and pulled her inside, closing the door as if he were trying to hide her arrival.

She blushed. "I'm sorry..." she murmured, uncertain what his strange reception meant.

"Did you see anyone as you came in?" he demanded, dragging her down the hall after him.

"One of your neighbors down the street was pulling into her drive...."

He waved a hand dismissively. "Not that. Did anyone see you pull in?" He stopped and punched in the security codes to the tunnel. "Where did you park?"

"Beside the garage."

He looked pained. "It's hard to see, but not impossible."

"Did I come at a bad time?" she asked, feeling utterly miserable. "I called, but the line was busy...."

"Never mind," he muttered. "It's too late. You'll have to hide."

"Hide?" She stared at his back as she stumbled down the hall after him. He still held her hand, and he was taking her into the elegant gunroom at the far end. She swallowed hard. "Are you expecting someone?" she ventured timidly.

"Yes. And they mustn't see you."

"Oh." She felt as small as Alice and rather like she'd been thrust into some sort of bizarre Wonderland. She was blushing in embarrassment and calling herself the worst kind of fool. "I'm sorry."

He had turned to look at her. She was wearing a red-and-peach colored blouse, black wool slacks, red leather shoes and a gold belt. A fine strand of gold was looped in a necklace at her throat, and the dangly gold earrings she was wearing caught the light and sent it glancing about the room.

"You look very beautiful," he said softly. He reached out to caress her cheek with his knuckles, but he was frowning. And worried. "Look... Sarmien and a couple of his friends are going to be here any minute...."

"Sarmien?"

He smiled. "You sound relieved. Who did you think?"

She tried to seem nonchalant. "Oh, I don't know...."

He laughed and pulled her close. "Don't tell me you thought I was already chasing another woman?"

She put her hands on his shoulders, and her eyes fixed on his throat. He was wearing a dress shirt with the sleeves rolled up and open at the neck. She could see his slow, steady pulse. It was all she could do not to lean forward and press her lips against it, snuggle against him.

"I love you," he reminded her softly, lifting her chin so she would look at him. "And I will never betray you. I'm a faithful husband, Daphne. A faithful lover."

She could see nothing in his amber eyes but warmth. Until he straightened and hustled her over to a side panel.

"I want you to stay in here," he said briskly. "Don't make a sound." He gave her a stern look. "Got that?"

"Yes, but..."

He pressed a small latch, and the hand-rubbed, oil-finished walnut panel slid open, revealing a secret passage between the two rooms it adjoined. He caught the back of her head firmly with one hand and kissed her on the mouth. As he withdrew, he breathed a sigh and murmured, "God, I needed that. I can't tell you how lonely it's been without you. Even for a day." He grinned at her boyishly. "I'll come back and get you when it's safe." The grin faded. "But it may be a while. An hour or two. Whatever you do... don't make a sound." He looked at her, realizing how little he was giving her in the way of explanation. "I'm sorry. There's no choice. You're going to have to trust me."

She caught his hand in hers and brought it to her cheek. The gesture of affection and faith made him catch his breath.

"I contacted Sarmien, told him I had some papers he might find very interesting, that you had cleaned them out and thrown them away, but I retrieved them. I offered to give him a look and sell them to him for a price. He's coming to look over the goods."

"Here?" she asked in dismay. "Why would he walk into your house? Wouldn't he guess it could be a trap?"

"He has no choice. I didn't give him a second location. I told him I was willing to earn some money as a government informant if he didn't want to pay me. He can't risk that." Danaker frowned. That could also make Sarmien very dangerous. He was cornered. "Yarbro and Foley have the place under surveillance." He grinned, a little embarrassed. "One of them's probably watching us on the monitor in my office right now. If anything goes wrong, stay put. They'll get you out."

Daphne grabbed him by the shirtfront, her eyes widening with fear for him. "What could go wrong?"

He shook his head and tried to laugh it off. "Nothing."

She threw her arms around his neck. "I don't want you hurt." He held her close and kissed her cheek, murmuring reassurances she didn't believe. "I love you," she whispered brokenly. "I came to tell you that. And that I want to believe you, to listen to whatever you want to tell me."

"Daphne," he murmured.

It was a sigh of gratitude and love. He kissed her mouth with great delicacy, wishing they had more time. When he drew back, his eyes were dark with emotion. "I'll never forget your faith in me. Always remember that I love you," he whispered huskily. He gave her a final quick kiss and pushed her firmly into the enclosure, shutting the panel after her.

She slid down to sit on the carpeted floor. To wait.

Sarmien brought two men with him. They were tall and silent, and their eyes were as deadly calm as the flat Sargasso Sea. Danaker would have bet that they were the killers who had gunned down Jamison. Sarmien smiled coldly. He did not introduce them.

"Are your friends interested in the files, too?" Danaker asked, looking them over, assessing where their weapons might be. They obviously hadn't come along to hold the door for Sarmien.

Sarmien smiled faintly. "No." He glanced around, his shrewd eyes taking in the security measures as they walked into the tunnel. "Before we sit down to discuss the…situation…we

would like to examine the premises." His smile hardened. "You
will understand, I'm sure."

Danaker nodded. He'd expected this. He took them into all
of the rooms and let them look around. The closed-circuit television monitors had been turned off in the office. It appeared
empty. Only Danaker knew about the sliding panels he'd had
installed in all of the rooms. Although Sarmien's men were
thorough, they didn't find anything amiss. Yarbro and Foley
remained undetected behind the panel.

They didn't find anything when they frisked Danaker, either.

When he returned the favor, they were suspiciously amiable
about it, placing their snub-nosed weapons on the table in one
of the gunrooms, as Danaker directed them to do. Sarmien had
a beeper in his pocket, but it looked harmless enough. Danaker had him place it on the table anyway.

It was all going too easily, Danaker thought, watching as
Sarmien examined the reports. When the man straightened to
leave, Danaker realized that Sarmien wasn't planning to pay the
bribe. He gripped the man's wrist and stared at him.

"You've forgotten something," he said in a deadly soft
voice.

Sarmien smiled with a silkiness that made Danaker's stomach turn.

"No," Sarmien retorted. He leaned forward, sure that Danaker wasn't wearing a wire because his men had searched him.
"But if you don't let me walk out of here right now, I'll see to
it that you're a dead man."

Danaker smiled coldly. "Like Jamison?"

Sarmien's eyes narrowed. "Exactly."

Danaker nodded toward the two men eyeing him like vul-
tures. "Am I supposed to be afraid of them?"

"That depends on the level of your intelligence," Sarmien
replied, coldly amused. "However, if you lack the necessary
discernment to be afraid for yourself, fear for the lovely widow
and her charming little boy."

Danaker's hand tightened on Sarmien's wrist. Sarmien's face
contorted in a spasm of pain.

"Let go of me, you fool," Sarmien snarled. "You're out-
numbered."

"Not quite." Danaker raised his voice.

The door to the gunroom was open, and Yarbro and Foley filled it, guns pointed at the men inside. Sarmien made a guttural sound of rage and turned furiously on Danaker.

"You have underestimated me," he hissed. "And it will cost you everything you hold dear."

Sarmien reached out quickly and pressed the beeper. His fingers connected with the button before Danaker was able to drag him to his knees. For a moment nothing happened. Danaker and the police looked at one another. Then they were plunged into darkness. The lights had been cut somewhere outside the house.

Danaker wrenched Sarmien's arm into a half nelson and dragged him in front of him. He whispered harshly into the man's ear, "Tell your dogs to lie down, Sarmien. If they shoot at me, the bullet's going through you first."

Feet scuffled, the sound deadened by the rug, as Yarbro and Foley leaped toward the table where the killers' weapons lay. Four men converged on the guns at once and struggled for them in the dark. The grunting and sounds of punches landing gave no clue as to who was getting hit and who was going down.

From her seat down the hall, Daphne could not hear anything. She didn't even know the lights had gone off, since she had a small, battery-operated flashlight that was permanently hung on the wall, and she had turned it on to get a better look at her surroundings. She pressed her ear against the wood, trying desperately to figure out what was happening.

Suddenly she felt the paneling shake hard, as if someone big and heavy had fallen against it. It happened again, and she leaped to her feet. Two men were struggling on the other side of the wooden door. They were throwing each other against it. She could hear them grunt with pain, could hear the sound of a fist striking wood when its intended target shifted away at the last minute. There was an infuriated cry from the owner of the fist. She didn't recognize the voice, but the stream of gutter-roughened profanities he spewed made her think he must be with Sarmien. The men must be circling one another around the table in the center of the room, she guessed, because they were no longer banging on the wall. She pressed her cheek against the wood, trying desperately to hear something that would let her know what was happening.

A shot rang out, and the wood splintered beside her cheek as a bullet pierced it. She screamed and pushed at the lock on the other side, intending to let herself out into the room where no one was fighting. As she lifted the manual latch, she realized a man was crying out in anguish.

"No!" Quinn roared in outrage and fear, thinking her scream meant she had been struck by the bullet.

"Quinn!" she whispered, terrified for him.

Another shot was fired, shattering the glass case just outside her tiny cubicle. She jumped away from the sound and accidentally hit the handle that opened the door Danaker had closed behind her. It flew open. The room was pitch-dark. She, however, was fully illuminated by the flashlight on the wall beside her.

"Move a muscle and I'll kill her," panted the man with the gun.

Danaker felt his blood run cold. "The hell you will," he growled, rising up directly in the line of fire. "You'll have to kill me first."

The man fired.

Daphne screamed as she saw Quinn jerk back a step. He'd been hit in the left shoulder. She doused the flashlight and rushed forward to catch him in her arms as he slumped to his knees.

Suddenly the room was filled with light again. Men wearing dark jackets labeled Police in yellow letters ran inside and disarmed the man who had shot Danaker.

Quinn looked up at Daphne, barely able to keep his eyes open, the pain in his shoulder becoming more unbearable by the second. "Are you . . . all right?" he whispered hoarsely.

"Yes." Tears filled her eyes, and she pressed her hand to his wound in an attempt to stop the bleeding. It was pulsing like a heartbeat. She was terrified the bullet had hit an artery. "You saved my life," she whispered, the tears sliding down her cheeks. She bent to kiss his face, turned awkwardly back to see her.

He seemed to relax, hearing that she was unhurt. He leaned against her and murmured, "Sorry, baby, I don't think...I..." Before he could finish what he intended to say, he passed out, falling heavily against her.

She was cradling him in her lap when the paramedics arrived.

"Please . . . can I go to the hospital?" she begged Yarbro as they loaded Danaker into the ambulance.

He pushed her toward a uniformed policeman. "Take her wherever the ambulance goes," he ordered.

* * *

When Danaker awoke in a hospital room hours later, Daphne was seated near his bed, holding his hand. As soon as he opened his eyes, he saw her. She was curled in the chair, sleeping, but her fingers were wrapped around his as if she intended to keep him.

"Daphne," he whispered.

Her eyes flew open, and she came out of the chair to hover over him worriedly. Seeing the clear look in his eyes, she relaxed. "Hi," she whispered back, smiling for the first time since she'd walked through his front door.

"Is everything all right?" he asked. "Did they get Sarmien?"

"The police took them all into custody, including someone in your house who pulled the circuit breaker on your electricity." She brushed a soft kiss across his lips. "Yarbo came by half an hour ago to check on you. He said to tell you everything's under control."

Danaker lifted an eyebrow. "It's about time." He noticed it was dark outside the window behind her. "Shouldn't you be home with Kyle?" he asked softly. He hated for her to go, but . . .

She shook her head. "He's spending the night at Crabby's. And he's already demanding to come see you tomorrow. He's very impressed with your heroism," she added with a smile.

Danaker laughed. He still felt a little groggy, and his shoulder was numb from pain medication, but he hadn't felt better in a long time. "You didn't have to stay with me," he said huskily. "Thanks."

She gave him a slightly outraged look. "You beastly man! Do you think I could have left you?"

He reached behind her and pulled her down onto his chest. "I don't know. Could you?" He kissed the corner of her mouth.

"Of course, not," she said, still shaken at the near miss he'd had. She framed his face with her hands and looked into his eyes. "No one ever offered to give up his life for me," she whispered.

"Will that help my case?" he teased. "It's not exactly a character witness, but I'm not above using anything."

Her eyes filled with tears, and she buried her face in his neck. She pulled away as she felt him flinch, feeling awful because she was sure she'd hurt him. "I'm sorry. . . ."

He held her fast. "You're not hurting me. They've shot me so full of pain killers I can't feel a thing," he murmured huskily. "Except the one thing that I need to feel every day of my life." He found her mouth with his in a long, peace-giving kiss. "You, Daffy. Will you give us another chance? Let me start all over again with you?" He grinned slightly. He knew it was unfair to pressure her when he was flat on his back in a hospital bed having taken a bullet to protect her, but he ignored his scruples in the interest of sanity.

"Don't you dare start over," she threatened him, smiling through tears of happiness. "I want you to pick up right where we left off."

He pulled her close and sighed. "Thank God."

She murmured urgently, "I almost forgot! Your friend Janisch? He came out of the coma tonight. Yarbro said he's asking for you."

He was tremendously relieved to hear that. "Would you come along when I visit him?" he asked gently.

"I'd love to." She smiled against his warm cheek. "How are you going to introduce me?" she teased.

He looked into her violet eyes, feeling as if he were drowning in them. He was barely able to whisper the answer to her question. "I'd like to introduce you as the woman I'm going to marry," he said achingly. "May I?" Another backward proposal, he realized. He held his breath, unsure what she would say, even now.

"A wise man once told me to trust my instincts," she reminded him with a smile. "They're all begging me to accept before you get away. We've had so little time together, and yet you've never felt like a stranger to me.... I feel like I've known you forever, my love."

She cupped his dear face in her hands and pressed her lips tenderly to his. Her answer was there for him to feel, and his good arm tightened around her as he deepened the kiss in eloquent and tender reply. *Yes, I will marry you. Yes, I will trust you. Yes, I am yours. I know you'll be faithful to me. You'll be mine. Forever.*

"Is that a yes?" he whispered unsteadily against her lips.

"Shall I tell you again, then?" she murmured teasingly.

He pulled her close and sighed. "Yeah. I want to make sure I heard it right the first time."

He got the answer he wanted, but it was repeated quite a few times and in very imaginative ways, considering the open door of the room. Daphne didn't care. And Danaker had entirely forgotten where he was. All that mattered was that she was in his arms again. And this time, she was there to stay.

* * * * *

NORA ROBERTS

Love has a language all its own, and for centuries, flowers have symbolized love's finest expression. Discover the language of flowers—and love—in this romantic collection of 48 favorite books by bestselling author Nora Roberts.

Starting in February, two titles will be available each month at your favorite retail outlet.

In February, look for:

Irish Thoroughbred, **Volume #1**
The Law Is A Lady, **Volume #2**

In March, look for:

Irish Rose, **Volume #3**
Storm Warning, **Volume #4**

Collect all 48 titles and become fluent in

THE LANGUAGE of LOVE

Ⓡ *Silhouette*®

LOL292

SILHOUETTE® *Desire*™

The Case of the Mesmerizing Boss
DIANA PALMER

Diana Palmer's exciting new series,
MOST WANTED, begins in March with
THE CASE OF THE MESMERIZING BOSS....

Dane Lassiter—one-time Texas Ranger
extraordinaire—now heads his own group of
crack private detectives. Soul-scarred by
women, this heart-stopping private eyeful
exists only for his work—until the night his
secretary, Tess Meriwether, becomes the target
of drug dealers. Dane wants to keep her safe.
But their stormy past makes him the one man
Tess *doesn't* want protecting her....

Don't miss THE CASE OF THE MESMERIZING
BOSS by Diana Palmer, first in a lineup of
heroes MOST WANTED! In June, watch for THE
CASE OF THE CONFIRMED BACHELOR ... only
from Silhouette Desire!

SDDP-1

MOST WANTED

Silhouette Special Edition®

salutes

MOMENTS OF GLORY

from Lindsay McKenna

In a country torn with conflict, in a time of bitter passions, these brave men and women wage a war against all odds... and a timeless battle for honor, for fleeting moments of glory, for the promise of enduring love.

February: RIDE THE TIGER (#721) Survivor Dany Villard is wise to the love-'em-and-leave-'em ways of war, but wounded hero Gib Ramsey swears she's captured his heart... forever.

March: ONE MAN'S WAR (#727) The war raging inside brash and bold Captain Pete Mallory threatens to destroy him, until Tess Ramsey's tender love guides him toward peace.

April: OFF LIMITS (#733) Soft-spoken Marine Jim McKenzie saved Alexandra Vance's life in Vietnam; now he needs her love to save his honor....

SEMG-1

Take 4 bestselling love stories FREE

Plus get a FREE surprise gift!

Special Limited-time Offer

Mail to Silhouette Reader Service™

In the U.S.
3010 Walden Avenue
P.O. Box 1867
Buffalo, N.Y. 14269-1867

In Canada
P.O. Box 609
Fort Erie, Ontario
L2A 5X3

YES! Please send me 4 free Silhouette Intimate Moments® novels and my free surprise gift. Then send me 4 brand-new novels every month, which I will receive months before they appear in bookstores. Bill me at the low price of $2.96* each— a savings of 33¢ apiece off cover prices. There are no shipping, handling or other hidden costs. I understand that accepting the books and gift places me under no obligation ever to buy any books. I can always return a shipment and cancel at any time. Even if I never buy another book from Silhouette, the 4 free books and the surprise gift are mine to keep forever.

*Offer slightly different in Canada—$2.96 per book plus 49¢ per shipment for delivery. Canadian residents add applicable federal and provincial sales tax. Sales tax applicable in N.Y.

240 BPA ADMD   340 BPA ADMR

Name _____ (PLEASE PRINT) _____

Address _____ Apt. No. _____

City _____ State/Prov. _____ Zip/Postal Code _____

This offer is limited to one order per household and not valid to present Silhouette Intimate Moments® subscribers. Terms and prices are subject to change.

MOM-91   © 1990 Harlequin Enterprises Limited

From the popular author of the bestselling title
DUNCAN'S BRIDE (Intimate Moments #349)
comes the

LINDA HOWARD

COLLECTION

Two exquisite collector's editions that contain four of
Linda Howard's early passionate love stories. To add
these special volumes to your own library, be sure
to look for:

VOLUME ONE: *Midnight Rainbow*
Diamond Bay
(Available in March)

VOLUME TWO: *Heartbreaker*
White Lies
(Available in April)

 *Silhouette Books*®

SLH92